"Christine Feehan has brought paranormal romance to a new high."
—*A Romance Review*

Praise for the Drake Sisters novels

TURBULENT SEA

"Book after book, the suspense has been building . . . Feehan's gift for compelling characterization is spot-on and makes the relationship between this combustible duo aces!"
—*Romantic Times*

"A terrific entry that the audience has been waiting for . . . The story line is action packed . . . gripping."
—*Midwest Book Review*

SAFE HARBOR

"Everything her fans have come to expect: action, gunplay, danger, bad guys, good guys, gorgeous women and magic."
—*Publishers Weekly*

"All I can say is—WOW! . . . A highly emotional love story, but also one packed with more action and suspense than any previous Drake series tale . . . I can promise you will be thrilled by the time you reach the end. Don't even think of missing this one. It's absolutely terrific and quite deserving of a Perfect 10!"
—*Romance Reviews Today*

"Action-packed . . . Christine Feehan provides a bewitching Drake thriller starring the pair fans have waited for."
—*Midwest Book Review*

continued . . .

DANGEROUS TIDES

"An excellent Drake Sisters tale." —*The Best Reviews*

"Enchanting. Smart, suspenseful, incredibly erotic."
—*Romance Reviews Today*

"A tempting blend of paranormal romance and mystery."
—*Booklist*

"Resonate[s] with passion . . . rich with enchantment and spiced with danger. Pure magic!" —*Romantic Times*

OCEANS OF FIRE

"Christine Feehan boldly goes where no writer has ever gone . . . Erotic, exotic, suspenseful."
—*Fallen Angel Reviews*

"Brimming with exhilarating action sequences and sultry love scenes." —*Publishers Weekly*

"Fascinating and mysterious . . . enjoy a little bit of magic, a dash of intrigue and all the romance to be found in *Oceans of Fire*." —*Romance Reviews Today*

"The Drake series is a complex blend of fantasy and suspense." —*Booklist*

Further praise for the novels of
"THE REIGNING QUEEN OF PARANORMAL ROMANCE"*

MIND GAME

"Swift-moving and sexually-charged . . . electrifying."
—*Publishers Weekly*

"[A] compelling and spectacular series. The amazingly prolific author's ability to create captivating and adrenaline-raising worlds is unsurpassed." —*Romantic Times*

"Explosive . . . An exciting, thrilling read . . . A phenomenal plot. Ms. Feehan has really outdone herself . . . a definite page-turner." —*Fallen Angel Reviews*

SHADOW GAME

"[A] swift, sensational offering . . . sultry, spine-tingling kind of read that [Feehan's] fans will adore." —*Publishers Weekly*

"Intense, sensual and mesmerizing . . . Feehan is a rising star in paranormal romance." —*Library Journal*

"Never slows down until the final confrontation. The story line is fast-paced and loaded with action."
—*Midwest Book Review*

"Sizzling sex scenes both physical and telepathic pave the road to true love . . . Action, suspense and smart characters make this erotically charged romance an entertaining read."
—*Booklist*

"Feehan packs such a punch with this story it will leave one gasping for breath . . . Guaranteed not to disappoint, and will leave one begging for more. A must-read book, only cementing Ms. Feehan's position as a genre favorite for yet another round." —*The Best Reviews*

WILD RAIN

"Readers . . . will be seduced by this erotic adventure."
—*Publishers Weekly*

"Ms. Feehan is unsurpassed in romantic fantasy; her imagination knows no bounds in creating unique and fresh tales that abound in steamy sensuality, fantastical imagery and lyrical prose." —*Rendezvous*

"A powerful tale that pumps up the adrenaline . . . A fabulous jungle love story." —*Midwest Book Review*

"Beautiful imagery, edge-of-your-seat suspense and passionate romance . . . The sex is spicy enough to singe your eyebrows." —*Romance Reviews Today*

"[A] terrific new series . . . Fascinating." —*Romantic Times*

Hidden Currents

CHRISTINE FEEHAN

J

JOVE BOOKS, NEW YORK

THE BERKLEY PUBLISHING GROUP
Published by the Penguin Group
Penguin Group (USA) Inc.
375 Hudson Street, New York, New York 10014, USA

Penguin Group (Canada), 90 Eglinton Avenue East, Suite 700, Toronto, Ontario M4P 2Y3, Canada
(a division of Pearson Penguin Canada Inc.)
Penguin Books Ltd., 80 Strand, London WC2R 0RL, England
Penguin Group Ireland, 25 St. Stephen's Green, Dublin 2, Ireland (a division of Penguin Books Ltd.)
Penguin Group (Australia), 250 Camberwell Road, Camberwell, Victoria 3124, Australia
(a division of Pearson Australia Group Pty. Ltd.)
Penguin Books India Pvt. Ltd., 11 Community Centre, Panchsheel Park, New Delhi—110 017, India
Penguin Group (NZ), 67 Apollo Drive, Rosedale, North Shore 0632, New Zealand
(a division of Pearson New Zealand Ltd.)
Penguin Books (South Africa) (Pty.) Ltd., 24 Sturdee Avenue, Rosebank, Johannesburg 2196,
South Africa

Penguin Books Ltd., Registered Offices: 80 Strand, London WC2R 0RL, England

HIDDEN CURRENTS

A Jove Book / published by arrangement with the author

PRINTING HISTORY
Jove mass-market edition / July 2009

Copyright © 2009 by Christine Feehan.
Excerpt from *Dark Slayer* copyright © 2009 by Christine Feehan.
Cover art by Dan O'Leary.
Cover handlettering by Ron Zinn.
Cover design by George Long.
Text design by Kristin del Rosario.

ISBN: 978-0-515-14647-9

JOVE®
Jove Books are published by The Berkley Publishing Group,
a division of Penguin Group (USA) Inc.,
375 Hudson Street, New York, New York 10014.
JOVE® is a registered trademark of Penguin Group (USA) Inc.
The "J" design is a trademark of Penguin Group (USA) Inc.

PRINTED IN THE UNITED STATES OF AMERICA

10 9 8 7 6 5 4 3 2 1

For Nicole Powell,
my wonderful niece,
who knows what the meaning of family is

ACKNOWLEDGMENTS

Many people helped with their expertise and I give them my heartfelt thanks. Any mistakes are solely mine.

Sheena MacKenzie participated in an auction for autism research. She won the auction to have her name as a character in my book. Much more research in autism is needed, and I appreciate her support!

Thanks to Morey Sparks, Brian Feehan, and Jack and Lisset for providing help with the various rescue scenes. Your help was invaluable.

Thanks to Lisset for her patience when I asked her a thousand questions about protection dogs.

Thanks to Morey for all the weapons and bomb advice. I know more than I ever thought I'd know about men who like to blow things up!

Mike Carpenter, a twenty-five-year veteran urchin diver, gave me incredible information on the local tides, rip currents, diving, sea life and hypothermia, as well as on boats and just about everything else to do with this coastline. He's a fountain of information and I could listen to and learn from him for hours.

Domini and Kathie, thanks for your hours of hard work in research and editing.

And thanks, of course, to Dr. Christopher Tong, my own personal brainiac who can do anything, and I mean anything. You always come through for me, no matter the deadline.

1

"HAVING fun, Sheena?" Stavros Gratsos rubbed his palms up and down Elle Drake's bare arms to warm her as he stood behind her at the railing of his large yacht.

All around them the sound of laughter and snatches of conversation drifted past her out to the shimmering Mediterranean Sea.

Sheena MacKenzie, Elle's undercover name—and her alter ego. Sheena could sit at any dinner table and rule, her polish and sophistication and air of mystery guaranteeing she'd get attention. Devoid of makeup, with her hair in a ponytail, Elle Drake could slide into the shadows and disappear. They made a nearly unbeatable combination, and Sheena had done exactly what Elle needed her to do—she'd lured Stavros and kept him interested long enough for Elle to poke into his glamorous life and see what she could turn up—which, so far, was . . . nothing.

Elle couldn't read Stavros's thoughts and emotions the way she did others when they touched her, and that amazed her. Her psychic ability to read thoughts was disturbing most of the time, but there were a very few who seemed to have natural barriers and she had to purposely "invade" if she wanted to see what they were thinking. Elle rarely ever intruded, even when she was undercover, but she would have made an exception in Stavros's case. She had been investigating him for months and had found nothing to either clear him—or to point toward his guilt.

She glanced over her shoulder at Stavros. "It's been wonderful. Amazing. But I think everything you do is like this and you know it." Stavros always put on the best parties and his yacht was bigger than most people's homes. He served the best food, had the best music and surrounded himself with intelligent people, fun people.

In all the months she'd been watching him, she had yet to discover even a hint of criminal activity. Stavros had been kind and generous, giving millions to charities, supporting the arts and working out deals with his employees in a hands-on discussion that avoided laying off an entire group of workers. She had come to respect the man in spite of earlier suspicions, and she was ready to go back to Dane Phelps, her boss, and write a very strongly worded report that the rumors concerning Stavros were wrong—except that his aura indicated danger and a strong penchant for violence. Of course, some of the men her sisters had chosen as their mates had that same vivid color swirling around them.

"I held this party in your honor, Sheena," Stavros admitted. "My elusive butterfly." He tugged on her arm to turn her around so that her back was against the rail and she was caged in by his body. "I want you to come to my island with me, to see my private home."

Her heart jumped. According to rumor, Stavros never took any woman to his island. He had homes all over the world, but the island was his private retreat. Most under-cover operatives would have relished the opportunity to enter Stavros's private sanctum, but her boss had been adamant that she not go, even if the opportunity presented itself. There was no way to communicate from that is-land.

Stavros took her hand and carried her knuckles to his mouth. "Come with me, Sheena."

She tried not to wince. Sheena. She was such a fraud. This was the man she should fall in love with, not the worm—he-who-could-never-be-named—who had broken her heart. Here was Stavros, handsome, intelligent, wealthy, a man who solved problems and seemed to care for many of the same causes she did. Why couldn't *he* be the man she fell madly in love with?

"I can't," she said gently. "Really, Stavros. I want to, but I can't."

His eyes darkened, became stormy. Stavros liked his way and was definitely used to getting it. "You mean you won't."

"I mean I can't. You want things from me I can't give you. I told you from the beginning we could be friends—not lovers."

"You're not married."

"You know I'm not." But she should have been. She should have been settled in her family home with the man destiny had intended for her, but he had rejected her. Her stomach churned at the thought. She'd put an ocean be-tween them and still he tried to reach her, his voice a faint buzz in her head, trying to persuade her to return—to what? A man who didn't want children or a legacy of magic. He refused to understand that was who she was— what she was. In rejecting her legacy, he rejected her. And she needed a man who would help her. Who would understand how difficult it was for her to face her future. She needed someone to lean on, not someone she had to coax or take care of.

"Come home with me," he repeated.

Elle shook her head. "I can't, Stavros. You know what would happen if I did and we can't go there."

His white teeth flashed at her. "So at least you've thought about it."

Elle tipped her head back and looked up at him. "You know how charming you are. What woman wouldn't be tempted by you?" And she was. It would be so easy. He was so sweet to her, always attentive, wanting to give her the world. She reached up and touched his face regretfully. "You're a good man, Stavros."

She was ashamed she'd suspected him of the heinous things she had—human trafficking among the worst. Yes, he'd started out smuggling guns in his freighters, years earlier when he had nothing. But he seemed to have more than made up for all of his mistakes, and as far as she could ascertain, he was truly legitimate. At least she could clear his name with Interpol and the other agencies around the world where his name kept cropping up. That would make her feel better about spending these past months working to befriend him and earn his trust.

"I'm hearing a 'but' in there, Sheena," Stavros said.

Elle spread her arms wide, taking in the yacht and the shimmering sea. "All this. This is your world and I can step into it occasionally, but I could never live in it comfortably. I've looked at your track record, Stavros, and you don't believe in permanency. And no, I'm not holding out for marriage with you. I just know myself. I get attached to people and breaking up is terribly painful."

"Who says we have to break up?" Stavros said. "Come home with me." His voice was soft, persuasive, and for a moment she wanted to give in, wanted to take what he was offering. He made her feel like a beautiful, desirable woman, when no one else had—but in the end, she wasn't glamorous, sophisticated Sheena. She was Elle Drake and she carried her baggage with her everywhere she went.

"I can't tell you how much I want to go with you, Stavros," she said sincerely, "but I really can't."

Swift impatience crossed his handsome face and he blinked, his dark eyes growing a little frosty. "The boats are beginning to take some of our guests back to shore. I need to speak with a few of them. Stay here and wait for me."

Elle nodded. Where was the harm in that? After tonight, Sheena MacKenzie was going to disappear and Stavros would never see her again. Maybe he already knew she was saying good-bye. She couldn't blame him for being upset. She'd tried to stay within boundaries, not lead him on, yet gain his trust enough to get into his inner circle. She'd attended his charities and his parties, and never once had she heard the whisper of illegal activity. If he was the criminal her boss suspected, he was amazingly adept at hiding it, and she no longer believed it was possible.

So why couldn't she fall in love with him? What was wrong with her? Certainly the worm—he-who-could-never-be-named—was not worth holding out hope for. Was she stupid enough to do that? Hope that he would come after her? That would never happen. He didn't want her. He didn't want her legacy—or her name—or her house—and he certainly didn't want the seven daughters that would come along with her.

No, she had stopped hoping Jackson Deveau would ever come to love or even want her.

Now she just had to stop hurting.

She watched Stavros as he talked to his guests, smiling and seemingly happy. As if sensing her looking at him, he turned his head and sent her a warm smile. Her heart did a funny little flip, not the way it did when the worm smiled at her, but because she knew Stavros was half in love with her and it was so unfair. The smile she sent Stavros back was sadder than she knew.

Could she live like this? This glamorous, whirlwind life? She was born with a legacy few others—if anyone—ever had or would know. As the seventh daughter of a seventh daughter, Elle's psychic gifts ran deep in her genes and would be passed on to her seven daughters. And her seventh daughter would carry that same bittersweet legacy. Would Elle fulfill her destiny? Or would the Drake legacy of magic die quietly with her?

Elle used to envision a life of laughter and happiness with her soul mate. That was before she'd met him. He was a morose, silent, brooding, very dominant male. She knew he could bring stillness and peace to her, or with one smoldering look, turn her veins to liquid fire. But he refused to accept who she was—refused to love her as she was. And if he didn't, she feared no other man ever would—or could. Not the real Elle Drake, at least.

She turned around, and leaned out over the rail, watching the boats coming in to take Stavros's guests back to shore. Night had long since given way to dawn and she was tired, suppressing a yawn as she tried to figure out what she'd do next with her life. Sea Haven, a small village nestled on the northern California coast, had always been home—a refuge. Her family house was there, a large estate overlooking the turbulent ocean.

The sea was so different here, like glass. A beautiful lure promising a sun-filled life of luxury, but she knew better than to think such a life was meant for her. Deep inside, she was a homegirl, a woman born to be a wife and mother. She loved adventure and spice, but eventually, her need to pass on her Drake legacy would grow so strong she wouldn't be able to ignore it. Did she have the right to deny the world someone like her sister Libby, who could heal with a touch of her hands? Or Joley, with her voice? Kate, whose books gave so many people solace and escape? Each of her sisters had incredible gifts passed down generation after generation. If she didn't fulfill her destiny, the line would end with her.

Movement caught her eye and she shifted her gaze to see the captain approach Stavros and whisper something in his ear. She was adept at reading lips, but she couldn't see his mouth clearly. Stavros frowned and shook his head, glanced at his watch and then over at Elle. She kept her face still, and turned her gaze back to the sea. Stavros's bodyguard, Sid, said something as well. He was facing her and she caught his words distinctly.

"It will be dangerous to have her on the island, sir. Think about this. Take her off the boat now and we'll give the driver orders to take her to your villa. They can hold her there until the meeting is over."

Elle's stomach tightened. The bodyguard was talking about her. Stavros shook his head and said something she couldn't catch, but the bodyguard and captain both looked toward her again and neither looked happy.

That built-in alarm, the one that had saved her numerous

times on countless assignments, shrieked at her, and she didn't hesitate. She moved quickly through the thinning crowd toward the side of the yacht where the boats were coming in to pick up the guests and return them to shore. Her purse and overnight bag were still in the cabin down below, but Elle was careful never to carry anything in her purse or her belongings that could betray her. She would leave the yacht and if Dane wanted her to return, she could use the retrieval of her things as an excuse to contact Stavros again.

She made herself small, trying to blend in with the other guests. As Elle she could disappear easily into the shadows, but Sheena stood out. Her heart sped up and a sense of urgency rode her as she wound her way to the departing boats. It wouldn't do to look back and check to see if she was being hunted; she already knew she was. She had one chance to step into the departing boat as it was taking off. She had to time it perfectly.

Elle slid through the last of the guests waiting for the next boat and stepped onto the platform, holding out her hand to the young man pushing off the departing boat. He grinned and guided the boat back into position so she could step into it. Just as his fingers slid around her hand, she felt another hand catch her upper arm in a firm grip, pulling her back.

"Mr. Gratsos would like the pleasure of Ms. MacKenzie's company awhile longer," Sid said smoothly, drawing her much smaller frame against him.

Elle inhaled sharply, feeling the burst of emotion spilling from Stavros's bodyguard. He almost wished he hadn't caught her—in fact he'd considered just missing her, but knew Stavros would have stopped the other boat. She allowed herself to be pulled back without a struggle. The bodyguard was bigger and much stronger than she was, and even if she could have caught him by surprise, what would be the point? None of Stavros's men were going to let her leave the yacht against his orders.

She smiled graciously at the driver and looked up at the bodyguard. He wasn't Greek. She wasn't certain just where he was from. He spoke with a Greek accent, but there was something off about him. And he looked terribly familiar, but she didn't know where she'd seen him before.

"You're hurting me." She kept her tone low, very low, her gaze on his face.

He let her go immediately, fast, as if her skin burned him. "I'm sorry, Ms. MacKenzie. Mr. Gratsos asked me to bring you back to him and I was afraid you'd fall into the sea if I didn't keep hold of you. I didn't realize how hard I was gripping you."

He'd been afraid she'd make a scene, but strangely, that was all she could get from him. Why was that? How was the bodyguard protected from her psychic abilities in the same way Stavros was? It couldn't be coincidence that two people who worked together had strong natural barriers, and yet Sid's barrier was as strong or stronger than Stavros's, although it felt different.

Elle flashed him a quick, forgiving smile, very much in keeping with Sheena's sweet personality. "I certainly wouldn't want to fall into the sea with this dress on."

He stepped back to indicate for her to make her way through the small knot of guests. Elle hesitated. "Sid, this is the last boat for shore and they're already boarding. I have to get off." Deliberately she glanced at her slim, diamond watch. "I have an appointment this afternoon."

"Mr. Gratsos will get you to your appointment in time," Sid assured.

That was a lie. He didn't like lying to her. Whatever protection he had built or had been provided for him, his more intense emotions slipped through—unless he'd allowed it, which was possible. She could do that. Sid was worried about her, and if he was worried, she needed to be. She stayed very still, measuring the distance to the boat. She was fast, but she doubted if the boat would take her against Stavros's orders.

Sid shook his head. "Don't try it, Ms. MacKenzie. If Mr. Gratsos wants you here, you'll stay."

It was a warning—a clear warning. Had he read her mind? She didn't think she'd given away her thoughts on her face. He looked at her directly, his dark eyes meeting hers. Her heart jumped at the caution, her mouth going dry. "Let me go now."

For a moment regret showed in his eyes, but she knew he wasn't going to cross his boss. "You'll have to take that up with him."

Elle nodded and made her way back toward the shipping magnate, very aware of Sid directly behind her.

Stavros held out his hand to her, closing his fingers around hers to draw her to his side. "I thought you were trying to leave me."

"I told you I couldn't stay," Elle reminded him. "I want to, Stavros, but I've already been gone long enough." She was careful to keep her tone light and regretful even as she deliberately opened her senses and tried to psychically read him.

Stavros was very used to getting his way, and trying to force her to comply to his will would be something he might do without thinking it was wrong. It was her first real reprimand, gentle as she could make it although she wanted to spit fire at him.

His eyes darkened to a stormy color. "I asked you to stay with me. To go to my home with me. Sheena, I've never brought a woman there."

She took a deep breath. He was taking her to his island and she would be cut off from all aid. Did he suspect her? And if he did, did that mean he had something to hide? Already the engines were starting to rumble and she could feel the deck vibrating beneath her feet. "Stavros, maybe I should meet you there later, tomorrow or the day after."

Stavros patted her hand and led her across the deck to seat her in a plush chair. "We need time together, Sheena. I want to spend a week together, just the two of us, and perhaps you'll change your mind about me."

"I don't have enough clothes for a week," Elle said, trying to be practical.

"I'll send for them."

"I'm not sleeping with you, Stavros. I told you I can't be in a relationship right now. I'm not ready."

"You told me this man broke your heart, Sheena. Who is he?"

She shrugged, suddenly concerned by the steel in his eyes. She had the uneasy feeling that if she named anyone, he might turn up dead. Which was silly when she had been very certain that Stavros was no criminal. But, then, if that was the case, why were all her internal alarms screaming at her?

"He's of no consequence."

"He must be, if you won't consider another relationship." Stavros drummed his fingers on the table. She'd seen him do that when he was deep in thought or very agitated. "Did you live with him? How long were you with him?"

"That isn't your business," Elle said firmly.

His eyes narrowed. "I can hire someone to find out these answers for me."

Her heart jumped. He'd had her investigated. Dane had told her to be prepared for that. They had meticulously built her life and provided everything down to college pictures and records as well as a detailed past, but would it stand up to the kind of investigation a man like Stavros Gratsos would demand? Was this the reason he was taking her to his island? He'd discovered that she was undercover?

"Why are you pushing me?"

Stavros leaned toward her, his gaze locking with hers. "I want you. I have never wanted a woman in the way I want you."

Was that the simple truth? She doubted it. Sheena was beautiful and a woman of mystery and intelligence, the type that would attract and intrigue Stavros, but he wasn't known for falling for women. He escorted them, spent time with them, but inevitably he walked away. Why was he so determined to claim Sheena for his own?

Elle sighed. "You're going to have to get over it, Stavros. I'll be as honest as possible with you. Birth control won't work on me. I have this anomaly that runs in my family. No form of birth control works. Even if you used a condom, chances are still very high that I would get pregnant. I'm not doing that to myself. Or to you, for that matter."

His eyes darkened even more as he searched her face for the truth. She actually felt his mind reach out to hers and she pulled back, afraid for the first time that he might be able to read her as she did others. She allowed only the truth of her statement in her mind where he might catch her thoughts. Not only did he look intrigued, he looked pleased.

"You speak the truth."

She nodded. "I have no reason to lie. I really can't take the chance and as I want children someday, I can't take care of the problem permanently."

"So you didn't sleep with the man who broke your heart?"

She shook her head and looked out toward sea. The shore was fading as the yacht picked up speed heading toward his private island.

Stavros let out his breath, drawing her attention back to him. "Then I will be your first. Your only." There was deep satisfaction in his purring voice.

"I told you I will get pregnant. Not *can*, Stavros, I *will* get pregnant."

"I want children," he said. "I have no problem with you getting pregnant."

Her heart jumped. There it was. Stavros was handsome, charming, wealthy and he wanted children. She was certain he was psychic. Why couldn't the Drake house choose him? Maybe there was more than one man who would fit with her, and fate had intervened to give her another choice. Stavros Gratsos, who was forcing her to accompany him home.

"Stavros," she said gently, "you are the sweetest man, but you're way out of my league. Half your guests wonder what you're doing with me."

"Let them wonder."

Sid approached in his silent way and leaned down to whisper in Stavros's ear. Stavros immediately patted her hand. "We'll be home soon. I have to take this call." He dropped a kiss on top of her head as if they had already settled everything and walked away.

Elle took a breath and let it out. She needed to try to

stay in character just in case her cover wasn't blown, but she needed to get word to someone where she was. She couldn't kid herself. She could easily disappear and Stavros could have a hundred people swearing they saw him drop her off.

She closed her eyes. She needed to reach her sisters and let them know where she was, but the distance was too great. They were back in the United States and unless the psychic link between them was shattered, they wouldn't feel her—but . . . There was the worm. Jackson Deveau. His psychic connection to her was strong and if she reached out to him, she might be able to connect and let him know where she was being taken. Did pride count when one's life might be in danger? Was she really that stupid?

Already the boat was moving the short distance to his private island. It wasn't that far from the mainland. As the yacht approached the island, she could feel a faint buzzing in her head. At first it was annoying, but soon began to swell in volume almost to the point of pain. Pressing her fingers to her temples in an effort to relieve the ache, she caught Stavros watching her. There was a gleam of satisfaction in his eyes, as if he knew of the pressure in her head. She glanced at Sid. Whatever she was feeling, so was he, but he hid it better. He kept walking with Stavros, his face turned away from his boss, but she knew that same pressure was in his head as well.

Elle took another deep breath and let it out. The island was getting closer and the pressure in her head increasing. It was now or never. She closed her eyes and blocked out everything but Jackson. The way he looked. Remote. Broad shoulders. Scars. Thick chest. Piercing eyes filled with shadows. *Jackson*. She whispered his name in her mind. Sent it out into the universe.

There was a brief moment of silence, as if the world around her held its breath. A dolphin leapt from the sea and somersaulted back under the glassy waves. Elle nearly screamed when Stavros jerked her from her seat. She hadn't even sensed him coming up behind her.

"What are you doing?" he bit out, his white teeth snapping together. Fury etched the lines in his face.

He knew. Elle glanced toward his bodyguard. Sid knew, too. They not only had natural barriers but they were sensitive to telepathy. *Both of them.* She was in way over her head.

"Sheena! Answer me."

"Let go of me." Elle jerked her body away from him. "I don't understand why you're behaving this way." Even Sheena, as calm and collected as she was, wouldn't put up with being manhandled. Elle glared at him. "I've had enough, Stavros. I want to go home."

She was never going home again. The thought came unbidden, but settled into her churning stomach. Once she set foot on that island, her life as she knew it would be over.

Elle? Where are you? Stay alive, baby, any way you have to. Stay alive for me. I'll come to you. I'll find you. Do whatever you have to do.

Jackson's voice was warm, a soft, intimate slide into her mind—into her body. He felt like home. Like comfort. She wanted to fling herself inside him and shelter there. He must have heard—or felt—the despair in her, the fear.

Stavros caught both of her arms and yanked her against him, giving her a little shake as he brought her up onto her toes. "You will stop this moment unless you wish Sid to put you to sleep. I know what you are doing."

Elle. Answer me. There was a hard command in

Jackson's voice, almost a compulsion for her to answer.
She gasped when Stavros's fingers tightened hard on her
upper arms.

"Don't!" he warned.

Had he heard? She doubted it. But he'd felt the energy
vibrating and knew she'd received a response.

*Damn it, baby. Just fucking stay alive. Whatever it
takes.*

Elle glanced at Sid. He held a syringe in his hand. She
forced her body to relax, not wanting to go to his island
unconscious. "You know about me." She kept her voice
even. Very calm.

"That you are telepathic? Yes, of course. I felt it immediately."

"Well at least I don't have to try to explain that to you,"
Elle said, spilling relief into her voice. "I hate hiding who
I am from the world, but people think I'm crazy."

His fingers relaxed their hold on her, although she
knew she'd have bruises. "You don't ever have to hide
from me, Sheena. I'm very much like you."

Elle studied his face. Stavros was a little too okay with
kidnapping to be as clean as she'd first believed him to be.

"We'll talk at my home," Stavros said, effectively stopping her questions.

Elle remained silent, determined not to allow him to
see that she was afraid. She let Sid help her from the yacht
to the pier and then into the waiting car. The island was
beautiful, lush and green under the late morning sun. She
noted the way as they drove along the road up toward the
villa.

Once there, Elle turned gracefully on the rich leather
seat of the chauffeur-driven car and extended her high-
heeled foot out the door, allowing the slit along her glitter-

ing gown to slip open and reveal her shapely leg just for a brief flash as she exited the car. Beside her, Stavros tucked her hand into the crook of his arm and guided her up the walkway to the enormous house built on the island overlooking the sea. He stroked her fingers and she glanced up at him, sending him a faint smile before turning her attention to his masterpiece of a house.

The structure was long, sprawling and multilevel and looked to be nearly all glass, so the views could be seen from any direction. Reachable only by small plane, helicopter or boat, the island afforded Gratsos as much privacy as he wanted. She knew he was trying to impress her, that she had intrigued him, because so far, nothing of his world had impressed her. He was used to women throwing themselves at him, and she was different enough to be a challenge. Well . . . that and he somehow had built-in radar when it came to psychic abilities. It was how he must have found his bodyguard and why he had been so drawn to her.

At least she knew why he was so interested in her now or it might have been difficult not to be flattered by his attentions. Stavros was a handsome, intelligent man and knew how to pull out every stop to seduce a woman. He was charming about it, but there was an aura of danger surrounding him, and she never discounted reading auras. He wasn't going to let her go. She was in trouble and she knew it. Stavros didn't like taking no for an answer.

Her heart beat a little too fast, and she took a couple of deep breaths to calm the flood of adrenaline. She was out of range of communication here, completely cut off from all help, especially with that bothersome pain growing stronger in her head. It had to be a transmission of some kind to block psychic energy. She wasn't certain it was even possible, but the moment she was alone, she was going to test her theory.

"Sheena?" Stavros rubbed the back of her hand again. "I wanted you to see my home." His voice purred. "Say you're not upset with me for kidnapping you and bringing you here." He paused on the intricate walkway leading to his magnificent home, tipping up her face to stare intently into her eyes.

Elle could imagine that his intent look would make most women feel a little faint. She just felt sick. Whatever Stavros's intentions were, he didn't much care if she agreed or not.

"Does telepathy run in your family?" She wanted him to think only of that ability and no other. She kept herself strictly under control, not giving in to fear when she wanted to raise her arms to the wind and use the force of it to gain freedom.

"Don't talk in front of anyone," he hissed, still smiling. "This subject is for us alone."

Another bid to join them together. She recognized manipulation when she saw it. At least he was still trying to be charming and gain compliance rather than force it. She nodded her head, unwilling to try to fight a losing battle. She'd much rather wait and see what Stavros wanted from her. Maybe she could collect information that Dane would find helpful, if she managed to make it out alive.

The door was opened by a matronly looking woman who managed to look right through Elle as if she wasn't there. "This is Drusilla. She's our housekeeper," Stavros introduced. "Without her we'd all be lost."

Drusilla beamed and smiled a welcome to Stavros while she nodded a little warily to Elle. Elle stepped inside the enormous multilevel glass room. "This is beautiful, Stavros."

"I'm glad you like it, as it will be your home."

Elle heard Drusilla's swift intake of breath and Stavros immediately sent her a glaring reprimand. Elle forced herself to step farther into the room, looking around her. The view was breathtaking, the most incredible she'd ever seen. It was an amazing silken cage, a prison beyond her wildest dreams.

She allowed Stavros to lead her through the long, starkly beautiful room and up the wide staircase to a large bedroom. He pushed open the door and gestured toward the four-poster bed. "This will be your room. Mine is just down the hall."

Someone had already placed Elle's small overnight bag on the bed. It looked ridiculous among the rich opulence of the room.

"Stavros, wait." Elle caught his arm. "I really can't stay. I have an appointment this afternoon and I can't be late."

"You're going to stay, Sheena, and you're going to have my babies. I've been looking for a woman like you for years. I'm not about to let you slip away now." He pushed her farther into the room and glanced at his watch. "You are to stay here in this room until I come for you. The door will be locked, Sheena, and you are to stay."

There was no missing the iron in his voice or the warning. Elle stood very still in the center of the room. He was showing his hand now, blatantly letting her know that not only had he kidnapped her, but that he expected total cooperation. She said nothing as he closed the door, waiting before moving until she heard the lock snick into place.

Elle opened her bag only to find it empty. Someone had already unpacked her things and put them away. After a brief search, she found her clothes neatly hanging in the spacious, walk-in closet. Elle stripped off her gown and changed into a pair of slim cotton pants and a snug cotton T-shirt. She swiftly braided her waist-length hair and pulled on her climbing shoes before going to the window.

Below her room, large boulders and rocks formed the cliffs leading to the dazzling sea. Ordinarily the sight would have soothed her, but the way the house hung out over the ocean made climbing dangerous. It interested her to find the window wired for security. She could open the window but an alarm would trigger if she so much as stuck her arm out. With the way the house was built, it would have been nearly impossible for anyone to break in, so was he keeping women prisoners here at his whim? Had he brought others here?

Elle studied the room carefully, gliding her palm over the walls and bed, seeking psychic energy left behind by any others. She felt nothing at all but that faint, annoying buzzing in her head. As far as she could tell, only the housekeeper had been in her room. Now that she was alone, she needed to send a message home and let them know where she was.

She opened the window and inhaled the sea and salt. The moment the salty mist touched her face she felt better—lighter, more hopeful. Elle lifted her arms and called the wind. Pain crashed through her head. She barely managed to suppress the cry welling up as stars burst behind her eyes and everything around her swirled black. She bent, retching, gagging, staggering toward the bed, pressing both hands to her pounding head.

Stavros was psychic and he had somehow managed to deploy some kind of energy field to prevent psychic energy from being used. Why would he do that? He wouldn't be able to use it either. Weak, she slid her back down the wall and put her head between her legs, breathing deeply to keep from fainting. She wasn't going to be able to summon help until she was off the island or she could find the source of the energy field.

Once she could breathe again, she rose unsteadily and dealt with the security, a small beam she redirected so she could slip through the window and cling like a spider to the side of the glass villa. And spiders were much better at clinging to glass than she was. She slid until her toes and fingers found purchase.

Elle clung to the edge, reaching with her toes, wishing she was at least another inch taller as she tried to gain the roof. For several heart-stopping moments she found herself staring down at the rocks and sea a good hundred feet below her, afraid she couldn't reach it and would fall. She studied the distance above her. She would have to lever her body up using the power of her legs and catch the edge. One chance. That's all she'd have—and she was going to take it.

Elle had climbed rocks and mountains all over the world. The slick roof was not going to be her undoing. She rehearsed every move in her mind and pushed off, using her powerful leg muscles to propel herself upward. Her hands caught, slipped and her fingers dug into the roof, holding. She let her breath out and gathered strength before drawing her leg up and over. Once positioned, she could pull herself all the way up.

She took a moment to recover and then ran lightly across the roof to the other side of the house where Stavros was conducting his meeting. She stayed low, knowing she would show up easily against the bright sunlit roof. She could see Sid escorting four men up the path to the house. Frowning, she lay flat. The men wore biker colors with patches, of the standard 1 percent symbol and an intricate sword with blood dripping down the blade. She'd seen the patches before.

Outlaw bikers from one of the most notorious clubs rising on three continents were the only ones who would dare to wear the symbol of the Sword. Some said the origins of the group were Russian, and it quickly spread across Europe to the United States. The recruits were brutal, prison-hardened and willing to kill over the slightest insult. She had run across them in several cases related to trafficking guns and drugs, as well as murder for hire. The club, known as the Sword, was fast gaining a deadly reputation that rivaled existing crime lords. Convictions were rare because only a handful of witnesses had ever agreed to testify against them. And of those few, not one had ever lived out the day after a death sentence was handed down from the club's notorious leader, Evan Shackler.

What would Evan Shackler or any of his bikers be doing on the island of a wealthy shipping magnate? And why was Stavros clapping him on the back as if they were old friends? More than old friends . . . Brothers? They greeted one another in a traditional Greek manner, kissing both cheeks, which wasn't a sign that they were relatives, but they looked uncannily alike. As they walked side by side, she could see a huge resemblance, although Evan looked wild and unkempt with his long hair and shadowed face beside Stavros's handsome executive image. They were close in height and weight and had the same mannerisms, even moving their hands in the same way. She'd have to look into the files for Shackler and meticulously check his background.

But if Shackler was in some way related to Stavros—which she admitted was a leap—could he be psychic? Had Stavros protected his island to prevent a relative from using psychic ability against him? That would make sense. If Stavros was psychic, he would want to be able to use his abilities just as she and her sisters did in the privacy of their home. Never once had she thought of constructing an energy field to prevent psychic talents from being used, so Stavros had to have a good reason for doing so.

Something bit the back of her shoulder, a vicious sting that was hard enough to send her spinning around. The sound of a gunshot registered almost before the fact that she had been hit did. Blood stained the front of her shirt and down her arm, bursting across the roof like an artist's spray.

Stavros was shoved to the ground by Sid, one hand preventing him from moving while Sid's gun tracked someone behind her.

"No one touches her!" Stavros screamed. "Kill him. Shoot him."

Sid's gun blazed and she heard a body fall behind her, realizing Sid's gun was trained on the guard who shot her, not her, and she scrambled back over the roof, crawling because she couldn't stand, couldn't use her useless arm. Breathing was difficult as she made her way to the edge of the roof overlooking the cliffs. Her body hurt so badly she didn't think she could make it back into the room even if she wanted to. She couldn't let Stavros keep her. She wouldn't be able to defend herself and she knew what he wanted now. He would keep her in this house—this prison—and she would be like the women she had tried to help—trapped in a world serving Stavros's will.

"Sheena!" Stavros was on his feet. "Don't!"

Sid went up the side of the house, moving fast, but her vision was blurring and she knew she had to jump while she could. He would reach her if she didn't get the nerve to take her chances in the sea and rocks below. Once away from the energy field, she'd have more power. She leapt out into space and lifted her arm to summon the wind.

The wind roared at her, shoving her slender body out away from the rocks to the welcoming water. Behind her, Stavros lifted his arms and sent his countercommand. As capricious as ever, the wind shifted, dropping her the remaining feet. She hit hard, her mind exploding into a million fragments as the cool water closed over her head, accepting her into its soothing arms. For a moment, she thought someone had landed beside her and that an arm brushed against her, but then she was sinking, not fighting, letting the sea take her home, far away from fear and a life she didn't believe would ever be hers.

Jackson. She whispered his name in her mind as she floated away.

2

JACKSON Deveau stepped through the doorway onto the front porch to stare up at the gathering clouds churning above the choppy waters of the sea. The storm was moving in faster than predicted, as it often did on the northern California coast. Fingers of fog, pushed by the building wind, reached shore ahead of the storm, covering the coastline in a wet, gray blanket.

She was out there somewhere. Alone. Alive. He knew she was alive. She had to be alive. Elle Drake, youngest of the Drake sisters, had been missing for a month now. Something terrible had happened to her or she would have reported in. Her undercover job had taken her into the seamiest side of life—human trafficking—and somehow her handlers had lost her. Her family had been told she was presumed dead, but he didn't believe it any more than her sisters did. He would know. They would know. The Drakes were psychically connected and, although Elle's sisters were devastated over her disappearance, the one thing they agreed upon was that she was alive. He wouldn't—*couldn't*—believe anything else.

So he had to find her. Today. If her cover had been blown as was suspected, whoever had her would keep her far away, out of the United States, if they didn't kill her first. Her family had tried numerous times, he had tried, but all of them had failed to even get so much as a direction on her. He had heard her soft voice nearly a month earlier and as many times as he replayed it in his head, he was certain she sounded afraid. And Elle wasn't afraid of much.

The storm would provide a much needed boost of energy and the plan was simple. All of them would gather together in Elle's protected house, home of her ancestors, gather the storm's energy, send it out into the universe and find her. And it was going to happen, because there was no other alternative.

He whistled and his dog, Bomber, bounded around the corner and paced with him to his truck. The big German Shepherd jumped inside and settled on the seat next to him. "Today, baby," he whispered softly into the wind, letting it carry his words away from him.

The drive through Sea Haven was familiar now. He'd moved to the small village on the coast after serving first as an Army Ranger and then in the DEA with his friend Jonas Harrington. Things had gone to hell more than once, both in the army when he was taken prisoner and later on an undercover assignment. Jonas had wanted to go home to Sea Haven and had talked Jackson into moving with him. He'd joined the sheriff's office and patrolled the coastline, not realizing for a long time what the inhabitants of Sea Haven had come to mean to him. He was a man of few words and even fewer friends, but he had been accepted in the small, tight-knit community.

The village was mourning Elle Drake, just as her family—and he—was mourning for her. There was a sense of quiet, of dread, as he drove through the streets. Everywhere he looked, he could see the small yellow ribbons on businesses and homes, waving from fences and trees. One of their own was missing and they all wanted her home. The wind continued to drive the fog until the coastal highway was thick and gray and mist covered his windshield. Gloom hung like a cloud as he continued down the highway until he came to the winding drive that led up to the Drake estate.

The multistoried house stood at the top of a cliff, surrounded by trees and a beautiful, colorful garden that even in the cold of winter grew and blossomed. The music of chimes in the wind hit him first and as the wind blew in from the sea, the various chimes danced and played an assortment of notes that seemed to ease the terrible weight on his chest. The wrought-iron double gate was closed and he sat at the bottom of the hill studying the symbols and the words etched in both Latin and Italian. *The seven become one when united.*

The Drakes had a magic that few possessed and when they came together, the things they could accomplish were extraordinary. Jackson found them all extraordinary women. Somehow he had been brought into their circle through Jonas.

Elle. He leaned his forehead against the steering wheel and breathed away his fear for her. He had been a prisoner of war, without too much hope that anyone would find him. He was moved every few days, and as a sniper with a reputation, his captors had no intention of returning him for even political reasons. The scars from those long weeks of torture were on his skin and ran deep beneath it as well. It wasn't as if he had much to live for back in those days, and he hadn't believed in much either. Until a voice began whispering in his head telling him to live, to fight, that he wasn't alone.

He had thought he was going insane at first. That voice was soft—feminine—and eventually over time, sensual. He loved the sound of her voice. *Elle.* His mysterious, elusive Elle Drake. In his pain he had somehow connected with her and she had been able to find him. He didn't understand their connection, but he knew she belonged to him. She was meant for him. He had followed Jonas to Sea Haven to see her, to know she was real. And once he had, he should have been man enough to walk away but he couldn't. He sighed. He had baggage, unresolved and far too dangerous, and he had to find a way to resolve those issues before he claimed the woman he knew was meant for him.

The large padlock on the gate fell to the ground of its own accord and the gates began to swing open. There was intense satisfaction in that. The Drake gate only opened for those who belonged. No one knew how it recognized the family and their men, but the house, capable of protecting those within, welcomed him.

"See, Elle?" he whispered. "Even your home says it's time." Past time. He should have acted a long time ago, started a war, or rather ended one, and then just locked her to his side. If he'd done so, this wouldn't have happened.

He drove up the road toward the house, noting how rich and green and beautiful everything always was. The house loomed ahead, old, standing in the wind and salt spray without a crack or chip in the paint, looking as if it had just been built. He drove around to the parking area up above where the yard overlooked the sea. He stood for a long moment staring down at the churning, dark water. Sometimes the ocean looked like glass, but this evening the sea appeared angry, in great turmoil, matching his mood.

Waves crashed against the rocks, spraying white foam high into the air, the sound like thunder, reverberating in his head. "Elle, baby, where are you?" He whispered into the wind, needing an answer.

"Jackson." Jonas Harrington came up behind his friend, knowing enough to say his name in warning and not come up behind him silently.

Jackson turned slightly and from the look in his eyes, he'd known Jonas was there all along.

"I should have stopped her," Jackson said. "I knew she was involved in something dangerous and I should have stopped her."

Jonas shook his head. "The Drakes aren't so easy to stop." But even as he said it, he knew Jackson would never agree with him. He was a throwback to the warriors of old. Elle was his woman and it was a duty, privilege and right to look after her. He didn't care about women's rights, or customs or society. Jackson had a code, an honor system. Elle was his woman and he was supposed to keep her from harm's way. He hadn't done it and no reasoning was good enough or ever would be for him.

"She's alive, Jonas, you know that, and her cover has to be blown, which means her life is in danger. Wherever she is, they're hurting her and they have to kill her when they're done finding out everything she knows."

Jonas studied his friend. Jackson was Cajun, with broad shoulders, roped arms, a heavy powerful chest and shrewd, cool eyes—black obsidian, glittering when upset, or absolutely flat and cold, showing no emotion whatsoever. His thick, unruly, wavy hair was as black as midnight. Scars ran down his face and neck and disappeared into his shirt. His features were etched with lines of hard violence and a stillness that belied his lightning-fast reflexes.

Jackson rarely spoke of his family, and from what Jonas had gleaned from the few times he'd mentioned them, they'd lived in the bayou itself, on a small island, boating to the mainland for supplies. His dad had been a fighter, a veteran of more than one war and a biker who left his family often because he couldn't settle, but returned just as often because he couldn't be away from them. From the things Jackson had let drop, his father had begun teaching him survival and fighting and the use of weapons at a very early age.

He seemed to love and despise his father, feeling as if the bikers he'd run with had been his family and Jackson and his mother had gotten the leftovers. Although the details were sketchy, Jonas knew that Jackson had been the one to provide for his mother. When she'd gotten cancer, his father had disappeared once again, unable to face the prolonged illness. Jackson had been fifteen when his mother died, leaving him to run wild in the bayou. He'd fended for himself until his father returned and Jackson was forced to accompany him to live in the biker camps, traveling with them as they moved. His father had died in a knife fight, taking four rival gang members with him just before Jackson's nineteenth birthday, and Jackson had joined the army. Jonas knew Jackson had a brush with that same biker club during his time with the DEA, but he never talked about it.

"We'll find her this time," Jonas said.

The black eyes flicked to him. "Yes, we will. I'm bringing her home. And she's done, Jonas. Be prepared for that.

I know how you are about the girls, but Elle's mine. And she's done."

"Jackson . . ." For the first time that he could remember in their long friendship, Jonas felt a stab of unease. Jackson could be quite ruthless and once he made up his mind, there was no turning him from his objective.

Jackson shook his head. "Let's just get a starting point. The storm's coming in fast. Are the girls gathered?"

That was like Jackson. He was done talking. Jonas sighed as they wound their way through the back garden. He'd never understood Jackson and Elle's relationship—or lack of one. Elle kept to herself, in the same way Jackson did. They were both strong-willed individuals and aside from Elle's bad temper, and Jackson's lack of one, they were very much alike—stubborn.

"Ilya's here. He has some information for us," Jonas said. "He prefers to tell us before we go inside."

Jackson glanced at him, his gaze sharp. Whatever Ilya Prakenskii had to say, he didn't want his fiancée, Joley Drake, or any of her sisters to know. And that meant it couldn't be good.

Jackson let out his breath, refusing to give in to the secret part of him that was filled with terror. He'd been a prisoner of war to one of the worst sadists in the business and he hadn't felt fear like this.

Elle. Baby. Stay alive for me. Any way you have to, stay alive for me. I'm coming for you.

The storm was the perfect conduit they needed to boost their energy. Wherever Elle was, she would be waiting, knowing they would never stop looking for her.

He walked around to the side of the Drake house where Ilya waited in the shadows for them. Ilya nodded to Jackson and glanced toward the towering house. "Let's walk."

"They'll know," Jonas cautioned.

The Drakes always knew. They'd been trying for a month to find Elle, uniting over and over to find their lost sister, and because they couldn't, they knew she was a great distance away and under extreme duress. Elle was powerful, probably more so than any of them. Jackson had seen her nearly bring a building down with the explosive energy of her temper. She was always carefully controlled, but if she couldn't get herself out of whatever situation she was in . . . Jackson closed his eyes again, his stomach turning over. She had to be injured. If she couldn't reach them, she *had* to be injured, there was no other explanation.

Elle hurt. The thought was terrifying. Elle in the hands of a man capable of human trafficking was even worse.

You know I'll never stop until I find you. Stay strong, baby. For me. For your sisters. For Jonas and Ilya and the entire damn village. Stay alive, Elle.

He wanted her to love him enough to live for him. He wanted to be her reason. She was his. She'd been his ever since he first heard her voice, soft and silky and so damned sexy. Something inside of him had come awake—had come to life.

He didn't have emotions the way Jonas had them. Caring for everything and everybody, every cause, that was Jonas. Saving the world, determined to save Jackson. Jackson glanced at Ilya. The Russian was much more like him. Controlled. Disciplined. Utterly dangerous. Sometimes he wished he could be more like Jonas, especially when it came to expressing his feelings to Elle, because if anyone was going to save him, it was Elle. He'd never wanted a woman for his own until Elle and she was as elusive as the wind.

He swore softly under his breath and turned away from the other two men. Both noticed every detail, and he didn't need their scrutiny right then. He should have just stepped up to the plate, been a man and taken what was rightfully his. He'd let her down.

Ilya stopped walking beneath a stand of trees and glanced up at the captain's walk. Three stories up, Hannah Drake Harrington, Jonas's wife, paced back and forth, her long blond curls spiraling in the strong wind. Several times she lifted her arms, drawing in the wind, calling to it as she did when she wanted to command it. Jackson knew she was gathering energy in preparation for their sending.

Ilya kept his voice low. "I've pieced together information from several sources who owe me. Elle's cover has been carefully built over several years, which explains her frequent disappearances. She used the name Sheena MacKenzie, a young, very attractive and wealthy socialite playing in the European circles mainly. She was known to be quite the adventurer, very skilled at everything from caving to mountain climbing."

"Which Elle is," Jonas interjected.

"By night Sheena MacKenzie was on record, suspected by Interpol of being a very high-class and successful thief."

"So she didn't infiltrate as a woman kidnapped and used in the trafficking ring," Jonas said. "Her people leaked the false information to Interpol? Or were they in on it? As far as I know she doesn't work for Interpol."

"If my informant has it correct, there was a loan and cooperation. The man they're after is a big fish," Ilya explained. "The main suspect is a man by the name of Stavros Gratsos."

"The shipping magnate." Jonas whistled softly. "He's

got more money than half the world. What would he want with a human trafficking ring?"

"It's a huge moneymaker, Jonas," Ilya explained. "More than likely that's how he got his start in the first place. He's been suspected, but no one has ever found proof. Human trafficking is second only to drugs and growing every day. One house can earn well over a million a month in one city. Imagine if you have a house in every city all over the world. It's global, not just one small area, and Gratsos has his finger in every pie. It wouldn't be difficult, and he's so far out of reach of authorities, he'd get away with it, and probably has for years."

"What exactly was Elle doing?" Jackson asked. Human trafficking. The thought of Elle in the hands of men like that left him shaken and cold and useless. He couldn't let his mind go there. He tried not to remember her voice, so shaken, reaching out to him and how he couldn't find her. She'd been in the hands of a madman for a month.

"She met Gratsos casually a few times," Ilya said, "and according to her handler, Gratsos seemed quite captivated by her."

Jackson closed his eyes briefly. He understood completely. Elle had that effect on people. She seemed elusive, out of reach. A combination of sexy and innocent that could capture a man's attention and not let him go. He knew better than most. Once he'd heard her voice, that soft bedroom voice that sank into a man's skin and settled in the pit of his stomach and gathered full force in his groin, he'd thought of little else. The obsession had only increased in her company.

She was short, the shortest of her sisters, with a petite, very feminine figure. Her eyes were as green as the sea, like two sparkling gems that enticed and promised. Her wealth of red hair was straight, without a hint of the curls that her sister Hannah had. The silken fall cascaded past her waist, a bright waterfall that took a man's breath. Jackson had a lot of fantasies about that hair—and her mouth, her perfect bow of a mouth. She seemed small and fragile, a woman to protect and cherish, so feminine a man might want to own her, yet there was steel inside her. She could appear cool and distant, yet any man would see the fire in her, the passion smoldering so close to the surface, passion a man would want all to himself. Yeah, he could see Gratsos being captivated by her. She was exotic and elusive and just out of reach. Someone used to getting anything he wanted would be more than intrigued by her.

"You think this Gratsos has her locked away somewhere?"

Ilya nodded. "Interpol and her handler believe she's dead. We know she's not. Gratsos might believe the cover story—a thief trying to steal from him. He might suspect her of being undercover, but he'd want to believe she was a thief, especially if he had the hots for her, which my informant said was obvious. Even believing she was an international thief might intrigue him further. If he's dirty dealing, he might be even more attracted thinking that she could be."

"He'd be angry with her, that she wasn't falling into his lap," Jonas said. "If he really was dealing in human trafficking, then he couldn't afford to risk that she was undercover and spying on him. That kind of charge, even for someone as powerful as him, would rock the world. He'd have to kill her."

Ilya nodded. "That would be the smart thing to do and Gratsos is a very smart man, but he's also very egotistical and believes himself to be above the law. He was penniless as a teen and built an empire from sheer guts and brains. Tragedy struck his family from the very beginning. His father married a woman, had twins, and she and the other boy died a month later in an automobile accident. The father was a mean son of a bitch, but Gratsos proved to be a very intelligent boy and he caught a few breaks from teachers. According to rumor, his first venture was smuggling and he was good at it. He had no compunction about operating outside the law then and I'm certain he doesn't have any worry over it now either. He owns tankers for transporting oil and freighters for dozens of other very lucrative contracts. Smuggling a few women on board wouldn't be a problem. If he's been doing this from the beginning of his career, he'd be very good at it by now. Keeping Elle might prove to be irresistible to him. He would like the idea of a woman like Elle under his thumb, right under the noses of the authorities while he carried on with his yachting and parties and business as usual."

Jackson clung to that, without thinking too much about what a man who held himself above the law and unscrupulous enough to deal in human trafficking, might do to a woman he believed he now owned. Elle was in trouble and if Gratsos was the man holding her, he had the means to keep her hidden from the world for a long time—until he tired of her.

He took a breath and forced his mind away from disaster. He had to think with a clear head. Find her first. Extract her. Keep her safe. Deal with everything else later. Just first find her. He looked up at the sky. Already he could feel the crackling of energy. Hannah was moving off the captain's walk back to the house, signaling it was close to time.

The Drake house towered above them, rising like an ancient dragon with widespread wings poised on the edge of the cliff. Water pounded below, sending giant sprays of white foam high up into the air, the water murky and dark, roiling like a witch's cauldron. The wind whipped across his face, lashing him with stinging droplets of seawater. Jackson tasted the salt along with his fear. This house would be his when he claimed Elle. Her legacy would be his.

Elle was the seventh daughter of a seventh daughter. She carried all the powers of the Drake family in her slender body, and with it, the ability to continue the line. Which meant birth control didn't work well on her.

She was to be the mother of the next generation of Drakes. He would marry her, but they would keep her name. Their seven daughters would possess the power of the Drake family. He had waited, letting Elle run, making her run, because he had been afraid. Not of the children he had no idea how to be a father to—he'd learn that—but of his own violent legacy. And how could he explain it to her without putting her in danger?

He wasn't a man able to relinquish too much control, and Elle defied him at every turn—more than defied him, she challenged him. He hadn't trusted himself enough not to lose her when they both were such strong personalities and in hesitating, she'd turned away from him—and eventually, she'd even given up on him.

Elle. Damn it. Where are you? Answer me. He put every ounce of command, of iron will—a will honed and shaped by violence—into the demand. *Answer me now.*

He rubbed his shadowed jaw and looked up as lightning lit up the darkening sky, lacing the brooding clouds with white-hot lances, spears that felt as if they pierced his eyes and went through his skull right to the back of his head. He dropped to his knees and pressed his fingers hard to his temples, his stomach churning, the pain in his head so intense he was sick to his stomach.

Everything receded into the background, Ilya's and Jonas's anxious voices fading away. The world around him curved and trembled. The ground shifted, became soft and giving beneath him. He heard a voice whispering and at first he couldn't make out words, but he reached and the voice became stronger. *Sheena. Look at me. Talk to me. Who are you? What are you doing here? Who sent you? Talk to me, Sheena, and the pain will go away.* Male. Persuasive. He'd heard voices like that before, molding their victim, holding hope just out of reach.

Jackson went still, afraid to move, afraid to hope. He'd touched her. He'd connected and if someone was questioning her as Sheena, her cover was still intact. He tried to breathe through the pain—her pain—and let his mind expand, reach out strongly to hers. *Elle. Baby? Can you hear me? I'm coming for you. We're coming. Stay alive for me, honey.*

He felt the faint far-off touch, just a slight stirring in his mind. Fragile. Tenuous, as if she was afraid to believe. *Jackson?*

Her voice sent a vise gripping his heart, squeezing until there was actual pain. For a moment he thought he might be having a heart attack. *I'm here. I'm with you. Tell me where you are, Elle.*

I don't know. I can't think straight. My head . . . She trailed off, and the connection between them wavered.

Don't! His voice was sharp. *Stay with me, baby. I need you to look around you. What do you see? Who's with you?*

There was a moment of hesitation. Lightning lit up the sky and thunder crashed close, the sound louder than the booming of the sea. White light burned behind his eyes and he had to close his lids tightly against the shattering pain.

A hand fell on his shoulder. "Jackson?"

Jackson shrugged off the distraction. "I've got her. I've got her," he snapped. It was difficult being in two places and he needed to be with her. She was slipping away, even as he reached for her. *Elle, no!*

She was gone, out of his reach and he stayed on his knees, breathing deeply, dropping his forehead to the ground and staying still until he got himself under control.

"She's alive," Ilya said. "We'll find her."

Jonas held out his hand and Jackson took it, allowing his friend to pull him to his feet. "Why didn't you connect with us and strengthen the bond?" he demanded of Ilya without looking at him, that cold coil inside of him that was dark and dangerous now, unfurling.

"I tried, Jackson," Ilya said, his voice utterly calm. "Whatever you two have together is a bridge that is solidly between only you. I couldn't join you."

"I couldn't hold her to me," Jackson said, frustrated. "If you can't join me, what are we doing here? How is this going to work?" Because it had to work. The pain had been her pain. She needed help. Wherever she was, she needed medical attention. "She was confused." Almost childlike, more fragile than he'd ever known Elle to be. And that scared him almost as much as her being in the hands of madmen.

"Jackson." Jonas put a steadying hand on his shoulder. "We'll find her."

Ilya gestured toward the house. "The women want us in now."

Jackson glanced up at the empty captain's walk. Hannah would know the optimum time to try to send the wind to Elle. If they were lucky, and all the elements fell into place, they would create a surge of energy capable of crossing great distances to Elle.

I'm coming, baby, he whispered to the night and followed the other two men up the winding path to the huge, sprawling house.

Sarah Drake stood at the door, holding it open for them. Her pale face was still, anxiety in her large blue eyes. The wind tugged at her dark hair, giving her an ethereal look, one Jackson often associated with the Drake women. Sarah was the oldest and engaged to Damon Wilder, a neighbor who owned the house just below the Drake family estate. His arm around Sarah's waist, Damon greeted the other men with a slight nod and, leaning heavily on his cane, turned and limped back across the living room to stand against the wall.

Jackson followed Jonas inside, Ilya trailing behind him. The atmosphere in the Drake home was usually one of warmth and laughter. Tonight it was heavy with tension and sorrow.

Joley, the sixth Drake sister, the musician of the family, ran to fling herself in Ilya's arms. It always astounded Jackson that a man as remote and unemotional as Ilya, lit up when Joley was anywhere near him. The Russian brushed a kiss on top of her blond-streaked head, his arms tightening protectively around her.

"Did you feel her?" Jackson asked Hannah. "I had a small connection to her just now, but then I lost her."

Hannah, tall and elegant with long platinum spiral

curls and wide blue eyes, spun around to face him at his question. An ex-supermodel, married to Jonas and already pregnant with their first child, Hannah was particularly strong in her talents and would be one of their greatest assets in trying to find Elle. Jackson saw the answer on her face, the complete blank look that told him she hadn't caught even a small ripple from Elle.

It should have made him happy that his connection with Elle was so strong, so much so that he had found her and not her sisters, even for just a few moments, but what mattered most, was getting her home safe and unharmed.

"You spoke to her? Are you certain?" Hannah asked.

The room went silent and all faces turned toward him. Kate the writer, serious and gentle, Abigail the marine biologist, Libby the doctor and healer, Sarah, Hannah and Joley, and the men who loved them, waiting, holding their collective breath.

"She's alive. Hurt." Jackson frowned. "A head injury, I'd guess. She was confused and the pain was excruciating. Someone was questioning her and they used the name Sheena MacKenzie, so hopefully her cover is still intact, although they wanted to know who had sent her and asked what she was doing there. They spoke English with a heavy accent."

"Greek?" Ilya asked.

Jackson shrugged. "I couldn't say one way or the other. I wasn't there, just heard it through her and I got the feeling of a great distance." He rubbed his shadowed jaw, needing to find a way to still his hands, to keep from betraying the terror building in his gut. Elle. Damn him for not taking charge. For not keeping her safe. *Baby, I'm coming for you. If you don't believe anything else, believe I'll come for you.*

He sent the message to her in the way he'd been whispering to her for the last couple of years. Soft. Intimate. Intense. He could tell her things across a distance he couldn't seem to say to her face. He could feel the emotions, so deep they shook him, across that same distance, but up close, he was always so carefully controlled.

"Come into the house," Sarah said, her voice gentle, almost as if she knew what he was feeling. "Standing in the entryway isn't going to help. You have to commit to us, Jackson. We can't help if you don't give us your full commitment, and it seems to me, as close as we are to Elle, you're her soul mate and you're the one that's going to find her."

There was that waiting again. The silence. He lived in silence. Understood it. These people in this room had opened their lives to him, shared their world, yet he had always stood apart by choice, refusing to go all the way with the very commitment Sarah was asking of him. He didn't understand people. He wasn't comfortable being around them. The desert, the mountains, the sandy dunes above the ocean were places he sought and understood.

Emotions were kept at a distance, yet this family, these people who always welcomed him, kept emotions close and intense, and every moment he spent with them made him feel both cared for and yet isolated and apart. For Elle he went deeper into the room, into the circle of her family.

The candles made a pattern on the floor, the flames flickering with life. He looked around the house. It would be his home. His life would be here when he married Elle. He walked across the room and laid his hand on the wall. It was an old house, yet always appeared new. He had seen the house come to life, protecting those who dwelled inside. When he laid his palm on the wall, he felt energy, strong and pulsing. Little sparks danced around his fingers and across the back of his hand.

If you're alive, the way the Drakes believe, help us find her. Help me find her.

Beneath his palm, the walls undulated, and for a moment he thought he heard the sound of feminine voices rising in the distance.

He turned to look at the Drake sisters, but they were looking at one another, their eyes wide, their faces slightly shocked. He dropped his hand and moved back to the center of the room. "The storm is nearly overhead. Let's get this done."

"The house spoke to you," Sarah said. "Jackson, do you know what that means?"

His dark eyes slid over her face, noting her astonishment. "Did you really think Elle didn't belong to me?" His voice was quiet. Low. Soft even. The menace there reverberated through the room, enough that Damon stirred from his place against the wall and limped over to Sarah, his cane supporting his weight as he put one arm around her.

"Jackson, we all know you're meant for Elle," Sarah said softly. "You're the one who is holding back, not us."

He felt the arrow in the pit of his stomach. Damn her, she was right. They said she could see into the future at times, and right now she looked a little fey. She was seeing too much and what was inside of him wasn't fit for a woman to see, least of all a Drake and the sister of the woman he was going to marry.

He could smell the scent of the herbs each sister had used to cleanse herself before the ceremony. The pentagram was laid out with the mosaic tiles in the center of the circle. Candles lit the way in four directions. He took a deep breath and forced himself forward when Hannah gestured to him to come take his place in the center. Each sister sat near a point of the star and Jonah and Ilya sank down beside their women, close, thighs touching. Abigail's husband, Aleksandr, threw open the double doors to allow the storm into the house. This was not his way, but it was the Drakes' way, as it had been for hundreds of years. It was Elle's way and he needed the strength of her family to send the summons, create the bridge and gain the information they so desperately needed.

Outside the wind shrieked and moaned, rising and falling like the churning waves. Jackson took a deep breath, drawing in the salty mist. The rain began to fall, a light drizzle, promising a much more ferocious downpour. Thunder boomed just as a wave crashed against the rocks and white water formed a geyser, hurling into the air. Jackson could see the white foam bursting above the cliff and then falling out of sight again.

Unconsciously he rubbed his palm along the floor, over the mosaic tiles Elle's ancestors had placed a hundred years earlier. He felt the life in them, warmth against his skin, as if the mosaic breathed. Once again he heard the soft feminine voices speaking from a great distance. Some speaking in an ancient tongue, others more modern, but all whispering to be strong, that they were with him. He had never sought nor wanted a family, or unity or the belonging. It wasn't for him. Yet here he was, the house, the family, the woman, and he had shoved it away.

Elle. Stay alive for me. Believe in me.

He was asking from her what he hadn't done himself. He should have believed in what Elle was offering. Love. Unconditional love. Elle had watched him quietly, waiting for him to recognize what was in front of him. He wanted, not unconditional love, but unconditional surrender. Her will to his. He didn't want to be out of his comfort zone, he wanted Elle to come to him, bending her ways to his. He hadn't wanted to give away the violence inside him. He'd wanted acceptance without having to give anything of himself.

And he had lost her. He even knew the exact moment she had turned away from him and had chosen to go her own way. She had left him behind just as he expected her to do, just as he'd pushed her to do. Jackson shook his head. He *had* pushed her. He wanted to remain the rolling stone, the man who refused to need anyone. He was determined to show her she was the one who would have to change. He wasn't going to explain himself to her or change for her. She had knocked on his door, stood just outside on his porch with the ocean roaring behind her, her delicate features soft and beautiful, her emerald eyes deep and fathomless, her long red hair blowing in the wind.

"My house was obviously wrong," she'd said. "You're not man enough to take on this task and I'm done waiting for you." She had turned away from him and walked away, never once looking back. Worse, he hadn't stopped her.

He looked around at her family, feeling the weight of the ancient Drakes who had gone before, measuring his worth. And right now, at this moment, he wasn't worth very much and he just couldn't give a damn that they would all see. Elle was too important. Getting her back was too important; he'd just have to sort the rest of it out later. Right now, none of his well-thought-out reasons for not believing in her lifestyle seemed to matter at all.

Outside the open door, lightning lit up the sky in white jagged streaks, illuminating the dark turbulent water of the ocean. Thunder crashed, immediately followed by the angry boom of the sea. The wind rushed into the house and swirled around the women, feeding into the building energy and power in the room.

There was no way not to believe in the strange magic the sisters had when they were together. He knew Jonas thought it was their love and closeness that somehow made them a powerful force, but Jackson knew it had to be more than that—they seemed elemental parts of the universe—perhaps blessings bestowed on the family at birth. Whatever one believed in, they were a force to be reckoned with.

Electricity crackled in the room. Power built until the walls undulated and the floor shifted.

3

ELLE could hear a woman weeping in the distance. Hopeless. Broken. The sound filled with despair. She wished someone would help the woman because the closer she came to the surface, the more pain wracked her entire body and the crying kept pulling her out of her cocoon. She couldn't imagine what had happened. She couldn't remember.

"Sheena. Open your eyes. Stop crying, sweet, I'm here now and it's going to be okay."

Her body jerked involuntarily at the sound of that voice. She knew him. Knew his scent. Knew his touch. He brought pain or took it away. He had become her world. She knew nothing and no one else but him. He fed her. He took her to the bathroom. He chose whether or not she could wear clothes, or have a shower. His punishments, when she defied him—which was often—were terrible. He never changed tone. His voice always remained calm and matter-of-fact. Very powerful.

His hand stroked over her hair. The tumbled mass of

red strands was the only place on her that didn't hurt. Her
back and buttocks were fire. Her breasts burned. And between her legs it throbbed and ached, so sore she didn't
want to move for fear her insides would fall out. But the
pain in her head was the worst of all.

It took a few minutes before she realized that *she* was
the woman weeping. Elle made an effort to quiet, to remember what happened. What had she done that had earned
another of his terrible punishments?

"Sheena, come on now. Open your eyes for me."

Her mouth went dry at the sound of his soft, persuasive voice. There was a metallic taste in her mouth. Someone touched her wrist and she knew instantly it was
Stavros. In all the weeks he'd kept her, she'd never seen
another human being, other than his brother that first day.
Not one. She hadn't heard another voice. He brought food
and water. He tied her up and used her in every way he
wanted. He whipped her repeatedly, left her alone until
she thought she might go insane and yet often spent hours
attempting to pleasure her with his hands and mouth and
body. She never knew what his touch would bring. Her
heart slammed hard in her chest and she tried to jerk
away.

"Shhh, my sweet. I'm going to carry you to the bathtub.
When I put you in the water, you have to stay on your
hands and knees for me. Can you do that?"

She felt him slip his arm under her legs. The moment he
made contact with her skin she suppressed a scream. Pain
flashed through her and her stomach lurched. She tried to
bring her hand up to cover her mouth, but her arms were
too weak and felt too heavy, as if she were weighted down.
Her wrists were burned and swollen.

His arm came up under her back and she screamed,

arching upward trying to avoid contact. Her skin hurt and every movement made the pain crash through her skull. Fear ate at her. She couldn't remember. She was so thirsty she could barely part her swollen, dry lips.

"Shhh, Sheena, stay still. You'll only hurt yourself more." He sounded sad, his voice almost sorrowful and disappointed. "You have to get control of yourself. You can do that for me, can't you?"

He gently set her in the bathtub on her hands and knees, the warm water lapping at her body. Elle managed to open her eyes to narrow slits. Blood turned the water to a pale pink. Her skin burned and stung, causing her to shiver uncontrollably.

"It's antiseptic, my sweet. It will help numb you." Very gently he wrang a warm cloth over her back. "Let me take care of you."

But he had done this to her. She remembered now. All of it. He'd been so angry, although he hadn't shown it, never raising his voice, but she knew him now, knew when she displeased him. He wanted obedience from her. She was his to do whatever he wanted. She knew that the weeks spent in his company, forced to turn to him for comfort, for companionship, food and water, even permission to go to the bathroom, was all designed to mold her and break her spirit. And God help her, sometimes she couldn't remember who she was anymore.

The island had some kind of energy field that prevented her from defending herself using her psychic abilities. She'd tried testing it over the weeks, looking for weaknesses, trying different levels of strengths against it, but every single time, she'd been defeated, her headaches instantaneous and so painful she would vomit. Sometimes the pain was so severe she bled from her nose or mouth.

Each time he'd forced her to have sex, usually daily, she'd tried to stop him, fighting physically and with her psychic talents. And each time had been a disaster for her.

First there was the pain in her head driving her to the floor where she could only writhe and weep. And then his retaliation, whipping her or beating her with whatever he chose, and he had a variety of instruments at his disposal, each worse than the other.

Her first time with a man had been with him. Shockingly, he had been gentle with her. He'd actually tried to make it pleasurable for her, and that was his way to break her. One moment he would offer comfort, taking care of her, seeing to her every need, and the next, if she in any way defied him, he would be ruthlessly frightening, punishing her swiftly and without mercy. She could never relax, never know what was coming next, fixing her attention on him the moment he entered the room, thinking about him when he wasn't with her, so that he was her entire world and nothing else mattered.

He washed her body gently. "Don't make me do this to you, Sheena. Accept that you are mine and that I am all you will ever need or want. I can make you happy and bring you more pleasure than you've ever imagined." The warm water poured over her body, helping to numb the terrible pain of the raw wounds crisscrossing her back and buttocks and thighs. "You were born for me, to please me, to bear my children, strengthen my line. I wouldn't have to punish you like this if you would simply obey me, Sheena."

His hand continued to gently wash her wounds, the warm water and caressing fingers providing a balm to her tortured body. She closed her eyes again, shuddering, shaking, completely dependent on him for his help. Her arms began to collapse and he had to wrap his arm around her waist to keep her from falling. Very gently he rinsed off the rest of her body and then pulled the plug in the ornate, sunken tub.

Wrapping her in a soft, fluffy towel, he lifted her into his arms, cradling her as if she was the most precious woman in the world. Elle's head fell back against his shoulder, and then she turned to bury her face against his neck. It was her first act of submission and it frightened her. She needed comfort, needed someone to hold and soothe her, rock her as he was doing. He took her to her bed and laid her gently on her stomach, massaging an ointment into the thin stripes covering her body.

She knew he had noticed her slip, that little drop of her head; she'd felt his heart jump and her eyes burned with tears. Her teeth chattered uncontrollably, but her brain was beginning to kick in again. This couldn't go on. She was going to be lost, or maybe she already was. There was no way out. Stavros was too powerful, his private island too isolated. No one knew where she was. She was tied or chained most of the time, locked in a room, and she couldn't use even the smallest psychic talent. Her body hurt every minute of the day. She was exhausted and worn from fighting him.

He turned her over and rubbed the ointment into her breasts and belly, lower still, following the thin stripes inside her thighs and across her painful bare mound. Unbidden came the humiliating memory of him shaving her clean, right before he took her virginity. She bit at her lip to keep from crying out, but tears squeezed between her lashes. He leaned down to lick them away.

"You look so beautiful, sweetness." His tongue traced a path to the edge of her mouth, down to one stripe across the swell of her breasts. "Your body will know only mine, and you'll always crave my touch."

She opened her eyes then to look at him. He seemed invincible. All powerful. She tried to make a sound, but her mouth was too dry and he immediately held a glass of water to her lips, helping her drink. He looked so caring she could almost believe him, but he had been the one to inflict the damage on her.

"Why do you keep hurting me?" She could barely form the words.

"You must learn obedience, Sheena. You are to serve me, at my pleasure. When I tell you to do something, you must never argue. You must obey without question." He lowered her back to the bed and stroked his fingers over her shivering body. "Sometimes it may please me to hurt you and you will learn to be happy to do this." He bent his head to her breast, his tongue flicking her nipple.

She hurt so much she couldn't stop the little shudder that went through her, but still, he had been training her body to accept pain and find pleasure there as well. Already his fingers were probing between her legs, and, ignoring her wince and small cry, he pushed his head between her thighs, letting the dark shadowed jaw slide across the whip marks.

Oh God, she couldn't do this anymore. She didn't have the strength to fight him. Her fingers clutched at the silken sheet, bunching it into her fists while tears poured down her face. There had to be a way out. She just had to think. To find it. To stop feeling helpless like the victim he'd made her.

Elle. Baby. Stay alive for me. Any way you have to, stay alive for me. I'm coming for you.

Her breath caught in her throat. Was Stavros playing a

trick on her? The voice was so familiar, so warm and caring—so achingly familiar. She went very still, trying not to respond, to open her mind. She knew if she did, pain would crash into her brain and she'd lose the tentative control she had going for her.

As if sensing her withdrawal from him, Stavros bit down on her so that she arched her body, a small cry of pain escaping.

You know I'll never stop until I find you. Stay strong, baby. For me. For your sisters. For Jonas and Ilya and the entire damn village. Stay alive, Elle.

She gasped. Jackson. It was Jackson. He was coming for her. She could hold out as long as it took, take whatever punishment Stavros wanted to deliver. Feebly she tried to move away from Stavros. He clamped his hand across her hips, deliberately pressing into the raw wounds, all the while his tongue and teeth ravaging her. Her body spilled out a helpless response, already trained to obey even when her mind screamed a denial.

"Stavros, no. I hurt." Maybe she could buy a reprieve with pleading.

"You live only to serve me," he hissed. "Have I not taught you that?"

He bit the inside of her thigh, leaving behind teeth marks and adding bruises to her already striped flesh and Elle arched away from him, screaming.

"Your pain pleases me, Sheena. Now I have your full attention, don't I?"

Elle. Damn it. Where are you? Answer me. Jackson's voice was pure command, all iron will—a will honed and shaped by violence—in the demand. *Answer me now.*

Elle couldn't have stopped herself from answering him if she'd wanted to. Jackson was everything to her now. He was hope. She was weak and he was a great distance away and with the energy field, she wasn't certain she could get through to him. She drew on every ounce of discipline and strength she'd learned over the years and opened her mind to the man who had let her walk away. *Jackson*.

Instantly pain crashed through her head, her body convulsed and she screamed out loud. She tasted blood in her mouth. Her brain rejected the abuse, and her body squirmed away from the pain, so that consciousness receded and the world turned hazy.

I'm here. I'm with you. Tell me where you are, Elle.

She braced herself, all too aware of what would happen, but determined to reach him anyway. *I don't know. I can't think straight. My head . . .* She trailed off, and the connection between them wavered as pain crashed through both of them. She needed to tell him about the energy field, but her head felt as if a thousand needles pierced her skull.

Don't! Jackson's voice was sharp. *Stay with me, baby. I need you to look around you. What do you see? Who's with you?*

Stavros jerked upright, for the first time his face darkened into a mask of fury. "Why are you so stubborn?" He slapped her breast hard and then the other one, rocking her body.

Elle sobbed brokenly, clutching at her head, unable to bear the pain crushing her skull. Stavros sighed, his fake smile ugly. "You have to learn, and I don't mind these little lessons if you insist on needing them."

She rolled away from him, staring out the window at the gathering storm. Her heart jumped and, for a moment, the pain in her body receded and time slowed down. Storm clouds roiled above the house and darkened the skies. Thunder rolled. Lightning flashed, turning the sky into a canvas of turbulence. Wind slashed and howled at the glass, spraying seawater over the windows.

"Jackson," she said, not realizing she whispered his name out loud. He was gone again, the bridge between them gone, and being alone was worse than before. She'd never felt so naked and vulnerable, stripped of everything she was—stripped of her courage.

The wind pulled back. Silence filled the space left behind. Elle became aware of a murderous rage pouring into the room. She held her breath as she turned her head slowly toward Stavros. His face had gone dark, brows together, his white teeth bared.

"*Jackson?* You dare to call another man's name in our bedroom? You filthy slut! After all the care I've given you, you dare to betray me like that?"

His hand blurred he moved so fast, his fist settling around her long hair. He yanked her off the bed backward and dragged her across the floor to the center of the room.

"Stavros, no," Elle pleaded. She couldn't take another punishment. And he was truly angry, his face a mask of brutality. She knew something terrible was going to happen.

He tied her hands with rope and jerked on the pulley, dragging her body into an upright position, straining her arms, and stretching her already painful body horribly.

"Please," she whispered.

He caught her hair, jerking her head back to stare into her eyes. "You belong only to me. You serve only me. You pleasure only me. If you ever escaped me, I would hunt you down and bring you back and you would be punished beyond anything you've ever known. I think it is time you learned just who you're dealing with."

Tears streamed down her face and she could barely catch her breath. She already felt broken, exhausted, so terrified she didn't know how to cope. Her mind felt chaotic and scattered, as if she'd misplaced her ability to think things through and all she could do was feel pain and fear. "Stavros," she tried again. "I don't know what I'm doing or saying. Please don't do this."

"You want another man? Is that what you want?"

She shook her head. "No."

"I think you do. I think you're such a little slut you want another man. I don't seem to be satisfying you."

"That's not true. I don't want anyone else." She didn't want anyone touching her. The thought of Stavros sharing her, forcing her to accept other men, made bile rise in her churning stomach.

Stavros stared down at her for a long moment while the wind lashed at the windows and lightning forked across the dark clouds. He leaned over, his face pressed close to hers. "I think you need to know who you belong to, Sheena. I think we need to drive that lesson home."

He waited and she knew he expected her to acknowledge his ownership. "Please," she said brokenly, "I can't think clearly."

He sighed and stood up, one hand trailing over her breast. Without another word he turned and left the room, slamming the door behind him. Elle couldn't stop crying, the pain in her head making it impossible to think, the fear of what Stavros might do choking her. She'd never seen him like that. And she never wanted to again.

She waited for what seemed like hours, but she knew it wasn't that long. Her arms ached and every bit of air on her skin intensified the pain. She wanted to give in to Stavros, just end it all before she lost who and what she was. She knew now how the women taken prisoner and forced into the human trafficking rings felt and it made her sick that she couldn't help them. She'd nearly sent word to Dane that she was certain that Stavros wasn't involved, and yet, he was. He had been all along. From the information Stavros had let drop, she knew his twin, Evan, was alive and that he, along with his bikers, kidnapped the women. Then Stavros used his freighters to send the women all over the world. Evan was alive after all, raised by his mother away from the father. She'd taken one twin and left the other behind.

The wind slammed into the window and she lifted her head to stare out at the raging storm even as she felt Jackson, much stronger this time, slide into her mind. She didn't want him there. It was too late for hope. There was only humiliation that Jackson would share everything that happened—that was going to happen—that he could see her like this, know what Stavros had done and was still doing to her. If she built enough energy and waited for her moment, she could use the storm and short-circuit her brain. It was the only way out that she could see.

You were there for me, Elle, when I was tied and beaten like a dog and thrown into that rat hole. You were there for me. Don't try to talk, and don't try to take your own life. I see what you're thinking, but if you turn yourself into a vegetable, what do you think will happen to your sisters? To me? Live, Elle. Believe I'll come for you.

Elle closed her eyes against Jackson's voice. Against the small flare of hope that lingered. Stavros was too powerful. He had too much money. No one could ever escape him, least of all her.

You're just tired, baby, worn out with fighting him. I know where he's keeping you now and I'll stay with you until I come for you. You aren't alone anymore.

She wanted to be alone. She didn't want him to see into her mind, the conflict there, to see the terrible things Stavros had done to her body and soul.

Be strong for me. I was strong for you when they ripped me apart and took everything I was. You know what they did to me. You're the only soul in this world that does. Be strong for me, Elle. I need you to be strong.

She was too tired, too far gone. There was little left of Elle Drake. She wasn't as strong as Jackson had been. She'd admired him so much, believed in him and then he'd just let her walk away. Was it the children he didn't want? Or her?

I wanted both. I still want both. You and our girls. I was a fool, Elle. I was afraid you'd get hurt. I have a death sentence hanging over my head and I didn't want it following us around. Just—

He broke off because, through her, he'd sensed Stavros's presence. Stavros had come back into the room and Elle was so tuned to him, so aware of him, she knew immediately. Her heart rate jumped and she began silently praying for strength. She jerked at the ropes tying her arms over her head. She could barely reach the floor with her toes and every muscle in her body was screaming in pain. She knew Stavros was watching her. Waiting.

She was so tired, so broken. Each time he came near her, she tried to use her psychic talent to defend herself, to keep him away. The pain was so intense in her head, she knew it was shattering her and if she continued, it would eventually destroy her brain. He was breaking her faster than she ever thought possible, using her own psychic defenses against her.

She tried to remain calm, to relax, and let the pain wash over her. It wasn't just about pain. It was about ownership and humiliation. Teaching her there was no hope. That he ruled her life, was her life and she had no other purpose than to serve him. How many countless women had gone before her? Been treated as a vessel rather than a human being? An object for a man to use?

Stavros touched her bare shoulder, a light touch of possession that made her stomach churn. "We have another lesson today, Sheena, and I hope you're paying attention to this one."

Her mouth went dry. She couldn't see him, couldn't turn her body, but his hands wandered over her, touching intimate places that he claimed were his and his alone. He stroked softly and gently over the welts on her back and breasts, deliberately delivering pain with each fake caress. Her body shuddered in spite of her resolve not to let him see her reaction to his torture. And Jackson knew. Jackson felt each touch, felt her soul cringing. She could feel his anger building, the need to retaliate, but he kept silent and stayed with her. A part of her was grateful, although she didn't know which was worse, him sharing the humiliation and pouring strength into her, or being alone and feeling hopeless.

The door opened behind her and she heard heavy footsteps. Her heart began to pound in alarm. So far the only other man Stavros had let in the room with her had been his brother, a sadistic man who enjoyed breaking the women they used in the prostitution houses they had in cities all over the world. Most of the women were kidnapped and he, as well as a team of his men, specialized in "training" them before placing them in the various houses. His brother had walked around her without touching her, but carefully instructing Stavros where he could hurt her most if she disobeyed, bragging how he could get cooperation in a matter of hours.

More than once he had tried to talk Stavros into letting him have her, but Stavros had been adamant that no one but him touch her. In the end, his brother left after the first day and she never saw anyone again other than Stavros.

A hand gripped her hair and jerked her head back hard. She found herself staring into Stavros's eyes. He bent close to her until his mouth was against her ear and he could whisper to her. "I want you to pay close attention to this lesson, Sheena. Very, very close attention."

He dropped his mouth over hers, kissing her hard, mashing her lips against her teeth and biting on her lower lip hard enough to draw blood. He pulled his head back and she cringed at the look in his eyes. Where was the handsome, sophisticated man now? He was one moment tender and caressing and then would switch to the other side so rapidly she could barely process it. It left her off balance and fearful, her attention always centered on him.

A man came into her line of vision. He was already rubbing his crotch in anticipation. It was clear Stavros had told him he could have her. Tall, broad-shouldered, he walked with a decided strut and stared at her striped body, licking his lips.

"You like what you see?" Stavros demanded. "My little slut has quite the mouth on her. I told you I owed you a favor. If you want to use this pretty little mouth, she's all yours."

"Hell yeah," the man responded.

Something terrible was going to happen here. Elle wanted to close her eyes, but was terrified to do so. Maybe if she gathered enough of the violent energy swirling around the room, she could either break free or kill herself. It was the only thing left to her, because she was not going to do this.

No! You will not try to defend yourself, Elle. Do you hear me? You do whatever it takes to stay alive. I'm here with you. Whatever he does to you, he does to me. You're not alone. Stay alive. That's all that matters.

Elle shook her head again, not knowing if she was trying to dislodge Jackson to spare him whatever might be coming, or whether she was refusing his demands. The storm hurled itself at the house, unrelenting and vicious like the men in the room with her. Jackson. Trying to get in. He couldn't save her, not now—not ever.

That's not true, baby. I swear I'm coming for you. I'll get you out of there. I swear it on every one of our children. Our daughters. I'll come for you.

Stavros walked around her shivering body, suddenly jerking her head back and mashing his mouth against hers, biting at her lips. Again she felt Jackson's reaction and his building fury, his pain easing hers and helping her to detach from what was being done to her. Abruptly Stavros lifted his head and wiped his mouth, smearing her blood across his lips.

"This belongs to me. I say who uses her, no one else." Stavros turned his head and looked at the man who seemed so eager to participate. "Drako. Come here. You want to help teach her to please me?"

Drako strutted forward with a grin on his face. "I'd love to help you."

Stavros caught Elle's long hair and dragged her head back. "He's going to teach you how to please a man with that mouth of yours."

The moment he released her hair, she shook her head and tried to kick out at Drako as he approached her. "I won't, Stavros." She refused to acknowledge the other man, refused to look at him.

The malevolence in the room grew. Outside, the fury of the storm increased. She could feel Jackson holding his breath, but it felt like he was holding her hand and she tightened her fingers hard around the rope.

"You'll do whatever I tell you to do," Stavros said. He lowered the ropes until Elle was on her knees, still shaking her head violently.

Drako grinned at her. "Maybe I should use that whip on her first, teach her manners, boss." He looked eager to hurt her.

"Shove your cock down her throat and show her what a man is," Stavros snapped.

Elle went wild, fighting to get away as Drako approached her. Stavros stepped very close, crowding Elle, trapping her legs with his, one hand on her hair, forcing her head back, the other hand behind his back.

Elle's heart pounded in fear. "Why are you doing this?" She hissed the words between her clenched teeth, keeping her gaze locked with Stavros. There was no mercy there, none at all, just a desire for power.

Drako's fingers pinched her nose closed, preventing her from breathing. The wind howled outside and slammed into the window. Elle fought the need to breathe, her lungs burning, her heart hammering. Drako was relentless and Stavros simply waited until survival kicked in. She wouldn't. She wouldn't. She'd rather die. She had to tap in to the storm and let it fry her brain, at least short-circuit it enough to snuff out reality. She'd be a vegetable, but it wouldn't matter what Stavros forced her to do.

No! You do whatever you have to do to live, Elle. Do you hear me? Please, baby. Oh, God, Elle. They aren't worth your life. I'll stay with you, right here in your mind. Lose yourself in me. Baby, please don't let them take you from me. Love me enough to live.

She could almost see him, tears on his face, in his voice and mind, his forehead pressed against the mosaic tiles of her ancestors. Her sisters' voices rising around him, holding the bridge, keeping it strong, unknowing about her fate and God help her, it had to remain that way, because she could never live with their knowledge of what these men were doing to her.

Her air was gone. Long gone. She had to make a decision. Live or die. Subject herself to the horror of this degradation or kill herself.

Live for me, Elle. Love me enough to live for me. God knows I don't deserve it, but love me enough to believe in me—that I'll come for you, that I'll fight for you with every breath in my body, every skill I have.

She gasped, drew in great gulps of air and Drako shoved himself deep, gagging her. Stavros's hand went from her hair to her throat, fingers clamping like a vise.

"Look at him, sweetness," Stavros commanded, his low voice almost like silk. "Look into his eyes."

Her gaze jumped to Drako's face. Stavros whipped out a gun, shoved the barrel into Drako's mouth and pulled the trigger. Drako's body jerked and blood splattered across the floor and on the walls. His body dropped to the floor at her knees. Elle screamed, but no sound emerged.

Stavros tightened his fingers around her throat. "Do

you understand now? Or shall I bring in another man? Because I can keep this up all night." His hand tightened, cutting off her air as he shook her. "Answer me. Tell me you understand, because there isn't a man in this world that would be safe if they touched you."

She nodded her head, tears streaming down her face.

"No one touches you. No one. Not ever. If another man dares to put his hands on you, or his mouth or his cock inside you, I'll have him killed. Do you understand me, Sheena? Are we clear? There is nowhere in this world you can go. No one you'll ever be safe with. You can stay on your knees and pray for forgiveness while you watch him rot."

He let go of her throat and walked out, leaving her with the blood streaming around her in a thick puddle. She heard herself screaming. Once she started she couldn't stop.

JACKSON heard his own raw cry, and he slammed his fist deep into the mosaic tiles. The floor softened under his punch, absorbing his flesh, allowing him to punch through as if the floor was gel and not solid. He swore, over and over, a vicious, steady, relentless spewing of every brutal term he'd ever learned in the bayou, the biker camps and the army.

Elle. Baby. I know where you are. I'm coming to get you.

He hit the floor again out of sheer impotence, seeing her broken, torn body, feeling her shattered soul. He had been a prisoner of war, brutally tortured, his mind fragmented, just as hers was. The Drakes had sent him soaring across the ocean so that he was in her mind, in her head, living her experiences and God help him, he wanted to murder someone. He found himself on his hands and knees, fighting not to vomit, feeling every humiliation, every lash, knowing exactly how broken she felt. He'd been there, exposed, brutalized and it had been her voice that had saved his sanity. *Elle*.

She kept screaming in her mind. He had to find a way to bring her back. Stavros was far closer to breaking her than he could imagine. She was trying to crawl inside her own mind and escape. Jackson could feel that she was partially there. Her sisters were worn-out and sooner or later the bridge between them would fail. It was only the tremendous love they had for their sister that kept them going past the point of sanity. Using the amount of psychic energy to bridge an ocean would leave the Drakes unable to move for hours, but he needed to stay with Elle as long as possible, at least until Stavros relented and took the body away.

Jackson didn't dare take his mind off Elle even for a moment to warn her sisters he needed to keep talking to her. He hoped they could see by his reactions that it was imperative to use every ounce of strength they had to hold the bridge.

I'm going to keep talking to you, baby. Concentrate on my voice and forget everything else around you. You aren't there. You're with me.

Jackson. The moment she whispered his name, seeking him, needing him, reaching out for strength, for hope, the energy field burned through her brain, an electric shock that had her screaming in pain.

Jackson felt the tears on his face. "Don't!" he pleaded with her, unaware he'd spoken aloud as well as in his mind. He even reached out for her, trying to touch her, to let her feel him. He took a breath and tried to keep himself together. *Don't talk, Elle. Don't try to reach me. Let me just be with you this way. The bridge isn't going to last, you know that. Your sisters are sending you love and strength and we have you now. Hold on for us. Jonas is here. Ilya, too. Matt and Aleksandr will be with us. You know we'll come.*

He felt the stirring in his mind, knew her thoughts, although she remained silent. She didn't want them to come. She was too afraid of Stavros. She believed he would kill them all—maybe even find and kill her sisters.

He shook his head. *You know Jonas. You know me. You've seen inside me, Elle. I don't kill so easy. None of us do. Take a breath, baby, don't look at the floor. Look out the window at the storm. We sent that to you, across the ocean, we found you and we sent you a storm.*

He felt her again and this time there was determination. She was building her strength and he held his breath knowing she was steeling herself for the crashing pain when she sent another message.

Stavros is psychic.

She screamed again and Jackson tasted blood in his mouth. The pain drove him down to the tiles again. A hand slid over his forehead, cooling, easing the terrible pain—easing it for both of them.

Powerful. Has a brother.

Each time Elle sent to him, the shocking current grew stronger. Libby gasped and jerked her hand away. They smelled the scent of burned flesh. The bridge wavered.

"No!" Jackson implored. "For God's sake, hold it." *Elle, stop. We'll lose the bridge. You have to stay quiet. Keep looking out the window and just let me hold you in my arms for a few moments.* Because the Drake sisters were trembling under the terrible effort. *When the next storm comes, baby, be ready. We'll be there to get you. All of us together may be able to short-circuit the energy field.*

He felt her sudden awareness of Stavros and he stayed quiet, waiting with her. Stavros wasn't alone and fear pounded through Elle, but then he felt some of the tension slip away. She recognized the other man. A bodyguard.

ELLE felt Jackson slipping away from her and she wanted to cry out, to reach for him and hold him inside her. Instead she kept her lashes down, trying to quiet the sobs escaping, trying to be as small as possible.

"What the hell have you done to her?" Sid demanded. "If you're going to kill her, put a bullet in her brain, don't turn her into a vegetable." He ripped the sheet off the bed and wrapped Elle's body in it, kicking Drako's leg out of his way as he removed the rope from her wrists. "She needs a doctor, Stavros. She's bleeding from her nose and mouth and around her ears. You know what that means? A brain bleed. You said you were going to keep her, not torture her."

Stavros rushed to the bed as Sid put her down. Elle rolled to her side and curled up in the fetal position, trying to disappear. Everywhere they touched her hurt. Her head pounded with agony. Her ability to think, to reason, was fast slipping away.

"Sheena," Stavros's voice was low, almost a caress. "Look at me, sweetness. It's going to be all right now. I've forgiven you and no one will hurt you again." He smoothed back her hair with gentle fingers, leaned down to press a kiss against her temple. "Don't fight me anymore, my sweet, just let me take care of you."

Sid wiped gently at the blood on her face with a warm washcloth. "Call a doctor, Stavros. You're going to lose her."

"If you're certain, but I'll have to kill him after he sees her."

"Pay him off like you do everyone else."

Stavros shook his head. "No one knows about her and lives."

Sid straightened slowly, his gaze ice-cold. "Is that why you killed Drako?"

"Not you, Sid," Stavros sounded genuinely shocked. "You're the only one I can trust. Drako died because he was betraying me to my brother. We do business together, but we don't trust each other. That's why I never talk to him unless we're here on this island. He's a strong psychic, Sid, and he wants power. He hates that I'm accepted in the world and he's chosen a life that keeps him on the outside. But he likes his image and the fear he instills in everyone."

All the while he talked, Stavros gently stroked Elle's hair, his hands almost tender as they moved through the silken strands. Anyone looking at him, at the expression on his face, would have thought he was deeply in love with her.

"Get rid of the body, Sid. I'll call a doctor." He kissed each temple and the corner of Elle's mouth. "Don't worry, sweetness, I'll take care of you." His fingers brushed at the tears sliding down her face. "It will be all right. Leave everything to me."

4

THE large ship anchored a few miles out in the Aegean Sea. A small bird—helicopter—sat on the pad waiting, sleek and black and very maneuverable. Men moved around, loading weapons in a quiet, controlled manner. A few smiled and made jokes, but most were silent, faces grim, dark stripes covering light skin, to match their dark clothing.

Jonas glanced at his watch. "So far everything is running by the numbers. The first storm took out his power with a nicely aimed lightning strike, and just as expected, the backup generator kicked in. But for fifteen seconds, his psychic barrier was down. Ilya tested it. It came on as soon as the generator kicked in. We intercepted his call for the electricians and our men will be going in soon." Jonas was proud of Hannah for that. She had created the storm and precisely aimed the bolt of lightning, scoring a hit first time out. That was his woman—deadly when needed.

"This is his home turf, his little empire, both on and

off the island. Did he buy the excuse that the storm was too dangerous and the electricians would come at the first break?" Sarah asked. She leaned against the railing and looked out toward the island where her youngest sister was being held prisoner. Her hand gripped the railing hard enough to turn her knuckles white.

Jonas wrapped his arm around her. "Hannah kept the lightning strikes close to his villa. So, yes, he bought it. Don't worry, honey, we'll get Elle back. We know what we're doing. Each man here is a good friend and trained in combat and rescue. We won't leave any evidence behind that he—or anyone else—could trace back to us."

"I know." There was determination in Sarah's voice.

"They've called for the electricians and our first team will make an entry in a few minutes. They'll go in and Gratsos will have guards to take them to the east side of the island where the power plant is. Four divers will move in with the boat, which will give us seven men on the island. The main dock is to the south with a smaller one on the north side. We're hoping to get lucky and have them direct our men to use the main dock. Our divers will have to hump it through enemy territory a shorter distance."

"Can we get the helicopter in the air to protect them?"

Jonas shook his head. "We can't risk it. If they bought the weather reports and the lightning strike, then we're good. And I don't see why they wouldn't."

Sarah watched him closely. "Who are you sending in to protect them?"

He inwardly cursed. "Matt's going." Matt Granite was Kate Drake's fiancé and hell on wheels in a fight. "He's leading the second team in."

Sarah laid her head on his shoulder for comfort, briefly

closing her eyes. "I hate this. That everyone we love is at risk, but this is for Elle. Has Jackson said anything at all to you?"

Jonas shook his head. "He won't talk, but he's back to the man he used to be before he came home with me. Colder. Edgier. Jackson is like Ilya, Sarah, and as much as I respect Ilya, he isn't an easy man."

"If these men deal in human trafficking, I'm terrified to think what could have happened to her this last month."

Jonas looked away. Jackson knew and his reaction had been scary. Sarah didn't want to know on some level, it was just too painful. Deliberately he glanced toward the cabins. "Hannah was sick most of the trip. I should have made her stay home."

"She would have followed us."

Jonas made a face. "That's why I didn't bother giving her an order. She never listens anyway."

Sarah smiled for the first time. "I'm sure that doesn't surprise you. Libby's with her and truly, we need her. She can command the wind like no one else; not even Ilya is quite as adept."

Jonas would have tried to stop Hannah if they were going after anyone but her baby sister. There would be no stopping his wife, pregnant or not. Not with Elle prisoner and Jackson losing his mind inch by slow inch.

"Team one is going in." Ilya's voice resonated in his ear.

"We have a go," Jonas announced aloud. "Tell the others to get ready."

Hannah would have to bring the storm in hard and they would have to trust Ilya's ability to keep a helicopter stabilized in violent winds if they were going to pull off the rescue, because they'd have to send it in later to back up the rescue team. But first, they had to bring down the energy field Gratsos protected himself with.

As if reading his thoughts, Sarah paused and turned back to him. "You know, Jonas, when that field comes down, Gratsos can use psychic energy as well. We don't know him, we don't know what he's capable of, so be careful."

Jonas locked his gaze with hers and a shiver went down her spine.

"I saw Jackson pounding the hell out of the floor, half out of his mind. Whatever that man did to Elle, he's going to pay, Sarah, one way or another. I don't give a damn how psychic he is. I'd bet on you against him any day of the week. Multiply that by your other sisters, and the man doesn't have a chance."

Jonas walked to Jackson's side where he was giving last-minute instructions to the team heading out in the boat. The three men going to the island to "fix" the power went in unarmed on a smaller boat. He knew these men, good friends willing to risk their lives to help Jonas and Jackson get Elle back. They were going into a war zone without a weapon other than their trained bodies.

"Team two will be right behind you," Jackson assured them, looking at the four divers, already in scuba gear, positioning themselves low in the boat. "Matt, you and Tom have to move fast. Our men will be at risk until you take out their guards and get their weapons to them, and we won't have anyone up in the air until you give us the signal." Jackson trusted Kate Drake's fiancé. He was a former Army Ranger and both Jonas and Jackson had worked with him numerous times.

Matt's eyes were cool. "We'll have them covered."

"Remember, we leave nothing and no one behind. This has to be quick and clean. Get in and get out. I don't think we have any civilians other than the housekeeper and the package." Jackson kept his mind away from Elle, it was the only way he could function. They weren't going in after his heart and soul, they were going in on a rescue mission and they would succeed. "The housekeeper has to know the setup, so if she gets in the way, she's an enemy."

Jonas cleared his throat. "We don't know that."

Jackson shot him a look. "Everyone on that island is an enemy other than Elle. We don't risk our men for any reason." His voice was implacable. Jonas nodded, knowing Jackson was capable of anything at that moment, including knocking him out and leaving him with the Drake women.

Matt lifted the sealed bag of weapons and explosives and slipped down into the boat. His team, in wet suits and scuba gear would stay out of sight in the boat until all four divers could be dropped off just before coming within sight of the island. He took over the instructions, making certain his team understood. "We all swim to the dock and split up," he reiterated. "Tom and I will make our way across the island to the small power plant and back up team one. We'll take out the guards and arm our guys before heading to the smaller dock on the north side. Rick and Jock, you make your way to the helipad. Team one will sabotage the backup generator under cover of the storm and then we'll all help with the boats."

Jackson bumped fists with him. "We'll need as much intel as possible sent back. Work your way into position as soon as you take out the boats, to cover our escape."

"It's done," Matt assured him. "We'll get her out, Jackson."

Jackson didn't want to think about "her," or what might be happening. He didn't dare connect with her until they had everything in place. If she believed they were coming in and something went wrong, it would crush her.

Jonas clapped Jackson on the back. "We made it faster than we expected, and the girls are waiting. The moment you give the signal, they'll call in the storm. Ilya's already been testing the energy field. He says it's strong, but we can bring it down under cover of the storm."

"Who did the recon?"

"Ilya," Jonas said, knowing Jackson respected the man. "Looks like Gratsos has a small army of his own. Only civilian that he saw was a housekeeper, but someone obviously keeps the grounds. He laid out what he could of the house. It's glass, which gave him a fairly good view of the ground floor, but he couldn't see much on the second floor, not the way it was designed. You'll be going in blind."

Jackson shoved small throwing knives into the loops of his belt. "I'll get her out."

Jonas let out his breath. Jackson had been different—harder, colder—on a thin edge since he'd gone insane on the floor of the Drake home. When they'd lost the bridge, he'd been a madman, swearing, fighting, ready to kill. Not at all the ice-cold man Jonas had come to know over the years. He'd been shaking, and, God help them all, weeping genuine tears, his hands balled into tight fists as he pounded the floor. Fortunately, the house recognized Jackson and somehow cushioned those punishing punches. But then he'd sat on the ancient tiles and rocked back and forth, hands covering his face, the sounds coming from him torn from his soul.

Jonas and the other men had had their hands full trying

to revive the Drake sisters, carrying them to bed, pouring tea down them. Ilya, even in his weakened state, tried to repair the damage done to Libby's hand from where she'd attempted to heal both Jackson and Elle from the electric burns in their brains. It had been a mess, but Jackson had been the biggest mess of all.

When he was finally rational, he'd looked at Jonas with cold, haunted eyes. "We're going after her immediately and we'll need every one of our friends. Call them in, Jonas, tell them it's personal and I'll owe them. Don't give any information to her boss. Not a word. Not a whisper. We don't want the law. We're going to have to extract her and it's going to be bloody so we'll need to be able to get out of the country immediately."

"Hit and run with no trace," Jonas agreed.

"We can't leave any trail back to us. That means no bodies left behind. Nothing that can be tracked."

Then Jonas had looked at Jackson and realized he was back—the same man who wasn't a man, who had returned from the prison camps just the shell of what he once was, nothing left but will and iron. In that moment, in that look, Jackson changed Jonas. The look in his eyes swept the feeling of right and wrong away. There was no right, there was only a mission with one single outcome. He knew what that was; he knew how to carry out missions. They were going to need weapons and they were going to need men.

"Our boys will come, you know they will. Everyone who ever called us friend, everyone who ever owed us. No trace will be found of any of us ever being there." Jonas's eyes locked with Jackson's. "We'll get her out the way we've always done things—together."

Jonas would never forget the look Jackson gave him.

Whatever gentleness Jackson had learned during the last couple of years while he'd lived in Sea Haven, was gone in that one instant. Jackson had returned to being remote, distant, rarely speaking, his mouth grim, his eyes cold. He cleaned his weapons often and practiced both shooting and throwing knives. He broke down and rebuilt his rifle hundreds of time until his hands were a blur as he did it, and he always practiced blindfolded.

Jackson turned away from Jonas and from the look on his face, a mixture of worry and regret. He didn't have time to reassure his friend—and he couldn't anyway. Something inside him that had only just begun to thaw had iced over until there was a glacier there. Elle mattered. She was the only thing—the only one who mattered in that moment—and there was no way to soften it, or pretend otherwise. He was willing to do whatever it took to get her back. He'd die if necessary—or kill. And he was fully prepared to kill a lot of people—anyone who got in his way.

He would never get the images out of his head—not ever—of Elle stripped naked, her skin covered in blood-red stripes, swollen bruises marring her soft skin. Worse, her brilliant mind shattered, her spirit nearly broken. He wanted—no, *needed*—to hunt and kill the animals who'd done that to her. There was no room for anything else in his mind or his heart. He would get her back and find a way to put her back together. She'd managed to glue him back together and he'd find a way to do the same for her.

The radio in his ear crackled. "Tell Hannah to bring up the wind," Matt's voice intoned. "We're approaching the island. Team two is entering the water and team one is going to be vulnerable as hell."

Matt slipped his earpiece into a waterproof container

and waited while his other team members entered the water. He looked at the three remaining. "Don't play the hero. If they don't let you onto the island, be agreeable to leaving immediately. These boys may be trigger-happy. We don't have any intel on them."

"Yeah, yeah, Mama," Kent Bastion answered. "We'll be good."

The three men looked at one another and snorted in derision. Matt shook his head and somersaulted backward into the sea. He swam away from the boat, gave them the go-ahead and the boat proceeded in the direction of the island. He glanced at the sky. Already he could feel the difference. The weather beginning to deteriorate, the wind picking up, the dark, heavy, clouds boiling angrily.

He signaled and his team went underwater, swimming the remaining distance to keep from being detected. They moved fast, knowing Kent and his men, James Berenger and Luke Walton, had no weapons if something went wrong. It took longer than he would have liked, and Matt was aware of every moment his teammates were without backup. The necessary wind Hannah brought in to aid team one ultimately hindered them as the waves built and the undercurrent grew stronger. He knew the first team would have to convince the guards that the regular maintenance crew was gone for the evening because of the storm and they'd been sent out instead.

Jonas was standing by to intercept another phone call if any questions were asked. Fortunately, Kent's father was Greek. It was a huge part of the reason they'd chosen him for the assignment. Not only did he look the part, he spoke the language fluently and had a reputation for talking his way out of any situation.

Matt sent up a silent prayer that he'd keep the guards

talking until they were able to get there and give backup to the three "electricians." As they approached the rocks, he signaled to Rick and Jock to break off and make their way to the helipad. Tom followed him to land, where they removed their swimming gear in silence, packing it into the bag they'd brought to secure everything and take with them when they left. A small detonator was put in the bag as a precaution. If they couldn't retrieve it, they would blow it up on departure. Slinging weapons over their shoulders and around their waists, they caught up the bag for team one. Matt and Tom took off running through the shadows to try to catch up with the other team, who had a good twenty-minute start on them and had been driving a vehicle.

The villa was on the west side with the power station beyond that to the east. The boat had docked on the southern side, so as they swam to shore, they'd angled just to the southwest, cutting the distance they had to run as much as possible. The wind hit them in blasts, although Matt had to hand it to Hannah—she angled the wind to aid their speed, rather than hinder it. He was always amazed at Hannah's abilities and precision when sending or calling the wind. And Kate—his heart turned over just thinking about his quiet, nonadventurous fiancée—she was a woman with a steel cord running down her spine, someone to stand beside him, not walk behind him. Each of the Drake sisters would give everything she had, everything she was, to get her youngest sister back.

Matt slipped his earpiece in, commenting as he and Tom maneuvered around guards. "From this angle I can see two men on the roof of the villa. They're not all that alert, the wind is really slamming them, but there might be more. Two on the southern side, in the rocks, but moving position up toward higher ground as the waves increase in height and strength." He gave the coordinates, knowing Jackson and Jonas would be mapping out each guard's position as information came in.

"We've got rolling patrols," Tom hissed and sank down into the shadows.

Matt dropped with him, lying prone, his gun in his fist as he watched the vehicle and guards go slowly by, flashing spotlights along the crevasses of the boulders and into the brush. He counted the seconds, each one ticking by a beat of his heart, each passing moment increasing the risk to the three men who had been driven to the mini power plant.

He was up and running the moment the vehicle had passed out of sight. Staying to the shadows, but increasing his speed over the uneven ground, avoiding the manicured drive he knew the roving patrols would most likely stick to in the storm. The waves broke over the rocks as the storm began slowly to increase in strength. If Gratsos had any psychic talent, the Drakes had to be careful, using a soft touch and making the storm as natural as possible so he wouldn't feel a sudden surge. Matt didn't know much about how it worked, but Kate said they could feel the brush of psychic energy when it was used.

The power plant loomed ahead, a small structure behind a chain-link fence. The gate was open, a vehicle sitting sideways by the open door. Tom and Matt slipped inside the fence and made their way to the door. Tom caught the handle and waited until Matt was in position before pulling the door open so Matt could slide in, gun steady in his hand while Tom covered him. He cleared the immediate area, moved forward to give Tom entry and cover. They went forward in standard search-and-clear formation as they moved through the rows of wires until they heard the sound of voices.

"Yes, Mr. Gratsos," the disembodied male voice said, "he's telling me they want to leave anyway. The weather is growing worse and they're afraid of getting stuck here. Our regular workers were unavailable, they'd already gone home in anticipation of the storm."

There was a short silence and then the guard sighed heavily. "Of course, Mr. Gratsos, we searched them. There were no weapons on them."

Another silence followed, this one briefer than the first. "There are three because one is serving an apprenticeship." The guard fought to keep exasperation out of his voice. "Yes, sir. They'll have to work fast to stay ahead of the storm." His voice lowered. "We may have to put them up for the night."

Matt crept around the floor-to-ceiling rows, trusting Tom to take out the guard when he finished his conversation with Gratsos. His entire being was focused on the safety of team one. The three men faced him, fingers locked behind their heads, all looking indignant. Kent looked especially annoyed, his brows pulled together as he glared at the guard who had his back to Matt.

"We can leave," he snarled. "This is bullshit."

"Have patience." The guard sounded bored. "He's checking your IDs."

Kent looked at the other two. "What does he think we plan to do? Steal with all you guards around?"

Something heavy fell on the floor in the direction of the guard who was calling Gratsos. "Clear here," Tom's voice confirmed in Matt's ear.

Matt cleared his throat. The guard pointing his weapon at team one swung around, his finger tightening on the trigger instinctively. Matt shot him. "Let's go. We need to disable the generator."

ELLE pried open her eyelids, forcing herself to take short, shallow breaths to ease the pain in her body. She'd tried to warn the doctor they'd brought in, and that had earned her another beating. She hadn't saved him. She hadn't saved anyone—least of all herself. She was certain Stavros might have killed her—he was enraged by her resistance—if it hadn't been for Sid. The bodyguard had once again stepped in and saved her, although she wasn't certain why. She had seen the look on his face, and for a moment she'd thought he might actually kill his boss when, hearing her screams, he had broken into the room, risking his own life.

Stavros killed easily, yet he refused to even argue with Sid when Sid intervened. Stavros had walked out, shaking with anger, but still, he'd left Sid to pick up the pieces, trusting the bodyguard with her when he wouldn't even allow his own brother to lay a finger on her. Sid had been gentle, washing her, checking her ribs, whispering to her in Russian, telling her to stop fighting, to just endure, to wait. For what? She didn't even have a sense of time anymore.

Elle wondered for the millionth time if she had dreamed Jackson's voice. If anything was real. Everything around her seemed hazy and faraway. What had roused her from her semistupor, an urgent feeling that wouldn't let go of her? She didn't want to actually feel, or think; she wanted to slip back into that place where no one could touch her. But . . . She turned her face toward the long glass wall and looked out to the sea.

The wind slammed against the building, rising to a shriek and then retreating, only to return with full force, knocking, again and again. Her breath caught in her throat. The wind. *Watch for the wind*. She tried to sit up and found she couldn't move. She pulled experimentally at the cuffs on her wrists. He'd tied her to the bed. Stavros didn't ever need a reason; he wanted her to know she existed at his whim—that whatever he chose to do, he would do, and she was powerless. He drove the point home to her often. He was tired of her fighting him, and in truth, she was tired of it, too.

She looked toward the glass again, moistening her dry lips. Had Jackson come? Had her sisters sent the wind to tell her they were coming for her? She didn't dare hope. A prickly sensation crept down her spine and she knew without turning her head that Stavros had entered the room. She let her head fall back on the pillow and braced herself for his touch.

"I thought the storm might be making you nervous," he said. "The glass always makes it seem as if you're out in it, when really you're safe." His voice was very solicitous and she wondered, not for the first time, if he really believed himself in love with her. And if he did, it was a sick kind of love—ownership she wanted no part of.

"It is a little nerve-wracking," she admitted, surprising him. His eyes went wide at her answer. She rarely responded to anything he said or did, her only real way of keeping control.

Stavros looked pleased. Immediately, as if to reward her, he crossed to her side and bent down to brush a kiss over her mouth. Elle forced herself not to turn her head. She didn't respond, but she let him have her lips again, a big victory for him.

"Were you missing me?"

She swallowed the bile rising. "I was lonely." She turned her head toward the glass. "And the wind . . ."

"Don't worry, my sweet. This house is a fortress. Nothing will destroy it."

He'd better hope his psychic barrier never came down, because if it did, she would take down his house and everything in it.

"I have to use the bathroom." She hated that she flushed red when she said it. He loved the humiliation of her having to ask. Sometimes he made her "ask properly"—asking "please" and thanking him afterward, even when he stayed in the room with her. She'd never detested anyone more in her life. At least she wasn't so apathetic that she couldn't feel her hatred of her captor.

"Of course, Sheena." His hands were gentle as he took off the cuffs on her wrists. "Good girl." He smiled, rubbing at the bruises on her skin. "You didn't fight this time and break the skin."

Only because she'd been unconscious, or asleep—she couldn't tell anymore. Elle glanced again out the window, trying not to hope, forcing herself not to reach out to see if Jackson or her sisters were close.

"Are you afraid of storms?" Stavros unlocked the cuffs on her ankles and rubbed her legs, his fingers lingering over her wounds.

Elle took a breath and let it out, letting him see how fragile and vulnerable she felt. If it lulled him into a false sense of security, she would concede to him almost anything. She nodded her head. "I try not to be. I know it's silly."

It was probably the most she'd exchanged with him since he'd first taken her prisoner. How long now? She didn't know, but it seemed as if he'd become her entire life.

Stavros helped her to sit up, holding her when she swayed a little, still holding the sheet over her body. "I've told you not to be modest around me," he reminded her. "I like to look at your body."

Involuntarily she tightened the hold on the sheet. At his look of annoyed impatience, she took another stab at playing to his ego. "I don't feel very attractive right now. My hair is tangled and my bones are sticking out." She'd always been thin, but now she looked like a scarecrow. "The doctor said . . ." She trailed off, looking away from him. "I don't like you seeing me like this."

"You're beautiful, Sheena. He doesn't know what he's talking about. You've been ill, that's all." Stavros tugged at the sheet until she reluctantly dropped it, and then he helped her to swing her legs over the side of the bed.

The room spun for a moment. She was weaker than she realized. She waited for the world to right itself and stepped upright onto the floor, leaning on Stavros a little more than she wanted. He wrapped his arm around her waist and helped her to walk to the bathroom. The wind slammed against the glass wall and Elle jumped, turning to look over her shoulder at the darkened sky. The clouds spun, whipping around, slowly forming pictures, taking her breath. Long hair blowing wildly with the wind, six distinct faces, looking left and right, searching . . . searching.

Elle's breath caught in her throat. She wanted to walk over to the long glass wall, not away from it. She could feel her entire mind reaching for those faces. *See me. I'm here.* But she didn't dare try to use telepathy, not with the barrier up and Stavros in the room. She could only hold her breath and pray that they would see her—feel her. The faces turned almost as one, eyes wide open and sharp, piercing the veil of the storm, hair swirling around in the clouds, as her sisters looked at her. And she looked at them.

Elle felt each distinct heartbeat in her body like a drum playing in her head. She felt each beat like thunder clapping in the sky. There was no mistaking her sisters. She sagged against Stavros, her knees going weak with relief. Tears burned behind her eyelids. They had come for her. It wasn't her imagination. She wanted to weep and laugh at the same time. Instead she forced herself to undergo the humiliation of using the bathroom with Stavros watching her every move. It sickened her that he needed such control over her, that he enjoyed his petty power issues. She washed carefully and made her way back into the room.

"May I sit for a few minutes?" She shivered, feigning cold, when it was sheer excitement. "I have a difficult time lying in bed when the wind is so strong."

She *never* asked for concessions and Stavros all but beamed, his dark eyes sliding over her with evident pleasure as he gallantly escorted her to the thickly cushioned chairs and settled her into one, retrieving a blanket to tuck around her.

She smiled wanly. "Thank you."

A bolt of lightning lit the sky and threw the grounds into sharp relief. Rain began to splatter against the glass in big, fat drops. Tears. Her sisters weeping for her destroyed soul. The thought came unbidden, but once she had it, she knew it was true. There was nothing left of the Elle that had left home so many weeks ago. She was gone and whoever was left in her empty shell of a body was lost.

"Was that so hard, Sheena? Asking for my help?"

She lowered her eyes and shook her head, cringing inside that she had to play this disgusting game. She wanted to think of it as she used to, her undercover persona outwitting her prey, but she no longer felt strong and in control. She wasn't strong. She might never be again. She continued to look out the window, not wanting to see Stavros's handsome face. He was the devil incarnate, and just looking at him filled her with fear. She thought him invincible and it frightened her to think that he might get his hands on her sisters.

"Sheena." His voice was purring softly and filled her with terror. "Look at me."

He couldn't possibly be reading her mind, the psychic energy barrier was in place. She could always feel that low hum, hurting in her head. She made herself look away from the hope the storm brought, to meet his dark, hooded eyes.

"See, my sweet, life doesn't have to be difficult, if you just do as you're told." Stavros swept his arms to encompass the room. "You can live a beautiful, privileged life here with me, having our children, having anything you want."

"Why me, Stavros? I'm not like the women you're usually with." Not tall and beautiful, just intriguing enough to get his attention to be invited to his parties. She wasn't one of the statuesque blondes he'd seemed to prefer.

He took her comment as a plea for reassurance. "Is that what concerns you, sweetness? That you're not going to hold my attention?"

Her stomach turned over. The last thing she wanted was to hold his attention. She forced her mind to keep up. It was so hard to think, but if she could just engage with him sitting a distance from her, not touching her, she could wait for a signal. Oh God. She could wait for the energy field to come down. That's what they had to be doing—taking down the energy field. Her heart jumped with anticipation. Stavros would be very sorry he ever laid a hand on her if that field came down.

Elle looked at the man, hoping he couldn't see her hatred of him. She forced a casual shrug, searching for the right words to appeal to his massive ego. "You're like a fairy-tale prince, and don't pretend you don't know it. Every write-up about you describes you that way, and look in the mirror. I'm no princess."

Stavros leaned toward her, looking more pleased than ever. "You're exotic, Sheena, a very rare jewel. And I know jewels. I searched the world over for a woman like you."

He had the purring quality to his voice again, meant to mesmerize her. He reminded her of a cobra hypnotizing prey. She suppressed the shudder and drew the blanket closer around her. Elle was thankful to her sisters as the wind slammed against the villa hard, drawing her gaze naturally so she could look away from those watchful eyes.

"I'm not, Stavros," she whispered and the shame in her voice was real this time. "I'm weak. I should have been able to keep standing up to you, to have pride. I feel as though I've failed some test you set out for me."

She rubbed the edge of the blanket against her trembling mouth. She wanted to go home—but home would never be the same—because *she* wasn't the same. She was no longer Sheena MacKenzie or Elle Drake. She didn't know who she was anymore. Her temples throbbed and the constant headache reminded her that she'd nearly burned out her talent fighting the energy field. What did she have left? Stripped of everything she was, everything she knew about herself, she felt like an empty shell with nothing inside.

"Sweetheart, this was no test for you. There was never a need to prove to me that you were strong enough or worthy enough."

Not for him. Never for him. To be a Drake. To pass on her legacy to seven women. To be strong enough to guide them over the coming years in the things they would have to learn to wield such power. She'd had power all her life, self-esteem, training, her body and mind fit, and yet now, at the first real test, she'd failed her seven daughters, her six sisters and every single Drake woman who had come before her.

She was broken and there was no fixing her. Even if they managed to get her off the island and away from Stavros, she would never get him out of her mind, or his touch off her body. He had done what he set out to do and she was changed for all time.

Elle shook her head and pushed back the tangle of bright red hair. She hated her hair because he ran his fingers through it constantly. He wrapped his fist around it and yanked her head back, forcing her to do his bidding over and over. There wasn't a part of her that felt clean, no part of her that felt as if it was hers. He had done that. Stavros. Even with the wild wind slamming into the villa and her sisters close, she felt terrified of him. He seemed invincible. Elle kept her head down, not wanting him to see her utter defeat at his hands.

"Sheena." His voice was deceptively gentle, compelling her to look at him, her heart in her throat. "I want your obedience. You will have to live here of course, but

I will make your world an incredible one. We'll have our children and our home away from everyone. You'll be protected and so will our children. Here, where I can make certain no outside influences adversely affect our lives."

He sounded so reasonable. She couldn't help but wonder, with her sitting there naked, wrapped only in a blanket, bruises and whip marks crisscrossing her body, how he could sound so sane and reasonable.

"You beat me."

His eyelids flickered and her heart jumped, frightened she'd pushed him too far. It was such an edge, a balance, trying to maintain a semblance of control when she really had none. Control was an illusion.

"I punished you, yes, because you misunderstood what I wanted from you. I want obedience, Sheena. I will take care of your every need, see to your wants and desires, even the ones you don't know you have, but in return, I need you to give yourself completely to me. Body and mind wholly into my care. My wants and desires should always be your first thought."

Like a slave. Like the women his brother had stolen and crammed into his freighters to sell into a life of hell. She felt resistance pouring through her mind and fought to hold back her natural use of power. She didn't need him to beat her again. Her breath left her lungs in a deliberate long rush and she nodded her head. "I thought you were testing me, testing my strength."

She shivered beneath the blanket and glanced again at the sky—at the clouds. Had it been her imagination? Was her mind playing tricks on her? The clouds looked like huge boiling cauldrons, a witch's ancient brew, roiling and whirling darker and darker as they spun. The rain lashed the glass, dimming the room even more. She hoped it hid her expression and the terror building inside her.

Stavros had known she was psychic—that was why he wanted her—not because of any attraction to her, but because he wanted children from her. It was the reason he hadn't allowed his brother too close to her. She closed her eyes and pushed her face into the blanket. She could already be pregnant. It was possible—even likely—that a child already lived inside her.

"Sheena?" Stavros left his seat and came to her, one hand sliding through the tangle of hair. She hated that. Hated him touching her hair. Hated having to sit, trembling, waiting for him to decide what she could or couldn't do. Whether she would receive pain or pleasure and she hated either from him.

The lights dimmed, went brown and she heard his swift intake of breath. Elle's head jerked up, triumph rushing through her, adrenaline pouring into her veins, filling her, giving her strength. She could feel the energy field wavering, the noise in her head receding and power seeping in.

Elle threw back the cover and half stood. Stavros still had his hand wrapped in her hair and he jerked her backward and down, taking her to the floor. Crouching over her, his eyes maniacal, his other hand fumbled in his pocket and he brought out a syringe, pulling the cap from the needle with his teeth. Elle fought him, but he knelt on her, one knee shoving hard into her stomach as he plunged the needle into her neck and depressed the syringe. Almost immediately the world began to fade, the edges getting blacker and blacker.

Stavros bent over her. "I will find you, Sheena, and I will kill everything and everyone you love. There is nowhere you can hide from me." His mouth mashed down on hers, splitting her lip, biting her hard, tearing at the soft flesh deliberately.

Mercifully the blackness spread until she couldn't hear, feel or see anything at all and she just let the dark take her.

5

JACKSON climbed into the helicopter and took his seat beside Jonas and Aleksandr Volstov, Abbey's fiancé and former Interpol agent. He glanced at Ilya Prakenskii, Joley's fiancé. It was up to Ilya now. He was an expert marksman, his reputation unrivaled, and he would need every bit of his abilities as a psychic as well as a marksman in the high winds. He would also have to use those abilities to keep the helicopter stable and depend on Hannah's precision with the wind in order to keep them all safe and provide the cover for the three men going in to rescue Elle.

The moment they were settled, the helicopter lifted into the storm. Jackson could see Hannah on deck, her arms outstretched to the sky, her sisters positioned behind her, feeding her energy as she orchestrated the storm. She directed the wind ahead of the helicopter so that Ilya could keep it stabilized as they shot through the air toward the island. The pilot skimmed the surface of the sea, the waves slapping greedily at them, dousing them with salt spray.

Where the waves had been four or five feet, the wind the sisters were generating pushed the waves into towering threats, powerful walls of crushing strength, whitecaps that Jackson could barely make out in the pitch black of the night. The helicopter only gave off a soft green glow as it made its way toward the island, bucking and rocking, tossed from one storm cell to the next with only Ilya's will to stabilize them. As they approached the island, they went total blackout, cutting all light so they could go in with silent stealth.

The pilot, Abel Williams, a man Jackson had fought three days and nights through thick enemy lines to get to when his helicopter had been shot down, looked grim and fierce as he struggled to keep the helicopter in the air. He'd come without hesitation, and never said a word when they told him he'd be flying in the black of night in the middle of a turbulent storm with choppy waves slapping at the bottom of the helicopter and occasionally washing inside through the open door.

The coordinates of the two targets Matt and his team had sent for them to take out before they could put Jackson, Aleksandr and Jonas in the field were coming up fast. The helicopter's safety was paramount before anything else. The first target was a complex tower built for obvious communication, but that would have gone down with the generator. More important, whoever sat in the bird's-nest view could virtually see the entire island and, with the right weapons, defend it from sea, sky or land attacks. The tower and anyone in it, had to go.

Abel came in hot, darting out of the sky, rockets blazing orange-red streaks against a purple-black sky. He took the little helicopter in fast, fired and maneuvered away, skipping below the cliff line to prevent retaliation should the rockets miss. If the blast and ensuing rain of fire were anything to go by, he'd been dead on target. He was already heading toward their second destination.

The lighthouse was next. Gratsos had a particularly large and well-manned lighthouse. Aside from the powerful lamp that warned off boats and ships from the jagged rocks below, the building housed several guards with high-caliber weapons and enough firepower to fend off a ship full of pirates. The guns boomed as they approached, shattering the night with a rumble like the clap of thunder. The wind howled and moaned and slammed at the lighthouse, ripping at the windows and roof as if trying to tear it open.

Ilya and Jackson both put weapons to their shoulders, hands steady, looking for the mark they needed to keep the shooters silent until Abel lined up his craft in the wicked wind. Almost simultaneously they squeezed triggers and Jonas calmly reported, "Two kills."

Abel fired several rockets, taking the lighthouse from several levels as he nosed the bird up and then down. They hit within moments of one another, lighting up the night, flames shooting into the air and lighting the grounds with a towering inferno. Wreckage rained into the sea below, coating the roiling water with blackened, charred debris, some floating on the surface and others sinking like stone.

The helicopter darted across the sky to hover directly over the grounds nearest the front door of the villa. Ilya took out a guard on the roof as Jonas dropped a rope through the door of the swaying helicopter. A bullet thunked near Jonas's head and he drew a weapon, but Ilya's rifle fired a second time and the shooter went down.

"Clear," Jonas snapped tersely. "Go."

Jackson went first, fast-roping down, weapons on his back and in his belt and boots. He was barely down when Jonas slipped out to follow him. Aleksandr came last, and all the while, Ilya continued shooting, clearing the area around them as the helicopter retreated.

"We're going silent," Jonas hissed into the radio. "Disrupt communication."

All of them shoved silencers on their weapons and slipped into the shadows. Ilya in the helicopter and the two ground teams would have to pull attention away from the villa while the rescue team went in to extract Elle. At the same time, Ilya would send out waves of energy that would interrupt all radio communication between Gratsos and his guards.

A man ran around the corner right into Jackson, his gun pressed tightly against Jackson's ribs. All he had to do was pull the trigger. Jackson drove his knee upward into his assailant's groin and dodged to one side, bringing up his own weapon and firing three rounds at close range. The body dropped away and he cursed, shoving the heavy corpse away from him.

Jonas flicked a glance at Jackson. "You hurt?"

"Just my pride. Let's move."

"We're going in," Jonas advised.

It was the call Matt and his teams had been waiting for. They needed to provide the distraction, keeping the guards focused on them and away from the house. Team two, Rick and Jock, were up now; they had to make their way to Gratsos's helicopter. Rick was a crack pilot and he'd be flying the bird out over the sea. Gratsos couldn't be allowed to use the helicopter to escape or follow them off the island and they could ditch the bird at sea and make Gratsos suspect for a short period of time that Elle had been taken out that way.

Jock and Rick, hearing the soft whisper, immediately set out over the rocky terrain toward the helicopter pad. It would be heavily guarded. It was Gratsos's fastest way off his island and he would want to keep it safe. With his tower and his lighthouse gone, he had to know they were under attack and if he was smart, he would tell his men to keep the way open.

They ignored the sporadic gunfire around them, staying low to the ground and heading for the helipad. Above them, Ilya's rifle was loud, a deliberate attempt to draw attention. Rick fired two shots, taking one guard down and winging a second as they ran.

Ilya finished off the second man before the guard could get a round off. The storm was slamming the island now, the wind frenetic, yet not coming near their helicopter. He marveled at Hannah's ability to command and direct the wind. On board the ship, Sarah was feeding her information, keeping track of each member of their teams. Hannah was working at keeping the storm directed at the enemy while aiding their own people.

Ilya had always admired the Drake sisters and the smooth way they fed each other energy, a blending of their skills and abilities so that when they worked, it was a seamless effort. He knew the kind of toll sustained use of psychic energy took on the conductor and the Drakes were pouring everything they had—everything they were—into the effort to get their sister back. He couldn't imagine what would happen to his Joley if they didn't get Elle back. Her bright, restless spirit would be quenched.

The helicopter lurched and slipped sideways as a mortar round came too close.

"Where the hell did that come from?" Ilya demanded, swiveling around.

Abel had already set the helicopter skimming through the sky, nearly heading straight into the wind before Hannah could adjust to their abrupt movements. She brought the wind around them. The sea looked dark and ominous, the storm creating mini water cyclones, twin columns dancing across the surf. He followed the performances as the cyclones made their way to the shore and touched down on a pile of boulders near the small dock.

A shadow moved in the darkness. Even with his night-vision scope he could barely make out the whisper of movement, but it had been there—someone flinching in the face of the sea's wrath. He was using thermal imaging, because in the heavy wind and storm, it would be easier to pick up body heat. The nest was below him and would be getting ready to fire off another round, their gun well hidden.

"Ten o'clock," he told Abel, his voice grim. "Take them out."

The pilot lined up the shot and took it. The blast flattened rocks and sent two men scrambling. Ilya shot them both and turned back to protecting his team. "You're clear, keep moving."

On the ground, Ilya could see Rick and Jock shimmying through the foliage toward the helicopter pad. There were two men between them and their target. Ilya shot one of them and instantly a third man rolled out of the foliage practically at Rick's feet, his gun flashing. Rick was already diving over him, his own gun bursting forth an orange-red glow while Jock fired several shots into the chest of the fallen man.

Rick and Jock systematically began to set up a field of

claymores surrounding the helipad to slow down anyone coming after them. Rick climbed into the helicopter, powering it up, needing to get it warmed up and ready for flight while Jock lobbed several flash-bang grenades into the air in a circular pattern designed to create the loudest, noisiest and most shocking distraction he could make, trying to draw attention to the helicopter area.

"Get this bird moving," Jock snapped, leaping in. "We're sitting ducks here."

It would take at least two or three minutes, maybe longer depending on how well the helicopter was maintained and they would be at their most vulnerable. They would have to depend on Ilya and their claymore field to protect them and it felt like an eternity.

At the generator, Matt and Kent separated and went at it from either side. Both slapped a block of C-4 on the sides of the large machine. The C-4 was already prepped with the blasting cap, detention cord and time fuse. Using hundred mile an hour tape—duct tape—they secured the blocks. Shoving the fuse igniter onto the time fuse, both twisted the ends until they were totally snug.

"Get ready to pull pin," Matt said. They looked at each other. "One, two, three, pull," Matt ordered.

Both twisted the rings a quarter turn simultaneously and pulled the pins. A soft hissing sound and a small amount of gray smoke accompanied by the familiar scent of time fuse burning told them they'd better run like hell. In one and a half minutes a man could run a good distance, even in the dark on uneven ground. Knowing the generator was going up behind them gave them both a rush of adrenaline, enough to help speed them on their way. Matt could hear Kent laughing as they ran, heading for cover, both counting almost automatically in their heads and then leaping at the last moment behind the rocks they'd already scouted for cover.

The flash was bright and hot and very loud. They both admired their handiwork, the orange-red glowing cloud with bright sparkles and then the concussion as the air surged toward them. The roar passed over them, their heart and lungs reacting. Kent laughed again. "Man, I could use a smoke about now. That was great."

Matt grinned at him and then glanced at his watch. "Come on, you whack job. We've got a lot more fun before we're finished."

Teams one and two were to make their way through enemy lines, creating as much havoc as possible to keep all attention diverted from the villa. They had to get back to the south dock and destroy the boats and the dock. Tom and Luke would take their boat and gear around to the small dock and everyone would rendezvous there.

It sounded easy enough, but as Matt and Kent began to make their way through the trees and rocks toward the dock, they found small groups of guards had set up some razor wire across roads and some of the more open meadows. Kent swore as he removed his favorite combat jacket to throw over the razor wire, stepped with his boot and leapt free. Matt followed.

"We have to take the jacket, Kent," Matt announced. "We can't leave anything behind."

Kent swore again. It wouldn't free easily and would come away in shredded chunks, slowing them down considerably. As they worked the material loose, they heard the small snap of a twig, just up ahead. The two men looked at each other. The razor wire was strung at the entrance to a field, one that most of them would have to cross in order to get through to the southern dock. The field was a perfect choke point. If Gratsos's guards had a nest set up to ambush anything moving through that field, it would be essential to take out the nest.

"Matt," a voice whispered in his ear. "We're coming up on your left."

"Razor wire," Matt reported. "Stay quiet, we've got bogies ahead. Get your ass in gear. We're running out of time."

Matt and Kent hunkered down to wait for Luke, Tom and James to catch up with them. As the three men emerged from the shadows, Matt signaled for a quick consultation.

"Kent, we're going to take the left side and make our way up to the nest." He pinned the other man with a hard gaze. "Stealth, my son. Pure stealth. No one gets shot here. Tom, you, Luke and James slide up along the right side and pound them with suppressive fire. Throw everything you've got at them. I don't want them looking our way or suspecting we're anywhere in the same vicinity. Pound the hell out of them. And if you bag a couple of them, all to the good. I'll owe you a beer."

Tom nodded his understanding. He was a man of few words, but long on action. He signaled to the other two men and they slid into the shadows and moved back to cross to the right side, using boulders and shrubbery for cover.

"In position," Tom reported.

"We're moving. Lay it down," Matt said.

The sound of the M-4s was unmistakable as the three men began to fire, a monumental distraction, drawing the attention of the men hiding in the nest. The volley lasted minutes, bullets streaking across the field to slam into trees and ricochet off the rocks, adding to the chaos.

Matt and Kent crouched low and took off running through the brush. Matt, taking the lead, swerved around trees until there was no cover left. He dropped down and signaled Kent to follow.

"Going to ground," he reported to Tom. "Forty meters out."

The sound of the battle never stopped. The M-4s continued and now the nest was answering. The RPKs, Soviet-made machine guns, roared back. The smaller, newer bullets were specifically designed to tumble end over end in the flesh, causing maximum damage to the human body. The sound of the guns reverberated through the night.

Matt and Kent began to crawl forward. With bullets flying overhead and a nest of enemies within plain sight, a fifteen-second crawl was a lifetime. Heart drumming in his chest, the blood roaring in his ears, Matt pushed with his toes and knees and pulled forward with his elbows all the while keeping his weapon clear.

At twenty-two meters out he held out his hand to stop Kent. Both men eased their weapons behind them onto their backs and drew the grenades from their vests.

"Shift fire. Throwing grenade," Matt said.

The M-4s continued firing but their aim had moved away from the nest, bullets hitting rocks just on the other side of it. Matt and Kent simultaneously exploded off the ground, pulling the pins and lobbing the grenades, dropping back down almost all in one motion. The blast was deafening. Rock, bodies, weapons and debris rained down. Both men rose, weapons ready, but the nest was silent.

"Clear," Matt reported.

Matt and Kent scanned the area carefully with their weapons while the other team raced to join them. The three moved ahead and covered, and they continued forward, first one team and then the second until they gained the southern dock.

Tom and James recovered the scuba gear left behind, stowing it quickly in the boat. Both men pushed away from the dock out toward the sea before climbing inside.

"Do your thing, Hannah," Matt said into the radio.

The wind shifted, slammed against the boat, shoving it out into deeper water. The waves rose and took it out around the bend. In the distance, the engine started up, but the sound was muffled by the wind and waves.

"Move it, we have to hump it to the small dock," Matt reminded Kent. "And we've got a lot of shit to blow to hell first."

"We've got three pillars on each side," Kent said, looking over the dock. He was their bomb expert and took a great deal of pleasure in blowing pretty much anything up. "So six pillars and three boats. Man! Look at that yacht. That little baby is going to get some real special attention. I'm getting a hard-on just looking at her."

"What do you want us to do?" Matt asked.

"We're going to use a satchel charge on all the boats. The little boats won't take much. Luke, put a three-pound satchel charge on each of the small boats. Position the charge right on the engine. There won't be anything left."

"Will do," Luke said and lifted a bag to go to work.

"It'll take you about three minutes or less to set the charges for the boat and you'll need to get back here fast and help Matt," Kent said. "Matt, set three pounds cutting charge per pillar."

Matt rolled his eyes. "That's not a little overkill?"

"Remember the golden rule, *P* is for plenty." Kent grinned at him. "With Luke helping, you should be set in five minutes."

Matt sighed and started toward the dock. He glanced back over his shoulder. "What are you using on the lady there?"

"I was thinking five five-pound charges. One on the engine, one on the gas tank, one on the front, one on the center and a really nice little charge for the bastard's bedroom." He looked especially gleeful. "This is going to be a real nice party."

Matt shook his head. He'd known Kent a long time. When the man set a charge, things went to hell fast. He glanced at his watch. "How long for you?"

"Give me seven or eight minutes. I'll get back, check the other charges and we'll blow shit to kingdom come."

Matt couldn't help but laugh. He watched Kent run toward the yacht and he turned his attention to the dock.

JACKSON burst into the villa, his gun spitting as he shot the guard standing near the door nearly point-blank. *Elle. Damn it, answer me.* His heart was pumping too fast, adrenaline riding him hard. The longer she stayed silent, the more afraid he was for her. Would Stavros kill her to keep her from being rescued? The son of a bitch might just be that spiteful. *Elle. Come on, baby, where the hell are you?*

The room was enormous, nearly all glass. Chairs were plush, the fireplace exotic, with a cherrywood bar to one side. Behind the bar was the only place anyone could realistically hide in the room. Jackson kept his M-4 aimed at the bar as he signaled to Jonas to move in and clear the room. Jonas pushed up against the wall and slid along it, staying tight, eyes on the bar as well. Aleksandr entered behind him and turned to face the one open entryway, the sweeping polished marble staircase that rose majestically in a semicircle. Beneath the stairs was an archway leading to more rooms.

Jonas stepped around to look over the bar. "Clear."

Jackson immediately switched attention, moving close to Aleksandr, Jonas falling back so that he was touching Aleksandr along his leg, back to him, moving with him as one unit. They could feel each other giving silent signals. Jackson had the fastest reaction times, was the best shooter and he was out front. Jonas guarded their backs. Moving together, they cleared room after room. It was slow going and with each succeeding empty room, Jackson's heart dropped more. Dread filled him and he tried to push away the thought that they might be too late.

Elle. Answer me. She had to be alive. He would know if she was dead, but even as he assured himself, dread spread through his body and a part of him felt panic. He shoved open a door, crouched low and swept the room, finding it clear. *Where are you, baby?*

She had to be there. If they'd already moved her, or Gratsos had taken her from the house when the generator had gone down, then she might already be gone. Matt hadn't reported a boat leaving the docks, but Gratsos and his bodyguard hadn't been spotted as of yet either.

Going up the stairs was tricky at best. They "stacked," bodies touching, Jackson leading, Jonas bringing up the rear. Jackson's site was straight up the stairs. Aleksandr faced sideways, aimed upward toward the balcony, continually sweeping right and left while Jonas backed up, leaning into Aleksandr so he could feel where they were going while he swept the areas below them.

They moved in unison, one stair at a time, visually checking each corner, every section over and over as they gained the second-story landing. Jackson faced the long hall. There were more rooms, more doors, more danger. And silence. Always complete silence. If she was there, wouldn't she be screaming?

The nearest room had the door slightly ajar. Jackson had a bad feeling about that and he brought his hand up in a slash across his throat, signaling danger to the others. He took a step toward the door, then a second one, Aleksandr matching his strides like they were dancing, Jonas right behind him, again facing the door opposite the one Jackson was stalking.

Jackson stepped to the side of the door, slammed it open with his arm and dropped in. He fired twice as he went down, rolling and coming up on one knee, tracking the room. A body dropped with a soft thud on the thick carpet, blood slowing pooling around it.

"Clear," Aleksandr said and Jonas kept his eyes on the door across the hall, gun steady.

Before they took a step, they heard a roar like a distant freight train. Then the earth shivered. Around them the villa rocked, furniture shook, walls cracked and the pressure vibrated through them.

"Dock's down," Matt reported in Jackson's ear.

"Fuck Christmas in Greece, welcome the Fourth of July. I say liberate the bastard straight to hell," Kent added unnecessarily.

"Crazy bomber," Matt muttered.

Shaking their heads, the three started down the hall-way, clearing each room as they went. As Jackson nudged open a door, a shadow loomed up in front of him in an open doorway, and he dropped and rolled, holding his fire until he was certain it wasn't Elle. A bullet spat, splinter-ing the wall just above his shoulder, but he was already returning fire, his aim instinctive and he heard the body fall. He shot again, leaving nothing to chance.

They had one room left. If Elle wasn't there, he was screwed. There was nowhere else for her to be. It meant they were too late and Gratsos had slipped past them, tak-ing her with him and they'd have to start all over again. Heart tripping, Jackson approached the last room. It was built to take up one end of the entire floor, the wall facing the ocean glass.

The door was slightly ajar as they approached and he heard movement inside. He froze, his hand cutting across his throat to signal the others. The door opened inward to the right, so they approached from the right side. Jackson waited, counting silently until they were all in position. Jonas kicked the door hard, slamming it open so that it crashed against the wall behind it and bounced.

Jackson went in fast, crouching low, sweeping the room with his gun, left and then instantly back to center to cover the two men standing in the center of the room, hid-ing behind Elle's limp body.

"Target," he spat out, his sites dead center between the eyes on the first guard—the one holding his gun to Elle's head.

Aleksandr had come in a split second behind, moving to the right, his gun on the second guard trying to shield himself behind the woman and his partner. Jonas came in nearly at the same time, deliberately moving to his left with Aleksandr to try to keep attention away from Jackson, their best shot.

"You take a step, she dies. Put your weapons down."

"Put 'em down, put 'em down now!" the other guard yelled.

"Stay cool," Jonas said. "No one has to die here. Just hand us the woman and walk away."

"Drop your fucking weapons now," the first guard screamed, panic in his eyes.

"Just shoot him," Aleksandr encouraged in a loud, obnoxious voice. "Take the shot. She's dead weight anyway. Do it now, take them out."

The guard behind Elle swore loudly.

"Take them out, take them out," Aleksandr insisted.

"Everybody calm down," Jonas said.

"Put your weapons down," the first guard said again, but now he was looking at Aleksandr, his eyes jittery.

Jackson never spoke. Never moved. Elle just hung in the man's arms. When he touched her mind, she wasn't there. He tamped down panic and took a breath. Let it out. Never once did his gun move from his target. He let everything recede into the distance but his target. The chaos of the shouting, swearing guards, Aleksandr prodding them, Jonas calming them, all of it disappeared until he was in that tunnel he was so familiar with. Ice cold water running in his veins, fire in his gut, his heartbeat in his ears and death in his mind.

He willed the bullet from his gun to the target, replayed it over and over in his head. All the while waiting. One moment. One split second. One mistake.

"Take them out, damn it," Aleksandr continued screaming, switching back and forth from English to Russian.

The guards yelled back, threatening, pulling Elle's limp body closer. "I'll kill her, I'll kill her, drop your weapons."

"Kill the bastards," Aleksandr yelled at the top of his lungs, his Russian accent very much in evidence. "We don't give a fuck about the woman. Just kill them."

The guard holding the gun to Elle's head swung the barrel toward Aleksandr and Jackson shot him between the eyes. Aleksandr squeezed the trigger and the second guard hit the floor almost simultaneously. Jonas leapt forward to Elle's side. Jackson was there before him, checking for a pulse, making certain she was breathing. For the first time, he let himself look at her, trusting Jonas and Aleksandr to keep their enemies off his back.

She lay on the floor, broken, like a doll. Her red hair was a mass of tangles. Her face was white. Not pale, but white, and dark ugly bruises marred her soft skin, around her eyes and cheek and even her jaw. Her face was swollen and when he bent and whispered her name, the robe they'd wrapped her in gaped open. His breath caught in his throat. His heart stood still. Bile rose, churned in his belly and clogged his throat. Behind him, Jonas made a sound like a wounded animal.

"My God, Jackson. Look what they did to her," Jonas's voice choked. There were tears in his eyes and he dropped down beside the woman he had always considered a baby sister.

Her body was crisscrossed with bloody, raw whip lashes and dark bruising. For one moment Jackson opened the robe and followed the trail up and down her body. There was no place that hadn't been touched. Even lifting her was going to hurt.

"We have to go," Aleksandr said. "Wrap her up, Jackson,

let's haul ass. We're on tight numbers here. The women can't sustain that storm forever. Put it away," Aleksandr counseled, putting a hand on Jackson's shoulder.

It took every ounce of self-control Jackson had not to knock that hand away from him. Instead, he wrapped Elle up, first in her robe and then the blanket they brought, dark like the night. He flinched picking her up, but at least she was unconscious, whatever they'd given her mercifully preventing her from feeling pain. He lifted her over his shoulder, letting her head fall down his back. He took his pistol in one hand and anchored her with the other.

"Let's move out." He could barely choke out the words.

They moved down the stairs, Aleksandr taking over lead position with Jackson in the middle and Jonas once more guarding their rear.

"We've got the package and we're heading home," Jonas reported into his radio.

"Head for the north dock. I'm on you," Ilya said as Abel brought the little helicopter around and back toward the villa. Ilya switched his thermal scope for night vision. Now it was crucial to identify his targets.

"Coming out now," Jonas said.

"You're clear," Ilya said as he squeezed off a shot and took out an enemy running toward the villa.

He caught glimpses of Matt bringing his team around to the north, working their way through the trees on the cliff side, trying to get into a position to give Jackson, Aleksandr and Jonas cover as they fought their way to the north dock with Elle.

Blast after blast came from the general direction of the helipad as the claymores went off. The helicopter rose in the air. Beneath it, the helipad went up in an orange-red fireball and rained down rubble.

"We're away," Rick informed Ilya, "heading out to sea."

"Six bogies at twelve o'clock." Ilya reported. He scanned the area and saw several enemies making their way up from the west side. "Four more coming from your seven o'clock."

The wind was building again, a prelude for the energy Hannah would need when Rick ditched Gratsos's helicopter at sea. Abel fought with the small bird, trying to bring it around to put Ilya in a better position to give covering fire.

Ilya put his scope on one of the four coming up behind Jackson's rescue team. He took out the leader. As the man fell, he saw movement, rather *felt* movement almost directly below. Fitting the rifle tight against his shoulder to steady the shot, he swept the area fast, expecting a round coming at him. For one brief second he caught a glimpse of the man he was certain was Stavros Gratsos. The man wore a suit and his bodyguard shoved him out of the line of fire and swept his own rifle to his shoulder.

Some unseen force kept him from pulling the trigger. He and the bodyguard stared at each other while time stood still. The features came into focus, sharp and defined. He was looking at the face of a younger version of the only relative he'd seen in a picture—his father. A chill went down his spine, his heart nearly stopped beating and then adrenaline pumped into his system. The bodyguard dropped the rifle to his side without taking a shot.

A streak of orange-red lit up the night like a whip of lightning, coming from the ground toward the helicopter.

Abel swore and the helicopter pitched away from the tracer round. Ilya fired off three rounds in rapid succession, taking out two of the three men.

In the distance, coming from the north side, scattered gunfire erupted, letting Jackson know that Matt's team had engaged the enemy, trying to clear the way for them to make it to the boat unharmed. A volley of shots and automatic gunfire reverberated as the enemy used the standard "pray and spray" assault. Every now and then a gun answered, a single controlled shot as Matt or Kent or Luke found a target.

Aleksandr went out of the house first, sweeping left to right, clearing the path to the first cover, a large fountain in the courtyard. Jackson came after him, pistol out as he carried Elle, with Jonas bringing up the rear. The sound of an angry bee zinged past Jackson's head and thunked into the fountain, burrowing a hole through the marble and spraying chunks out the other side.

Jonas hissed a command and Aleksandr and Jackson hit the ground while Jonas swung around and returned fire on full auto, spraying the area behind him, uncertain where his target was. While Jonas laid down a rain of fire, Aleksandr and Jackson sprang up and ran for the cover of the grove of trees forty meters away. Jackson shifted Elle off his back to the ground and came up on his knees behind a small nest of boulders, bringing his rifle around.

"Move," he snapped to Jonas. "Got you covered."

Jonas took off running toward him, and Aleksandr and Jackson sprayed the area behind him. Jonas leapt the last meter.

"Where is that son of a bitch?" Jonas demanded. "Is he dead?"

"I don't know. Ilya? Are we clear?" Jackson asked.

A bullet whined past, this time coming at them from the villa's second floor.

"I thought you cleared that house," Ilya growled.

"That sneaky son of a bitch," Jackson cursed. "He could hold us here forever."

"I'll get him," Ilya said. "Abel, come around."

The helicopter zipped through the sky. Jackson crawled around the pile of boulders, using his knees and toes and elbows, rifle ready, circling around to get in a better position. Jonas fired a couple of shots to lure the target out. As soon as he slid back behind the rock, the enemy popped his head up to take the shot. Jackson shot him.

"Clear," he said. "The son of a bitch can go to hell."

"You're clear here," Matt said. "Move, move, move."

Aleksandr took the lead, Jackson with Elle tight behind him and Jonas, as usual, brought up the rear. Overhead, Ilya in the helicopter did another pass over the area, looking for Gratsos and his bodyguard. They'd gone into a hole somewhere and Ilya was fairly certain that if it was a Prakenskii guarding him, no one would find the Greek.

Matt and his team fell in behind the rescue team to protect them, spacing themselves a small distance apart. Abel kept the helicopter above them as they ran out onto the dock and boarded the waiting boat. The wind had really picked up and ripped and tore at their clothing as they positioned themselves for best protection.

Jackson went down in the bottom of the boat to cover Elle, shielding her body from the others as they made their way out to sea. The waves rose up, choppy and merciless, and the rain poured from the sky. Several hundred meters from shore, Tom detonated the charges on the small dock. It went up in a blaze of fire.

Kent grinned at Tom. "That was a thing of beauty."

The waves rose up behind them, hurling them through the water, throwing the boat as fast as the wind pushed at them. All of them had night-vision glasses to their eyes, keeping the helicopter in sight, speeding to the rendezvous point.

"Dropping Jock now," Rick said.

"Man over," Matt called. "Move this thing."

Rick hovered almost low enough for the skids to touch the water to allow Jock to bail out. He went into the sea and Rick took the helicopter up fast to give the boat time to move in quickly and retrieve his partner. His heart was beating fast. He was relying on the word of two army buddies that the women could force the helicopter away from him when he bailed out.

"You can do this?" His mouth was dry.

"Go when I say," Sarah said. "Don't hesitate." Hannah would have to direct everything they had to push the helicopter away from the pilot without catching him in the wind. That meant precise timing.

The pilot made the sign of the cross and brought the helicopter in low again, over the roiling waves. For a moment he was afraid he might not be able to move, but then the adrenaline kicked in. "Hail Mary," he shouted, half in prayer, half in bravado.

"Go!" Sarah shouted.

He burst into the air. Folding arms over his head, keeping his body pencil straight, he leapt out away from the helicopter. Behind him, the wind howled and blasted the side of the helicopter with hurricane force. The roar hurt his ears, but the blast pushed the big body of the metal bird sideways as it fell from the sky.

The water closed over his head.

The helicopter crashed into the water a good distance away, but he felt the drag on his body as he kicked strongly to the surface.

"Second man in the water," Matt reported.

The wind howled and moaned. Jonas frowned as a wall of water nearly took them out. "Sarah, tell Hannah to back off. We're getting slaughtered out here. The waves are nearly swamping the boat."

"She's trying, Jonas," Sarah snapped. "This isn't easy. The storm's taken on a life of its own."

It took both Matt and Aleksandr to haul Rick into the boat. They wrapped a blanket around him and he wedged himself beside Jock, a rifle in his hands.

Elle came to, fighting, gasping for breath, unseeing, fists flailing. Jackson held her to him, cradling her against his chest, rocking back and forth, although he was fairly certain it was to comfort himself, not her. He had been in her mind, knew what they'd done to her, but seeing her broken body, her face swollen and bruised, the raw wounds of the whip marks across every part of her body and the evidence of manacles around her wrists and ankles made him sick. He'd actually been sick, heaving his guts out over the side of the boat, his eyes burning and the air choking in his throat.

"You're safe, baby," he crooned softly. "I've got you safe. Open your eyes, Elle, look at me. I've got you safe." He repeated it like a mantra, a litany.

Her lashes fluttered. She groaned. The boat bumped hard on a wave, throwing them all around the boat. Several of the men swore as seawater poured over them.

Elle gasped and looked around, obviously not comprehending. Jackson bent closer and used the much more intimate form of communication. She seemed drugged, disoriented, very far away. *We've got you safe, baby. We're away from the island and heading for the ship.*

She stared up at him for what seemed an eternity and then recognition kicked in. For a moment, tears swam in her eyes. *Where is he? Stavros? Did you get him?*

We will. We have to get you out of here.

Elle's expression changed. Her eyes turned emerald bright, like two jewels pressed into her pale face. She struggled out of his arms and stood up, ignoring the men in the boat. Facing the island, she raised her arms high. At once lightning forked across the sky. The wind funneled straight through the arc she formed with her arms and headed in a concentrated rush for the villa.

The air pressure in the boat was tremendous, pressing down on them, the force of the wind vibrating through their bodies as it passed overhead and hit the villa head-on. Glass and steel exploded as if charges had been set on the very foundation. Elle refused to stop, even with Jackson pulling at her. She faced her enemy and flattened everything standing on the island with the force of her rage. Trees exploded. Cars and trucks flew into the air and crashed back to earth.

"Elle, stop," Jonas said. "She's bleeding, Jackson."

Jackson could see her face now. Blood streamed from her eyes and mouth and nose, even from her ears. He felt the pain ripping through her head as lesions opened in her brain, but she refused to stop, lashing out at the man who had nearly destroyed her.

"Holy shit," Kent said. "Look at that. I'm in love here."

Jackson caught Elle's arms and dragged her back against him, pressing his mouth to her ear. "Stop now,

Elle, or I swear I'll knock you out. You aren't killing your-self over him. Stop now, damn it."

Elle slumped against him. *Don't let my sisters touch me. Too dangerous. And I can't bear if they feel what I feel. Promise me.* Blood pumped out of her nose. *Only you, Jackson, no one else. Swear it or I keep going.*

Jackson closed his eyes. "I swear it, Elle."

6

"THIS is ridiculous, Elle," Sarah said, her voice sharp. "You have to go to a hospital or at least to one of our homes where we can take care of you. You're not in any shape to stand out here arguing, let alone take care of yourself."

Elle kept her arms wrapped around her waist, rocking her body back and forth as if to soothe herself while she looked up at the Drake house. "I'm not going in there, Sarah." She shook her head, ducking to hide her expression, but Jackson caught the sheen of tears. "Don't tell me I don't have a choice. I've had enough of that for a lifetime."

The sisters had been arguing for fifteen minutes and Elle was so pale Jackson was afraid she might faint if they kept it up. He took over, using his hard, authoritative voice, one that brooked no argument, one that signaled he meant business—and he did. "You have lots of choices, Elle. Stay here in your home. Go to one of your sister's homes. Go to the hospital or come home with me. Any of these will work for us, but you going off alone is not an option. Pick something and let's get it done."

Elle felt small and lost in the middle of her family. The house loomed over her, the windows lit, watching her. They were all watching her. *Seeing* her. She needed to get away from them before it was too late. Her sisters. She loved them so much and she couldn't do this to them. Not to Libby, who would try to heal her, or Hannah and Joley, who were both pregnant and already sick. They would feel what she'd felt, see the internal damage, not just what was on her body, but the depravity, stamped so deep into her soul she had no hope of washing it away.

Elle looked helplessly at Jackson. *They can't see inside me. Not all of it. Not like it happened.*

You're wrong, baby, but come with me then. You can't be alone right now. You know that. You should be in the hospital.

It hurt to use telepathy. Her head throbbed and ached, but she didn't want to hurt her sisters any more than necessary. *I'm probably pregnant with his child.* She held his gaze. Looked straight at him, refusing to look away, wanting to see his rejection, his disgust. Instead his ice-cold eyes warmed and he reached for her. Elle stepped back and shook her head. *Birth control doesn't work and he used me . . .*

His gaze slid over her and she shivered a little under the piercing stare, drawing the blanket she was wrapped in closer around her, as if she could hide from him—from them all.

"Elle's going home with me."

Sarah stepped toward her younger sister, but stopped instantly when Elle shrank away from her. A mixture of emotions crossed Sarah's face and Elle looked as if she'd been struck.

Jackson stepped between them, his body partially blocking Elle from her older sister's view. "I know this is difficult, Sarah. She needs medical attention, and obviously Libby's touch to heal her psychic scarring as well, but right now she needs a little space."

"From us?"

There was a wealth of hurt in Sarah's voice and he felt Elle's instant reaction, as if in her mind, she'd curled up into the fetal position and held herself tightly. "Sarah," he lowered his voice, tried to be gentle, inwardly cursing that he wasn't a gentle man and probably the least equipped of all of them to deal with their combined emotions. "All that matters right now is Elle and what she needs." He turned and swept Elle into his arms before she—or anyone else—could protest. "I'll see that she's taken care of tonight, and tomorrow we'll sort all this out."

Elle shocked him by not protesting his authority—something she would have fought to her last breath before. Her sisters parted ranks for him as he took Elle away from the Drake sister estate, back to his pickup. He was gentle as he deposited her on the seat.

"Let me get your seat belt for you, baby," he said and reached across her, careful not to bump her body. She hadn't let anyone touch her on the ship or on the airplane, not even on the small plane that Joley had hired to take them back to the landing strip close to their hometown. She'd barely spoken, looking fragile—looking broken. He ached inside every time he looked at her.

Elle caught his hand to prevent him walking around to the driver's side. "I'm not the same."

His fingers curled around hers. "It doesn't matter, Elle. I've been there, remember? You're never going to be the same. It doesn't work that way." He caught her face in his hands and looked into her eyes, waiting until she stopped avoiding his gaze. "We'll do this together. We'll get through it together."

She swallowed hard, her expression so sad it was heartbreaking when he hadn't realized he had a heart to break. "And if I'm pregnant?"

"Then it will be our baby. I know you'd never give it up or get rid of it, so I'm with you on this one all the way. Ours, Elle, not his."

"You're sure? When I don't even know what I'm like anymore?"

"I'm sure. Give me a chance, Elle."

She shook her head. "I'm so broken, Jackson. Inside and out. I don't know who I am anymore. You don't have to do this."

His mouth tightened. His jaw set and a muscle ticked there. He stared her down without blinking. "Make no mistake, Elle, I'm helping because I do have to do this. You're mine. You were always meant for me . . ."

She put a trembling finger against his mouth. "Elle Drake was meant for you. She's gone—dead. She's not here anymore."

The hands framing her face tightened. "Whoever you are, whatever you want or need is standing in front of you, Elle. I'm not asking for anything right now, only that you let me help you through this. We'll sort the rest out later."

"Protect my sisters, Jackson. That's what I need from you right now. They can't touch me until I can build my defenses. They can't be inside my mind."

His fingers slid reluctantly from her face, so thin now,

so ravaged. Her eyes were too old, too sorrowful, dark circles under them. He shut the door and signaled to his dog to come around to the driver's side. Aunt Carol had looked after the animals for them all while they'd been gone, and she stood, along with the Drakes, tears in their eyes, watching from the porch. Even the house seemed to be weeping. He glanced around the yard, overgrown with vines and flowers and shrubbery, an explosion of color and a wealth of herbs. Every plant seemed to be looking toward Elle, even in the dead of night. As he looked at the house, he swore it trembled, as if it already knew the legacy was fading away.

Swearing under his breath, he refused to look at the sisters, holding hands, watching him take their sister from them—from her home. He slammed his door and started the truck.

"You're certain this is what you want, Elle? To be with me? You've had a hell of a time and you need someone gentle. If you put yourself into my care, I'm going to take care of you. I'll do what I believe is right." He stared straight ahead, not wanting to see fear—or distrust—or even acquiescence. He had wanted Elle Drake to come to him without the legacy, without her sisters, without him having to accept everything that came with her, and here she was, huddled so small and vulnerable in his truck, delivering herself into his hands and he felt the wrongness of it. If she came with him, he was going to make this right. He was going to do everything in his power to make the prophecy of the Drake family happen. "Elle?" he prompted. "Your choice, baby. Can you feel their love for you?"

"I can't feel anything but what he did to me, what he took from me."

"You're not allowing yourself to feel." He pulled down the driveway slowly, giving her time to change her mind, but when she said nothing, he turned onto the narrow highway overlooking the ocean and picked up speed.

Elle didn't answer, burrowing deeper into the blanket instead, closing her eyes, allowing herself to drift away. Her head ached, and she could barely draw breath with every movement of the truck. She wanted to crawl into a hole like a wounded animal and hide from reality. The world seemed too big, too open, as if she didn't know how to move in it. She could feel the house pulling at her, wanting her to come back. The wind touched her face through the open window, beckoning to her, calling with faint feminine voices, and she hated herself for causing her sisters to cry.

She could feel Stavros, hear his voice. He was inside her mind, her body, maybe even her soul and she would never be able to get him out. All the times he'd touched her—hurt her—forced her to do things . . .

"Stop it, baby," Jackson said gently. "That doesn't help."

"He's all over me. In me. How am I ever going to get away from him?" There was despair in her voice. Without being aware of it, her fingernails tore at her skin as if trying to rip Stavros off her.

Jackson reached over and laid his palm gently over her hand, stilling her. At once her mind was flooded with him. His scent. His strength. He poured into her mind in much the same way she'd poured into his so many years earlier when he'd been a prisoner of war. A victim of brutal torture, of unspeakable things, and his mind had been close to shattering. She had come to him and when there was nothing left of him, she had filled his mind with all of her, with her strength, her unique scent. Her will to survive. She had given him everything she was.

Now he gave himself to her just as completely, filling every corner of her mind, saturating every cell with his masculine presence, with every emotion, holding nothing back. Not keeping back the details of his capture and torture, not even the worst of the depraved acts committed against him. He opened himself to her, allowing even his rough, raw sensuality and his fears that even after all her experiences, he would be too much for her to handle inside her mind. He shared his life, his thoughts, letting her see the stark, painful childhood and the wild running through the bayou, as well as the violence of the biker camps his father raised him in. He hid nothing from her and Elle soaked in his strength, in his honesty with her.

He knew he had nothing else to give her but who he was. He'd shared those moments of depraved brutality when Stavros had killed a man he'd forced her to touch. He knew she was terrified Stavros would find her and drag her back—no—kill everyone she loved. And she was risking his life by being with him, trading his life for that of her sisters.

"I'm sorry, Jackson. I am. I'm not strong enough to be alone and you're the only one I have that might be able to stand up to him. Jonas could lose Hannah or I'd go to him . . ."

"Don't, baby," he soothed. "We're in this together, we always have been whether we wanted to admit it or not."

"He'll kill you. You know that, don't you?" Her voice shook just thinking about Stavros and her mind felt shredded. She clung to Jackson's strength, to the darkness in him. He was brutal and raw, with a violence that more than matched Stavros's. Unlike the Greek, he didn't bother to hide it—certainly not from her. It wasn't the truth that she would have risked Jonas, and she couldn't bear the lie between them. "I shouldn't have implied that Jonas . . ."

"Don't explain, Elle. I'm in your head. You're in mine. We share the same skin right now, and your risk, being with me, is just as great. I have a threat hanging over my head as well," he reminded her quietly. "My father crossed another gang and they killed him for it. I took several of them out before they got me. I didn't die and they know it. They've been looking for me and anyone with me is in danger."

Elle's gaze slid over him. He was looking straight ahead, out the window, ignoring her and the ocean below them as they wound their way along the ribbon of highway toward his home. "And you're just telling this to me now?"

"There was no need for you to know before."

A small stirring in her mind told Jackson Elle Drake was not completely gone. She'd always had one hell of a temper to go with her bright red hair, and he felt a small spurt, like a weak firecracker going off. "There was every need. You know what I thought."

"I know what you said you thought. You blamed me for your running off."

Her lips tightened and she ducked deeper into the blanket, averting her face, inhaling the wind. The breeze ruffled her tangled hair. She pushed at it. "You didn't want me enough to take me the way I was, Jackson."

He felt the punch of her words in his gut. "Don't fucking tell me I didn't want you enough, Elle. Don't ever say that to me. I may not be Jonas, all smooth and saying whatever a woman wants to hear, but I sure as hell wanted you with every cell in my body and you knew it. You wanted me to change. You wanted me to be a yes man."

She swallowed hard. "I'm not doing this with you. It doesn't matter anymore. We had our chance and we lost it."

"And don't fucking say that to me either."

"Maybe I just shouldn't say anything."

The scenery blurred as she stared out over the ocean. Waves pounded against great rocks, throwing geysers of water into the air and dousing the rocks with white foam. There was a semblance of peace in the familiarity of the coastline, wild and untamed, the ocean unpredictable, yet always constant. Like her family.

Jackson cleared his throat. "I don't know how to do this right, Elle. You're exhausted and hurt and—"

"*Damaged*. Just say it. We both know it. I need honesty from you, Jackson. I'm counting on your honesty to tell me when I'm screwing up. Because I feel so . . ." She trailed off. She rubbed her chin on the blanket. "Angry. Wanting to hurt someone. I hate myself for this but better you than them."

"Don't you think I know that?" He pulled the truck into his drive and took them up to his home. "I knew what I was asking when I begged you to stay alive, Elle. I've been there, I know better than anyone what you're feeling right now. I'm well aware you'll do anything to protect your sisters."

"Including putting your life in danger?" There was a note of challenge in her voice.

"I shared your mind when he shoved a gun down some-one's throat."

Elle squeezed her eyes closed tightly, but she couldn't stop the vision of a complete stranger towering over her, shoving his penis into her mouth, or the sight of Stavros slamming his gun into the man's mouth and pulling the trigger. Her throat closed, as if a hand squeezed like a vise around it, taking her breath until she fought, thrashing to get air.

Jackson slammed on the brakes and reached for her, ripping her seat belt free so that he could spin her around, catching her by the shoulders. Her hands were at her neck, trying to pry unseen fingers from her throat. Behind them, in the back of the truck, Bomber was barking frantically.

"Breathe. Take a breath," Jackson demanded, his voice calm, although his heart was stuttering. Her eyes were glazed, far away, not seeing him.

He kept her mind flooded with him and he tried again. *Elle. Take a breath. Breathe with me.* He pried her fingers loose from her neck and pressed her palms flat over his lungs as he inhaled deeply and then let out the air. *That's it, baby, with me. Feel that. We're together. The same skin, honey. You breathe and I'll breathe.*

She was following his instructions, huddled, sheltered inside him, fearing Stavros reaching for her from a distance. Jackson leaned down and brushed the top of her head with a kiss. "We're okay now, Elle. You're home. You're safe." He drew her into his arms, cradling her against his chest, blanket and all. "Sarah will bring some clothes over for you tomorrow. In the meantime, you can wear mine, but they'll be a little big. We'll make do."

Elle clung to him for a moment, trying not to feel those fingers at her throat. A panic attack? She'd never had them before. Or had it been real? Had Stavros found her already? Sheena MacKenzie had ceased to exist. There was no way he should be able to trace her back to Elle Drake, and certainly not that fast. It had to have been a panic attack. She rubbed her throat, feeling bruised and sore. "Maybe I'm losing my mind, Jackson."

"And maybe you're traumatized, Elle." He kicked open

the door and swept his hand toward the interior, signaling the dog to enter and search. Even with Elle in his arms, he had one hand near his weapon, tucked into his belt. The German Shepherd poked his head out a few minutes later and gave a short bark, signaling all-clear. Jackson stepped inside and put Elle down in the center of the room. "It isn't all that clean, honey. I didn't expect to bring you home with me."

Elle turned in a slow circle to take in the room. It was a man's room. High ceilings, all gleaming wood. The front of the house was a series of cathedral-like windows rising to the high beamed ceiling in panels, framed in the same polished wood. The floor matched the ceiling and walls as if the entire long open room had been hewn from the same piece of giant redwood. She walked over to the stone fireplace, again a very impressive piece that seemed masculine.

"It's beautiful, Jackson. And very open."

"I don't like to be closed in."

Her gaze jumped to his. A ghost of a smile touched her mouth. "Neither do I."

"You're welcome to look around, Elle. Treat the house as your home. I'll run you a bath." He kept his voice absolutely expressionless. "I'll have to look at your wounds and get them cleaned up and we need to do something with your hair."

Her hair. Her crowning glory, her mother called it. She hated her hair. She hated the feeling of Stavros running his fingers through it. "I think I'll cut it off. All of it." But he could still do that. Still slide his hands over her hair. Her stomach lurched and she was afraid she'd vomit.

"That's a bit drastic, Elle. I can comb out the tangles for you."

But Jackson was in her head. He knew. He saw. He was always going to know that Stavros would color everything she said or did for the rest of her life. She met Jackson's eyes and knew she couldn't hide from him. She wanted to weep for being so weak, for allowing Stavros to touch her . . .

"Don't! You didn't *allow* anything, Elle."

"Maybe if I'd fought harder. I don't know. I could have jumped off the yacht before it reached the island. Why didn't I?"

He crossed the room and gathered her into his arms. "You know better, baby. You're stronger than he thinks you are. You got away."

She pressed her face tightly against his heart. "I didn't though. He's inside of me. He's all over me. He's in my head."

Jackson framed her face with his hands, forcing her to meet his gaze. "There's no room for him in your head, Elle. *I'm* there. I'll always be there and if he tries to come in I'll drive him out until you're strong enough to do it yourself. And there was never room for him in your heart because I was already there. He couldn't touch your soul. It belongs to you and no one else unless *you* decide to share."

"I know you need space, Jackson, but you can't leave me alone."

It cost her to say it out loud and he never would have made her. She was trying to atone, trying to give him something back when she was putting him at risk, when she knew she was going to lash out at him.

"You never have to do that, Elle, not with me," he said, meaning it. "I don't need that from you. I'm not going to be perfect here, we both know that. I'm mean as a snake most of the time and I like my own way. I haven't changed just because your disappearance scared the hell out of me. Don't worry about me."

"I can't," she said. "I can barely survive right now. You're the toughest man I know and I trust you with my sanity. I'm giving myself to you, Jackson, my soul. You said it was mine to give and you're the only one I know that is mean enough and tough enough to guard me, to guide me through this."

He knew what she meant. She was basically calling him a cross between a bastard and a saint. He was a bastard, but the saint—he'd have to see. He touched her hair and she jerked her head away.

Elle shook her head, upset that she couldn't control herself. "I'm sorry. He did that. He liked my hair. I can't stand to look at it."

"So you want to cut it off? I can do it for you, honey, but it won't look so good."

She pulled the blanket tighter around herself, grateful that he wasn't arguing. "I still don't know if I could take looking at it." She shuddered trying not to feel Stavros trailing his fingers over her scalp.

"You could always do dreads." Jackson flashed her a grin as he lifted the mass of red tangles. "You'd look pretty damn cute in dreads."

She lifted her head, her eyes going very green. "Dreads? I never thought of dreads. I wouldn't have to cut my hair and nobody could run their fingers through it."

Jackson went very still. It was the first time in three days Elle had shown a glimmer of interest in anything at all. "Think about it, baby. I could do them for you."

She studied his face. "You hate the idea."

"I'm in your head, Elle. You'd know if I hated it. I don't

give a damn what you do to your hair. If you shaved your head it wouldn't make me feel any different about you. You want dreads, we'll dread your hair."

"My sisters might be horrified."

He grinned at her, a slow, deliberate conspirator's smile. "I think they're already pretty horrified that you're here with me." He indicated the way to the bathroom with his chin. "I have to feed Bomber. It takes hours to do dreads, especially with your hair, so think about it tonight and if you really want to do it, I'll get the supplies we'll need and we can start tomorrow."

Elle nodded and watched him saunter away to what presumably was his kitchen. Her heart instantly began to pound too hard. She wanted to scream after him—*don't leave me alone, don't leave me alone*—but she pressed her fingers against her mouth and listened to her heart hammering out a protest.

Jackson stuck his head back around the corner, his eyes dark and shadowed. "Can't you feel me, Elle? I'm with you every moment. You don't have to use telepathy, I can feel you. I'm not going anywhere."

She let her breath out, not realizing she'd been holding it. This was like walking through a minefield, every moment pure terror. She had to find a way to live again, figure out who she was, live with what had happened. She could taste Jackson in her mouth, his strength, his determination, and his ferociousness. Her gaze assessed him as he stepped fully back into the room. He wasn't as tall as Stavros, but he was built stronger, with wide shoulders and defined muscles. With his scarred face and his strong jaw, he wasn't handsome like the Greek, but there was something very compelling about Jackson. Where Stavros smiled at every opportunity, Jackson rarely did. Stavros rarely swore and Jackson, with his rough background, often slipped up, using crude terms that sometimes made her flinch.

Jackson crossed the distance separating them, rubbing the side of his face. "Do the scars bother you?"

His voice was flat, expressionless, and his eyes gave nothing away. Elle reached up with her fingers and traced the small jagged white lines. He didn't flinch under her touch. "Of course they don't bother me. I've always thought they were badges of courage."

He caught her hand and nipped at her fingers, giving a small derisive snort. "I wasn't feeling very courageous when I got them."

Elle took a deep breath and dropped the blanket. "Neither was I."

She was wearing his shirt still, the one he'd given her on the ship, along with a pair of soft sweatpants borrowed from one of her sisters and nothing beneath it. He could tell the material hurt her skin when she moved and there were traces of weeping blood crisscrossing the shirt and pants. She was trembling, her body still in shock.

He drew in his breath sharply. He'd seen a glimpse of her broken, bruised body when he picked her up off the floor, wrapping her in the sheet, but her robe had covered most of her. She'd stayed hidden after that, refusing to allow anyone to go near her. They'd all respected that because her eyes had been so hollow, so filled with sorrow she'd nearly torn their hearts to shreds. But he couldn't stop his slow steps forward, his hands from reaching out to slowly unbutton her shirt until it began to gape open.

Elle stayed still, holding her breath, her head high and he knew it cost her, that small show of courage. Jackson swept back the shirt to reveal the whip marks, some cut so deep he knew they'd leave scars. There were bruises and bite marks marring her soft skin. Without a word, he pushed the sweatpants down over her hips to see the slashes cutting across her hips and buttocks, down her thighs and even across her feminine mound. His breath burned in his lungs and rage erupted like an exploding volcano, but he shoved it down until it seethed below an ice-cold glacier, a boiling mass of brutal need for retaliation.

"I should take you to the hospital, Elle," he said, his voice a soft ribbon of sound, completely monotone. At her instinctive withdrawal, he locked his fingers with hers, preventing her from covering up. "I've seen worse, though, so I think we can deal with it ourselves. I do want your sister to give you a shot of antibiotics and then prescribe them for you."

"I don't want her to see."

He tugged her sweatpants up, careful to keep the material from brushing her body. "She won't intrude. You know Libby, of all your sisters, is the least intrusive." He began moving her toward the bathroom. The hallway was wide and opened up to a large bathroom with a sunken tub and a wide window with an ocean view. He saw her gaze shift to it and look hastily away. "Does it bother you that half the house is windows?"

She shook her head. "Not in the sense that Stavros's villa was glass. I know even if a boat was out there, no one on it could see me like this, but still, it feels as if I'm exposed to the world." She looked away from him. "To you."

"Don't feel that way about me, Elle. Whatever I know about you, you know about me. We're in this together. You have to look at it that way."

"I don't have a choice. I can't let you out of my mind and I think I'm afraid to let you out of my sight." She flashed a ghost of a smile.

He tugged on her hair. "Bath or shower? We have to wash those wounds and make certain you don't get an infection." He frowned as he pushed the shirt from her shoulders. "He either wasn't very experienced at this or he's a true sadist."

"What do you mean?"

"What was his goal? To force compliance? To punish you? Why leave permanent marks on you? If he was a dominant, he wouldn't have done that, not unless he really likes hurting people."

"His brother showed him how to 'punish' me when I didn't comply. I had the feeling he was giving him a crash course in 'breaking' a woman, although he took to it very fast."

"His brother?" Jackson prompted, his voice carefully neutral. "You haven't said much about the brother." He only knew she'd spoken of him that once with such fear and loathing.

She didn't want to think about Stavros's brother with his dead eyes and his hungry expression. Now there was a sadist. He definitely liked to inflict pain on women, and she had been so terrified of him, she'd actually looked to Stavros for protection. She was ashamed of that—horrified even—and didn't want to see Jackson's reaction. He had been in her mind and had seen that moment when her breath had caught in her throat and she had made an involuntary move toward Stavros. She'd seen the triumph in the Greek's eyes, but right then it hadn't mattered, only his protection of her from his even crueler, far too hungry brother.

"It wasn't because I was a desirable woman," she mused aloud. "They both sensed I was psychic, yet I didn't know they were. I just thought they had natural barriers as some people do, but I underestimated them."

Jackson chose the shower for her. Already she was swaying with weariness, but she couldn't comfortably sit in a bathtub. He was going to get very wet holding her up, but his comfort didn't matter—only hers. He stripped off his shirt and shoes, leaving on his jeans for her modesty, before checking the water temperature. "Stavros doesn't usually play with whips?"

"I didn't get that impression, but his brother obviously not only played, but really enjoyed playing."

"Do you think they run a human trafficking ring together?" Again he kept his voice casual, not wanting to trigger a panic attack. He was feeling his way with her, but her mind was like a minefield—one wrong step and she might retreat back into the sanctuary she'd found for herself. A place she could huddle deep and hold herself away from the brutal crimes committed against her.

Elle let the soft sound of the water and Jackson's reassuring presence soothe her. She was safe. Back home in her beloved Sea Haven. Her ocean, with its pounding waves and wild, untamed seascape, was right outside. If she wanted to, she could go sit on the sand and watch the waves breaking against the rocks, in a timeless display of power and beauty. She took a breath and let it out.

"One minute at a time, baby," Jackson said, turning her so he could gently remove the shirt where the blood had dried and stuck to her skin.

He kept his eyes on her face, on the mass of red hair, focusing on the wounds rather than on her soft skin and the curves of her body. He wanted her to feel as comfortable as possible when he knew already she wasn't. She was acutely aware of his hands touching her, of the washcloth sliding over her as she leaned against him for strength. She kept her head down, not wanting him to read her expression, although she never once pulled her mind from his.

Her nudity made her feel vulnerable, but the stark wounds on her body made her exposure far worse. Jackson knew she was thinking of how the whip marks and long lines of bruising had been put there and what Stavros had done to her afterward and hated him seeing the images burned into her mind. He kept his thoughts still, holding only strength and warmth flowing from him to her, grateful for the ability to push rage deep beneath the glacier of ice in the pit of his soul where she couldn't find it. There was only his need to protect her, to help her through her trauma.

The water poured over both of them, Elle resting her back against him while he washed her breasts and rib cage.

"Can you lean against the wall, baby?" he asked her, gently moving her into position so he could wash the rest of her body, down her abdomen where his child should be nestling, lower to the wicked marks dissecting her feminine mound. He forced himself to keep his mind from straying toward vengeance, holding only care for her uppermost.

Elle brushed the top of his bent head with her palm. "I know this is difficult for you, Jackson. You don't have to hide your reaction from me. I get angry and then want to cry a river. I don't expect you to live through this with me and never let on how you feel."

He glanced up at her from where he was kneeling on

the tiles, the water pouring over him as he washed off the crusted blood on her thighs. "I don't think you need me scaring the hell out of you with my inventive ways to torture and kill him."

She might have laughed if it hadn't been for his eyes. There were no traces of humor, only those dark, deadly pits where hell reigned. She shivered, her fingers tightening in his hair. "I'm grateful you care enough to want to torture and kill him. I'm glad you won't."

"I would," he said gruffly. "Never fool yourself into believing I'm a nice man, honey. If given the chance, I wouldn't kill him clean, let's just say that. He'd suffer, and I know a lot of ways to make a human being suffer a very long time before welcoming death."

He bent forward and pressed a kiss along the angry raw line, a soft brush of his lips moving against her skin. He transferred his gaze back to her thighs, his touch gentle, his hand trembling as he took care not to hurt while he continued washing, and she wanted to cry for both of them.

"Some things are better for you not to have to know about me, honey. I think my thoughts on Gratsos and how I would like to see him in agony before he dies might be one of them." His voice was matter-of-fact, but there was no humor in his mind and she knew he wasn't joking with her.

Elle took a breath, her fingers tightening on his shoulders to hold herself up. "Has he destroyed both of us?"

His gaze jumped to her face again. "Absolutely not. That son of a bitch doesn't have the power to destroy us, Elle. We're down, but we're not out. We'll be getting back up stronger than ever."

His mouth curved in a humorless smile, but it caught at

her heart. "I was already this way long before Stavros came into our lives. I just never let you see the real me."

"I like the real you," Elle whispered.

His eyes went warm. He reached up and shut off the water. "The antiseptic is going to sting, honey." He wrapped her in a soft towel and blotted the water from her, trying to keep from touching any of the wounds, but it was impossible.

"You're not hurting me," she assured. Her body shuddered under the brush of the towel, but she held on to him and kept her chin up.

"You don't have to protect me, Elle. I know it hurts, I've been there, remember?" No one had washed his wounds or sterilized them. Flies and mosquitoes had flocked to the raw, seeping injuries and feasted. He pushed the thought away quickly, but knew by her swift inhale that she'd caught a glimpse. He fought back the need to pull his mind from hers, to hide his past and the monster it shaped from her.

"Don't," Elle said. "Please don't. I need you. I need this. I need to know you survived and became someone useful and I need to see you as you really are, so I have some hope." She ducked her head, avoiding his eyes as she confessed. "I don't have much hope in me right at this moment. You're a deputy, you're not a monster. You've chosen to help people, not hurt them. I need you so much right now, Jackson. Don't hide from me."

He brought both of her hands to his mouth and kissed her fingertips. "Whatever you need, princess, you know I'll do it." He led her to the bed and gestured for her to lie down on her stomach so he could apply the antiseptic and bandage the worst of the still weeping wounds. His gut was in hard knots. He may have chosen to be a deputy on the surface and wear a badge, but deep down where his soul was, he was capable of things Elle should never have to think about. In his way, he was as violent and twisted as Stavros.

Elle's breath hitched in her throat. "You're not. Don't think that. You're not."

He hoped to hell she was right.

7

JACKSON came awake, gun in his fist, his gaze already searching the room for a target. He didn't move, aware of Elle curled beside him, wearing only his shirt and bandages. The noise had come from her, a small distressed sound that was heartbreaking. He let his breath out and slipped the gun back beneath his pillow, turning carefully so as not to brush against her wounds.

Elle sat up abruptly, hands going out defensively, striking at some unseen attacker, her breasts heaving beneath the thin shirt as she fought for air. She twisted her head, searching frantically around the room before dropping one palm on his chest.

Jackson. He's here.

Her voice, so thin, filled with terror, along with the stark panic on her white face, gave him a chilling moment. Fingers of fear slid down his spine and his belly knotted in response. He glanced at the German Shepherd lying across the doorway. The dog was alert, fully aware of Elle, but giving off no alarm. Jackson relaxed.

"Look at Bomber, honey. He's highly trained. He'd alert us if there was an intruder."

"I heard his voice. Whispering to me." Her hand crept to her throat, fingers stroking restlessly, as if her throat was sore. Even her voice was strained, as if it hurt to talk.

"What did he say?" Jackson sat up and pulled her into his arms to steady her, careful to keep from rubbing his body against hers, afraid he might hurt her.

Elle frowned. "I was thinking about you. How safe you made me feel and then I couldn't breathe and I heard him whispering in that voice—purring with satisfaction like he always did." Both hands fluttered at her throat. Her voice sounded distant, thin, very scared.

"It was a dream. Just a bad dream, Elle. You're going to have plenty of them."

She moistened her lips. "I don't think so, Jackson. He knows how to find me. He said he'd kill you in front of me, and that it would take a long time for you to die."

He wrapped both arms around her trembling body. "It was a dream. He thinks you're Sheena MacKenzie. There's no way for him to trace you, honey. And I don't die so easy, remember. Even if he did come after us, he wouldn't expect me. He has no way of knowing what kind of man I am, but you do." He nuzzled the top of her head with his chin. "You know what a bastard I am."

A single sob escaped and he felt the shudder that ran through her body. Jackson buried his face against her neck. "You're safe, Elle. You're here with me and you're safe. Just lie back down and try to sleep."

She shook her head adamantly. "I'm afraid to close my eyes. When I do, he's there." Her voice was the sound of despair. "I swear, Jackson, I'm having panic attacks like Hannah has. I've never had one in my life, but I can't breathe and my heart is beating too fast because you went to sleep and I couldn't feel you in my head anymore." She wrapped her arm around his waist and pressed her body tightly against his, uncaring of her injuries.

He tipped her face up, brushing at her tears with his lips, tasting them. He followed the trail to the corner of her mouth and stopped when he felt her recoil. "What is it?"

"I'm embarrassed to tell you."

A ghost of a smile softened the line of his mouth. "I don't think we have much more to hide from one another. You know more about me than anyone and I think I know more about you."

"It's still embarrassing." Elle found some of the tension leaving her body. Something about Jackson made her feel strong when she knew she wasn't.

"Be brave."

"The minute you went to sleep and left my mind, all these images poured in. Of him. His mouth on mine." She touched her fingers to her lips. "I didn't want to remember, to taste him, or feel him on me, so I looked at you, at your face. Your mouth." Faint color stole into her cheeks. "I imagined what it would be like to kiss you. What you would taste like. What your lips would feel like against mine." She blinked back tears and rested her forehead against his. "Just like earlier, I couldn't breathe, Jackson. I felt his hands on my throat squeezing the life out of me and I could hear him whispering that he would kill you in front of me. His voice was so real." She lifted her head and stared into his eyes, wanting—willing—him to believe her.

Jackson looked down at her for a long time without speaking, his eyes fathomless. His hand came up to the nape of her neck, curled and rested there with a hint of possession. Elle's heart began to pound. He dipped his head down toward hers. Slowly. Giving her time to move. She didn't, but he felt her body tighten. Tasted fear in her mouth. *I can't.*

"This isn't about sex, baby," he whispered, his lips against the corner of her mouth. "This is about you and me. How I feel. How I taste. So you don't have to imagine— you know. And any time you need to erase his memory, you have another one to put in its place."

His scent was pure masculine. His aura surrounded her, merged with hers. The colors were darker than most people's, but he didn't try to hide that from her. His lips, featherlight, touched her skin, brushed against the corner of her eye, feathered down her cheek to her mouth. Each stroke of his lips was light, breath on skin, soft yet firm. She could feel herself, held so tight inside, muscles locked and corded, terror ruling her, melting with each individual kiss. So light as to almost be nonexistent, unhurried, lei- surely even, as if they had all the time in the world—as if there were only the two of them and no one else in exis- tence. With each touch of his mouth on her skin, the ten- sion slipped away, kept melting until she felt almost boneless, until she lifted her arms and circled his neck and leaned closer.

Jackson's mouth settled on her. He didn't pour lust or even love into her mouth. There were no demands, no pres- sure, just that featherlight brush of an artist—a poet— masterfully plying an instrument so that she wanted to weep with joy. She felt him in her mind, filling every dark place with care, with strength, with a slow-burning passion that made her feel alive, when she'd been dead for so long.

His kiss deepened, slid seamlessly from one to the

next, his hands sliding up to her face, framing her, holding her, *cradling* her as if she was the most precious treasure in the world. Her melting continued, as if the intense heat he generated thawed the ice-blue glacier inside her. Her mouth moved on his, wanting more—even needing it.

The moment she participated, the moment she took from him, her throat closed, as if fingers tightened relentlessly and her lungs burned for air. Panicked, she tried to pull back, tried to pry the unseen hand from her neck.

Jackson didn't back off. "Open your eyes, baby. Lift your lashes and look at me." The words whispered against her mouth, into her mouth, his lips never lifting from hers.

Elle snapped open her eyes and found herself staring into his. She'd never noticed the intensity of the color, how they looked like black obsidian. There was absolute resolve in his eyes, a dark promise of protection and something else she wasn't certain she wanted to see—the need to destroy her enemy.

"Now breathe with me. Just the two of us. No one else is here. Draw the air into your lungs, Elle, and breathe with me."

His hand slipped from her face to slide down to her rib cage, his palm resting there while his other hand pressed her palm to his rib cage. She felt his breath. In. Out. The mechanics of it and his mind tied them together, bound them, made them one so that her body automatically followed his and she drew the air from him. His mouth to hers. She felt her throat relax. Felt her lungs draw the life-giving element deep inside her. She tasted Jackson. Felt him in her. Knew he was real and solid and would fight at her side, stand in front of her, protect her back, whatever it took to keep her safe.

"How did I doubt you?"

"How did we doubt each other?" Jackson corrected gently. He brushed his lips across hers one last time and lifted his head. "We're in this together, Elle. You have to think of us as a unit. If you do that, we'll make it."

"Right now, I think of us as sharing the same skin," Elle admitted. "I know you need space, Jackson, and I really appreciate you staying in my mind."

He held her, listening to her quiet weeping until Bomber pushed his head against both of them in an effort to comfort her, too. He patted the dog's head. "How strong are you? Do you feel like a midnight"—he glanced at the clock—"well, three a.m. walk? Are you up for it? We can take a couple of chairs and go sit and watch the sun come up."

"But you need to sleep."

He shrugged. "Actually, baby, I took a leave of absence from work. I was due a lot of sick days and personal time and figured now was a good time to take them, so we can sleep during the day and stay up all night and live like a couple of vampires, minus the sucking necks, although later, when you're up to it, we might include that in our nighttime activities."

"Would you really dread my hair for me?" Elle lifted her head from his chest, tired of crying, tired of feeling out of control. She could be afraid, she could even be mean or angry or feel the need to find Stavros and put a bullet in his head, but she had to stop bursting into tears. She'd turn Jackson's life upside down and he wouldn't utter one word of complaint.

He lifted the mass of tangled red hair. "I don't think we have to do much to get it done. You're one giant dread already." He stood up, padding across the room in his bare feet, his jeans low on his hips, the top button not done.

Why had she noticed that particular detail? And why had her mouth gone dry? She couldn't ever want a man to touch her again, not like that.

Jackson turned his head, looking at her over his shoulder, his eyes two black, merciless pits. "When I touch you, Elle, you're going to feel love. You'll be ready some day and when it's right, we'll love each other."

She hated what she'd become, what Stavros had made her. She had to give him something. "I've always loved you, Jackson. From the first moment your mind connected to mine, I loved you."

"Hell of a time to tell me, baby," he said, coming back to her and leaning down, his hand spanning her throat in a brushing caress. "But thank you. I don't know how the hell I got so lucky, but I'll take it."

"I'm the lucky one." And she was. She had Jackson. She had her sisters waiting for her, ready to help and support her. She had an entire village of people who had watched her grow up and wished her well. So many other young women weren't as lucky. They had no one to help them through the trauma of rape and assault.

Jackson gripped her hand and tugged. "Come on. Let's go watch the sun come up."

Elle stood up slowly, letting the sheet fall away, standing in his shirt and her bare skin. "Why haven't you asked me why I don't let you wash my hair?"

Jackson released her and padded over to the drawers to pull out a pair of drawstring sweatpants. He handed them to her, his gaze moving over her with a disarming gentleness she'd never have associated with him. "You're not ready. When you're ready, you'll tell me."

She touched her hair. "I always loved my hair. Mom said it was my best feature, my crowning glory."

"Your eyes are your best feature." He tipped his head to one side to study her. "Maybe your mouth. You have a killer mouth. Your smile can stop traffic. But I love your hair. All that fiery red reminds me what a little stick of dynamite you really are."

"Not so much anymore." She pulled on the sweat-pants.

"You're down, Elle, not out." He shrugged into a shirt and picked up a blanket and two sweaters, indicating she precede him out of the bedroom.

Bomber pushed against Elle's leg as if to guide her and she dropped her hand on his head, feeling reassured by the dog's presence.

"I've got two more dogs coming," Jackson announced as he pushed open the door, his hand over her head.

Elle frowned as she went under his arm to step outside. "Two more dogs? What do you mean?"

"Protection dogs. I've worked with them quite a bit. A friend of mine trains them. The two coming are very skilled and I've worked with them before. Lisset sells them, so I asked that when she was ready to let them go, to give me first opportunity."

"Lisset?" She'd never heard him talk about another woman. Not once. She'd never heard a whisper of him dating, or seen him get a phone call from a woman. Jonas had never mentioned another woman.

Elle really looked at him. His broad shoulders, his flat abdomen and narrow hips. He had a very nice butt, which she'd noticed often.

"Stop it."

She raised her eyebrow. "You're pretty darned good-looking."

"No, I'm not." He caught her hand as she started toward the path leading to the beach. "Not down there. We'll sit up here under the trees and watch the sun come up."

"I thought we were going down to the beach." She had missed walking on the beach with the cool sand on her toes and the wind coming off the ocean in her face.

"We can't take a chance of getting sand in your wounds."

"Yes, we can." She tilted her chin at him. "I don't mind a little sand."

It was the first time she'd really acted like Elle. The green eyes deepened to a sparkling emerald challenge and Jackson felt his heart contract. "I'm sure you don't mind, honey, and as soon as your sister Libby gets her butt over here and heals those open wounds, you can roll in sand if you want. In the meantime, we'll just sit under the trees and look at the sea from up here."

Her mouth tightened. "Jackson, it's no big thing."

He reached out with deceptive casualness, curled his fingers around the nape of her neck and drew him to her, one slow step at a time. "If you had been a smart girl, you would have stayed with your sisters. Then when you wanted to walk on the beach with open wounds, they would have argued with you and eventually given in because they want to give you anything right now. I do, too, Elle, but not at the risk of infection. You chose to be with me, and you have to suffer the consequences. I haven't changed and I'm not going to change. We do what's best for your health. If you want to be angry with me, and we both know you need to be angry with someone, then all right, I can live with that. And I've given you far more of an explanation than I've ever given anyone in my life."

"Is that supposed to win you points?"

Again that faint, ghost of a smile came out of nowhere and his white teeth flashed briefly. "Maybe. I don't much care about points. I don't mind picking you up and carrying you to the trees either. So decide."

"You're such a white knight." She pushed past him and headed along the worn path for the wind-blown cypress trees overlooking the ocean.

"I'm guessing that might have been sarcasm." He placed the blanket on the ground just on the rise of the small slope leading to the dunes separating him from the sea.

Elle sank down onto the blanket, sighing heavily to show him she wasn't as happy as she would have been walking on the beach. "You guessed right."

Jackson dropped a sweater over her head, his hand gentle as he put her arms through the sleeves. She'd given in too easily. Elle Drake would have withered him on the spot for daring to dictate to her, even for her health, but at least she'd made a protest, token or not. "Libby can come tomorrow, maybe with Sarah or Hannah so you aren't overwhelmed."

Elle's breath caught in her throat as alarm slammed through her. "No." She shook her head. "Absolutely not. I don't want them to know."

"Baby," he said softly, picking up her hand, his thumb making lazy circles inside her palm. "They already know."

She caught his fingers and held tightly. "No, they don't. They know as in, oh, poor Jackson, he was tortured. How terrible. And of course they feel genuinely terrible for you. They have tremendous compassion, but they don't know what it's like to be stripped of all dignity, all humanity, to feel like less than an animal, crawling naked and blind on the ground, a body to be used in any way someone else sees fit. Knowing you can be raped, brutalized, sodomized, beaten, starved, forced to commit any depraved act just for someone else's entertainment. Unless you've been through it, you can't *feel* it. It isn't stamped into your soul so deep you're branded for life."

Jackson raked a hand through his hair and shifted, the knots in his gut hardening. He knew what she meant. The knowledge, the bitterness, the rage. He could taste it in his mouth and hear his own screams. Sweat beaded on his skin and he looked away from her.

"Don't." She hissed the command between clenched teeth. Her hand caught his face and forced him to turn his head back, to look at her. "If you know every single detail of what that man did to me, then don't turn away from me because I know what they did to you. If you can see me and accept my degradation and pain, then don't take it away from me that I share yours."

He leaned down and brushed his lips across her mouth, jolting her. "Men think we protect women and handle it, that we should handle it." When she continued to stare up at him he sighed and brushed a soft kiss over her mouth again. "All right. I've got it. I do, Elle."

"Before, when you were captured and we were connected and I asked you to live, I knew what it meant, I knew what I was asking of you and what it meant to me. When you asked me to live, I expected that you knew what it would entail. I knew we'd be sharing the memories in our minds, that you'd know every detail of what happened to me at his hands, and I'd know every detail of what happened to you when you were captured. Does it bother you so much that I know?"

His gaze flicked over her face. Had there been a note of

hurt in her voice? Was there a difference? He knew what Stavros had done to her, using her body, forcing her compliance, and even pleasure, and he knew she felt shame because of that. To him, it was all part of the humiliation and degradation process Stavros had used to beat her down. Of course he needed to know what Stavros had done, what she suffered, so he could help her. He wanted to help her. He had told her he wouldn't leave her alone and he meant it. He'd known, from the moment he'd asked her to live for him, the extent of the commitment he was making—even more than she did. She would go through all the stages of recovery with him—what recovery she would manage—and anger would be a big part of that.

He was locked in her mind during every waking moment, something that'd be uncomfortable for a loner like him, but for the first time in his life, he hadn't felt starkly alone. He was different. He'd been different from his earliest memory, and now, keeping his mind intertwined with Elle's, something inside him was changing. He found himself growing more empathetic with her. He knew almost before she did what she was feeling. He felt as if his mind wrapped more and more into hers, binding them together in ways he hadn't expected.

"Jackson?"

Her soft inquiry brought his gaze jumping to hers. "It's happening to you, too, isn't it? You see inside of me more and more, even into the dark places I try to shield you from."

Elle nodded and leaned into him. "You don't have to shield me, Jackson. I have a few dark places of my own."

"Is it the legacy? Is this how it works? Binding us so tight we can't exist one without the other?"

"I have no idea how it works, only that there is one."
Elle sounded bitter. "It didn't save me, and it didn't save
you, Jackson. I don't even know who Elle Drake is anymore."

He wrapped his arm around her. "I know who Elle
Drake is, and right now, one of us knowing is enough. We'll
take this one day at a time."

"I'm going after him."

He was silent, working through the protest. He wasn't
letting Elle anywhere near Stavros Gratsos, not now, not
ever. He had plans to take the man out himself, but he
needed distance. Time and distance. Memories were long
and a sniper had a certain method recognizable to those
around him. Even with Elle's testimony, they had no proof
that Stavros was involved with human trafficking. The
most they could get him on would be kidnapping and rape
charges, and chances were the man had enough money to
get off. Everyone had seen the shipping magnate with
Sheena MacKenzie. They were thought of as a couple.

"I am, Jackson. He isn't going to get away with this.
I'm going to start training and then I'm going to get
him."

"Let's just take one day at a time, Elle. Living for revenge isn't a very good way to go. I know. I've been there
and it eats away at you until your humanity is gone."

"He already took that from me."

The dog shifted closer, and laid his head in Elle's lap.
She dropped her hand onto his head and stroked the fur.
Jackson smiled. "There's no way he could ever take that
from you, baby. But we'll train. And we'll get stronger."
His arm tightened, drawing her closer beneath his shoul-
der. "I'm going to ask Libby to come."

She jerked away, or tried to, but he held her firmly.

"Just listen to me. I've been thinking a lot about this. If you stay connected with me, between us we should be able to hold a barrier to prevent Libby from feeling the emotional ramifications of what happened to you. She's seen your body, she knows intellectually already, so helping you heal will only make her feel better, not worse. Your sisters love you, Elle, and they have to help you. It's in their natures, just as when Hannah was attacked. All of you needed to help her. If we stay connected and build the shield together, I know we're stronger than anyone else. We just need to try it."

Elle took a deep breath and looked out over the pounding sea. Always the same. Always different. The waves crashed against the rocks relentlessly, shooting white foam over the boulders, smoothing and polishing them even as the waves wore them down over centuries. She loved the sound of the sea, and the colors, the deep blues and greens depending on the mood. Right now the sun was climbing in the east, and along the horizon orange glowed just below the fog bank. The colors made the horizon appear striped where the sky and the sea met.

"Here with you I feel safe, Jackson, like I can hide from the world for just a little while. I know its not forever. I know I have to face my family, our friends, even my boss, but right now, sitting with you, I can feel safe. Is that so terrible to ask for just a little time before I have to see pity in their eyes? Knowledge? Before I have to really look at what happened to me, the how and why of it?"

He brushed the top of her head with a brief kiss. "No, of course not, Elle. I don't mind having you all to myself." But even as he said it, he knew it wasn't true.

He might have wished to have her all to himself before, but now he knew better. Elle Drake was part of something huge. Magical. Something called family—something he'd never had and hadn't thought he wanted.

Elle looked up at Jackson's face, carved and set, his mouth firm. "You have trust issues." She'd caught glimpses of his childhood, but his history was buried deep and he didn't like looking at it. Unlike her. She loved her memories of her sisters. She rubbed her hand over the German Shepherd's head, and then scratched his ears. "Do you think we can do it? Keep Libby from feeling, from really knowing what happened to me?"

"Yes. I think we're strong enough together, Elle, but she'll recognize whip cuts and she has to check you internally for damage." His hand covered hers, his fingers in the dog's fur alongside hers. "We need to know if you're pregnant."

Elle stiffened, refusing to look at him, staring out at the colors streaking the horizon over the ocean. The fog bank had darkened and was moving slowly toward them, casting purple stripes through the orange and dulling the colors. Fingers of white mist reached out over the choppy waves, throwing shadows over the beach below them.

"He might not know who I am, Jackson, but he's real and he's coming after me. I don't want him to find my sisters." She swallowed hard, fighting to keep her mouth from trembling. "I think his brother is even more violent—worse than he is—and Stavros didn't want him alone with me. I think they're both looking for someone psychic. If his brother finds out I'm gone, he could come looking as well. My sisters are all psychic and that would put all of them in danger."

"Staying away from them isn't going to save them, you know that. Everyone in the village knows there are seven of you. Anyone coming into town and asking questions is going to hear about your family. Joley is a superstar. Hannah was a supermodel. Just because she quit modeling doesn't mean there aren't a thousand articles about her. And Kate is a bestselling author. Your family is in the public eye."

"But no one knows about our psychic abilities."

"There has been more than one article written about Libby healing people. She was in the tabloids right along with Joley. If they come, Elle, they'll find your sisters and I think we need to be prepared for that."

"No one can prepare for him."

"I disagree. It's going to take him a while to find your identity, but he will. He'll track down Sheena MacKenzie and hopefully buy your cover story all the way, that in the end, Interpol suspects you of being a very high-class thief. He'll move on that and eventually figure out Sheena MacKenzie doesn't really exist. He has enough money to buy off several people who might know your real identity."

"Only Dane knows. I was on loan and he was the only person who knew me. There are no paper trails and no electronic ones. I never went to his office. No other agent saw me. That was the deal. Dane was the liaison between me and everyone else. We knew if Stavros was involved he had to have the local police and customs officials paid off. Dane worried he would have people in every branch of law enforcement and frankly, I believe he's right. We were careful. All Sheena's clothes, everything she owned was brand-new so nothing could be traced back to me."

"He'll find Dane. We need to warn him."

"As soon as Dane knows I'm alive he'll come here. Nothing will stop him."

Jackson felt his gut tighten. He turned his head slowly,

locking his gaze with hers. "He's in love with you. Damn it, Elle."

"He only thinks he is, it's not the same thing."

"You were taken. You've always been taken."

"You never made a move, Jackson." She jerked her hand away from him and stood, wincing as the wounds pulled and stretched with her action. "I went out with him a couple of times and then told him it wasn't going to work."

"That there was someone else," he prompted.

"There *wasn't* anyone else," she denied. "You didn't want me."

"I've always wanted you. I moved to Sea Haven for you. Don't give me a load of crap, Elle." He stood up, too, stepping close, crowding her. "You wanted me on your terms."

"You should have wanted me on any terms," she snapped. "If I mattered, then the circumstances shouldn't have."

"What the hell am I to you, Elle? A legacy. Someone your damned house chose for you. You wanted a yes man to go with your little fantasy about seven children and—"

"How would you know what I wanted?" she interrupted. "You never took the time to find out. You found out about my family and you just stepped aside. You didn't want me but you didn't want anyone else to have me."

"So you go off and put your life in danger? What the hell kind of crap is that? You're so fucking stubborn, Elle. You get your mind set on something and you don't want to change it for anyone—especially me."

"You wanted to take over my life."

"No, you thought I wanted to take over your life. I wanted you to see what you were getting into, not what your legacy dictated. I'm not the nice guy your daddy picked out for you. I'm not going to say yes when I don't think it's right for us—or for you. You didn't want that. It's not politically correct in this day and age with strong women, is it? I'm a throwback to the cave days and you wanted me to change for you."

"I just wanted you to want *me*. The real Elle Drake, with her crazy family and her seven children and the house from hell. I wanted you to love that Elle Drake. Was that really wrong for me to want you to want me as I am?"

"I do love Elle Drake, her family and her seven children and even the house from hell. But I'm going to be me, Elle, and you're going to have to accept who I am and the baggage that comes with me."

She threw her hands up into the air. "You think I don't know you? I know exactly how you think. You're so damned bossy and you think you know what's right for me."

"For us." His eyes glittered down at her as he corrected her. "I want you to argue with me, Elle. I don't mind heated discussions, but I'll be damned if you walk out on me every time you're pissed."

She gasped. "I didn't do that."

"The hell you didn't. I've had a lifetime of that and I won't take it from you. You stand and fight with me, baby. All or nothing. Do you understand me? You're not going to have one foot out the door because you don't like me telling you what to do. You'd better make up your mind that I'm your man and then you stick."

"I'm not the one with commitment issues," she snapped. "That would be you."

His eyebrow shot up. "Really? Because I believe every time I came near you, you ran like a rabbit."

"Maybe I needed you to help me face what I'm supposed to do, Jackson. Did you ever once think I might need you? You think you have a difficult time thinking about becoming part of my family and having seven daughters, but has it once, just once, occurred to you it might be difficult for me? I heard your voice and I knew your mind. I've walked there, wrapped myself in you and you still were far from me. You didn't want me there, inside of you."

"Damn it, Elle." He shoved his fingers through his thick, wavy hair. "You saw what they did to me. And there's my childhood, so different from yours. The torture." His hand crept to his face, traced a path down his chest as if feeling the trail of blood. "Did you think I wanted that for you? I was protecting you."

"I don't want your protection any more than you want mine. I need to be your partner, Jackson. I need to be able to see inside you the way you see me."

"I can't be anything but what I am, Elle. If you want a man who is going to treat you like a broken doll, you sure as hell came to the wrong place. And if you expect me to step aside and let you make decisions that are ultimately going to harm you, then, baby, you definitely have the wrong man because I protect my woman. Right or wrong, politically correct or not, I stand in front of her when there's need. You got that?"

Elle studied the lines in his face, the dark shadows moving in his eyes. A frisson of excitement went down her spine, and in the pit of her stomach, birds took flight. He might be a throwback to the old cave days, but he was a man who would stand strong when there was trouble— any kind of trouble. Whether it was fighting an enemy or parenting teenagers or trying to provide a living for a large family. Why had she seen his strength as a weakness? *She* had to be equally as strong, standing with him, up to him, carving out a place by his side, not leading the way.

"Elle? Fucking answer me."

"I got it. And watch your language, Jackson. You can clean it up if we're going to be having seven daughters. Can you imagine me having to explain to the school why they all talk that way?"

He shrugged. "Some of us weren't raised so genteelly."

"Well some of us can just learn and grow along the way. That's an excuse." There was a bite in her voice, but in her mind, a faint hint of laughter.

He opened his mouth and then closed it again with a small sigh. Retrieving the blanket, he sent the dog forward with a small hand gesture. "You're always going to have the last word, aren't you?"

She waited for him, moving beneath his shoulder, matching her shorter strides to his longer ones until he laughed and slowed down for her. "Yes, because you have a foul mouth and you're always going to leave yourself wide open when we argue."

"You could try not arguing with me, Elle."

She shot him a look from under long lashes. "Yeah. That's going to happen. Just like you learning to clean up your language."

"It's just a fucking word, Elle. What the hell difference does it make?"

"See? You can't help yourself," she said smugly. "I'm always going to win."

He sighed heavily. "I'll learn. Especially after our daughters are born."

"You'll learn before."

A seagull screamed overhead just as Bomber stepped

across and in front of Elle. Uttering a sharp, short bark, head pointed toward the front of the house, ears up as he alerted Jackson to an intruder.

Jackson's gun slid smoothly into his hand and he pushed Elle behind him.

"I want a gun," she hissed.

"You might shoot me if I say 'fuck,' and I'm bound to slip up. You've got a nasty little temper there, baby," he pointed out as he signaled her to slip into the shadows.

Feeling a little defenseless without a weapon and with her body in such a fragile condition, Elle went without protesting, although she took a firmer grip on him with her mind. She watched the dog as it bared its teeth and went into attack mode at Jackson's softly spoken command. Jackson gripped the collar and held him, but Bomber looked terrifying, all teeth and intent, barking, snarling, lunging at the end of his collar in a charge.

8

INEZ Nelson rounded the corner and came to an abrupt halt, holding a box of groceries in her arms. She went pale and stayed still, waiting for Jackson to give the release command. When Bomber settled she took a deep breath, only then seeing the gun Jackson returned to his shoulder holster.

Inez owned the local—and only—grocery store in Sea Haven. She'd been a part of the Drake sisters' lives as long as Elle could remember. She looked fragile with her graying hair and slender body, but she was already smiling at the dog.

"Good job, Bomber. You protect our girl. I brought some things I thought you two might need," she said in greeting, her sharp eyes inventorying Elle as she emerged from her hiding place in the bushes. "Hi, honey, I didn't think you'd be up so early. I was going to leave the box on the deck."

Elle felt her color rising in spite of her efforts to control it. She couldn't stop herself from looking down, to see if all the wounds were adequately covered. Jackson's sweater was long on her, but it was white and some of the bandages showed through. There were a couple of spots where blood had wept through, staining the material. She lifted her hand to touch the tangle of dull red hair, still matted from lack of care.

Jackson caught her wrist and tugged, pulling her beneath his shoulder, his body shielding hers just slightly, making it more difficult for Inez to get a good look at her.

"That's so sweet of you, Inez," Jackson spoke into the brief silence.

He could feel Elle's discomfort, her sudden irrational fear, and her distress at treating an old friend with such a lack of warmth. He rarely talked to anyone in the village for more than a couple of terse sentences. But, if Elle couldn't visit yet, then it was up to him to cover for her. He flashed a friendly smile and indicated Inez precede him up the stone path to the deck. He kept his arm firmly around Elle's waist, urging her to walk with him.

"When did you put etchings on your stones, Jackson?" Inez asked, looking down at the path. "I never noticed that in all the time I've brought you groceries."

Elle glanced quickly up at Jackson's face. *She brings you groceries?*

The moment she used telepathy, her brain seized, squeezing her skull like a vise. She gasped and clung to Jackson to keep from falling. He put his hand on the nape of her neck and pushed her head down so she could draw in deep breaths to keep from fainting.

Libby told you not to use telepathy. You have to let your brain heal, Elle. If you keep this up you'll destroy your talent completely. Fear made his voice edgy and gruffer than he intended.

Elle tried to jerk out from under his hand, glaring up at him. "I know that. Don't you think I know that? I forgot."

"Forgot what, dear?" Inez turned with a smile on her face, but gasped when she saw Elle's face. "You're bleeding, Elle."

"Am I?" Elle touched her mouth and nose. Her fingers came away smeared with blood. "It doesn't hurt, Inez. I'll just go in and wash up and be right back." Keeping her head down, she hurried into the house, sliding the screen closed behind her. Bomber just managed to slip through at Jackson's signal before the screen slammed shut.

"Should you go in with her?" Inez asked. "I can leave, Jackson."

Jackson's first reaction was to have her go. He'd always been uneasy around people, but Inez had known Elle from birth, she'd attended the baby shower for her. He could see concern in her eyes, and the lines in her face deepened as she put down the groceries and regarded him.

"Please stay. Have a cup of tea with us this morning." He sent her a small grin. "Or coffee. Don't tell Elle, but I have coffee in the kitchen."

Inez smiled back. "Coffee would be fantastic. I haven't had my quota for the morning yet." She glanced at her watch as she settled into a glider. "I have just enough time before I'm supposed to open the store."

"I'll just take these inside and bring you out a cup. Sugar and cream?"

She shook her head. "I like it black and strong. And maybe we shouldn't mention that to Elle either."

Jackson gave her a thumbs-up and hurried inside to check on Elle. She had already scrubbed her face and was desperately trying to tame her hair. Tears ran down her face. He caught her frantic hands and held them still. "Tell me."

"Look at me. I'm a mess."

"No, you're not, Elle. You're the most beautiful woman in the world. Pull your hair back and do that thing you do—you know, twisting it up and sticking a pencil in it. It really brings out the shape of your face."

He was thinking about her skin and mouth and her bone structure. Not even in a sexual way, she decided, her tears drying up instantly. Just in an abstract way and he truly did think she was beautiful. Just the way he thought made her feel as if she might be. She took a deep breath, unconsciously following his breathing pattern and did as he suggested, twisting the mass of hair into an ornate roll and sticking a pencil through to hold it in place.

"Inez is going to have a cup of—er—something with us this morning before work. You can catch up on all the happenings in Sea Haven."

Elle caught his sleeve. "Am I covered up?"

"All the way, baby." He leaned down and brushed a soft kiss across her trembling mouth. "A little too much if you ask me, but then I'm rather fond of looking at you."

Jackson went back into the kitchen and poured two cups of coffee from his automatic coffeemaker, which he loved. New technology was wonderful sometimes and to have coffee ready when he woke up was one of his joys in life.

"I know what you're doing," Elle called out from the other room.

The tea kettle began singing, although Jackson had not yet turned on the burner. "Damn it, Elle. You're not supposed to use psychic powers at all. Do you not comprehend what *at all* means? Because I can help you understand it."

"Don't threaten me, Jackson," Elle warned.

He heard the water running and knew she'd bled again around her nose and mouth. Her brain was far from healed. "It wasn't a threat, baby. It was more like a promise. Knock it off." He made a small pot of tea and put a tea towel over it to steep while he carried the coffee out to Inez. "Sorry it took so long."

Inez glanced toward the house with a small smile. "I think you've got your hands full with that one, Jackson. It's going to take a strong man."

He flashed another grin at Inez, actually feeling amusement, something rare for him. He sprawled his legs out in front of him, taking a long, careful look around. "I like her being a spitfire. She looks so deceptive you know, a little thing, young-looking, people never take her seriously, but she's got that brain, she's smart as hell, and when she gets going, it's a thing of beauty."

Inez laughed. "She's been that way since she was two." She turned her head and looked straight at him. "She'll get through this and be all the stronger for it. She doesn't think so now, but Elle's a fighter. And we'll help. You see anything at all we can do, you let us know."

He raised his coffee cup to her. "You're doing it, Inez. She needs to know she's surrounded by people who love her."

Inez looked away but not before he caught the sheen of tears. "The Drake girls have been a bright light in our village from the moment they were born. They've helped most of us in one way or another. This is a tight-knit community and we're close. I know you're worried about her." Her faded eyes turned shrewd. "You think she's still in danger, don't you?"

Jackson kept all expression from his face. Inez had no way of knowing where Elle had been or what had happened to her, and he wasn't about to clue her in. Elle would hate that.

"Oh, don't worry, you don't have to tell me," Inez said, as if reading his thoughts. "But if she's in danger, we'll all protect her. She's ours as much as yours."

"Thank you, Inez," Jackson said.

"When did you put in all these new plants?" Inez changed the subject, indicating his yard with her chin. "The last time I was here delivering groceries, none of those plants were there."

Jackson frowned as he regarded his yard. Dark green vines twisted up his fence. Several green shoots were nearly knee high and thick with buds all up and down the walkway, lining the stepping stones. He looked closer at the stones. Inez had commented on the symbols etched into the stone. They hadn't been there before. Neither had the plants. It wasn't spring, yet plants were shooting up all over and he saw more birds flitting through his backyard then he'd ever seen before.

He was staring thoughtfully out to sea when Elle stepped onto the deck. Two dolphins leapt into the air, somersaulted and returned to the water. He leaned forward and took another slow look around his yard. Birds flitted from branches, stripped of leaves for the winter, yet he could see the buds forming on the bare limbs. He drew in his breath as he stood to settle Elle in the most comfortable glider and tuck a blanket around her slender form.

"Do you often bring Jackson groceries, Inez?" Elle asked.

Inez nodded solemnly, ignoring the teasing note in Elle's voice. "Someone had to make certain he ate properly."

With deliberate intent, Elle studied the defined muscles

in Jackson's arms and chest. "You're right, he looks to me like he's been starving." She flashed the older woman a smile and blew on her tea.

Inez looked stern. "That was sarcasm, young lady."

Bomber pushed his head under Jackson's fingers for a scratch. Elle suppressed another smile. "I think you've spoiled him, Inez. Do you have any idea of the big bad reputation he has that's going to be gone when this gets out?"

Inez looked at Jackson fondly. "He just thinks he's big and bad. Did you know that he looks in on young Donny Ruttermyer nearly every single night and goes over his money with him to make certain he's paying his bills?"

Elle knew Donny had Down syndrome and when he turned twenty had begun doing odd jobs for several businesses, determined to make his own way. She could see faint color stealing up Jackson's neck and he carefully refrained from looking at her. "Does he now?"

Inez nodded. "Donny really looks up to him."

Jackson squirmed in his chair. "Actually Old Man Mars looks after Donny. He brings him produce and he was the one who persuaded Donna over there at the gift shop to rent the boy a room. And Mars goes over his bills with him, I just double-check things."

"You give him the money if he's short." Inez gave him away without a qualm.

"He's not short all that often," Jackson defended. "The kid makes his own way."

Elle exchanged a glance of amusement with Inez. "Yes, he does, Jackson." She took a deep breath. "So what's the latest rumor on me, Inez? I'd like to know what the village suspects happened to me."

Inez shrugged. "You're gone so often at first no one

had a clue anything was wrong, but then your sisters stopped talking weddings and began gathering in that house of yours. We could see Hannah on the captain's walk and knew something was wrong. The general consensus is that you were exploring somewhere and were lost."

Elle nodded, meeting the older woman's gaze and holding it for a moment. That "general consensus" had come from Inez, who possessed a knack for influencing the people around her in what she wanted them to believe about the Drake sisters. "I was traveling in South America and I fell while climbing a rather sheer rock face and was injured, but I'm recovering nicely."

Inez glanced at her watch and set down her coffee cup. "Donna will be wondering where I got to this morning. She's such a nosy woman, and she'll be calling Jonas, reporting I didn't show up for work this morning. She spends half her life looking out that gift shop window to see what I'm doing." There was affection in her voice as she groused about her best friend.

Jackson rose with her. "Thanks for the groceries, Inez. It's always a pleasure to see you." He stepped between the older woman and Elle, smoothly walking with her down the steps. "It meant a lot that you came."

Inez glanced back at Elle. "She looks very thin and tired, Jackson. You take care of her."

"You know I will."

"One more thing." Inez caught his sleeve, halting him, lowering her voice even more. "That horrible Reverend RJ person has been in town for a few days. He's renting a beach house and trying to get followers. He brought a few people with him, a woman and her daughter from San Francisco I think. He's been asking about the ribbons the village had up. He was told they were for one of the local boys overseas, but I had the feeling he was really here to cause mischief with the Drakes. Jonas and you were both gone, so I didn't say anything until now."

"You're certain he's still in town?" The Reverend RJ had caused trouble for both Hannah and Joley. Jackson couldn't imagine that he was in Sea Haven for any other reason than to stir up headlines for himself and the last thing they needed was publicity.

"I haven't seen or heard about him for a couple of days now, Jackson."

"How old is the woman's daughter?"

Inez frowned. "Young, fifteen maybe. It's hard to tell these days with kids. She dressed in the goth fashion, all black, lots of piercings, hair hanging in her face, but she looked cute. She didn't talk when they came into the store and she looked sad. I felt sorry for her. Do you want me to ask around about him?"

Jackson shook his head. "No, just keep your ears open. If he's around, someone will mention him to you. Don't act overly interested, but call Jonas, Ilya or me."

Inez nodded solemnly. "Don't you go worrying about me, Jackson, I've been around his kind a time or two." She waved to Elle and stalked off, her thin shoulders stiff.

Jackson watched her go with a small smile, shaking his head as he turned back to Elle. "She's a very nice woman."

Elle nodded. "She looks after half the village." She watched him come toward her, the easy fluid way he moved, whisper quiet, his eyes watchful, restless, shifting from sky to ground, even out to sea. He made her feel safe. "That's nice—what you do for Donny."

Jackson shrugged. "He's a great kid and I got the time.

He likes to talk about law enforcement. The boy doesn't have a mean bone in his body. I've got him keeping an eye on both Donna and Inez. I told him they were getting up a bit in age, although neither wanted to admit it, so he carries heavier boxes for them." He gave her a quick, embarrassed grin. "Then I told them I was trying to help Donny learn manners so if he asked to help them carry things, it would be doing him a favor to let him."

"Very clever, Deveau. I'm going to have to watch you. What was all that whispering she was doing? What's going on?"

"She just warned me that I'd better look after you. And she said RJ was in town a few days ago."

His voice was very casual, but Elle stiffened, tension rising in her enough to trigger the dog into going alert, his head up and ears cocked, listening for trouble. His eyes remained focused on her.

"It's no big deal, Elle. RJ coming into town isn't unusual. Joley and Hannah and even Kate generate news coverage. He wants it. We'll just keep a low profile."

She nodded, forcing air through her lungs. "I don't know why I'm so nervous. I'm just not ready for my name to be public in any way. I still have to contact Dane and file a report, and even that scares me. Being held prisoner in his house, I realize every passing day just how much power Stavros really has. It's not only his money—and believe me, he'd buy his way out of anything—it's his psychic ability. He subtly influences people. I didn't even recognize the flow of energy for what it was until we were on the island and he couldn't use it on me anymore."

"How does he influence them? What exactly are his psychic abilities?"

She rubbed at her temple. Her hand was trembling and

she twisted her fingers together in her lap. "I don't know, Jackson. He obviously knew I was psychic and I never suspected he was. I couldn't read him and just thought he had natural barriers. But I couldn't read his bodyguard either or any of the men in the room with us. I should have suspected, but I never felt energy at all around him."

"Could that be his only talent?"

"He was afraid of his brother and with that psychic barrier on the island, I'd guess that his brother can be more lethal, but I don't know." She rubbed her temple again.

Jackson stepped behind her and dropped his hands to her shoulders, massaging her, feeling her small bones. He couldn't understand how Stavros could have hurt her the way he had. Elle needed someone to love her, to understand her, to admire and respect her. Why try to break her down?

Her hand came up to cover his fingers. "He isn't you, Jackson, and he never will be. He doesn't want a strong woman. He doesn't want a partner. I don't know, maybe he's into the entire dominant and submissive thing and I didn't really understand it."

"I doubt it, baby. From what I've heard, a true dom loves and appreciates his woman. He wants her happy and satisfied. A submissive gives him or herself to her partner. No, he was breaking you, forcing dependency. Tell me what you know of his brother."

A seagull cried and another answered. He glanced up at the sky. The fog was beginning to thicken, coming in off the ocean, misty fingers trailing along the shore, moving toward them.

"His brother came into the room once and he really frightened me. There was evil in his eyes and in his aura.

Stavros is right to fear him. He likes hurting people, not just women, but anyone. And he looked at Stavros with the exact same look he gave me. Cold. Calculating. He told Stavros how to 'break' me to his will. When he talked, he made certain I heard every word. He showed me the whips and cane and described each instrument in detail and how it would hurt. He described the bruises or wounds each would make and how to teach me to serve him sexually. He said he enjoys breaking in the women for their clients."

Jackson tugged at her hand. "You're shivering. Let's go into the house."

Elle shook her head. "Not yet. I like being out in the open where I can see something coming at me."

He didn't like the look of the fog, dark and damp and much heavier than usual. He glanced at Bomber, noting the dog was alert, staring out toward the choppy water, his body between Elle, Jackson and the incoming fog. The Shepherd was standing, his ears up, his eyes focused, his hair up and tail down, poised and ready, stretched toward an unseen enemy.

Elle's fingers crept up to her throat. Jackson caught her hand. "Why did you do that?"

She swallowed. "I don't know. Just for a moment, my throat closed. I think talking about Stavros puts me in a state of panic. I'm sorry, Jackson. I don't mean to be such a baby."

"You're no baby, Elle." He leaned down and brushed his mouth over the top of her head. He was beginning to get a bad feeling and every single time in his life he'd had that same churning gut, something bad had happened. "Your home is safer than mine. I've got the room where I stash my weapons, and you'll be relatively safe there if we get you in it, but your house eats people. It actively protects you. And there're more people to look after you."

"I have to be with you right now, Jackson. I know no one else understands it, but I know I won't be safe without you."

He couldn't pull out of her mind and he didn't want to think too much about the why of Elle's belief that she was safer with him, not until he could be alone with his thoughts. Something wasn't right and Elle had more psychic gifts than most people. If she didn't believe she was safe without him in the Drake house, with Ilya and Jonas and Matt to protect her, then whatever threatened her had to be more than physical—and he had a really bad feeling about who was behind that threat.

"Jackson?" Elle's voice quivered.

"We'll be fine, baby. You want to stay with me, then you'll stay. I've got a couple of friends—the woman I told you about who trained Bomber, and her husband—who can give me a few tips on keeping you safe. She's sending me the two dogs I told you about as soon as they're ready. I've already made the arrangements. One in particular is for you."

Elle slid her palm over Bomber's head. "He's comforting."

Bomber gave a short bark. Jackson's hand slid smoothly inside his jacket. "Show me."

Bomber started toward the trail leading to the beach just below the house.

"It's my sisters," Elle said. "They're on the beach."

Jackson called the dog back to him and Bomber instantly responded, coming to heel, sitting at Jackson's side. Man and dog shielded Elle while Jackson peered through the thickening fog, trying to make out the figures taking shape on the sand.

The six women looked ethereal. He could just make them out in their long, flowing skirts, bare feet and loose hair. He could hear feminine voices rising on the wind and the crackling of a fire as they lit pieces of wood they drew into a fire pit. Arms raised toward the graying sky, they sang, feet dancing a pattern in the cool sand.

Elle came down the stairs of the deck to stand beneath his shoulder, her smaller body pressed against his. Jackson wrapped his arm around her, drawing her close to shelter her as they watched the flames, orange and red, glow bright through the heavy fog. She slipped her arm around his waist, her fingers curling into his shirt like a fist.

"You want to be with them." He made it a statement.

"Yes." She rubbed her face against his ribs. "They're determined to heal me one way or another. Please stay in my mind, Jackson, just in case."

He didn't like the way she was shivering, as if the piercing cold went straight to her bones. "I'm not leaving you, Elle." His voice went gentle, shocking him. He wasn't a gentle man. Demons rode him hard and he often was abrupt to the point of being rude, yet Elle brought out the best in him—the best he didn't even know he had. He felt at once protective and soft inside where she was concerned. "Your sisters aren't trying to get inside of you, honey, they're just trying to give you strength."

"I know." She kept her head low. "Once I know we can shield from Libby, I'll ask her to help me heal faster. I don't want her in my brain though, not even to help with the psychic healing."

"Isn't that more Kate's thing?"

Elle did look at him then, shocked that he knew. Libby's ability to heal was famous in the small town, but few knew of Kate's ability. "How?"

"Last Christmas, when the town was attacked by the entity in the fog, Kate brought peace to everyone. Matt and Jonas brought her to my house, thinking I needed peace like the others, but I was going through a rough time and I was worried for Jonas, that I might do something crazy. So I tried to burn out my talent." His voice was low as he admitted it to her.

She raised her head, gasping. Her fingers tightened in his shirt. "Jackson. Where was I? How come I didn't know?"

"You were off somewhere, South America maybe. Who knows. And Kate and the town were in trouble so your attention was centered there."

Elle let out her breath. She hated that. Hated that she hadn't known he was in such trouble that he might think about psychic suicide. "You couldn't stand to touch anyone."

"I don't just get emotion that way. I'm different, Elle, and I don't know how to explain it. With you I have telepathy, we're on the same wavelength, but with everyone else, I know things some of the time and mostly it's things I don't want to know. It can be very disturbing, especially if I've had a bad day at work." He looked down at her, his gaze locking with hers. "But then you know that. You've had the same overload many, many times in your life. You try never to touch others, but it doesn't always help, not even with your family."

She pressed her forehead against his chest. "No," she admitted. "It's overwhelming to feel so many emotions bombarding me day and night. How did Kate help you?"

"She talked to me, which I'll admit was soothing, but then, right before she left she shook my hand and wished me peace. But she took some of the shadows I live with, the darkness, with her, and I realized afterward, my brain was on overload and she eased . . ." He stopped and caught Elle's chin, pulling her head up to look into her eyes. "You think she can heal you psychically."

"There's a chance."

Jackson let out his breath in a rush of excitement. Stavros might be powerful, but he wouldn't be a match for the Drake sisters. Not with Elle truly healed. He'd been worried for their future, for their children's future.

"I don't know if I want her to try." The admission came in a small voice. "If she takes on the burden, or the illness in the same way Libby does, what would it do to Kate?"

They both looked out at the six women dancing around the bonfire. The wind came in off the ocean and blew the fog from the shoreline, corralling it and shepherding it back out to sea. Soft melodic voices lifted, the notes pure and beautiful, bringing a sense of peace to both Elle and Jackson. Bomber reacted as well, his ears cocked forward, his eyes bright and focused, following every movement of the dancers.

The bare feet stomped each step into the sand, creating a pulsing rhythm they could feel building in their blood. Hannah, recognized easily by her height and the platinum curls, raised her arms toward the sea while the others continued moving in a circle. Jackson felt the wind shift, a subtle difference. He felt the ocean, tasted salt, the fine mist of the sea itself on his face. Elle lifted her arms, moving away from his body to stand directly in the stream of air coming in from the beach.

It took Jackson a moment to realize what was in that mist. Hastily he pulled the sweater Elle was wearing over her head, and, ignoring her protest, dropped it into the sand.

"Take off the sweatpants," Jackson ordered, already

moving behind her to grasp the waistband, pulling them down over her hips.

"I don't have anything on," she protested.

"Who gives a damn?" he snapped, his voice rough. "It's not like I haven't seen you and they're staying a distance away. I'll send Bomber to the front and he'll warn us if anyone is coming. Get them off."

He signaled the dog and yanked at the sweatpants simultaneously, not really giving Elle a choice. If her sisters were willing to try to heal her physical body from a distance, he was going to take them up on whatever they could do. It was painful to see her body so bruised and cut and welted. And she was ashamed, as if she could have somehow stopped Stavros from torturing her.

Elle drew in her breath sharply, but allowed Jackson to hold her arms out from her sides, and slowly turn her around so the steady stream of mist could coat her entire body, front, back and sides. She felt the burn of the salt in her wounds, but then a soothing heat followed, and deep inside, where no one but Jackson could see, she wept at the sheer joy of being joined, even just through the wind, with her sisters again.

Jackson could feel love and warmth pouring in along with the healing mist, but he was looking out beyond the sisters, out over the foaming sea. He expected dolphins and even perhaps a breaching whale, but instead, there was a thick gray fog bank hanging back from the shore, but threatening nevertheless. He swore something moved in the fog, stretching icy fingers toward the beach, but Hannah's wind kept the invasive tendrils at bay as her sisters danced.

Just what was Stavros's psychic talent? Could he project himself across the sea and hover offshore? Had he established a connection with Elle the way Jackson had? The thought upset him on more than one level. He didn't want any other man to have a psychic connection with Elle.

The fire crackled and snapped, glowing bright orange and sending flames skyward. The feminine voices slowly drifted away and the dancers fell exhausted into the sand. Hannah was last, holding the healing mist as long as possible before she, too, collapsed on the beach. Behind her, the sea was rough and choppy, stirred up from the high winds fighting to get past her to reach shore.

Jackson flung the blanket around Elle. "Go into the house, baby, and get dressed," he said. "I'll start the tea water and get your sisters."

"I can make the tea," she offered. "I'm tired, but I feel better already." She shivered a little as the fog crept closer to the beach. "I don't like them lying helpless in the sand with the fog coming in, especially Hannah. She's too close to the edge of the water."

"I'll get her." He didn't like the way the fog bank was so dark, or the way fingers stretched, elongated, looking eerily as if a hand reached toward them. "Go in the house, Elle. Get dressed and stay warm. Bomber is a trained protection dog and will protect you rather than property. I asked Lisset to train him with Russian commands because the family all speaks Russian and I figured it would be easier for any of us to direct him when necessary." He gave her a list of commands and made her repeat them back to him. "Dress warm, baby. It's cold out today and the fog is moving in fast." He signaled the dog. "Go with her, search."

Bomber's ears cocked forward, his eyes focused on the bank of heavy gray fog moving toward the shore. He whined, communicating his anxiety but he obediently preceded Elle up the steps to the house and disappeared inside.

"Wait for him, Elle. Let him clear the house. He'll signal when it's safe for you to go in. Always wait. You have to start taking precautions."

"I'm not used to this." She shivered inside the blanket.

"I know, but it will become second nature. It's better for us to learn how to take care of ourselves and our children. We both have something dangerous hanging over our heads that could affect our lives." He kept his voice matter-of-fact, as if it was nothing to live under a death threat. The one thing Elle's kidnapping had taught him was he had to grab ahold of life with both hands, and not watch it pass him by because he was afraid for Elle or for his children. Bad things happened all the time, but he was missing the good things while waiting and he was determined for Elle to see they had a future no matter what.

Bomber poked his head out the open door and gave a short bark. "Praise him and go in with him."

"I'll put the kettle on and get dressed," Elle said, grateful to be of some help.

Jackson waited until Elle and the German Shepherd were safely inside before he started down the worn path. The small stretch of dunes separating his property from the beach rolled gently, little plants pushing through the sand, dotting the landscape with bits of vibrant green.

Once on the beach, he crouched beside Sarah. "You okay?"

"Just a little drained. Did it work?" Sarah glanced toward the sea, a small frown on her face. "I don't like the look of that." Her voice was thin and she didn't move, not even turning her head, but shifting her gaze to look at the brooding fog.

"I think you really helped her, Sarah. If nothing else, she felt better surrounded by you all. She's making tea. I'll help you into the house, but don't let any of your sisters try to get inside her head. She doesn't want that."

"We figured that out," Sarah said.

Jackson's stomach was beginning to tighten into hard knots and a frisson of awareness crept down his spine. He turned from Sarah to watch the sea. The waves receded, pulling back into the thick bank of fog gathering out at sea in an eerie calm. A dark channel of water ran from the shore to the sea, the deeper color pushing into the ocean water, staining the blue a muddy green right through the middle. Out at sea, a wave gathered force and began a rush toward the beach.

Jackson leapt to his feet, shouting a warning to Hannah as he ran, pounding through the sand toward where she lay, one arm and leg outstretched in the damp sand. Hannah was pregnant, Jackson knew, although only a small rounded bump on her thin frame gave evidence of the fact. Her eyes were closed and her body limp, drained from using psychic energy to direct the healing mist to her youngest sister. The waterline closest to Hannah was much shallower than it should have been, creating the illusion of utter calm. He was nearly to her as the water hit and the long thick arms of the tubular kelp reached up out of the fast approaching wave and wound itself around Hannah's wrist and ankle.

With the wind driving the wave onto shore with such force, the backwash, with nowhere else to go, was pushed to the side—surrounding Hannah completely as the water sought to return to the sea. The hidden current, much stronger on the surface than underneath, gathered in strength, and beneath the murky water, the returning kelp jerked hard and Hannah's slim form slid toward the open sea. Water foamed around her body, splashed over her face, and her eyes snapped open in panic. She began to struggle, but her movements were feeble and no match for the power of the retreating rip current as it dragged her out to open water.

Jackson dove after Hannah, catching her arm, holding on as the wave sucked both of them under, rolling them violently as it rushed them into deeper waters. He hung on grimly, refusing to give her up to the sea.

Don't fight it. Stay calm, Hannah. He had never used telepathy with anyone but Elle, but Elle was with him, directing the communication in his mind. He could feel her, the fear, the knowledge they were in terrible trouble.

Rip currents, hidden beneath the surface of the water, caused more deaths than any other natural disaster except floods and extreme heat.

Let it take us out to sea. Swim parallel to shore. The current isn't that wide.

He kept his fingers locked like a vise around Hannah's arm. Already the cold was invading his body and his jeans were heavy, trying to drag him down. He couldn't imagine what it would be like for Hannah as thin as she was. The ocean was cold and hyperthermia would set in fast.

She's already exhausted, drained of all energy by the healing she performed, and trying to move her arms and legs is impossible. Elle's voice cut in, very calm.

Tell her to turn over and float for me. Jackson was fighting the strong current that kept trying to rip Hannah away from him. He swore the water around them was alive, ripping and tearing at them both. He knew fighting was useless, they had to let the current carry them as far out as it went.

The kelp has her trapped. You have to free her, Jackson.

For a moment, in the dark sea, with the icy cold and strong current pulling at him, it didn't feel possible, but still retaining possession of her arm, he stopped swimming, abandoned trying to pull Hannah along in the grip of the riptide, and jerked the knife from his belt. At once he felt the rush of powerful water pulling them farther out to sea, but he closed his mind to everything but freeing Hannah from the kelp.

Somehow the thick tubes of kelp had wrapped Hannah's arm and leg repeatedly as they tumbled over and over in the churning water, sand abrading exposed skin as they were swept through the sandbars out to sea. He slashed through the rubbery fronds along her arm until she waved her arm freely. He kicked strongly, holding her clothes as he fought his way to her leg and the kelp she was entangled in. It had been uprooted and was a deterrent to swimming, so he slashed through that as well and caught her hand, tugging to get her going in the right direction.

Jackson was nearly out of air and knew Hannah had to be terrified. *Tell her we'll be fine, to swim parallel to the shore.* He kicked out strongly, taking Hannah with him, praying she wouldn't fight. They broke the surface and both gasped for air. *Tell her not to look at the beach, to just keep swimming.*

9

ELLE put on the teakettle, resisting the urge to use her abilities to instantly heat the tea. She hadn't realized how often she actually used psychic talent in everyday life. Hastily throwing on a clean pair of sweats and finding a comfortable sweatshirt in Jackson's bureau, she started into the kitchen when Bomber gave a short, alarmed bark. She turned toward him when the first wave of panic hit her. Something was terribly wrong, and Jackson had inadvertently pulled out of her mind. And when she reached for him . . .

Her throat closed and she gasped and fought for breath. Fingers closed tightly around her throat and pressed deep, choking her. Her eyes rolled back in her head and she found herself on the floor, dizzy and weak, gasping, tears burning in her eyes as she tried desperately to pull nonexistent fingers from her throat. Was she losing her mind? She tried to reach for Jackson. Dimly she could hear Bomber barking.

I'll kill everyone you care about if you don't come

back to me. Do you hear me? I'll keep killing until you come back to me. The voice whispered in her head, a soft menace that filled her mind and amplified her fear to the point of terror. She felt herself slipping, letting go and then Bomber's wet tongue slapped her face repeatedly. When she opened her eyes, Jackson was there, flooding her mind with need, with a strange calm, with a demand that she aid him.

Hannah. She whispered her sister's name, reached out and found Hannah shivering uncontrollably, afraid for her unborn child, for Jonas, for all her sisters. She could hear Hannah's silent scream as she joined with her and immediately felt the impact of the cold water. For a moment they were together, swept out to sea, trying to peer through the heavy veil of fog and unable to make out the shore. *Kick. Swim,* Elle urged, and Hannah tried to help Jackson by using her long legs, but she was so weak.

Elle felt Jackson there, strong, fierce, and it steadied her. She took a deep breath, sat up, using the dog to help her stagger to her feet. Patting him, she sent Hannah warmth and strength and reassured her that help was on the way. She touched Jonas's mind, and knew it was true, he was coming at breakneck speed, Ilya following close behind. Because they were locked so tightly together, there was no way to hide from Jackson the way her brain misfired, the tiny electrical shocks that jolted her. She could feel the blood trickling from her mouth and nose and she accepted the fact that she wasn't simply risking her life to aid them, she was risking becoming a vegetable. Her brain desperately needed healing, and she was only adding to the stress it was under, deepening the lesions, ripping open the wounds in order to save Jackson and Hannah.

Damn it, Elle, pull back, we'll make it.

I can't do that. You know I can't, not when both of you are in danger. Don't fight me, Jackson. Because she couldn't survive without him. She didn't say it to him, not even telepathically, but she knew he felt it, because he immediately stopped all resistance and let her flow easily into his mind.

I'm trying to get her to stay calm. She can't panic. Have her swim parallel to the shore.

She can't. She's already exhausted, drained of all energy by the healing she performed, and trying to move her arms and legs is impossible. Elle made certain to keep her voice very calm, not wanting him to feel the pain lashing through her head. She moved outside and headed swiftly to the beach.

Tell her to turn over and float for me.

Elle pushed the command into Hannah's sluggish mind. Hannah tried, but something was wrapped tightly around her leg and arm, refusing to let her go. For a moment the image of a monster octopus was in Hannah's head.

It's the kelp, Elle told him. Now she was on her knees in the sand, holding her head. *The kelp has her trapped. You'll have to free her, Jackson.* She tasted blood in her mouth and her eyes stung as her vision blurred. She wiped at them and her fingers came away stained with blood.

She waited for what seemed like forever, feeling Jackson's mind, the icy invasion, slowly creeping into his brain, slowing his thoughts and reflexes. She couldn't keep both of them going, so she had to help Hannah, so much weaker than Jackson, although everything in her reached for him. It felt dark and cold and lonely where he was and she could feel his lungs burning. At last he seemed to reach for air.

Tell her we'll be fine, to swim parallel to the shore. Tell her not to look at the beach, to just keep swimming.

With a sinking heart, Elle realized Hannah couldn't possibly swim. She had already slipped from the first stage of shaking uncontrollably to a much deeper sleep state. Her mind had slowed way down and the continual shivering had nearly ceased, a bad sign as the shivering was the body's way of trying to keep her temperature up.

She can't swim, Jackson, she's too far gone. There was despair in her voice. *I'm coming for you in the dory.*

No! You're not strong enough, Elle. You couldn't get either of us in the boat. Jonas will come. You know he'll come.

Even in her mind, Jackson's words slurred, but he was still holding Hannah to him. She did the only thing she could think to do, send him and Hannah as much warmth as possible.

Bomber went into a frenzy of barking as first Jonas's sheriff car and then Ilya's truck, nearly bumper to bumper, slid around the corner of the yard. The dog nearly went insane, snarling and barking as the two men bailed out, running past Elle for the shore. It took Elle a couple of minutes to remember to give him the dismiss command, stopping the dog from barking and adding to the chaos of the moment. Ilya stopped to lean over Joley, who waved a feeble hand toward the fog bank. Jonas actually leapt over Sarah's body sprawled in the sand as he made for the small double-ended Oregon dory Jackson kept aground on the higher dune.

The dory was hitched to an old four-wheel-drive truck Jackson kept only for the purpose of launching the boat into the surf. He yanked open the door and started the truck immediately, not waiting for Ilya as he drove backward into the waves. He was grateful that Jackson always had his equipment in top running order. Leaping from the truck he released the boat and Ilya jumped into the driver's seat to pull away from the boat.

"Hurry, Jonas, I can't keep them safe much longer," Elle called. Blood streamed down her face like tears. It matted in the hair near her ears and she could taste it in her mouth.

"Hold them, Elle," Jonas commanded. "Don't you let Hannah die."

The surf caught at the dory as Jonas primed the pump with three pulls before he ripped at the cord to start the engine. Cursing when it didn't start the first time, it caught the second, roaring to life just as Ilya flung himself into the boat. Jonas turned the throttle and the dory reacted fast, cleaving through the surf out toward the sea where he knew Hannah was barely holding on. He could feel her in his mind, her thoughts sluggish, her body freezing.

Although pregnant, Hannah was thin and not far along. She couldn't last long in the cold water without much body fat. It was only Elle, sending her warmth, trying to keep Hannah's body temperature up that was giving them the few extra minutes needed.

Jackson, Ilya and Jonas are coming for you. Hannah, just float. I know you're cold, but Jonas is coming in the boat. Hang on a little longer. Elle's brain felt as if it were shredding from the inside out. She could barely breathe through the pain. She went down to one knee and ducked her head low to try to gulp air when she was dizzy and near fainting.

Bomber lunged at something and she caught sight of her sister Sarah, crawling toward her up the path. She hissed the command to disengage, remembered she needed to speak the command in Russian and repeated it, still breathing deep, fighting waves of dizziness.

Jonas opened the dory full throttle and took them out to sea, straight into the unnatural fog bank. *Elle. Give me a direction. Hannah's too far gone and I can't reach her.*

Jonas felt the sudden impact as the rest of the sisters joined what strength they had left to feed Elle so she could reach Jackson. It was a shaky bridge at best. He felt Jackson's direction more than getting an actual signal from him. But it didn't matter, he took the dory over the surf, slicing through the waves and the heavy fog in a straight line to them. Jonas prayed that Jackson had Hannah, as he couldn't feel her in his mind at all.

Slowing the boat when he knew he was getting close, he chugged along, trying not to panic, his gaze frantically searching the sea. A hand came up out of the water to the right of their position and his heart nearly exploded in his chest. Through the choppy water and the heavy veil of fog, he could just make out Hannah's body stretched out on top of the water with Jackson's arm hooked around her neck, holding her to him. Jackson shivered uncontrollably, but he kicked strongly to keep them from going under.

Ilya knelt up in the boat as Jonas pulled alongside them. Jackson tried to help Ilya pull Hannah into the dory, but his movements were slow and clumsy.

"I'll get her," Ilya said, his voice tight with apprehension.

Hannah was ice cold as Ilya hauled her into the boat. He took the time to throw his jacket over her and then reached back to get Jackson. The man weighed a lot more than Hannah, and his body was almost dead weight. Jackson set his jaw and looked up at Ilya, nodding to indicate he was ready and as Ilya heaved him out of the water,

Jackson surged upward to give himself the momentum to get into the boat.

Jackson sprawled on the bottom of the boat, shivering, teeth chattering, his brain refusing to work. Jonas switched places with Ilya, stripping off his shirt, covering Hannah's body with his own, rubbing her arms and talking to her in a voice raw with love.

"Hold on, Jackson," Ilya said. "We'll get you warm."

Jackson couldn't answer, but he held on to Elle, afraid to pull out of her mind, afraid of letting go of her in much the same way he was certain Jonas was afraid to let go of Hannah. In spite of the icy cold, and the way his brain cells refused to function properly, he could still feel her pain, like a thousand needles piercing his skull.

Elle, baby. Hold on for me. Just hold on for me. He was more afraid for her than he was for himself. He was still shaking, shivering, his teeth chattering, which meant he was still functioning, but Elle was fading away from him, as if she might be passing out.

Ilya ran the dory right onto the beach and leapt out, reaching to help Jonas with Hannah. They ran her up to the house, where Jonas stripped her clothes off and covered her with blankets. He tore through Jackson's kitchen to find plastic bottles, filling two from the hot kettle and wrapping them in towels to put under Hannah's arms and a third on her stomach. Jonas covered her head with another blanket and cranked up the heat.

"I'm making you tea, honey, stay there for me," he encouraged.

Hannah shivered uncontrollably, a good sign that her body was reversing the process of hypothermia, a very dangerous condition, but Jonas was taking no chances, and he caught up the phone and demanded an ambulance.

Hannah wasn't going to be happy with him, but it didn't matter; she was going to the hospital.

Ilya stumbled in, bent double with Jackson leaning on him, barely able to walk. "I'll strip him," he told Jonas. "You get Elle, she's covered in blood," Ilya continued, "and then help me bring the others inside. That fog bank is moving this way and it feels wrong to me. The dog is becoming more and more agitated as it looks out toward the sea. Bomber isn't like that, he doesn't spook easily."

Jonas swore, took one last look at Hannah, obviously reluctant to leave her, and then he ran back outside to get Elle. Bomber went into attack mode when he approached.

"Call him off, Elle," he snapped impatiently. She was on her knees, her head down, the tangle of red hair covering her face from where it had slipped from the loose knot. He saw her hand move, sliding into the dog's fur and she whispered to him, settling the dog in place so he gazed at Jonas happily. "Yeah, that's right, boy, you recognize me. I'm your friend. The one who lets you tear into me on occasion for great fun."

He stepped past the dog and lifted Elle's slight weight into his arms. Immediately he smelled blood. "Let me look at you."

Elle roused herself enough to respond. "Just get my sisters off the beach before the fog is all the way in." Something was in the fog, searching, seeking, and she knew that something was Stavros. It sounded insane. They'd think she was crazy if she told them, but she knew it in her heart. This was Stavros. Maybe she was creating a larger than life villain out of her fear of him and his absolute power, but she believed he could use the fog to look for her. After what had just happened to Hannah, she wasn't going to take any chances with her family.

"Elle, look at me," Jonas insisted.

"Trust me, Jonas, you don't want to look." Her voice croaked hoarsely.

Every step Jonas took into the house jarred her. Jonas set her down beside Jackson and the sight of Jackson shivering uncontrollably beneath blankets, his face pale and his hair wet, smelling of the sea, set her heart pounding with fear. *He could have killed you.*

Jackson's head came up alertly, his hand reaching unsteadily for her, brushing aside the mass of hair. He gasped when he saw her blood-streaked face. At once, his eyes glittered like two polished black diamonds. *Stop using telepathy. You're burning yourself out and I'm damn well not allowing it. Stop it, Elle, or I pull out of your mind and disconnect right now.*

She gasped with the cruelty of his response. She had *saved* them, using everything she was and she hadn't been trying to burn herself out—not on purpose. Not to prevent Stavros from wanting her. She wouldn't do that. Jackson was thinking that way, a kind of psychic suicide, but she had been trying to help them—hadn't she? Elle covered her face with her hands, unable to look at him or Jonas and Ilya as they brought in Sarah and Joley and laid them in chairs.

In the distance Elle heard the scream of a siren and knew the ambulance was on the way. Hannah wouldn't like it any more than Elle would have, but she was pregnant and no one, least of all Jonas, would ever take a chance with either of their lives. She made an effort to push herself to her feet, but was physically drained after the use of psychic energy, her arms and legs like lead. She forced herself to crawl across the floor out of the kitchen, not wanting anyone to see her so bloody and ravaged. The paramedics would insist on checking her out and she couldn't bear that.

Jackson caught her ankle and held her. His fingers were icy cold and he was shaking nearly uncontrollably. She halted, not because he was stronger—his hands were gentle—but because he didn't want her out of his sight. One big advantage of having him wrapped so tightly in her mind was that she could feel his emotions as if they were her own.

"Stay with me, baby. Get under the blanket and get me warm."

He was so cold. Icy cold. Deep inside where his soul should be, he was icy. She rolled beneath the blanket and over the top of his body, aware of Jonas and Ilya bringing in Abbey and Libby. Jackson's arms went around her and held her tight against his naked form. "I didn't mean it, Elle. I'm sorry I said it."

"I need you," she whispered against his ear, ashamed, aware of the ice cold of the wide expanse of skin covering hard muscle. "I've never needed anyone. I should choose you because I want to be with you, not because of a legacy, or because I was raped and beaten. I shouldn't need you so desperately."

His arms tightened around her so hard he nearly drove the air from her lungs. "Do you think I don't know need? I need you, Elle, just to survive intact. You've known that from the beginning and it's part of what made you run. You knew I'd hold you too tight and the thought of a short leash was something you couldn't live with. I know need. Just let it be. Whatever it is between us, for now, let it be."

The uncontrollable shaking was lessening and he was beginning to be more aware of his surroundings, of

Bomber alerting to strangers outside in the yard, of Ilya depositing Sarah on the couch and covering her with a blanket.

"Ilya," he called. "Get us into the other room before the circus starts."

Ilya hesitated, glanced toward the paramedics rushing up the path and leaned down to help Elle and Jackson to their feet. He simply lifted Elle off her feet and half carried Jackson with his other arm, taking them to the bedroom.

"You should let them examine you," Ilya cautioned Jackson. "Both of you. Elle's covered in blood."

"You know it's a psychic bleed," Elle said. "What could they do other than give me a brain scan and tell us what we already know?"

Ilya swore and put her on the bed, steadying Jackson with one arm. "You certain you're all right?"

"Get us some tea," Jackson said, and collapsed next to Elle.

Ilya covered him with blankets. "Your body heat will warm him faster than anything, Elle," he said. "I'll bring in hot water bottles as soon as possible as well as tea. Give me a minute."

"Shut the door," Jackson called after him, signaling his dog to the bed. Bomber climbed up and lay against his side while Elle lay on top of him.

"Thank you for saving Hannah."

"There's never been a rip current there, Elle. Never."

"I know." She nuzzled his throat. He smelled of the sea, a comforting scent in spite of the near tragic incident. "It was *him*. Stavros."

His hand slid over her back to the nape of her neck, his fingers doing a slow massage as he turned her conclusions over in his mind. She was grateful he didn't just dismiss them as paranoid hysteria. She kept rubbing his arms and chest trying to warm him. Between her, the dog and the blankets, he was coming back fast. His mind had gone from sluggish to sharp almost before his body responded. She found she could breathe easier, some of the tension leaving her.

"You think he attacked Hannah? How would he have found you so fast? It's possible, even probable, that he will find you, but not this fast. How could he?"

"Bribe someone maybe?"

"One of our team? I doubt it. It could happen, but it's doubtful."

There was speculation in his voice and she could feel his mind working quickly, processing and discarding names of the men who'd aided them. All good friends. All men he'd gone into combat with. Men he had risked his life for many times. "Maybe," he repeated, but this time she felt the doubt in his mind.

Elle didn't say anything, but her body shuddered, just once. She doubted if he could feel it with all the shivering his body was doing, but his fingers continued that soothing, rhythmic massage.

"Maybe it was something else altogether, Elle. Maybe we're giving him too much credit."

"Maybe." She knew better, but whatever. She wasn't going to argue with him. She'd felt Stavros's fingers on her throat again, heard his voice, that soft monotone that never changed, not when he was hitting her with his fist, or carving up her body with a whip, beating her with a cane, and not when he was being gentle, his hands and mouth roaming over her as if he owned her. A sob escaped before she could suppress it.

"Kiss me."

"I can't."

"Look at me, Elle." He waited until her gaze met his. There was shame. Pain. Humiliation. Panic. Most of all a deep sorrow for everything she'd lost.

"Kiss *me*. Feel *me*. He's not here with us. I won't let him be. He's a monster that took you and you had no choice but to give in to him . . ."

"No! I should have fought more. I should have done something. I'm trained, damn it. I've been trained in martial arts, in weapons. I have a hell of a psychic talent. It shouldn't have happened to me. How could I let him do those things to me?"

"You tell me, baby. You tell me how, with all my training, with my psychic talent, with my strength and my ability with weapons, I fell into enemy hands and allowed them to do those things to me. Explain it then, because I don't understand."

"You're such a bastard, Jackson. Why do you have to talk like that?" She tried to lay her head on his chest, wanting to hide.

"You're fucking going to kiss me first, Elle. He's not standing between us. You understand me? I won't have him standing between us. You fought a good fight. You survived. That's what you were supposed to do. You survived."

Her teeth sank into his shoulder and her tears burned against his skin. "I shouldn't have," she whispered. "I should have had the courage to end it and maybe him."

His fingers tightened on her neck and he pulled her head back so he could stare into her tear-drenched eyes. "Don't you ever fucking think that, let alone say it. Would you want me to have died? Or Hannah? Or Abbey?"

She shook her head. "But this is my fault—what happened today. I heard him. I heard his voice. He said he'd kill everyone I love if I don't come back to him."

"You listen to me, Elle. He's the one who needs to be afraid, not you. You're not locked in by his psychic energy field. He doesn't have you trapped. You're strong and you're lethal. Your sisters are as well. Don't you dare sell any of them short. Hell, baby, your house makes people disappear. And we're not going to talk about me, but if that son of a bitch thinks he can take you from me, let him come and try. You're down, but you're not out. Do you understand me? Do you, Elle? Look at me. Don't turn away from me and pay lip service to what I'm saying. I'll kill the bastard for you right now. Say the word and I leave and go to work. It's what I'm best at anyway. There's nowhere he'll be safe and if you think I don't want to, you're very wrong. I dream about it, I think about it, day and night and none of what I do to him is pleasant or civilized. If you want to be scared of someone, you're scared of the wrong fucking man."

She stared down into his black, glittering eyes knowing every word he said he believed. She leaned forward and brushed her mouth across his. "Stop saying 'fuck.'"

Jackson had been furious at the thought of Stavros possibly reaching across the ocean and frightening Elle. Could he do that? Could the son of a bitch really come at her psychically? He and Elle had first touched mind to mind across an ocean. He wanted to wrap her in bubble wrap, put her somewhere no one could find her, hire an army to guard her, get ten dogs. He wanted the bastard dead. And then she'd kissed him. Not a real kiss, just a brush of her lips against his. And scolded him in that prissy little lecture tone of hers he loved.

"It's just a word, Elle." It was deliberate provocation, but he couldn't help it.

"It's not a nice word, Jackson and you don't need to say it."

"You think I don't know you were born into a high class, elegant family and I came from the biker camp from hell?"

"It doesn't matter where anyone comes from, Jackson. Once you're grown up, you still have a choice about who you want to be and how you want to live."

Now she really sounded prissy and he couldn't stop the small grin that welled up from inside him.

His hand curled around the back of her head. "I love you, Elle Drake. In case I haven't told you lately."

Elle blinked. She looked startled, like a panicked deer caught in the headlights of a hunter's truck. "You've never said that before."

"I'm sure I have."

"I'm sure you haven't. Believe me, I would have remembered."

"You probably weren't listening. I especially love your nasty little temper. In case you haven't noticed, I'm a lot warmer and I'm completely naked under here. Things are beginning to perk up and I wouldn't want you to get all scared on me." His hand slid down her back in a slow glide that didn't ask for anything at all, simply took her in.

"I'm not afraid of you, Jackson," she whispered. "I'm not going to let him do that to me. I won't." But maybe she was. A little. A lot. What if she couldn't do with him the things that she'd done with Stavros?

He spat out an ugly curse. "You're not going to do anything with me you did with him, Elle. When we come together, we'll be making love, not fucking. Hell, what he did wasn't even fucking. What he did to you was rape. Control. Power. That is never going to happen between us, honey. When I look at you, when I want to touch you, it's because I love you and I want to show you that."

She pressed her forehead against his, closing her eyes. "What if I can't do the same back, no matter how much I want to? What if he keeps coming between us? I've heard that happens, Jackson. Before I went on the assignment, of course we thought if I was captured they'd kill me, but in my research on human trafficking I read about long-term effects on women who are subjected to physical and emotional abuse over long periods of time. The trauma affects them their entire life, even with counseling."

Jackson noticed she'd said "them," not "us" or "we." She still could not identify herself as a victim. "Of course it would, Elle. Do you think I'm not affected every damn day of my life? I wake up in a sweat, my heart pounding and adrenaline rushing. I have a gun in my fist tracking the room before I'm fully awake. I have a room full of weapons and I practice shooting nearly every day. I work out with weights and run to stay in shape, not because I want to look good, but because I want to be prepared. I worry that I'll be a paranoid husband and father and drive you insane. And don't tell me you haven't worried about it either, because we both know you have."

"But you can make love, Jackson. I can see it in your eyes, feel desire in your mind and hunger in your body. What if I can't satisfy that?"

He rolled over, gently putting her aside. His face was smeared with her blood. "We've got to clean up before anyone sees us and freaks out. Let's take a shower."

Elle sighed. Still weak, Jackson, who had already gone

through so much, had to carry her into the bathroom and set her in the shower. She managed to remove her clothes while he turned on the water, blasting them both with heat.

"That feels so fu— er . . . good," Jackson said and wiped the blood from her face with a washcloth, his touch tender. "I'm going to wash and condition your hair, Elle."

She swallowed hard, unsure which would win, the rising panic, or her wish to please him. He hadn't asked her, but she knew if she put up her hand and stopped him, he wouldn't protest or question, he'd let her be. Her hair had been so important to her. Blazing red. Thick and long and feminine. It was her only feature she thought truly astounding and Stavros had made her hate it.

She braced herself, waiting for bile to rise in her stomach, but Jackson's hands felt soothing in the mass of tangles, the pads of his fingers massaging her scalp as the fragrance mixed with the hot water.

"Lean against me, Elle, you're swaying."

His body was hard, his erection unashamed and he was a big man, intimidating to her. She held her breath and hesitated before easing her body closer to his, until they were skin to skin, her back to him, the small of her back resting against his thick groin. She felt his heat radiating through her, his hunger, deep and strong, but just as equally his control, his need to love her as gently and tenderly as he knew how.

Jackson didn't think of himself as gentle or tender, she knew he worried about that in himself. His mind was only on her, on healing her body and mind, on finding a way to make her love her hair again, on accepting if she wanted to go through with dreading her hair when he loved the long silk of it shining in the sun. To him, her hair was as much a part of her as her temper, her intelligence, her tenacity, all traits he loved and admired in her.

"I won't dread it," she said, wanting to give him something back, "but you'll have to try to get the tangles out. It might take hours."

"I don't mind, baby, but do me a favor and stop thinking of me as a saint. I want you. Know that I want you. Get used to it. That's just reality and yes, I think you're sexy as hell. I always have."

Elle frowned, glad he couldn't see her face. She used to feel sexy and special and worth something, but Stavros had taken that away from her. She didn't want to think about anything but Jackson's fingers rubbing the conditioner into the tangles and the way his body made her feel safe instead of terrified.

"This smells like my favorite conditioner."

He held the bottle in front of her face for a brief moment before returning to his task. "It is yours. Sarah put a box of things in my truck before we left to go get you. Tea. A few clothes. Your personal things. I found them when I went to get the blanket."

Elle let her breath out. "She knew. She has precog. She knew I wouldn't stay with them. Why would she argue so much?"

"She didn't expect to see you covered in wounds, black and blue, your face swollen. You're her baby sister, Elle. Of course she wanted to take care of you."

"I'm sorry I hurt her—hurt all of them." She took a deep breath and blurted out the truth. "I'm afraid without you, Jackson."

"I know you are, baby. Don't you remember what it was like those first few days when I escaped the camp and was waiting for retrieval? You stayed in my mind and my heart beat so hard you were afraid I'd have a heart attack. I didn't want you leaving me, not for a moment, because you represented home and freedom and, above all else, safety to me." He skimmed his mouth down the side of her face. "Tell me you remember staying awake seventy-two hours because I was afraid to close my eyes. And when I finally did, the nightmares ate us both alive." His body shuddered against hers and his arms went around her waist, pulling her even closer, burying his face against her neck. "I'm still afraid without you, Elle."

She turned to face him, her bare skin sliding over his, her arms circling his neck as she pressed against him, giving herself to him, holding him, aching inside for both of them.

Something banged against the bathroom door and she jumped. Simultaneously, Jackson shoved her behind him.

"Tea's ready. Do you need help?" Ilya's voice called.

"You want to scrub my back?" Jackson asked.

"I think that was the American version of sarcasm," Ilya responded. "If you're feeling better, I've got five women out here. I could use a little help."

"Hannah?" Elle asked, turning her head up to the water so it washed the conditioner from her head.

"Jonas took her to the hospital just to make certain she's all right. Come get your tea."

"Give us a couple of minutes," Jackson said, helping to massage the conditioner from the thick mass of red hair. He reached past Elle and turned off the water.

She put a hand on his belly and he felt the jolt slam right through his muscle and bones. His hand trapped hers—inches from his groin, now full and heavy and pulsing with need. He cleared his throat. "What is it, baby?" He tried to sound normal, but his voice came out gravelly.

"I heard his voice, Jackson. I need you to believe me. Yes, I panicked when you pulled out of my head so fast and I could feel you being swept out to sea. My throat closed and I could feel his fingers tightening around my neck, closing off my windpipe, but I know it wasn't just a panic attack. Maybe he programmed me, I honestly can't tell you, but I heard his voice, very distinctly. He told me he would keep killing everyone I loved until I came back to him." She looked up at him, her green gaze begging him to believe her. "I'm not crazy."

His large hands framed her face and he looked straight into her eyes. "I don't think for one moment that you are, Elle." His tone was one of absolute decisiveness. "He can't have you." It was a decree—a promise—his word. His head lowered toward hers.

Again he took his time giving her every chance to pull away, but she didn't, watching him come closer and closer until she could see his long lashes, the straight nose and wickedly sexy lips, parting just enough to catch a glimpse of strong teeth. She took a breath and closed her eyes just as his lips touched hers, brushed back and forth in a soft, coaxing manner. She went still inside. A thousand butterflies took flight in her stomach. Her toes curled. The sensation of his lips against hers set off an electrical current that started with a small sizzle and built like a fireball rushing through her veins.

His hands held her face and she pressed her body close, skin to skin, melting into him, crawling inside his head, closer than two people could ever be. His mouth moved and hers answered. Deep inside, where her soul resided, she felt him there, holding her, sheltering her. She lifted her head. "He knows I love you." She touched his face, her fingers trembling. "He knows, Jackson. He can't get in when I'm filled with you and it's making him angrier. He's never denied himself anything and he believes he owns me."

"Well he's wrong, Elle. No one owns you."

Jackson bent his head and his mouth touched a long slash that curled over her breast. Her breath slammed out of her lungs and she went utterly still. She felt the gentle brush of his lips, featherlight across the torn flesh. He followed the line of whip marks with his kisses, so soft they were barely there, yet each set off a seismic reaction inside of her. Her body, so numb inside, nearly dead, no longer feminine or hot or needy, felt each of those kisses in her deepest core.

She closed her eyes tightly and held on to him as he kissed every wound, even dropping to his knees to plant kisses along the stripes inside her thighs and over her abdomen, deeper even where two or three times the whip had slashed through her most private, most sensitive spot. Again, she didn't feel as if his actions were in any way sexual, yet he was waking her body with love.

The intensity of his feelings shook her. How could she not have known how he felt about her? She kept her hands on his shoulders to steady her, fingers digging tightly into his muscle for an anchor. She hadn't expected the pooling of heat, or the wild beating of her heart. She hadn't expected the sizzle and burn of joy rushing through her veins, heating her body and making her breasts ache and her groin weep. She didn't even know if she wanted to be alive.

Jackson stood up and brought both of her hands to his mouth, kissing her knuckles before reaching for a towel and wrapping her in it. He took his time with her hair, toweling the moisture from the long strands.

"Get dressed, Elle. Something that will cover most of the lash marks so you'll be more comfortable. I'll dress and find a good brush to start on your hair while you visit with your sisters. And don't worry, I think we're growing together in strength and no one will be able to penetrate the shields in your mind."

She stood there a moment, just looking at him. Jackson Deveau. The badass from the bayou everyone was so afraid of. *Her* Jackson. The man who was slowly, carefully, bringing her back to life.

Jackson smiled at her and caught her chin, kissing her again, making her stomach do a funny little flip. "Go, honey. I'll catch up with you."

Elle nodded, uncertain how to voice the emotions welling up.

10

ELLE found her sisters sprawled out around the spacious living room. They smiled at her wanly, Libby still pale and weak, but the others were clearly stronger. Ilya looked a bit harassed and she felt a little sorry for him. Her family could be very overwhelming at times. Bomber remained by the bank of windows staring out to sea, his ears forward, his body still, eyes focused on the unusual fog surrounding the house.

Sarah beckoned to her to come join them. "You scared us, honey. You nearly burned out your talent completely, but thank you for saving Hannah and Jackson."

"You all helped," Elle pointed out. "I'm not certain I could have helped Jonas pinpoint their location without you. And thank you. I appreciate you coming over and working so hard to heal me."

"Of course we'd come," Sarah said. "In spite of everything, you do look better this morning. I can see Jackson is taking good care of you."

Elle blushed, her color creeping up her neck into her

face. She didn't know why. Jackson had been more than a gentleman. She realized that her fingertips had gone to her tingling lips and she hastily pulled them down under her older sisters' watchful eyes. She tasted Jackson in her mouth and it hit her then, he had miraculously managed to replace the touch and taste of Stavros with something good, something exciting. He didn't demand anything in return. He didn't even ask for anything. *Jackson*.

A stabbing pain shot through her head and he stuck his head through the doorway, black eyes half concerned, half furious. "Knock it off, Elle," he snapped, his tone low and mean.

Her sisters all swiveled around to stare at him. Tension rose in the room. They had no idea. Elle burst out laughing. He really was big bad Jackson, but hidden underneath all that steel muscle and the cold black eyes was something altogether different that no one, not even her sisters, suspected. He hid the gentle giant very well beneath that blue-jeaned devil.

"I didn't mean to."

He gave her another glare and disappeared again.

"Same old Jackson. I see his social skills haven't improved much," Sarah said. She waved her hand toward the teapot and it floated across the room and poured another cup of tea into the mug she was holding. "The man really needs to join the twenty-first century. I thought he might have improved while you're so fragile."

"Jackson is careful with me."

"Yeah, that sounded like it." Sarah rolled her eyes.

Elle looked around the room at her sisters, all obviously in agreement with her older sister's opinion of Jackson. She could have defended him, but it seemed more important to guard him, to hug his secret side to herself.

She simply shrugged her shoulders. "Has Jonas called about Hannah?"

"The baby is fine, and Hannah is much better. Jonas said she warmed up fast in the ambulance. Both of them are very grateful to you and Jackson," Sarah continued. She waved the teapot in Elle's direction.

Elle pointed to a mug sitting on the coffee table. Sarah waved her hand again. She'd already forgotten Elle wasn't allowed to use her psychic talents. "Thanks, Sarah." It was embarrassing not to be able to use her skills. She rubbed at her throbbing temples. She'd had a headache for so long she'd forgotten what it was like without one. Jackson never forgot that her brain was shredded and every time she used her talent, she was at risk.

"We're all very grateful to Jackson. He did an amazing thing."

Elle lifted an eyebrow. "So you're saying he's a cretin, but a heroic one."

Sarah nodded. "Very heroic."

Jackson stepped into the room looking sexy with a black tee stretched tight across his broad shoulders and heavy chest. His jeans fit him like a glove and now that she knew what he was hiding there, she couldn't help but notice the front of his jeans. "Elle saved us both," he corrected, pouring tea the old-fashioned way. He wasn't adept at levitation or parlor tricks. He just needed something hot to chase away the last of the cold lingering inside him.

He stirred in honey and drank the first cup down before pouring a second and moving to Elle's side. He sat on the floor between Elle's legs, half turning so he could take her bare foot onto his lap. "She shouldn't have, she was risking too much, but she kept us warm until help arrived.

Thanks for giving her the push at the end. It saved us." He sipped the tea and brought Elle's foot against his belly.

It felt intimate to have him hold her bare foot. Elle could see that Ilya had started a fire to help heat the room and give more of an illusion of warmth. The crackle and popping along with the flickering flames added to the coziness of Jackson's living room. She glanced up the walls and could have sworn that for one moment they undulated, as if alive, as the walls of the Drake home sometimes did when ancestors settled into the walls to help make it a fortress.

Brace yourself, baby. It was all the warning he was going to give her. Her sisters were looking her over, trying to see inside her, trying to look past the bruising on her face and the few raw wounds they could see to what they couldn't see. He was going to confirm some of their worst suspicions.

"Elle is afraid she might be pregnant."

Sarah lowered her teacup and looked at her youngest sister with a small frown. Ilya shook his head even as he laced his fingers with Joley's. If it was possible for Libby to lose any more color, she did. Abigail and Kate exchanged a long look.

Elle tried to pull her foot away, ducking her head and allowing the mass of tangles to tumble down around her face, hiding her.

We need to know what to do to take care of you. Jackson was unrepentant.

"My understanding is that the seventh child can share the legacy but only with the right partner," Ilya said. "And with that partner, birth control doesn't work. With anyone else, pregnancy is very difficult."

Elle gasped and sat up straighter, looking at Sarah. "Can that be true?"

Sarah nodded. "It's recorded in the diaries."

"Mom is a snake," Elle hissed. "A total snake."

"She probably didn't know. In those days," Sarah explained, "women rarely slept with a man before marriage. It probably didn't come up."

Jackson tugged at her foot. "Trade places with me so I can work on your hair." *It might be easier for you with your sisters here.*

Her heart began to pound again. She hesitated and then slid from the chair to give it to him. Jackson settled her between his thighs, another intimate position she hadn't considered.

"I could examine you," Libby offered. "You should be treated, Elle."

"Not until I'm stronger. My head is so messed up, Libby, that I'm afraid I can't protect you. I'm not willing to risk you."

"It's my risk."

Elle shook her head. "You've helped me just with what you did."

Jackson began the slow process of dividing the mass of long hair into strips. His hands were astonishingly gentle as he began to slowly pick the tangles from the ends of the thick strands and work his way patiently up toward her scalp.

"So you really don't think Elle is pregnant?" He kept his voice matter-of-fact.

"I'd be shocked," Sarah answered. "Do you feel pregnant, Elle?"

Elle shrugged. "I have no idea what it feels like."

"Sick," Joley said and glared at Ilya. "Sick to your stomach."

"Not everyone gets sick," Libby pointed out. "I'll get you a pregnancy test."

"Thanks, Libby," Elle said. The tugging on her scalp made her feel loved and cared for, instead of reminding her of Stavros grabbing her head and forcing her to do his bidding. There was something very soothing about the purposeful way Jackson combed out the tangles, always holding the hair tightly between where he separated the snarls and her tender scalp.

"Bomber, what are you looking at, boy?" Jackson asked.

The dog turned his head, gave a short bark and turned back to stare out the window at the dissipating fog. Jackson took a drink of his tea while he observed the dog. The animal still appeared on the alert, his body still, his eyes focused and ears cocked forward.

"We all know Gratsos and his brother both have psychic talent." Jackson looked at Ilya and Sarah over his steaming mug, the fingers of his other hand holding on to Elle's hair as if to give her an anchor while he asked questions. "Is it possible he could reach out from a great distance without knowing where Elle is and choke her?" He didn't want to think it was possible for Gratsos to communicate with her, but he already knew it was because he had done so himself over great distances. "And the fog, could he be fishing? Throwing out a psychic trap, so to speak."

Ilya hitched closer and exchanged a long look with Sarah. "Interesting idea. Sending out his energy to search for her. I suppose it could be done. I've never heard of it before. I couldn't do it. What about you, Sarah? You read all the history."

Sarah chewed thoughtfully at her lower lip. "I've not read about it, nor could I do it, but that doesn't mean it's not possible. Hannah can send the wind. Why couldn't he send fog? Or something else?"

Elle inhaled sharply. "Like a hidden current? A rip current?" A shiver went down her spine. That was exactly what Stavros had done. She was suddenly certain of it. Oceans away, he'd still sent the fog and the psychic trap hidden within a current. "Hannah can do all sorts of things like that. She can build and direct a twister. Anything to do with weather. Maybe with Stavros it's the sea. He has a shipping empire. He owns an island. I researched him thoroughly before I went undercover and he only travels to cities near water. Every house or villa he owns overlooks water. It was a small thing but it came up and we actually discussed it."

Ilya drew in his breath and looked at Jackson. "That's why the sea was giving us trouble during the rescue. We thought Hannah had lost control of the storm, but maybe she was battling Stavros without knowing it. He can hide his energy."

Jackson's hands were once again tugging at her hair, a gentle steady rhythm that calmed her pounding heart as Elle looked out the window. Bomber backed away and turned and came to Jackson's side, lying down, pushing his head into Elle's lap. "The fog is gone," she said, pressing her hand into the Shepherd's fur. *It's interesting that Bomber is very relaxed now that the fog is gone. Do you think . . .* "Ouch!"

Jackson's hands gripped her shoulder hard and gave her a little shake. "Keep it up, Drake. You'll find yourself over my knee. Why the hell do you have to be so fucking stubborn?"

There was a small shocked silence. Sarah cleared her throat. "Are you actually threatening to strike my sister? We don't believe in corporal punishment in our family. My parents *never* struck us."

"Well, maybe if your father had, Elle wouldn't be such a little hellion," Jackson said.

Elle tipped her head back. "Stop saying the 'F' word. And Sarah, Jackson would cut off his arm before he actually hit me. He just likes everyone to think he's a badass."

"I am a badass, damn it," Jackson said. He picked up the comb and carefully started on the next thick strand of hair. "You seem to be the only one who isn't aware of it."

Elle laughed. It wasn't a huge laugh, but she couldn't help the small spurt of amusement at the idea of big bad Jackson combing the tangles out of her hair.

"She's always been a little hellion. What's she doing this time?" Sarah's voice choked with emotion; the sound of Elle's laughter caused tears to well up in her eyes.

"Using telepathy again. Her brain has to rest, to heal."

Elle made a face at Sarah and rolled her eyes. Jackson leaned down and whispered into her ear. "I saw that."

"No, you didn't."

"Okay, I felt it. I saw it in your mind."

Kate stirred in her chair, picked up her mug of tea and blew on it, looking at her younger sister over the rising steam. "Jackson is right on this, Elle. You have to stop using anything to do with psychic energy until your brain heals."

Kate's voice was gentle and kind, her eyes compassionate. The tension in the room immediately dissipated as if it had never been.

Jackson smiled at her. "Our Kate. The peacemaker. You can heal psychic burnout, right?"

A collective gasp went around the room. All eyes turned to Kate. Ilya leaned toward her in his chair and Elle drew back, away from the others, nearly climbing into Jackson's lap.

"Only that one time with you, Jackson," Kate admitted. "It's not like much of that goes around, you know?" She sent him a small smile, faint color on her face. Kate had never liked much attention on her and she was definitely under scrutiny. "Libby heals illness and has a lot of people to practice on. I just winged it that day."

"You helped me and you weren't even trying," Jackson pointed out.

"No," Elle said firmly. "I won't even consider this."

Jackson lifted her onto his lap and settled his arms around her, letting her curl into him. His chin nuzzled the top of her head, but he kept his gaze on Kate. "If Gratsos can use psychic energy to travel and he's fishing right now, he'll find Elle faster than we counted on. She'll need to be at full strength to fight him. We all will. He's got a big sea here to use against us."

"It's all speculation," Elle protested. "We don't have a clue if this was anything but a natural phenomenon. They do occur all over the world. Right here on this coast, we have several places where rip currents occur."

"But not here," Sarah said. "We've lived our entire lives here, Elle, and never once has there been a hidden current off this particular part of the coast. The physical makeup is wrong."

"We don't know that," Elle denied. "The ocean floor changes all the time."

"You're grasping at straws," Jackson said. "The point is, there is a possibility and even if it's a low one, we need to consider that it was an attempt to find you."

"How would he know to come here?" Joley asked.

"He wouldn't have known," Sarah said. "He'd use the fog the way Hannah does. He'd send it out and when it tapped in to psychic energy, the fog would build into what you saw, seeking a user of that energy, and then the trap would be sprung. He wouldn't even need the ocean, a lake or river could be just as treacherous."

Joley frowned. "But he's taking the chance of killing Elle. What if Elle had fallen by the water's edge instead of Hannah?"

"I doubt the trap would have been sprung," Ilya said. "He has to have Elle's psychic fingerprint. He'll know her energy when he feels it."

Jackson frowned. He didn't like Stavros having anything at all to do with Elle, let alone having her psychic fingerprint. "Is it possible he's choking her, Ilya?"

"You tell me," Ilya said. "What can you do?"

All eyes turned to Jackson and there was another uncomfortable silence. He could stroke Elle intimately in her mind, bring her to orgasm, share his entire being with her, every sensation, and the flip side of that, of course, was that he could cause her pain, and yes, choke her, hurt her, possibly even kill her.

He didn't want them to know. Not her sisters. Not Ilya. His gaze flicked to Kate. She looked down at her hands, the only one not looking at him. She knew, all those months ago, that he had tried to burn out his talent. When the devil rode him too hard, and he detested the world around him, he feared he might harm someone.

I'm sorry, baby. I didn't want you to be afraid of me.

I will never be afraid of you.

For the first time he didn't reprimand her for using telepathy, even when a small trickle of blood appeared at the corner of her mouth. He wiped it away with the pad of his thumb.

Elle's fingers tangled with his. "We're talking about Stavros and what he can do, not Jackson. If Stavros can choke me from a distance, but he doesn't want to kill me, why would he keep doing it?"

"Control," Jackson and Ilya said simultaneously.

Ilya waved his hand toward the kitchen and the kettle floated to the sink to refill with water. "If he can frighten you enough, he'll keep you from your friends and family and especially any men you might have in your life. From the beginning, Gratsos has wanted control of you. He must have sensed your psychic ability and planned to keep you for his own purposes. He had the island already prepared with a psychic shield so you couldn't use your talent."

"But neither could he," Elle pointed out. "Or his brother."

"How old is that villa?" Sarah asked. "Did he buy it himself?"

"It had been in his family, and his father sold it to pay off debts. Stavros bought it back when he became wealthy," Elle answered.

"Where is his mother?" Sarah continued.

"She was supposedly killed in an accident when Stavros was a baby along with Stavros's twin brother, but it turns out she left her husband, faked her death, and took the twin with her," Elle said. "She drowned in a lake a few years ago. When Evan, that's the twin, was in my room that first day, they talked quite a lot about their past. Both seemed bitter."

There was a small telling silence, all of them thinking the same thing. Could Stavros have had something to do with the death of his mother?

The teakettle whistled and Ilya poured the water into the teapot with another wave of his hand, adding several scoops of the healing tea to further energize everyone.

Jackson sat back in his chair, watching the cozy fit over the teapot without a single hand touching it. Cups and mugs lined up on the kitchen sideboard next to the pot. He looked around his open living room at the Drake sisters sprawled out in his various chairs. Ilya sitting beside Joley, her body draped over his in a casual, comfortable manner. What had happened? It looked like a scene from the Drake home, not his quiet house.

He let his breath out slowly, and pulled Elle closer into him as he studied her sisters—his family. *Family*. He tasted the word, rolled it around in his mind. He hadn't known what a family could be until he met the Drakes. They all had opinions, they all got into one another's business and they all were fierce in their protection of each other.

Elle tipped her head back to look up at him, feeling his emotions, sharing them with him, the wonder and miracle of family. They exchanged a small smile and felt—complete.

Sarah sighed. "Elle, can you check that website you like to research all the time? The one that records all the strange events around the world? I'd like to see if the fog showed up in more than one place and if so, were there other rip currents around or near it at the same time."

"What website?" Ilya asked.

"I found it by accident a few years ago when I was researching. The website's at HiddenCurrents.com. A reporter has gathered all sorts of information from various online sites and newspapers, as well as magazine sources. She writes her own articles as well. The site covers all kinds of things from weather to earthquakes, remote viewing, experiments, other anomalies—anything odd happening anywhere in the world, you can find it there. She named it Hidden Currents because she thinks all these things are running on the surface of the earth and we just don't connect the dots. She's trying to connect them."

"She isn't a government agent?" Ilya asked.

Elle shook her head. "Just an inquisitive reporter, very sharp, who began noticing unusual weather patterns. At first she was looking for global warming signs, but she began speculating about psychic events and whether or not something else was going on. I became intrigued and began studying the various events myself. I think, like all of us, I just thought we were the only ones in the world like us, but Ilya and Jackson are proof we're not. Now Stavros. There are more lines than just the Drakes that have psychic abilities."

Jackson, without thinking about it, pulled his mind from Elle's. He didn't want her to feel his reaction, but every single time she used Gratsos's more familiar given name, his gut clenched and knotted and he wanted to hurt somebody. Ashamed that he couldn't control such a visceral reaction, he hid it from her. His arms stayed solidly in place, holding her against him, still gentle, when deep inside where no one could see, he raged at the need for action on his part.

"It makes sense that there would be," Sarah agreed. She looked at Ilya. "You've been all over the world, have you met others?"

"No, but I don't think true psychic ability is all that common," Ilya mused. "People have flashes, moments of intuition, some act on it and are perhaps a little more sensitive, but that isn't the same as true psychic talents. The abilities the Drakes have are enormous." He looked at Jackson. "Was your mother or father psychic?"

Jackson's hands tightened against Elle involuntarily. She didn't attempt to slide into his mind, not now when he was so uncomfortable with the conversation and clearly didn't want to talk about his family, but she found herself uneasy without his touch. She had become dependent on the continual reassurance of his mind. Without him, she felt completely alone in the room filled with her family.

Elle pressed her hand tightly against his until Jackson laced his fingers with hers. She wanted to surround him with warmth the way he did her, but she forced herself to stay out of his mind and away from his childhood memories.

Jackson shrugged his broad shoulders and rubbed his chin again against the top of Elle's head. Elle recognized it as a sign of nerves as well as a simple need to touch her. She saw Kate glance at Jackson and then away, as if they shared some secret she wasn't aware of.

"If Gratsos is fishing to find the whereabouts of psychics, then he would have sent his energy out and every place he found psychic energy, the fog would have developed," Elle said into the silence, diverting attention from Jackson. "I'm certain it would show up on the website. I'll check it this evening and see if there are any reports anywhere else."

Jackson, showing his appreciation, leaned down to feather kisses down the side of her face to the corner of her mouth. Elle felt the familiar tingle start in the pit of her stomach. He could do that to her in spite of everything that had happened, make her feel beautiful and wanted and even sexual when she wasn't at all certain she was any of those things anymore.

Bomber lifted his head, looking around the room and then suddenly focusing on her. He leapt to his feet and barked, a sharp, threatening note, ears forward, eyes piercing. He barked a second time. Elle felt the brush of fingers along her throat, faint, almost as light as Jackson's lips as he pressed kisses across her face to her ear. Non-threatening. Barely there. She coughed, her throat contracting.

Jackson's tongue touched her ear, flooding her body with heat. She had never realized she was so susceptible, her body suddenly alive, every nerve ending screaming at her, wanting him and she reveled that she could have such feelings. Jackson was so wrapped around her soul, so a part of her heart and for the first time since escaping, she thought she might have a chance at a seminormal relationship.

Bomber barked again.

The fingers brushing her throat pressed deeper. "Jackson," Elle's hand went to her throat to remove his hands, all of sudden feeling a little too vulnerable.

Jackson sat up straight, looking at Bomber, nearly giving him the dismiss command, but he was circling the chair, his eyes focused totally on Elle. She coughed again and reached for her neck, saying his name again, but this time it came out in a hoarse whisper, as if she couldn't quite talk.

She gasped. Wheezed. Pulled away from him and slipped from the chair to the floor, on her knees, coughing more. Without warning her body was picked up as if she weighed no more than a feather and flung backward. She landed on the hardwood floor practically at Ilya's and Joley's feet. Joley screamed and slid to the floor to crouch protectively over her sister even as Ilya caught Joley and pushed her behind him, using his own body as a shield.

Bomber barked ferociously, darting in toward an unseen

enemy. Sarah, Kate and Abigail reached for Elle's writhing body. Elle fought her invisible assailant, slapping at nonexistent hands, at her breasts, her thighs, screaming now, kicking as if she was trying to dislodge a hidden attacker. She rolled across the room, actually hit the dog, who snapped his teeth at empty air, up close near her throat.

The room erupted into total chaos. The five Drake sisters leapt to help Elle. Ilya was there before the women, kneeling beside Elle, but not touching her. When Joley tried again to get past him to her sister, he firmly pushed her back behind him. Joley struggled to get around Ilya, the dog barked continuously and Elle fought anything that came near her, screaming and crying, hitting out with her fists and drumming at the floor with her bare heels. Her fist struck Sarah's arm, skidded off and nearly caught Kate in the face.

Elle's body lifted a second time, this time by the top of her head, as if the unseen hand grasped her long hair and yanked her up. She stumbled back, coughing, kicking, tears pouring down her face. Jackson could see the marks on her skin now. Fingers sinking into her flesh. Bomber continued to bark, wanting to attack, acting as if he could sense the entity.

Elle fell again and tried to crawl across the room, away from her family, away from the dog, toward the door. The floor of the house undulated, a long roll that added to the chaos. Tea spilled. Elle flipped over on her back, kicking and fighting, sheer concentration mixed with terror on her pale face.

"Join with us, Elle," Sarah demanded. "You're shutting us out. We can fight him off with you." She approached her sister again, this time more cautiously, Kate, Libby and Abigail behind her while Ilya kept Joley across the room.

The four sisters touched hands, and Sarah laid her palm on Elle's forehead. Elle rolled away from her, knocking into an end table. A lamp crashed to the floor. Kate burst into tears and began sobbing. Joley buried her face against Ilya's chest.

"Elle, please," Sarah pleaded. "Come on, honey, you have to let us in. We can help you."

Elle shook her head, her body shuddering as she was half lifted up and slammed back to the floor, the breath driven from her lungs. The attack was brutal and vicious, a punishment, an act of ownership, clear to everyone in the room.

Jackson stood then. Everything had happened in moments, and during that time he'd studied his enemy. He was certain he knew what to do. He flexed his fingers, his heart beating hard in his chest, too hard, the sound like thunder in his ears. His gut hurt, it was knotted so tight. He could see bruises forming on Elle's delicate skin, around her throat, the fingers pressing hard into the swell of her breasts beneath the thin material of her shirt. There would be bruises there as well, he knew. He pushed through the circle of women and signaled to the dog to cease barking.

Elle looked at him, shaking her head, pushing backward with her heels in an effort to keep away from him.

"You're scaring her more, Jackson," Sarah said. "Can't you see she's terrified?"

He ignored Sarah's restraining hand and straddled Elle's small body, catching her flailing fists and pinning them above her head, settling his weight on her to pin her to the floor. She bucked wildly, trying to throw him off.

"Jackson!" Even Libby, the quiet one without a mean bone in her body, tried to pull him off Elle.

He could feel, as if from a distance, hands pulling at him, fists pounding on his back, but his entire being was centered on Elle.

"Elle." Jackson said her name calmly, his voice soft, very low. He remained straddling her, pinning her wrists to the floor ignoring her sisters who continued to try to shove him off her. "Elle, open your eyes and look at me." He waited a heartbeat. Two. Certain she heard him. She thrashed underneath, fighting, crying, begging, shredding his heart, but he refused to give into his own fears.

He was her one refuge. He focused on that, not on what was happening to her. "Elle. Look at me." This time he put more command in his voice, although he kept his tone low and soft.

Her lashes fluttered. Long. Wet. Heartbreaking. Her emerald gaze met his. Recognized him with a jolt of terror.

"Give yourself to me."

She shook her head violently.

He leaned closer. Sarah tried to pry him off by grabbing his hair. Ilya caught her around the waist and pulled her physically off him just as Bomber rumbled a warning.

"Give yourself to me, Elle." He said it again. Calm. Implacable. A relentless demand. Ignoring everything else around them. There was only the two of them. Elle and Jackson. No one else. Nothing else.

Her eyes pleaded with him. He knew what she was afraid of. She believed if he joined with her mind that Gratsos would be able to harm him. She feared the same for her sisters. Elle, his Elle, courageous as always, was protecting everyone she loved.

He slowly shook his head, holding her gaze. "Give yourself completely to me, Elle. He can't hurt me. I'm stronger than he is. Together we're far stronger. Give me your heart and mind and give me your body."

Now the room around him was so silent he could hear breathing, was able to distinguish each sister, the dog, Ilya, especially Elle's terrified rhythm. He forced his own air to be slow and steady, his heart and hers, his lungs and hers. One and the same. "Come with me, baby. Give yourself to me."

He bent down toward her face with infinite patience, infinite slowness. Time seemed to stand still. His vision tunneled. His hearing faded to center only on Elle. For him, there was no one else in the room. It was only the two of them. Elle and Jackson. "Your body, Elle, trust me. Give yourself to me, baby."

She took a breath, let it out, and visibly made the effort to relax beneath him. She stopped her frantic struggling, her gaze locked with his. He could see fear, but there was trust. Her muscles relaxed. Whatever Stavros was doing to her, she simply accepted it. She allowed her heart to beat slower, to match the steady rhythm. She forced her lungs to follow the pattern of his. Her gaze never wavered from his and her body became his—melting into his strong frame, soft and pliant while he stretched out over the top of her, his weight settling, his heavier muscles blanketing her.

"That's my girl. Now your mind. One mind, baby, that's what we are, what we need to be. Open up your mind and let me in."

The room around him was absolutely quiet, still, as if everyone held his or her breath and waited. Jackson didn't look away from Elle. It was only them. The two of them and no one else in the world. He waited for her to let go of her fear and turn herself over to him. It was a huge step for her. Fighting, she at least felt as if she had a semblance of control. She swallowed hard, blinked several times and then her barriers came tumbling down, as if she removed them fast so she wouldn't lose her nerve.

He flowed into her mind, filling every space, wrapping himself in her tightly, claiming her, pouring strength and resolve and building her resistance to Gratsos. Jackson caught her head in his palms, framing the little heart-shaped pixie face with his large hands and he lowered her head to his.

Her breath caught in her throat. Her lips parted. She watched him come to her. Jackson. Her other half. Her strength. Her one and only love. He filled her mind, filled her heart and soul. Flooded her body with need and heat. There was no room for anything or anyone else in her mind or heart. In her body or soul. There was only Jackson. He came to her with exquisite gentleness, with disarming tenderness.

His lips touched her, firm and cool, velvet soft, heating fast. His tongue stroked along the seam of her lips, teased and seduced, drove out every depraved brutal act Stavros had committed and replaced it with something altogether different. She burned inside. In her mind. In her heart, deep in her body where she craved only Jackson. She opened her mouth and drew him in.

Jackson, for the first time, felt the other man. Oily. Evil. A thick ooze of a human being rotted from the inside out. The handsome shell covered a poor excuse of humanity, with a sense of entitlement Jackson had never encountered before.

Try me, you son of a bitch.

He issued the challenge, knowing Gratsos was already retreating, fleeing Elle's mind, leaving her shaking, nearly convulsing on the floor, sobbing with relief and clinging to Jackson. She slid her arms around his neck and pressed her face against his throat, weeping uncontrollably, unrestrained, something none of her sisters had ever seen her do before.

"It's all right, baby," he said gently. "He's gone now. He ran like the coward he is." He slid from her body and onto the floor at her side, although she continued to cling to him. He put his arm under her knees and lifted her, carrying her to the high-backed recliner on the far side of the room. "You're stronger than he is, Elle, you're just burned out right now. Once you're at full strength, I'm telling you, he won't be able to get inside you."

She held him tighter, her fingers digging into his muscles, trying to burrow under his skin and lose herself there. Jackson hated that they had an audience, even if it was her family. She seemed too vulnerable, too fragile, and Elle would hate that. He looked at them, his eyes burning, fierce, but he couldn't help it. He knew he looked intimidating, but this was Elle—*his* Elle—and he wanted only to protect her.

Sarah hung her head. "I'm sorry, Jackson. I should have known you were helping her. She wanted you, trusted you, not us."

Her voice was so sad, his heart ached. Elle remained in a fetal ball, curled into him, still weeping, but silent now, trying to come to terms with that fact that Gratsos had managed to attack her from across an ocean.

"You're wrong, Sarah," Jackson said. "Elle trusts you with her life, with her soul. She was protecting you from him. She's been protecting you all along."

"He can't hurt us." Sarah bit her lip, stopping the rest of her sentence. Jackson was glaring at her, knowing she'd been about to blurt out that they were too strong for Gratsos, yet Elle had been the strongest among them and she'd been captured and tortured repeatedly.

It was Elle who answered, lifting her head, her chin up, eyes a bit defiant. "He can, Sarah. He can hurt all of you. You can't conceive of his kind of money or power. No one ever tells him no. He wants something and he gets it. The police are his, the politicians are his, and now we know he has psychic abilities. He isn't afraid to hurt anyone and he's going to keep coming after me. It's bad enough that I'm risking Jackson, I'm not about to risk any of you."

"He got in our home," Jackson said. "If we were at your house, would you be protected?"

Elle shrugged. "I can't go there until my brain heals."

Sarah frowned. "Why, Elle? I don't understand. The house can protect you much better than this place. You know that. And why won't you let Libby—"

"Not Libby," Jackson interrupted. "Libby can heal brain injuries and she can heal the body, but Kate heals the psychic burnout, don't you, Kate?"

"Don't answer that, Kate," Elle defended fiercely. "It's a moot point anyway as no one is going near my mind. It's too dangerous and you all just witnessed why."

11

KATE looked down at her hands when all eyes turned to her. To Jackson, Kate Drake had a certain regal quality. She was the quietest of the Drake sisters, a little shy and rarely brought attention to herself. She loved her books and curling up in her home on a stormy day with her family the most. That and Matt Granite, the rough, tough ex–Army Ranger who just happened to be her fiancé.

"You and Jackson are strong enough to shield me from anything you're afraid of, Elle," she said, her voice soothing and confident. She walked to the window and looked out over the sea. Far away she could see tendrils of dark heavy fog receding. "I won't do anything you don't want me to do, but, honey, it's very obvious to me that when Jackson lets go of your mind, this man, this enemy, has found a way in."

Elle frowned and rubbed at her bruised throat. "But how? I don't understand how he can take me over like that." Like he was possessing her somehow, crawling inside her mind and raping her all over again. She could feel the touch of his hands, the way he chose to hurt her, the way he taunted that he could bring her pleasure. She hadn't wanted Jackson to hear that, to know or feel it, yet he had.

She looked at Jackson with despair in her eyes, feeling it with terrible dread in her heart. "I'm so sorry," she murmured.

"Do you really fucking think I would ever blame you for the things he did to you?" Jackson spat out, shaking with rage before he could contain it. He made a visible effort to gain control, letting out his breath and burying his face in her neck for a long moment. "Stavros Gratsos has nothing to do with what is between you and me and he never will have. He doesn't know what love is, or pleasure or giving and sharing one's body. He wants to possess you and control you, force you to be whatever he chooses for you." *He might have forced your body to react to him, Elle, but he never had you. He'll never have the real you.* "You're my heart and my soul, baby, and whatever he did was all about him and nothing about you."

"I can try," Kate said. "I'd like to help."

Elle took a deep breath and shook her head regretfully. She wasn't strong enough to shield Kate from the emotional trauma of what had happened to her and she wasn't about to let her gentle sister experience a man as depraved as Stavros. Jackson had saved her.

You saved yourself by taking that leap of faith. You trusted me enough to give yourself to me wholly. And Jackson had been humbled by Elle's faith in him. After all she'd been through, she'd still believed in him enough to let go of everything and hand herself over to him. He kissed the top of her head, trying not to crush her in his arms. He had the need to hold on to her with everything he was, every last bit of his strength, and shelter and protect her, make certain nothing could ever touch her again.

Elle stirred, pressing closer, but she didn't respond. Her mind moved against his, a warmth, a feeling consuming him that he was unfamiliar with. Love. It felt like love flooding his mind.

"Everyone needs to rest," Ilya said. "We should go back to the Drake house and let Jackson and Elle have a little time to recoup before we make any decisions. Kate, before you do anything, you need to discuss it with Matt."

Her chin rose. "I can help my sister without consulting my fiancé, Ilya."

His eyebrow shot up. "Really? Not when you're risking burning out your own talents."

Joley scowled at him. "It's bad enough that you want to boss me around, but I swear, Ilya, you're turning into another Jonas. Don't be telling my sister what to do."

Ilya caught her chin in his hand and leaned down to brush a kiss over her upturned mouth. "Believe me, honey, it takes both Jonas and me to keep the lot of you in line. It's a full-time job for us."

Elle tried to smile as the ribbing started. Ilya had successfully moved the attention from her, but now she could dwell on what had happened as she looked around the room and saw the broken lamp and the overturned furniture. She felt every bruise and her throat was sore. Was she letting Stavros have access to her by just simply thinking of him? Letting him into her thoughts and mind? If so, how could she possibly stop? He'd done terrible things to her, things she couldn't help but remember in vivid detail. Worse, what if she was just plain crazy and none of it was real? She was asking Jackson to believe her, but could her mind be so hysterical that she was somehow doing this to herself?

No! I felt him, too. And Bomber knew he was here. I think he has access whenever my mind leaves yours. You're too broken now, your natural barrier's in shreds and he waits until you're defenseless and then he pours in like the ooze he is.

Another man had assaulted his woman in front of him. If Gratsos could have, he would have raped her to show her she had no control, that she was nothing and he could get to her anytime he wanted. Rage was a living, breathing entity deep inside and Jackson breathed it away, forcing his mind from that dark place where he'd lived for so long. What Gratsos didn't understand was, Elle was far more powerful than the shipping magnate could ever conceive. And combined with Jackson, when she was back to full strength, he was certain Gratsos wouldn't stand a chance. In the meantime, he had to keep her safe.

It was surprising how small of a ball Elle could curl into. She took up very little of his lap and felt small and light in his arms. He wanted to be alone with her. "Maybe we should let Elle rest," he agreed with Ilya. Jackson was busy examining the damage done to Elle without trying to make it obvious. Gratsos was angry with her. He'd wanted to hurt her and he'd done so. She was shaking and trying to hide it from her family.

Libby crossed the room to stand in front of them. "I know you don't want me to feel anything that happened to you and I respect that, Elle. But I'm a doctor as well as your sister, and I can heal."

"You've done that. I can tell my wounds are already better," Elle said in a small voice, without looking up. She burrowed closer into Jackson.

Libby sighed. "That isn't good enough, hon. I have things I have to check for and you know it. We can't wait. I don't think I'll need to touch you, not unless I find something." She waited. Elle remained silent and Libby stepped even closer to her sister and held her palms outward, starting throat high, as if she were a machine taking an X-ray. Very slowly she ran her hands down Elle's body, hovering for a long while near her groin.

Elle could feel warmth pouring into her. She curled her fingers around Jackson and just held on. It was humiliating to her that she couldn't stop Stavros, that he had managed to kidnap and subject her to a monthlong torture and rape. She couldn't imagine the women who had been taken and used as sex slaves for months and years on end. How hopeless they had to feel, how small and insignificant. How ashamed.

Stop it, baby. They have no reason to feel shame and neither do you. The people who do this kind of thing to others should feel shame. Jackson brushed kisses over the top of her head.

Libby dropped her hand, staggered and Sarah wrapped her arm around her sister's waist. "There's no disease, no pregnancy, and I healed the tears and bruises as best I could without touching you, Elle," Libby whispered, her voice choked. She turned away leaning heavily on Sarah.

Elle's sisters gathered around Libby as they started toward the door. "We'll be back to do another healing session and this time, we'll be much more careful," Sarah promised. "Ilya's taking us home. You know you're welcome to come."

"I can't yet. Give me another couple of days," Elle pleaded. "I'll be stronger and then maybe Kate can help a little and I can deal with the house."

Jackson looked around his home, at the subtle difference in the walls. He didn't want to believe it, but he was beginning to think maybe the Drake house was moving locations. "Don't worry, Sarah," Jackson promised. "I'll take good care of her."

Sarah nodded, her eyes meeting his. "I believe you will, Jackson. Thank you for what you did."

Jackson watched the Drake sisters follow Ilya out. At once the tension drained out of Elle. She nearly went limp in his arms.

"I was so scared for you. Terrified." Elle pressed her face tightly against his chest. "You risked so much. What if he'd gotten into your head? What if he could cause you pain, or even kill you, Jackson? You're so reckless."

He stroked her damp hair, only partially combed out. "I knew he couldn't. You welcomed me. You invited me. He's an intruder and he doesn't belong. You don't have faith in your own abilities anymore, Elle, because you think they failed you, but you're still strong."

A small shudder ran through her. "I wasn't strong enough to keep him out."

"Let me look at you. How much damage did he do?" He lifted her away from him, forcing her to stand on the floor.

He could see the smudges of fingerprints on her throat. He tugged the top of the shirt lower. The dark bruises formed a pattern across the slope of her breasts and he could see faint teeth marks. She was holding still in his mind, waiting for his recoil, waiting for his reaction, so he gave her none, tamping down the raw edge of violence that had been a legacy from his father. He had patience and he would find and kill Gratsos, but right now, Elle needed reassurance and Jackson was determined to provide whatever Elle needed.

"Not too bad. The bastard. And I want you to notice I didn't call him a fucking bastard this time. I'm learning."

She smiled just as he knew she would. "I don't think you're quite getting the concept I'm after." She stroked Bomber's head and rubbed his ears. "You're such a good dog. Thanks for trying to save me."

"Maybe we could use that," Jackson said suddenly. "I'm going to make you tea the old-fashioned way and finish your hair while I think about this."

"About what?" She watched him gather teacups and carry them into the kitchen, following a short distance behind. "What are you thinking about?"

"Bomber and his instincts. He obviously spotted Gratsos's psychic energy long before we did. Each time you've had a problem, he's alerted before. I didn't recognize it right away, but that's what he's doing." He glanced over his shoulder at her. "You hungry?"

She smiled again, this time her eyes lighting up. She'd been upset not wanting her sisters to have to heal her, but she was grateful to Libby. She had felt so unclean, and Libby made her feel whole again, not quite so dirty and used. "Jackson Deveau, you're going all domestic on me. You really aren't such a badass after all."

He grinned at her, a little embarrassed. "I'm a total badass. Don't you go ruining my reputation around here."

"My sisters are going to uphold it. They get hot under the collar when you yell at me."

She sounded smug—and teasing. He liked that. It gave him a warm feeling in the pit of his stomach. He'd always wondered what a loner like him would do with a woman around permanently; now he knew he wanted her with him.

"I'm reading your mind," she reminded, walking on

bare feet into the tiled kitchen. "Tell me about your great plan."

He sighed and picked her up, putting her on the counter beside him as he put away the groceries Inez had brought them. He held up several bags of Elle's favorite dried fruit—tangerine. "That woman is so sweet sometimes."

"I never thought I'd hear you say that about Inez. You don't talk to her."

"I talk to her." He cleared his throat and looked away from her, a faint flush of color rising up his neck. "She brings me groceries sometimes."

"Without you ordering them?"

He shrugged and pulled out the makings for sandwiches.

"Jackson." Elle waited until he looked at her. "Why does she bring you groceries?"

"I don't know. I tell her it's not necessary, but she thinks she owes me or something."

She could tell by his color and reluctant tone that he really was embarrassed. Elle moved in his mind. Her eyebrow shot up. "You loaned her money?"

"Damn it, Elle. Don't say it out loud. No one knows and I didn't exactly loan it to her. She's a very proud woman and she helps people out all the time. Too much. She insisted on keeping Frank Warner's art gallery open. He's getting out of prison any day now."

"How could he be? It hasn't even been a full year." Elle was shocked. Frank Warner had allowed the Russian mob to use his art gallery to smuggle in illegal items and launder money. She'd felt a little sorry for him in that he hadn't known what he was getting into, but through his greed for money, he had allowed a dirty bomb into the country by opening up the smuggler's route.

"He was only sentenced to three years and he got time off for good behavior. Inez was very instrumental in his receiving the lightest sentence possible. Frank was huge on charity and helping out the local food drives as well as the programs for school kids, the shoes, the field trips, and he participated heavily in all the auctions, donating some great works. She worked tirelessly to help him. They'd been friends since grammar school."

"How did you know all that?"

He handed her a sandwich and poured the boiling water into the small teapot. Before Elle had come into his life, he didn't even know what tea was. Now it was a staple. Worse, he actually knew the differences in teas.

"I was doing a drive by her store late one night and found her sitting outside in the back in tears." He couldn't help the embarrassment creeping into his tone and in his mind. He glanced at her as if half expecting her to say something.

Elle remained silent, a funny melting sensation in the vicinity of her heart. This was a side of Jackson she never saw. He was such a loner, and acted as if he didn't want to speak to or get involved with anyone or the community if he could help it, yet she was finding out interesting little stories about him that told her more than he obviously wanted her knowing.

"To make a long story short, she'd invested a great deal of her own money in the art gallery, buying in with Warner and becoming partners with him, but the gallery really suffered the first few months after his arrest and she was behind a little on her own mortgage payments. The store was doing fine, but she was working most of the hours. She couldn't figure out how to pay someone to work the gallery to keep it going, as well as the grocery store and still have enough for her home. Frank's apartment is over the gallery, so as long as she made the payments on that property, his home was safe."

"And you lent her the money?" Elle prompted.

He squirmed. "She wouldn't let me loan it to her." He looked around as if someone might overhear. "She insisted I buy into the grocery store. I didn't want to, but she wouldn't take the money any other way and I couldn't figure out how to save her home."

"You own part of the grocery store?"

He shrugged. "Eat your sandwich."

"How big a part?" Elle persisted.

"Okay, maybe half. I don't know. I just signed whatever the hell Inez drew up. It didn't matter to me and it did to her so I just did it." He confessed it like a sin, in a small rush.

A slow smile lit her eyes. "Jackson Deveau, you have a soft streak in you, don't you?"

"Hell no. Inez's just different. She doesn't have any family and she needs someone looking out for her is all."

"Like Donny Ruttermyer," Elle pointed out with a raised eyebrow.

"Eat your sandwich and stop bugging me." He handed her a glass of milk.

Elle smiled at him over the glass. "You really hate being the good guy."

He scowled at her. "I just don't want you getting the wrong impression about me, that's all. I like my privacy and I think most people are just plain ridiculous."

"Really?"

The little teasing edge to her voice did something to the pit of his belly. In spite of himself, his body stirred, an aching, relentless need that wasn't going away anytime soon. "Really," he confirmed.

He needed a little respite from being in such close proximity to her. Elle wrapped in his mind was intimate, and listening to her voice, soft and melodious, was stroking nerve endings he didn't need stroked. And then there was the brush of her body, her soft curves and glorious skin. He had to stop thinking about her. Right now, and maybe for a long time, she was going to need healing and care, not someone trying to touch her. But it didn't stop him from aching to slide his palm over her skin.

Elle moistened her lips with the tip of her tongue. Jackson was trying so hard to keep from having any sexual thoughts toward her, but the images crept into his mind and washed over her, until a part of her was almost feeding his deepening hunger. She heard the come-on note in her voice, knew she was flirting with him, but the drive in her was becoming stronger.

There was a part of her that knew some of her desire was for the wrong reasons. She loved Jackson and she wanted to know that she could please him, that in spite of everything that happened, he found her attractive. There was a doubt in her mind. It shouldn't have been there when he'd been so supportive and she could read his growing hunger for her, but still, she worried that he would think about the way Stavros had touched her, had forced another man to touch her and might not want to be with her.

"Don't do that, Elle," Jackson's voice was low. Husky. Sexy. "Never doubt that I want you and will always want you."

"This is crazy. You can't have private thoughts and neither can I because the moment you pull away from me, he attacks." She tried not to be upset that he knew, but it was humiliating, just as his knowing everything that happened to her in vivid, brutal detail was humiliating. Just as he knew that Stavros had succeeded in forcing her body to respond to him.

"Elle. Why are you thinking about him?"

"I can't help it. I hate this. I hate wondering if I'm ever going to have a life with you, whether I'm capable of it."

"We'll have a life together, Elle." He flashed a small cocky grin at her, one that turned her heart over and made her stomach do a funny little flip. "Don't count out my skills of persuasion."

"You have skills?"

"A lot of skills."

Elle took a breath. She had skills now, too. She hadn't thought about that aspect, only that she might be afraid to be touched. If she didn't think about being afraid, if she could let herself relax and just go with her natural instincts with Jackson—her gaze dropped to the front of his jeans—she could work magic maybe.

"That's it. Go into the other room," Jackson said.

She could see the bulge in the front of his jeans growing. He turned away from her to busy himself cleaning the counters and pouring the tea for them.

"Well, it's the truth, you know. I did learn some things. Used the right way they might be fun." And Stavros could go straight to hell. Everything he wanted for himself, every service she'd learned at his hands could be given in love instead of forced from her.

"Elle." Jackson's voice was pleading. "Do you have any idea the pictures you're creating in your head?" He glanced over his shoulder and studied her face. "Go sit down before you fall down. You're so pale you look like you're going to faint. I'll bring us some tea and then I'll work on your hair some more."

"Jackson." She waited until he turned back from the tea to look at her. "Stop ordering me around."

He shrugged his shoulders, completely unrepentant. "Someone has to, baby, and it might as well be me. You're a spoiled little thing and stubborn as hell. Besides, I promised Sarah I'd take good care of you and she scares the crap out of me."

Elle sighed and went back to her favorite chair. It was large enough to accommodate a big man and she could curl up in it, drawing up her legs and making herself into a small ball where she felt safe. "What do you think about moving inland?" She tried to keep her voice from trembling, and her mind from giving away the fact that Stavros terrified her.

No matter what Jackson said, she didn't feel strong or even particularly brave. She still felt his hands, powerful and filled with anger, around her throat and on her body. He would never let her go. And now he knew about Jackson. That would only fuel his intense rage. He hadn't wanted any other man near her and the memory of him murdering the guard after forcing her to service him was burned forever into her mind. The guard's face kept changing. Elle on her knees, her mouth sliding over Jackson's shaft, looking up and seeing the gun shoved down his throat. She blinked rapidly to try to stop the burning tears.

"Stop it. I mean it, Elle. If you're going to think about that then let's just get it out in the open. You're terrified that you won't ever be able to give me pleasure by sucking my cock."

She winced at his crude terminology, but that was Jackson. His voice was hard, his dark eyes glittering as he

strode across the room to tower over her. She felt intimidated, threatened, when she stared at the twin columns of
powerful thighs and then up a little higher to the thick
outline of the evidence of his desire. She'd been thinking
about what the taste and feel of him would be like.
Whether she'd be afraid or excited or both. And she'd
aroused him. Now she realized she might have done it on
purpose.

Elle shook her head. "I'm sorry, Jackson. I can't help
but worry about it."

"You worried about kissing me and we kiss just fine,
Elle."

"He took everything away from us."

"He didn't take anything." His hands dropped to the
buttons of his jeans.

Her gaze jumped back to the front of his jeans, mes-
merized as he slowly unbuttoned the fly. Her heart began
to pound and she moistened her lips. "What are you doing?"

"What are *we* doing, you mean." He shoved his jeans
down and stood there, large and even more intimidating
than she remembered from the shower. "We're going to
know one way or another whether or not if you put your
mouth around me, I die."

She swallowed hard and closed her eyes briefly, tightly.
"Jackson, I don't think . . ." He stroked himself, a casual
easy movement not only with his physical body, but with
his mind. She felt the wave of pleasure course through
him, through her. Her body stirred, nerve endings going
on alert. Her mouth watered. She wanted the taste of him.
She wanted to replace every bad memory with Jackson, to
fill herself with him, but this . . . Again she shook her head.

Jackson didn't move. He didn't step forward. He didn't

drag her to her knees by her hair, he simply stood there, his hand circling his heavy erection, and he looked as sexy as sin.

"What if I can't?"

He shrugged as if it didn't matter either way, but it did—it mattered to her. Jackson was everything good in her life, in her soul, and if she couldn't bring him pleasure . . .

He laughed softly. "Silly woman. Pleasure starts in the mind. He can try to tear it from you and force you to accept him by training your body to a certain response, but it will never be what we have together. You give me pleasure already. I can feel your tongue stroking along the shaft, right here."

She followed the line of his finger, with her eyes and then in her mind. She almost tasted him. Warm. Male. Wholly Jackson. Her tongue curled and he jumped.

"See, baby? It's about love, and giving and not about control and serving. I have no doubt that you can bring me all kinds of pleasure anytime you want to."

Elle didn't take her eyes from his shaft and the large mushroom head already glistening with a small pearly drop. She wasn't sickened—just the opposite—she was fascinated. She could feel his breath moving in and out of his lungs, the heat coursing through his body and gathering into his very core. Her hand moved tentatively and she cupped his heavy sac, almost without realizing she'd done so.

Jackson let out his breath in a long rush. Her fingers stroked the velvet texture. He didn't move, standing perfectly still under her exploring hands. Fire streaked through him when she nuzzled him gently, her warm breath exquisite against his sensitive skin. She felt his reaction as if it were her own, his erection engorged and growing heavier and thicker, burning and aching with need now. She let her tongue run over the broad head just to taste him. His entire body shuddered in reaction. His shaft pulsed and jerked. She felt the explosion of ecstasy bursting through his mind.

"Tell me who has the real power, Elle," Jackson whispered, his voice hoarse. "This is all you, giving me pleasure. So fuck him. He can't take anything away from us." He actually stepped back away from her, trembling a little, but determined not to go any further.

Elle didn't want to stop. She wanted to see for herself. She hadn't taken him in her mouth, stroked her tongue over him or felt him slide his shaft down her throat. She needed to know if it was possible without turning the act of giving, of love, into something depraved. Her hands stopped his backward step, fingers digging into his thighs.

"I want to feel you inside my mouth."

"Baby . . ."

Jackson's voice was gentle, but it shook, just a little, telling her he wasn't nearly as composed or in control as he wanted her to believe. It should have scared her, but it filled her with elation. She ran her fingers down his thighs and back up again, stroked the tight sac and leaned forward to nuzzle the base of his shaft.

Jackson's heavy erection jerked and pulsed against her face. He gasped and a groan slipped out. "You don't have to prove anything to me, Elle."

She could see in his steady gaze he meant it. This would have been enough for him, he felt she could build confidence from there, but it wasn't enough for her. He stood there, so sinfully masculine, so giving and tender and she wanted him to feel that explosion of ecstasy again and again. She wanted to be the one to bring it to him. And she wanted to wipe the memory of how it felt to be forced into service rather than lovingly give it.

Her hand circled his wide girth and she slipped to the floor, on her knees in a submissive position. Jackson winced visibly and caught her shoulders. "I'm telling you, baby, this isn't necessary." But it was becoming necessary.

His entire body was on fire. What man didn't love to see his woman on her knees in front of him wanting to give him pleasure? He was afraid to let her, afraid of touching her, afraid of triggering a negative response in her, yet the moment her mouth moved over him, he knew he was lost, caught forever in her spell. The only avenue left to him was to share how she made him feel. He flooded every corner of her mind with sizzling fire.

Kneeling, Elle looked up at him. His face was a mask of desire, lines etched into his skin, white lines around his mouth. His eyes were closed, as he savored the feel of her hands stroking his heavy, thick erection. She felt his lust rising, his desire spreading and it should have scared her, but his love was woven so tightly into every image, into every thought, that she only wanted to feel more, to please him more, to give him—everything.

Hunger invaded, sharp and relentless, a need to feel Jackson, to know the shape and texture of him, to have his shaft filling her mouth, and feel his need of her—for her—filling her mind. She leaned into him, one hand sliding up his inner thigh, the other massaging his balls. She licked along the broad head, a curling sweep of her tongue, teasing him a little, feeling the jerk, the pulse that followed as she licked him like an ice cream cone.

Jackson's jaw was set, his hands balled into two tight fists, a mixture of such longing and restraint incredibly beautiful to her and such a sexy turn-on. He didn't grab her hair and thrust his aching cock deep into her throat, recognizing her need to be in total control, but she could tell she was driving him insane with her sensual exploration, her tongue laving and sliding over and around, exploring the hard length of him. His breath left his lungs in a rush as she skimmed her mouth up and down the heavy shaft.

There was no room for anything in her mind but bringing pleasure to Jackson. She wanted to prolong the time, savor it, revel in the way his body became hers. He gave himself totally to her, but a soft growl escaped, and his jaw tightened more, teeth clenching in an effort to stay under control when his desire and need raged like a wildfire.

Keeping her gaze locked with his, Elle parted her lips and, with infinite slowness, took him in, drawing the flared head into the moist velvet heat of her mouth. His body shuddered again. His hips jerked hard, his muscles going tight under her fingers. Even his balls drew tighter in reaction. She moaned, vibrating around his shaft as he slowly sank his length deeper. She heard the heavy rasp of his breath, hoarse and needy.

Love exploded through his mind, hot and hungry and so mixed with lust she didn't know where one started and the other left off. The two emotions were darkly woven together, inseparable, and she realized she wanted it that way. She wanted this, her gift to him, a treasure she could give him, worshiping his body and not allowing ugliness to touch them. His hunger fed hers. Her mouth tightened around him, tongue teasing and probing while she suckled strongly.

Jackson dropped both hands on her shoulders, fingers tightening. "Baby. You have to stop. We're getting out of hand here." His voice was rough, almost unrecognizable.

Oh, yeah. He liked it. He more than liked it. Triumph swept through her. Elation. She ran her tongue up and down his shaft and over the head, teasing at the underside before drawing him deep again, suckling strongly. She was giving everything to her man, showing him love, and no part of Stavros and his ugliness touched them—or could touch them. A kind of euphoria seized her and she engulfed his shaft with her tight mouth, her tongue working magic.

He gasped. "Elle." This time his voice was demanding. His hips shifted. "Feel what you're doing to me." He could barely get the words out, a groan escaping as he tried to keep his body from reacting. It was impossible with the demand of her hungry mouth.

Elle reveled in his slipping control, the way his heart beat into her mouth with every stroke. He filled her, her lips stretching around his girth, his shaft pulsing and jerking against her tongue as she urged him closer, her hands on his hips. He tasted a mix of hot, sexy passion, love and lust and sinful desire. She rubbed her tongue back and forth all along the rigid length of him, paying particular attention to the sensitive spot just under the flared head where he jumped and fireworks exploded in his head each time she concentrated her attention there.

She kept her gaze locked with his, wanting not only the pleasure in his mind, but to see it on his face, in his eyes. The haze, the opaque glitter, the lust rising, the harsh breathing. Her tongue stroked and caressed, teased and danced, all the while she watched his face and the expressions of pleasure chasing through him. She kept up a firm suction even as she bathed the head of his shaft with her tongue, then slowly pulled back until she was sipping on the very tip, watching him carefully. He swore under his breath, his tone ragged, shredded, his eyes flaring with heat as she, just as slowly, took him deep into her mouth.

"Damn it, Elle. You have to stop." Because he couldn't. He should, but he couldn't. He didn't have that kind of strength, not when her mouth felt like heaven and it had been so damned long and he'd been terrified of losing her. "Son of a bitch, baby, I'm losing it here."

The harsh tone fed her own desire, his entire focus, his whole being centered on her, on how she was making him feel, her tongue a hot velvet lash over the sensitive bundle of nerves on the underside of his shaft. The more she felt his pleasure the more she wanted to give him. She was drowning in the need to give herself wholly to him.

She suckled slow and easy until he was groaning, then switched to fast and hard until his hips pushed deep and he growled a warning.

"You're pushing me over the edge, honey. You have to know I'm not going to be able to stop." Jackson didn't want to stop anymore. She was driving him insane with her hot sexy mouth and the way her gaze locked with his the entire time, wanting him, worshiping his cock, loving him with every single stroke of her tongue.

Elle felt as if she might be going up in flames, burning from the inside out. Her breasts ached, felt swollen and sensitive, and between her legs she was wet, drenched with hot need for him. There was a desperation in her, a drive to exorcise every sexual demon she had. She had to feel Jackson in her body, hot and hard and so real, the love in his mind driving him deep to settle in her and live there, filling her up so no one else could ever touch her.

She felt empty without him, needy and urgent. She had thought she would never feel desire again, never know what it was like to burn for a man, but her body craved Jackson's, her mind twisted and burned through his, frantic for his touch, for his claiming her. She wanted him to replace the feel of depravity with love, cruelty with tenderness.

There was a roaring in her ears, thunder beating through her heart as she felt Jackson's swelling, his heavy erection growing even harder and thicker. His hips picked up a rhythm with her suckling and he pushed forward, deeper. She relaxed her throat to take him deeper. The moment he felt the muscles wrapping tightly around him, his mind went into another place. She felt the burst of pleasure shaking him, taking him over, the fireworks exploding.

Then his hands were gripping her hair and he was thrusting, driving forward and her lungs burned for air and the room tilted and she couldn't breathe, was frozen, helpless, paralyzed, uncertain where she was or what was happening around her. Rage and fear mixed and she began fighting, hitting, kicking as his body erupted, jetting thick ropes of hot seed splashing in her mouth. Her fist landed close to his groin, another struck his thigh.

Jackson jumped back, his legs rubbery, his body drained of strength. He stumbled, caught by the jeans around his ankles and went down hard. He laid there for a moment on his back, trying to breathe when his lungs burned for air and his body was still singing with fire. He wasn't entirely certain what had gone wrong, his brain still wasn't working very well. There was a roaring in his ears that slowly began to fade as he tried to piece together what was going on.

Elle scrambled away from Jackson, crawling backward until she felt the wall behind her. She pressed her hand tight against her mouth, her chest heaving, her throat raw. She realized she was screaming and forced herself to stop. She'd hit him. Hurt him. She'd destroyed something beautiful and priceless and she didn't even remember doing it until she found herself beating at him with her fists.

She had to leave. Run. There was no place to go, nowhere to hide from herself, from what she'd done. And she didn't even know what had happened. She curled into a ball and sobbed, wishing the ground would open up and just take her away.

12

JACKSON slowly sat up, very slowly reaching for his jeans and dragging them up over his hips. Elle was a distance from him, her body in a tight ball, her tangle of hair hiding her face, her weeping heartbreaking. Bomber pushed close to her, trying to comfort her, whining anxiously as he circled, trying to figure out what to do.

"I'm sorry. I'm really sorry." The words were muffled, but Elle just continued to repeat the apology over and over.

Jackson sighed and ran both hands through his hair, taking stock of the situation. He sat there, knees drawn up, looking at Elle, shaking his head. She'd withdrawn from his mind, and when he touched her tentatively, her barriers were strong, strong enough that he figured she'd be able to keep Gratsos out as well. She didn't want anyone sharing her thoughts, her recriminations. He knew Elle, she'd be hating herself and blaming herself for what had happened.

"Elle. Stop crying and sit up." He put demand in his voice.

She moved, flinching a little at his tone.

"I mean it. Sit up and look at me. You wanted to come home with me and now you have to put up with the consequences. Stop crying and look at me."

Elle raised her tear-streaked face, shoved back with her heels, her back pressed tight against the wall and sat, drawing her knees up to partially hide her face, but she was looking at him—and listening and that's what he wanted.

"I'm not dead."

Elle frowned and wiped the tears off her face.

"Look at me." He held up his hands, turned them over and over. "I'm not dead."

"I don't understand."

"You were afraid if I put my cock in your mouth I'd somehow wind up dead. Well I didn't. You gave me pleasure and I'm still alive."

She winced visibly. "But . . ."

"Come on, honey. You wanted to see if I was attracted to you and I was. You wanted to see if you could bring me off and you did." He tilted his head to one side. "Hell, baby, rockets went off. So much so that you knocked me on my ass." He grinned at her.

"That's not funny."

"It's a little funny. Me exploding all over the room and getting tripped by my own jeans around my ankles and landing on my ass. It was a hell of a ride, Elle. You don't do anything by halves."

She was silent. Brooding. Wanting to see it his way, but feeling a failure. "I don't even know what happened. One minute I was having the time of my life, loving what I was doing to you, wanting you with every cell in my body and then everything just went wrong. I don't remember anything but needing to fight." Tears welled up in her eyes again. "I'm sorry. I know I hit you."

"Baby, I wasn't feeling much but the rockets going off. I think you could have used a two-by-four and I wouldn't have felt it."

She pressed her fingers against her eyes. "I wanted you, Jackson. I did."

"I know, honey." His voice was gentle. "It's all going to come right. Have patience with yourself."

She shook her head. "I just want to be normal, is that so much to ask?"

"What the hell is normal?" Jackson said. "Kids all over the world are abused, Elle. Women are raped and kidnapped and forced into sex trafficking. Not just women. Little kids. Boys, teens. It happens everywhere. Parents die. Children are murdered. Illness happens, all sorts of bad things."

He stopped. Took a breath. He had been captured and tortured, but he had a far different background from Elle. He had seen women beaten. He'd seen men murdered. He had grown up thinking his lifestyle was normal. Elle was ill prepared for what had happened to her. She had grown up in a loving family where everyone was safe and protected and parents didn't hit their children. There were no drug deals and no murders. No father coming home drunk and beating her mother.

"Elle, think about it. The scars on your body haven't even begun to fade yet and the worst ones are where you can't see them. They aren't just going to disappear. They're there, a part of you. Sometimes everything will be fine, and other times it won't. That's just going to be a part of our lives. I can live with it. And you'll have to live with my scars. Believe me, baby, I have plenty of them."

Elle sat on the floor, pressing her back against the wall, looking at the man across from her. He was strong and caring and deserved so much more than she felt she had to give him. He wasn't going to walk away from her no matter how rough things got. And maybe the one thing she could give him was living. To keep going even when she felt she was down and out. He could have been ranting at her and she felt she would have deserved it. He'd told her to stop. He'd tried to get her to back off, but she'd wanted him— wanted his desire—wanted that intensity, the love and lust wrapped so tightly together and only for her.

"Are we good, Elle?" Jackson asked.

She knew what he was asking. She wanted to hold him. The love she felt for him was overwhelming when she realized he was giving her acceptance. Just as she was. Flawed. Broken. Uncertain and fragile. Jackson accepted her. She nodded slowly. "We're good."

"I made a mess all over the floor." He looked ruefully around. "We'd better not have any company for a while."

"I didn't think about that. Jonas will probably be showing up to check on us. You know how he is." Elle scrambled to her feet. "We need another shower. And I have to light candles. Do you have any with strong fragrances? Where're your cleaning products?"

He climbed to his feet and reached over to draw her close, pulling her into his arms. "Kiss me, Elle."

She hid her face against his chest.

Jackson took a hold of her chin. "Kiss me."

She turned her mouth up to his. She expected his gentle, coaxing kiss, one filled with tenderness and love. She got something altogether different. Jackson's mouth came down on hers, his tongue sweeping away resistance with masculine demand. He poured sex and sin into her mouth, hot passion and sheer erotic hunger. His arms crushed her, steel bands, his body rock hard, pressed tightly against hers so that she seemed to melt around him, soft flesh, curves pressing deep against heavy muscle.

When he lifted his head, she felt weak with wanting him. Her gaze met his. She took a breath because it felt as if she were drowning. His hands framed her face.

"What do you see when you look at me, Elle?"

His gaze burned over her. Her breath hitched in her throat. She moistened her lips.

"Tell me."

She couldn't look away. She wanted to, because the way he looked at her made her ashamed. There was no mistaking the look in his eyes.

"Say it. Out loud. Say it."

"Love. I see love." Her voice was low, barely above a whisper.

"What else?"

"Hunger." That wasn't beginning to describe the intensity of the desire burning in the depths of his eyes. "Lust."

"For who?" he prompted.

"Me."

"I love you, Elle. I love you with every breath in my body. There's no room for another woman. No thought for one. You're it for me, everything. All the rest, the sex, whoever is after us, the legacy, all of it doesn't matter if you don't feel the same way. You have to love me with every breath you take. I want to know that you do. Before we go any further. Before you decide you're too broken, you have to stand up now and say I'm worth fighting for. Say it now. To me, with me looking you straight in the eye."

She blinked. Opened her mind to him. Flooded him with everything. Her fears. Her shame. Her love and need for him. Her desire for him. She held nothing back and still he kept looking at her. Waiting. Elle took a breath and traced his lips with unsteady fingers. "I love you, Jackson. With every breath in my body. I'm not going to run, not from Stavros and not from myself because you're worth fighting for. *We're* worth fighting for."

A slow smile lit his eyes and he lowered his head again and this time his kiss was infinitely tender.

"What was this about?" she asked when she could talk.

"I just wanted to prove a point."

Her eyebrows shot up. "What point?"

A small satisfied smile softened the hard edge to his mouth. "That we really are fine."

She touched his lips, traced the definition there. "I'm glad you have so much faith in me, Jackson. I'll get it back."

"I know you will. In the meantime, that's what you have me for, to remind you often." He let go of her and then had to steady her when she rocked back on her heels. His grin flashed again. Masculine. Satisfied. "And you can find the candles while I mop up the floor. I've got some of those scented air things Inez brought me a while back. I think she thought my place was too much of a bachelor pad. Look under the sink in the bathroom. Or maybe in the closet. I think in a box on the floor."

"Good place for them." Elle found a small smile hovering as she hurried into the bedroom. "Do you want to take a walk after we shower? I'd like to get outside for a little while."

"You want to walk around town?" Jackson sounded skeptical.

Elle poked her head around the doorway to see him rinsing a mop. "No, silly. There's no fog. I thought we could walk on the beach. You practically live on it. We can't very well avoid it. And Bomber can let us know if anything creepy is around."

Jackson didn't answer so she went in search of the candles. She opened the walk-in closet and was surprised to find it very neat. He had several sheriff uniforms and lots of soft, faded jeans, one suit and a dress shirt. The wall behind the clothes had a security keypad on it. Elle frowned and ran her hand over it.

"Jackson, what do you have locked up in here?"

There was a small silence. She turned her head to find him leaning one hip lazily against the doorjamb. "Weapons. Lots of weapons."

She shook her head. "You're so crazy."

"I'm hopping in the shower. The candles should be in one of those boxes."

He sauntered over to her and reached past her to grab a clean pair of jeans. Elle inhaled his scent. She didn't think they needed candles, she liked the way he smelled, but maybe she was just a bit prejudiced.

He laughed and kissed the tip of her nose. "You are, but I like it."

"Stop reading my mind."

"I can't help it since I'm in it so much."

"Don't flatter yourself."

He laughed again and left her. She stood waiting for the sound of the shower, realizing she had a smile on her face when she honestly believed she'd never smile again. How could Jackson take every bad situation and make it not only bearable, but good? Why hadn't she seen him the way he really was before she'd gone off on her undercover assignment? Would she have taken such a dangerous job?

Elle sighed. Yes. She would have taken it because someone had to stop the monsters of the world. Elle had believed in herself, in her abilities, in her psychic talents and her training. She would have gone even had Jackson asked her not to go. She had set out to prove she didn't need him—that no legacy was going to dictate to her. And she'd wanted him to follow, to come after her, to love her that much. What she hadn't realized was that he did. He loved her enough to let her choose her own way.

She'd seen ownership. She wanted partnership and Jackson might be a man to stand in front of her when he deemed necessary, but he would always be her partner because he respected her right to choose. She closed her eyes for a moment and wrapped him in love from a distance—because she could. Because she needed to.

The warmth and emotion came back tenfold. She felt it in her mind, moving through her body until her veins flowed with it. "Jackson." She breathed his name out loud because she was forbidden to use telepathy and just the thought of that made her smile. She had thought him a dictator because she didn't understand the difference between responsible caring and forcing one's will on another.

Elle pulled out a box and glanced through the contents. Evidently Inez brought Jackson quite a few items he probably had little use for. Little fragrant soaps, scented lotions, potpourri, which she had to laugh over, certain he had no idea what it was, and cuticle cream. The second box contained flashlights and every type of battery possible, all neatly packaged. She closed the lid and pulled out the last box. Pushing the lid off, she went still. Medals.

Lots of medals. Including a purple heart. How did a person get so many medals? What kinds of things had he gone through in order to be so recognized?

The water in the bathroom was turned off. Elle put the lid back on the box and put it carefully away. "I didn't find any candles, Jackson."

"Maybe the candles are in here after all," he said. "Let me look."

Elle went into the bathroom. The door was open and he had a towel loosely wrapped around his hips. His hair was damp and water still beaded on his skin. She had the urge to lick it off, but she wasn't going there again, not after the last disaster. He crouched down, peering under the sink, a small frown on his face.

"Take your pick. I think there's a hundred in here. All scented." He sounded a little disgusted, as if he thought Inez was trying to turn him into a girl.

Elle could barely breathe with the way she felt just looking at him. Every time he moved, muscles rippled subtly beneath his skin. He turned his head and looked at her and she blushed, knowing she hadn't hidden her thoughts from him.

"You're going to get yourself in trouble, woman," he said. "You're playing with fire."

"I don't know what's wrong with me. I can't stop thinking about you."

"We're sharing the same mind, Elle. It's rather hard not to." He shoved several candles into her hands. "Here, go light them while I put on some clothes. Fast."

"I could stand here and watch you."

"You could behave yourself and stop thinking I'm a damned saint." He reached out and touched her face, skimming the pads of his fingers down her cheek before dropping his hand and turning away to look at his bearded jaw in the mirror. "I need to shave."

"Don't. I rather like it. Just trim it up."

"Are you sure? I grew it when I was helping out another county. And then I didn't bother to shave when we went looking for you."

Undercover, he meant. "I like it," she reiterated, and took the candles into the living room and kitchen. Her entire life her family had simply used their talents to light candles from a distance and make tea and pour it. It felt strange to perform the simple act of lighting a candle and pouring herself a cup of tea. At first it made her feel ill, half of a Drake, cut off from her talents, but as she poured a cup of tea for Jackson and added milk, she found herself feeling domestic.

Jackson came in barefoot, wearing just his jeans, moving up behind her and circling her waist with one arm, pulling her back against him as he buried his face against her neck. "Is that for me?"

She leaned against him—against his strength, her body fitting against his perfectly. "I thought I'd bribe you to get the rest of the tangles out of my hair."

He brushed a kiss along her neck and then teased the sensitive lobe of her ear with his tongue. "I'm easy enough to bribe."

Elle let the feeling of comfort and desire wash over her. Instead of being afraid of it, she just absorbed it because Jackson didn't ask anything of her. He just accepted her and that left her able to enjoy being with him, enjoy his touch and the way he ached for her.

"You're easy enough to love."

He grinned at her and took the cup of tea. "I'm going to remember that when we have seven very naughty little girls running around the house and you're trying to get them all settled down for bed."

She followed him to his chair where they could sit and brush out the last of the tangles. "And just what are you going to be doing while I'm chasing them around the house?"

"Stirring them up, of course." He flashed another grin. "I'll be the papa bear, scaring the hell out of them."

Elle sat on the floor in front of him, catching the picture in his mind of Jackson, hands up, fingers curled into claws lumbering around the kitchen chasing screaming little girls with red hair and bright, laughing eyes while she stood there, hands on her hips, trying to look stern. She laughed. "You're so crazy. Of course you'd do that and get them all worked up before bed. And they aren't all going to have red hair."

His hands were gentle as he tugged at the tangles. "Yes, they will. And so will our poor son."

"Whoa. Back up the train. A son?"

"Well you wouldn't want me to have to live in an all-girl household would you?"

"Yes." She turned her head fast and yelped. She glared at him, but he shrugged and turned her head back around, but not before she caught his smirk. "That's *eight* children, Jackson. That's a *lot* of children."

"Well, look at it this way. Ilya and Joley will probably have seven boys. And Jonas won't keep his hands off Hannah and he's competitive, so who knows how many they'll have. We can't be slackers."

She choked. Jackson stiffened and jerked her around to face him. She burst out laughing. "I'm sorry. I didn't mean to scare you. You're just so *bad*. We are not competing with Jonas to see who has the most children. After the first one, I'm certain you're going be shaking in your boots. You'll start thinking about the dating years and freak out on me."

"I have weapons, honey. Lots and lots of weapons. And I know how to use every single one of them. I don't mind scaring the hell out of teenage boys."

Elle was silent for a moment, replaying the picture of Jackson chasing their daughters in her mind. She frowned. "When you were thinking about having little girls running around the house, it was the Drake kitchen, not this one." In fact, the house had been very detailed in his mind, as if he knew the entire layout already.

He sighed. "That's just my personality, Elle. I have an eye for details."

For security he meant. He noticed people as well as things. He could lay out the Drake home exactly from furniture to items on their walls. He had that kind of memory.

"Why the Drake house?"

"It will afford them more protection than just the two of us can give them. I wouldn't mind being in it now, with you. And as the youngest daughter, it's your inheritance. You deserve it and so do our daughters."

She looked around her. Jackson's home felt safe to her. "I like your house, Jackson."

"That's a good thing because we'll be retiring here when we hand over the legacy to our youngest daughter. I think your ancestors are moving in. Have you noticed all the new shrubbery? It wasn't there a couple of days ago."

She turned her head again, earning another sharp tug on her scalp. "Are you certain?"

"I'd know if I planted those vines and flowers, Elle. I'm not really a gardener."

Elle settled back. "If you don't garden, who does? You have one of the prettiest properties around here."

He worked on a particularly difficult tangle until it was smooth. "I think we're done. You can take another shower and condition your hair."

Elle burst out laughing. A real genuine laugh. "Jackson the hairdresser. I swear, you have more surprises than any man I know. I'm betting Jonas doesn't know what conditioner is."

"Maybe not before he married Hannah, but he's sure to know now. She makes all that stuff. I know, because he brings it to me by the boxful."

"You have some of Hannah's conditioner under your sink? You should have told me earlier!" Eagerly, Elle jumped up and rushed into the bathroom.

Jackson picked up his tea, took a sip, and found it too cold to drink. Smiling, he shook his head. He really had wondered how it would be living with Elle. He'd been alone all of his life. His mother and he had been happy for brief times together in the bayou, when she wasn't pining for his father. And there were even a few times he could remember enjoying his father's company, but those times were few and far between. Mostly he was alone, long days and nights, running in the bayou and avoiding the truant officer as much as possible.

He'd kept to himself in the army, getting the job done, until he'd met Jonas. No one avoided Jonas. And through Jonas he'd found Matt. His circle of close friends widened, but Jonas was always the center. They had been through hell together and fought back to back to make it out. Jonas had gotten free, but Jackson had been captured. A fairly routine mission gone wrong and then he was really in hell. Weeks went by and he knew he was lost until he heard a voice.

He would never forget Elle's voice wrapping him up in satin sheets and hope. She'd found a way to light the darkness and give him the strength to make his escape. They'd planned it together, that soft feminine voice and he. She was with him through countless tortures, the pain and anguish, the humiliation of being helpless and having monsters amuse themselves with finding how much a body could withstand without killing it. They tortured him and used his body until he was nothing more than a monster himself with the need for vengeance.

She was there. In his mind. Refusing to leave him even when he begged her to go. She saw him through it all and he had come out on the other side, when he had believed it would be impossible to survive intact. It was the first time in his life he hadn't been alone. It had been the worst— and yet the best time of his life. Elle had shared his mind, shared his pain and his hope and ultimately saved his sanity and life. He had followed Jonas to Sea Haven to meet her.

Though he'd known the moment he met her family that he was nowhere good enough for her, that he came from a place she would never understand, it didn't stop him from wanting her. Still, he hadn't known how, after so many years of being alone, he would feel with her living under the same roof. Now he knew.

He inhaled her scent drifting from his bathroom. The water was off now and he could hear her moving around. He liked the sound of her in his home, the fragrance that was all Elle. For a moment he closed his eyes and savored the idea of her with him. When a man had been alone, adrift, with nothing in his life but duty, he realized finding Elle was a miracle. She was his life. His reasons for honor and code and everything he held on to.

She came into the room, looking so feminine, so heart-breakingly beautiful he ached with emotion. His heart actually hurt and it made him feel like a damned fool, but he still didn't care.

"Are we going for a walk?"

He sighed. He'd been hoping she would forget, but he knew part of it was defiance, thumbing her nose at Gratsos, refusing to allow him to control her life in any way. And he was proud of her for that. He looked outside at the clear sky and let his breath out. He'd keep her from the water's edge and walk high, closer to the dunes than the water.

"Come on, Bomber." He signaled the dog. "Let's go for a walk. My lady wants to go, we go."

She deftly wove her hair into one thick braid that hung to her waist as she followed him outside. At once she lifted her arms to the sky and smiled. "I love the ocean."

"So do I." He couldn't imagine living anywhere but here on the wild northern California coast, with the stormy sea and the close-knit community. Artisans and fishermen coexisted and worked together to keep their environment as pristine and preserved as they were able.

She didn't seem to mind walking along the dunes, up above the expanse of beach, throwing sticks to Bomber and skipping along, free to run when she wanted or just walk beside him, holding his hand as they made their way down the curving coastline.

Birds flew in lazy circles looking for a meal and out at sea two dolphins leapt and chattered. They paused for a moment to watch them.

"Those are Abigail's dolphins," Elle said eagerly. "I know they are. Well, not Abigail's, of course they're wild, but all the same, they actually call to her with a signature whistle. It's very cool. Two males, Boscoe and Kiwi often come by to coax her into swimming with them. Kiwi has that scar on him from when he saved Abbey's life. She'll be happy to know they're back." She glanced toward the Drake house, but from where they were she couldn't see the captain's walk. "I'll bet she's up there now."

"If she was up there, her dolphins wouldn't be out here following us as we take our walk." Jackson was much more practical.

"Unless she sent them to keep an eye on us," Elle said.

Jackson grinned at her. "That's such a Drake thing to do."

She kicked sand at him and threw driftwood down the beach for Bomber. "You mean everyone doesn't have dolphins to watch over them?"

"Not ones they can communicate with."

"Abigail can talk to any animal," Elle said.

"Can you?"

She shrugged. "Not like she can. I can a bit. I have all the talents, but because I have so many I haven't developed them all to their full potential. I chose the things I needed to use the most and worked on them. Everything takes practice and work. It's not automatic."

"But you could connect on some level with Bomber?"

She frowned, realizing he wasn't just making conversation. "I might be able to. Why? What are you thinking?"

He took the stick from the dog and threw it again, watching as Bomber happily chased it. Bomber had a strong prey drive and would play for hours with his favorite work toy, a ball on a rope that Jackson used to keep him in good shape along with his other training. "Just that if you can connect with Bomber, and he can sense a psychic attack, we might be able to strike back."

Elle stopped. Overhead seagulls skimmed over the water, throwing dancing shadows along the sand. The wind carried the sound of the dolphins chattering back and forth as they played in the water. "How?"

"I haven't figured that part out yet, Elle, but so far, he's been having things his own way, mostly because you need to heal. In another day, you'll be strong enough to let Kate and maybe even Libby really work on you. Once you're at full strength, I'm certain when I'm not in your mind, you'll be strong enough to keep him out, but when we're together, we'll be able to attack him if he comes at you."

Elle bit down on her lip as they began walking again. "You have a lot of faith in me."

"I keep telling you, you're down, baby, you're not out."

She inhaled the scent of the sea and once more slipped her hand into his. "I love Sea Haven, Jackson. I love everything about it."

"When do you want to move back home?"

She glanced at him quickly. "Not yet. Give me a little more time. I want to make certain I'm strong enough that when all my sisters are around me, I don't accidently slip up and let them feel what I'm feeling. My emotions are all over the place. Sometimes I feel like I've cried so many tears I don't have any left. And other times I want to fight someone, or just scream." She took a deep breath, her fingers tightening around his. "I'm afraid to be without you, Jackson." She made the admission in a low voice. "I can't remember ever being really afraid in my entire life."

"I'm still afraid to be without you," he said, "but probably not for the same reasons."

In the distance a couple walked toward them, just coming around the rocks, their footprints in the wet sand. When they spotted Jackson and Elle, they changed course to intercept them, although they walked at the same slow, leisurely pace.

"What does that mean?"

"It means sometimes I want to take a gun and shoot people I think don't deserve to live. Like Gratsos. And maybe without you in my life, I'd do it."

"Jackson the badass." She smiled at him. "You're not at all like you think you are."

He brought her hand up to his mouth, kissing her knuckles. "You keep thinking that, honey. I don't mind."

The couple approached them as they walked along the dunes, the sand soft under their feet. As they neared them, Elle recognized Clyde and Marie Darden. Clyde was well-known for his beautiful garden and his entries in the fair each year. He was fiercely proud of his hybrid flowers and guarded his gardening secrets carefully. More than once, as a child, Elle had gotten in trouble for taking a dare to climb over the fence and walk through Mr. Darden's garden. She'd even picked one of his prized flowers one time. She'd really gotten in trouble for that. Darden had marched her home to her father, threatening to box her ears every step of the way.

She gripped Jackson's hand tighter as the couple came straight up to them, blocking their way, obviously meaning to talk. Jackson stopped, drawing Elle under the protection of his shoulder.

"Clyde. Marie. How are you?" Jackson asked, shocking her. No one called the Dardens by anything other than Mr. and Mrs. Darden. Mr. Darden demanded respect at all times.

"Wonderful, thank you, Jackson," Mr. Darden said. "I see you have our girl home at last. We kept our ribbon on the tree for you the entire time you were gone, Elle."

Mrs. Darden nodded. "We had a candle lit in the window, too. And we prayed for you, for your safe return."

"Thank you," Elle said. "Everyone's been so kind."

"If there's anything we can do for you, Elle," Mr. Darden said. "Just let us know. Marie makes incredible chicken soup."

Mrs. Darden nodded, her face brightening. "What a wonderful idea, Clyde. I'll bring some by for you, Elle, for both of you."

"We'd love that," Jackson said before Elle could respond. "Your soup saved the day for me when I was getting that cold."

Elle looked up at his face, but he was carefully avoiding her gaze. Now she knew who did Jackson's gardening for him. No wonder he had such a beautiful yard with Mr. Darden at the helm. The man could grow anything anywhere and it would blossom and thrive.

Mrs. Darden beamed. "You're such a sweet boy, Jackson. Thank you for the cord of wood. It really helped us when the electricity went out."

Jackson frowned. "I thought you had the generator."

The Dardens exchanged a long look. "I should have told you," Mr. Darden said, "but you were so worried about our Elle. Something went wrong with it and it went out completely in that last storm."

Mrs. Darden patted Jackson's arm. "We knew you'd worry about us, so we didn't tell you. The fireplace kept us warm enough."

"How did you cook?"

"We ate sandwiches, dear," Mrs. Darden said. "The electricity was only off for a couple of days."

"Three days," Jackson corrected. "I'll come by later and take a look at the generator."

"If you insist," Mr. Darden said. "And while you're there, a board needs replacing on the stairs. Mrs. Darden nearly fell through it the other day."

"On the back stairs?" Jackson sounded stern. "I told you those stairs had to be replaced and you told me Lance was going to do it."

"Lance hasn't gotten around to it," Mrs. Darden said. "We asked him right after you told us, but he keeps pushing the date back. I think he may be ill."

Elle knew that was code for Lance having fallen off the wagon. He was a binge drinker and went months without drinking, but then would stay drunk for weeks on end.

"I'll take care of it," Jackson said. "Next time call me right away. You can't take chances with falling."

Mr. Darden nodded. "In the old days, I would have done it myself."

"Oh yes, dear," Mrs. Darden agreed, looking up at her husband with shining eyes. "You always did the household repairs. Even the roof," she explained proudly.

"Well there's no need for that," Jackson said. "Marie always supplies me with soup and takes care of me when I'm sick. I can do something in return. That way I don't feel bad that she has to come by and feed me."

"Now, Jackson," Mrs. Darden scolded, as if he was a young boy. "You're hardly ever ill and I don't mind at all."

Bomber suddenly gave a short bark, his body going still, facing out toward the sea. Goose bumps rose on Elle's arms as she saw the dog's ears go forward and his eyes focus beyond the waves. Slowly, afraid to look, she turned her head. Jackson had already moved, sliding his body easily between her and the sea. He caught Mrs. Darden's elbow and began urging her to walk up toward the dunes.

The wind shifted and blew toward them. Out at sea, the fog had begun to gather, a dark gray mass that thickened as she watched it.

"Jackson."

"I see it, baby. Don't panic on me."

"What's wrong, Jackson?" Mr. Darden asked, surprising Elle again. He glanced at the dog, at Elle's pale face and then out to the sea. "I don't like the look of that fog."

He didn't look upset, but rather protective, falling in step on the other side of her, as if he, too, was shielding her from the sea. The seagulls overhead screamed. Out in the waves, the two dolphins leapt in the air and somersaulted, smacking the water hard to draw attention. Both rose up on their tales, speeding backward and whistling in agitation before plunging back beneath the water.

"Where's your car, Clyde?" Jackson asked.

Mr. Darden glanced toward the road. "About a quarter mile back. It was such a lovely day we thought we'd walk to your house and say hello to Elle and then walk back."

"We brought you a card, dear," Mrs. Darden added.

"Thank you," Elle said, trying not to sound nervous. "That was so thoughtful of you."

"Maybe we should all just get home," Jackson said, sounding like the authoritative deputy. "The fog can get pretty bad and I'd rather you were safe. You know how thick it can get and I wouldn't want you driving in it."

"Do you think it's going to get that bad?" Mrs. Darden asked, looking out at the sea, obviously disappointed that the weather might spoil her visit. "I looked at the forecast and it didn't say fog."

"Elle needs to rest anyway. I'll bring her with me when I come to look at the generator," he added.

The couple beamed and quickly agreed. Jackson watched them until they were safely around the bend and out of sight before he urged Bomber and Elle toward the house.

13

THE fog stayed where it had gathered a distance offshore for most of the evening. It was dark and just hung in the sky like a heavy pall in spite of the wind picking up. Jackson kept Elle indoors, forcing her to play cards with him and crowing when he thoroughly trounced her.

"I thought you were supposed to be so good at this," he teased.

"Yeah, well, I'm not a professional card shark. Sheesh. What did you do? Go to school for this? No one wins every single hand at gin rummy."

"I do," he said with a little smirk. "I made a lot of money playing most card games in the army."

"And now you own a grocery store."

He scowled at her. "You'd better not mention that to anyone. Or bring it up again. It's embarrassing. And Inez just won't stop with the groceries. She brings me all sorts of things." He sounded exasperated. "I tell her not to, but she doesn't listen. I can't eat all that food."

"What do you do with it?"

He shrugged, his scowl deepening. "I don't know."

Her eyebrow shot up and amusement crept into her expression. "Does it find its way to the Dardens?"

"Elle," he said her name in warning, jumped up and busied himself pouring them both a cup of tea. Adding milk, he carried a small tray of cookies to the table and set them in front of her.

"You make cookies, too? Is there anything you don't do?"

Another faint flush spread up his neck as he seated himself opposite her. "I didn't make the damn things. But they're good so eat them. You're still too thin."

"I'm just right." But she took a cookie anyway. "These are great. Who did make them?"

He sighed. "Marie did."

Elle's grin widened. "With the ingredients you brought her from the groceries Inez brings you? You lead a very complicated life, don't you?"

"I'm a very complicated man." He took a cautious sip of tea and tried to look casual.

Elle burst out laughing. "You've got this entire circle of people you look after. All this time, all of us thought you were such a loner, but you're surrounded by people."

His scowl was back. "I'm a deputy. I'm supposed to help people when they need it."

"I thought your job was to shoot bad guys."

"Well, that, too. Technically, I'm supposed to arrest them. Jonas frowns on us shooting people, but once in a while, just to stay in practice . . ."

She laughed again, amazed that he could make her do so when the fog hung heavy out the window and the dog paced restlessly up and down, keeping a wary eye on the fog. Bomber could sense the psychic energy looking for a target, and yet Jackson had still managed to distract her. She leaned across the table. "How in the world did you get so involved with these people?"

He shrugged. "People rarely check on the elderly in bad weather and long cold spells. Sometimes they don't have heat or they can't drive their cars to get to the store, or they don't have a car and they can't walk. I just like to check on them and make certain everything is going fine for them. No big deal."

She sat back, regarding him with shining eyes. Jackson looked away from her. "Don't look at me like that."

"Like what?"

"Like I'm a fucking saint, Elle. I'm not."

"Don't worry, until you stop using the 'F' word, no one is going to mistake you for a saint."

He grinned at her. "You get that little schoolmarm tone in your voice whenever you scold me."

"You like it," she said.

"It's cute."

She made a face at him. "Just for that I'm telling my sisters you're 'good-deed Jackson.' They'll never let you hear the end of it."

He groaned. "You wouldn't dare."

The smile faded from Elle's face. She froze, turning her head in the direction of the Drake house. She suddenly leapt to her feet, nearly knocking over her teacup. Jackson, uncertain what was happening, rose to his feet as well, reaching for the gun in his holdout holster. Elle's face had gone pale and her eyes were enormous. She looked wildly around the house and then started for the door.

Jackson was there before her, inserting his large, immovable frame between her and the exit. "Talk to me, baby. What's wrong?"

"I don't know." She frowned and shoved a hand over her silky hair in agitation, her expression far away, eyes a little fey. "Abbey. She's upset. She's heading into . . ." She looked over his shoulder toward the spreading gray mass, now closer to shore. *"That."*

"Are you certain?"

Her gaze came back to his face and this time she looked annoyed. "Of course I'm certain. She's my sister. We're all tied together. Can't you feel her, too? Through me?"

Jackson allowed himself further into Elle's mind and Abigail's alarm was wrenching. She was in a near state of panic. The phone jarred both of them. "Get it, Elle."

"But Abbey may need me."

"Get the phone. I'll go to Abbey." He already knew exactly what Abigail was doing and no way was he allowing Elle anywhere near the sea. "That will be Aleksandr. Tell him to get over here now and guard your ass. He was working out near Fort Bragg." He gave her a small shove toward the phone and sprinted for his bedroom.

When he returned minutes later, he was in his wet suit, flippers in hand, his scuba gear and diving belt on his shoulder. "I want you in the house. Do you understand me? You stay inside with the door closed and the dog with you. Swear it to me, Elle, or I don't go."

"But I should—"

"Swear it to me, damn it," he said, cutting her off.

Abigail's distress increased and both of them could see her now. She flashed past the house running toward the ocean.

"I won't leave the house, I promise. Help her, Jackson."

Jackson caught the nape of her neck, kissed her hard and turned and ran outside. "Abbey, wait. I'm getting the boat. It will take less time."

Abbey was at the water's edge, belting on her tank. "Hurry, Jackson. Boscoe's caught in a net, or something. He's going to drown."

Jackson leapt into his old truck and fired up the engine. He launched the dory into the surf within minutes. Abbey was in tears, looking out to sea. The engine started on the second pull and they sped off.

"Thank you. I wasn't certain how I'd get back. He's a distance out."

He didn't give her a lecture. She'd been around the sea all of her life. It was growing dark. The wind had picked up and even with the Drakes' help, she couldn't fight a stormy sea at night. Not to mention, and he wasn't thrilled with the idea, the bigger predators that came out this time of night to feed.

The dory cut through the surf, bumping as he increased speed. Abbey looked out toward deeper waters, whistling every now and then. He could barely hear over the engine, but she directed him, following the instructions of Kiwi, the other male bottlenose, as he emitted a series of squeaks and clicks. It was unusual that the male dolphins and their group spent so much time near Sea Haven, as it was common for them to swim up to fifty miles in a day, yet they "hung out" to be close to Abigail.

He slowed the dory when she signaled to him and turned on the spotlight, directing it into the muddy waters below. "Try to use as little psychic energy as possible, Abbey," he cautioned. "Gratsos is out here, riding in the fog, and he's seeking a target again."

"I don't care about that. I'm going in."

"Wait!" He said it sharply, catching her shoulder and holding her in spite of her efforts to somersault into the water. "We go together and we go tied together. The water

is going to be very cold, very dark and now, more dangerous than ever, and we have no idea what we're going to
find down there." He shoved a webbed harness for her
ankle at her. "Put it on."

"I have a knife already." She touched her belt.

"Fucking put it on, Abbey. We aren't taking any
chances."

A brief smile flashed at him as Abbey strapped the
harness to her leg so the knife fit snugly. "You have such a
foul mouth, Jackson. Wait until all your little girls talk
like that." She accepted the end of the six foot length of
rope and clipped it to her belt so they were loosely tied
together.

Kiwi leapt from the water, dousing them both, his head
bobbing as he scolded Abbey, urging her to hurry. His
body slammed back into the water and he circled the
boat.

Jackson thrust a light into her hand, watched as she put
in her mouthpiece and motioned to her to go in. He followed right behind her. The dolphin slipped close, brushing their bodies once, twice and then angled so Abbey
could reach out and catch his fin. He dove, taking her with
him. Jackson felt the pull of the rope and swam down, following. The dolphin was incredibly strong and fast, dragging them both through the sea, deeper and deeper.

It was dark and the beam from their lights barely cut
through the murky water. The world was cold and foreign, instead of the way Jackson usually saw it when he
dove. There was a feeling of dread, of danger building
and twice Abbey looked back at him and he knew she
was feeling it as well. Jackson allowed the dolphin to do
the work, looking around below and above, doing his
best to provide a guardian for Abigail in the hopes of see-

ing anything deadly coming before it actually reached them.

The dolphin swam out from under Abbey abruptly and circled a struggling mass. Boscoe, tangled in a fisherman's net, was bleeding from his nose and fins as he fought to free himself. Jackson pulled his knife out while Abbey put her hands on the dolphin, calming him.

He felt a small surge of energy in the water, almost electric, as she communicated with the animal and knew they were in real trouble now. By using psychic energy to keep the dolphin calm while he slashed and cut through the thick netting, she was calling down another psychic attack on them. He had no idea what form it would take, but they were extremely vulnerable there in the cold ocean at night. Abbey began helping him, although it took a great deal of strength to cut through the netting. They circled the dolphin as fast as possible, pulling the net away from him as they went.

It seemed to take a long time—too long—with the dark water surrounding them and the dolphin occasionally thrashing out of desperation in spite of Abigail's reassurances. There was no telling how long he'd been fighting and he was exhausted and needed air. The moment he was free, he surged toward the surface, Kiwi abandoning them to help Boscoe. Jackson kept the knife in his hand and signaled to Abigail to go to the surface.

She nodded and began to swim, kicking strongly in an effort to hurry. Jackson stayed right behind her, and he felt the first tug on his body, a powerful flow of water backwashing against the tide. Swearing to himself, he used his strength to try to keep them going in the direction they wanted—up—but the wash of water caught them both and tumbled them much like a spinning washing machine.

Jackson flung out his arms in an effort to snag Abigail and bring her in close to him, to help protect her from the debris churning with them, but he could only feel her suit as she tumbled beneath him toward the sea floor. His body smashed against the ocean floor. He rolled over and over, his tank scraping, the force of the water trying to strip his body of all gear. He made himself relax, letting the water take him, feeling the pull of the rope anchoring him to Abigail. He knew with the force of the turbulence, the rope could snap.

Jackson pushed off the bottom and began to swim perpendicular to the shore. It was difficult to figure out exactly where he was when he'd been spinning and tumbling. The rope stretched taut and he applied a little pressure, knowing Abbey was far more familiar with the sea and its dangers than most people. She was a marine biologist and spent a great deal of her time underwater. There wouldn't be any panicking for Abigail.

He felt the rope slacken and immediately she brushed his leg, indicating she was swimming with him. They should have been able to pull out of the undertow, but another powerful backwash caught them again. Jackson had the impression of a bowler striking, using the hidden current to take them down and under. They rolled together this time, Jackson and Abigail gripping each other's arms and thighs to try to lessen the damage. Again he pushed off the floor, using the strength of his legs. There were sometimes rip currents aplenty along the northern coastline, but not this—not an undertow. Gratsos had attacked.

Something large and heavy bumped them. He drew away, but Abigail reached out eagerly. He realized the dolphin was back and she'd seized the fin. Kiwi used his powerful body to drag them out of the undertow and back up toward the surface. The water sucked at them for a moment and then they were swimming free.

It seemed to take forever to rise to the surface. When he broke through the water and looked around, the dory was a good distance away and the wind had kicked up the waves to several feet high. They began to swim in the trough between waves. Something brushed his hand as he pulled on a downstroke. Abigail gasped.

"Look out, Jackson. Oh my God. Stay still for a moment."

He did so, swiveling around, trying to make out what had upset her. All around them, like a forest of giant mushrooms, jellyfish floated up from the bottom, hundreds of them. He'd never seen them so large. He'd been in the ocean often enough to see wide populations of jellyfish moving through the water, but none like these. The pink mushroom caps were large, like strange monsters of the deep. Tentacles stretched out in the water from so many jellyfish moving together, the long feelers created a forest of toxic limbs reaching for anything unsuspecting in their path.

"Don't touch the tentacles," Abbey cautioned.

"How the hell am I supposed to do that?" Jackson demanded, turning around, searching for a way through the dense field. "What are these things?"

"Jellyfish, an entire army of them. I swear they're trying to find us, and they aren't supposed to do that."

"Fucking tell that to them, Abbey, because they don't seem to know it. How are we getting out of here?"

They tried not to move because the slightest wiggle of an arm or leg brought the creatures closer, as if the movement of their bodies drew attention to them.

"Do you feel the energy surrounding them?" Abigail asked.

Waves splashed over him and he nearly choked. When he could, he shook his head carefully. "No. But if there's psychic energy it has to be that bastard coming at us."

"We have no choice but to fight fire with fire," she said.

"Not Elle, Abbey. She'll burn herself out. She needs to rest."

"The rest of us don't. And he's not getting our sister— or you." Abigail splashed water with the flat of her hand in disgust, directing it away from them and watching the jellyfish swarm where the water fell. "Elle could totally kick this amateur's ass if she was at full strength."

They bobbed in the waves, trying not to move too much. "So how do we get out of here, Abbey? You're the expert."

"We can't go below, they're coming up from below us. He's set some sort of a trap, but as you can see, it's not specific toward us. He's using the traces of psychic energy to trigger his attacks. I was using it on Boscoe, both to calm him and to heal him. I didn't want him getting infections." It was difficult to talk and both were getting tired, trying to let the waves come and go without throwing them around. Abbey looked toward her home.

Almost at once Jackson could feel a subtle difference in the wind. It shifted direction, a soft ruffling rather than a roar, carrying a sweet feminine voice with it. Joley Drake. Superstar, with a voice like a siren's, calling to the jellyfish, beckoning them across the water. A spell singer, Joley could persuade anything or anyone with her voice. It drifted like kelp, peaceful and serene, melodious and haunting, and all the while the strains of melody whispered and cajoled the jellyfish, summoning them to her.

Tentacles lashed the water, the current of psychic energy exploding in answer to Joley's song, but the huge group of jellyfish moved away from Abigail and Jackson, toward Joley's voice, propelled by their need to answer. Jackson and Abbey waited for the migration to pass and then began to swim back to the dory.

Jackson had taken two strokes through the water, with Abigail on his left side, when suddenly her body jerked hard, the rope between them pulling taut. She clenched her fist and began beating on something unseen beneath the water, striking it over and over, before gasping and going under, her eyes looking at him, desperation and horror on her face. Jackson shoved his mouthpiece into his mouth and dove with her, following her body down below the surface.

The water was dark, and he could barely make out a massive fin and the torpedo-shaped body, a single, round eye and jaws clamped around Abbey's leg, her fist punching at its nose and eyes. The water churned and clouded more, obscuring his vision.

Kicking strongly, Jackson tried to turn, realizing the shark had released Abbey and had disappeared from his sight. He turned to see a huge gaping mouth, the double rows of teeth looking like a circular saw, wicked and primitive and far too massive to avoid. It charged past Jackson and hit Abbey again, hard enough that her body jerked and was propelled forward. He saw her hand flash as the water erupted into a churning mass of bubbles and debris, once again obscuring his vision.

His body was drawn through the water rapidly, pulled by the rope tying him to Abbey. He swam faster, trying to catch up, knife in his fist as he approached the huge shark, trying to get around it to the head. The jaws were clamped around Abbey's back and stomach, the metal tank crushed in its mouth, Abbey trying to fight as he came up on its left side. He sank the knife deep into the animal's eye and it reared its head back, opening the wide jaws to release Abigail.

Another large body shot past him and rammed the shark in the belly from underneath and Jackson caught Abbey around the waist and shoved his airpiece in her mouth as he kicked away from the shark. A second dolphin took up the attack, slamming hard into the shark's belly. As soon as it streaked away, a third and then a fourth took up the fight, the dolphins protecting Abbey, playing a dangerous game of tag team to give them time to escape.

Jackson didn't waste the precious moments the dolphins gave them. He swam hard, taking Abigail with him, pausing only to take a breath as he angled their escape toward the dory. He tried to keep them in the trough between the waves, and stay out of Gratsos hidden traps of psychic energy.

At the dory it took several tries with both of them using full strength to get Abbey out of the water. Jackson wanted his body completely out, but with his gear and his strength nearly gone, it was a fight to get himself in the boat. In the end he had to remove his weight belt and then his tank. Even then it took him several attempts before he managed to drag himself inside.

"Are you all right," he asked as he started the engine. "How bad is it?" He didn't want to take off her suit to look. The tight compression would help slow any bleeding.

Abigail, half sitting and half stretched out, gave a high-pitched whistle to signal to the dolphins to get out of the area before replying. "I was lucky. It was a juvenile Great White, and by the way, attacks from juveniles are very rare. I've only heard of it a couple of times. Now I'm wondering if something disturbed it, if Gratsos or someone like him used the sea to set psychic traps."

"Tell me how bad, Abbey," Jackson insisted as he started up the dory.

Abigail took a breath and forced herself to look at her body. There was a gash on one arm that would require stitches. Along her thigh she had quite a laceration, much larger than the one on her arm, but again, not life-threatening. She looked up at him. "I think he got his mouth around the tank when he grabbed me and there's a burning sensation, a pressure in my abdomen, and there're tears in my suit with blood on it, so I honestly don't know how bad that one is, but the others aren't so bad."

"Aleksandr is going to be one pissed-off Russian."

She sighed. "I know. He'll make me go to the hospital even though Libby could probably take care of everything at home."

The dory flew over the waves back toward shore. Around them, the fog thickened and rolled, darkening in color, blotting out all light until the shore itself disappeared. Jackson swore under his breath. Large boulders rose out of the sea all around them and visibility had just gone to zero. He could hear Abigail's breath coming in small gasps and, although she'd assured him she wasn't hurt too badly, he wasn't as certain and wanted to get her to a hospital as soon as possible.

He slowed the dory, a chill going down his spine at the same time Abbey hissed low. Their eyes met and then both began to try to pierce the veil of darkness closing in around them for the next threat. They both felt it, something malevolent stalking them, riding on the hidden current just on the surface of the water. The wind began to pick up, pushing the waves higher, so that around them the sea began to churn violently.

"Hold on, Abbey," Jackson said grimly, "the bastard's coming at us again."

"I'm fine," Abigail assured him. "Don't worry about me."

Mostly he was worried that Elle would try to help them and Gratsos would recognize her psychic energy. It concerned him that first Hannah and then Abigail had been attacked after using psychic energy. That had to be the trigger for the attacks, and the way they used their talents had to have some of Elle's signature stamped on it. Was Gratsos aware that he was actually attacking Elle's family members? He'd told her he'd kill everyone she loved unless she came back to him and Jackson had no doubt the man was vicious enough to try to carry out his threat if he found her and no one stopped him.

"Are your sisters connected to you right now?"

"Yes, of course."

"So they know about the shark attack?"

"Yes. And they know we're being stalked."

"Don't answer them. Don't in any way use psychic energy until we're safe on shore."

Abigail turned her head toward a roaring sound to their left as a waterspout shot up, whirling violently, the long tube spinning and picking up strength as it pulled more and more of the water around it into the tall column. Jackson threw the dory in reverse in an effort to avoid running into the water twister just as a second burst from the water. The water tossed the little boat from side to side as the twister erupted around them as if hunting prey.

From the direction of the Drake family home came a fierce blast of wind that raced over their heads and met the turbulent cyclones head-on, pushing the columns of water back and away from the dory, clearing out a section of fog around the boat. Jackson didn't hesitate, trusting the Drake women as he took the boat into the gap. The wind continued, blowing everything in its path out of its way, forcing the twisters to back up and dispersing the fog enough to give Jackson a clear line toward shore.

Lights sprang up along the beach, several high-powered spotlights pointing toward the sea, beckoning Jackson in, and he knew Elle and Aleksandr had rigged the lights to try to pierce the thick veil of fog. Using the bright lights as a beacon, he headed home, not slowing when first one, then another waterspout whirled close to them. The ferocious wind hit just in front of the boat, forcing the cyclone away from them and continued to keep the path clear.

He ran the dory onto the beach as Aleksandr rushed toward them. The Russian lifted Abigail into his arms, cradling her tight against his chest, his face a mask of fury as he whirled around and headed back to the waiting ambulance, ignoring Abigail's protest every step of the way.

Jackson pulled the dory higher, well aware of the cyclones held at bay by the Drakes, but they were losing energy and the wind was fading. He heard Bomber barking ferociously and his heart jumped.

"Stay back, Elle. Get the hell away from the sea. Go indoors, I'll be there in a minute," he used his no nonsense voice, praying she'd listen. One never knew with Elle and she didn't take to orders well.

"Behind you, Jackson," Elle yelled.

He knew better than to turn his back on the ocean, but he'd been focused on her and the sleeper wave came roaring at him, looking like a twenty-foot wall of water. The cyclones had merged together and Gratsos was making his last brutal attack.

Jackson's heart sank. He had no chance, the wave would sweep him out to sea and he was already too exhausted to successfully fight it. He just stood waiting for it to consume him.

Elle ran forward, her arms up in the air, her face turned toward the sky, palms out. She chanted something the wind whipped up and away so he couldn't hear, but they were connected, welded mind to mind, and he felt power move in her, through her, a burst of energy so strong he expected the night to light up. He felt the impact of her rage, a well erupting, an explosion of pent-up violent energy slamming into the wall of water with the force of a volcano.

Her energy was red-hot and the air hissed and sizzled up and down the beach. Lightning forked in the sky. The wave rocketed upward, a solid sheet of superheated water that burst into the fog, spread like wildfire, consuming everything in its path, so that overhead, great mushroom clouds streaked upward. Flames of red and orange licked along the edges and rolled like fireballs inside the churning mass, to rain back over the sea, dropping liquid fire into the depths to find the hidden current beneath the water and channel the ferocious energy seeking retaliation.

The fog was gone as if it had never been, the sky clear with stars scattered everywhere. Silence settled along with the flames and only the sound of the waves remained, a steady ebbing and flowing that brought a sense of peace with it. Elle's knees caved and she went down, face first into the sand. Bomber rushed to Jackson, then turned back toward Elle, anxious, uncertain which one to go to.

Jackson stood swaying beside the dory, one hand on the boat's side to steady himself. He looked around him, dazed, exhausted, trying to find the strength to move, to get to Elle. The water was calm, the beach peaceful, and other than Abbey's steel tank and diving belt having teeth marks, there was little evidence of the fight for their lives.

"Elle?" He staggered his way up to her and sank into the sand beside her.

Elle rolled over and stared up at him. There was blood trickling from her ear and the side of her mouth. "You scared me again, Jackson," she whispered.

"You disobeyed me again." He stretched out beside her, reaching out an arm to scoop her up so her head was pillowed on his chest and her body was tight against his. "Very inappropriate behavior for the woman of a bad-ass."

"I just saved your bad ass, buddy," she pointed out.

"Yes, you did. Remind me to thank you properly later."

"Stavros really made me angry this time."

He turned his head and looked down at her pale face. "I've got to tell you, honey, when you're pissed off, you're hot as hell. That fire in the sky was a major turn-on for me. If I wasn't so damned tired, I'd be showing you just how much." Very gently he wiped the blood from her face with his hand. "Do you have any idea how bad Abbey is? She said she was all right, but there was blood and, although she said it was a juvenile, it looked like a big son of a bitch to me."

Elle pressed her face closer to him. "Thank you for saving her."

"I wish I could take the credit. It was her dolphins. They came back to help at just the right time."

"Abbey's getting stitches in her arm, not very many, but the gash on her leg requires a lot more. Maybe twenty or so." Elle frowned, concentrating for a moment, listening to the flow of information from her sisters. "Her abdomen is very bruised and she's got a few gashes there as well, but they think something, possibly her diving belt, saved her."

"It has teeth marks on it."

Elle shivered and pressed closer. "You're all wet."

"And too tired to do anything about it." He brushed kisses over her face. "I suppose we could try crawling back to the house." He was silent a moment. "Do you remember your idea about moving inland, away from water? I'm beginning to think it might just be a good idea after all." He tipped her chin up until her gaze met his, the brief spurt of amusement fading from his eyes. "He isn't going to stop, you know."

She blinked, her eyes going from sea-green to a mystic emerald. "I know." She sighed softly, her fingers sliding over his wet suit, brushing little strokes over him, reassuring herself he was alive and well. "I'll call Dane tomorrow and report in. Maybe we can put our heads together and come up with an idea for a sting operation. There has to be a way to catch him, to get enough evidence he can't make go away. Something very public."

He was silent for a moment, hesitating before he told her what he knew to be the truth. "He won't stop coming after you, Elle, not even from prison." He was trying to tell her, without saying the words aloud, that he knew what had to be done.

"Jackson, he isn't worth it."

"*You're* worth it to me, baby, more than worth it. I can't let that son of a bitch terrorize you for the rest of your life."

"You can't let him force you to do something you know is wrong. Murder is wrong."

"We'll have to agree to disagree over what executing him would be called."

Elle closed her eyes. "This has been a really bad day."

"Evening," he corrected.

She put her head up to look at him. "What?"

"It was a good day, honey. I enjoyed every minute with you. Not so much with your sister though. I think I'll skip swimming with Abbey next time she wants to go diving."

Elle laughed softly and snuggled closer. "I think we're going to have to learn teleportation. Wouldn't that be cool?"

His hand came up to rest in her hair, massaging her scalp. "You're scary enough, Elle. You don't need to be able to walk on water or go through walls."

"Don't you know Sarah's the one who walks on water?"

His gaze widened. "Don't tell me things like that."

"When Damon first came to town, he heard all sorts of rumors about Sarah. He was very grumpy apparently and all the rumors annoyed him so he made up one of his own and it spread through the village like wildfire."

Jackson laughed. "I can see Damon doing that." He rolled over. "Can you make it into the house?"

"It looks a long way away."

"Tomorrow, Kate is going to try to heal your talent."

She shook her head and forced her exhausted body into a sitting position. The moment she moved, her head felt as if it exploded. They were so closely tied together Jackson grabbed his own head and bent nearly double in an attempt to combat the pain and dizziness. His gaze met hers.

"Don't go all stubborn on me, Elle. We can't take any more chances on you burning out completely. You keep this up and you could end up damaged permanently. Until we get out from under Gratsos and his attacks, you're going to keep using your abilities and your head is a ticking time bomb. You know it is."

"I don't want it to be a ticking time bomb for Kate. None of us has ever tried to heal a psychic burnout. It's my problem, not hers."

"She healed me, so I know she can do it."

"When Libby heals, she takes a part of that illness or wound into herself and her body has to deal with it. It's probably the same for Kate. I'm not trying to be stubborn, Jackson, I just couldn't bear it if something happened to any of them on my account."

He crouched in the sand beside her and framed her face with his hands. "If you don't allow her to try, even in small daily increments, just a little at a time to speed up the process, we're all in danger. Every time he comes at us and he succeeds just a bit, it strengthens him and weakens us. This time you sent him back a hell of a message. Wherever he was, he got a backlash. There was no way he didn't and you're nowhere near your ability. We need you in this fight, Elle. You're going to have to allow Kate to try."

"I'll think about it." When he continued to look at her she sighed. "I promise, Jackson. I'll talk it over with Libby and Sarah and see what they think before I ask Katie. Matt's very protective of Kate and he may object."

"All of us object to the things you girls do, but you do it anyway. If Kate decides she can heal you without harming herself, nothing Matt says will change her mind." Jackson caught her shoulders and helped her to her feet.

Elle swayed unsteadily, her head screaming at her. "I'm going to have to lie down."

"Me, too. Let's just get into the house in case Gratsos tries something else."

"I don't think Stavros will be in any shape to try anything against us for a while. He's going to need a little medical attention." Elle smirked at him.

Jackson wrapped his arm around her waist tighter and began to walk her toward the house. Bomber dropped into position at his side, his body relaxed, which helped Jackson breathe a little easier. If Elle said Gratsos was done for a while, he wanted it to be true, but he wasn't going to take any chances. The man just kept coming at them.

"You're going to let your handler know you're safe? Are you certain that's wise?"

"I have to, Jackson. It isn't fair to him and he might be able to come up with a plan to help us with Stavros."

Jackson remained silent. He had his own plan for Gratsos and it didn't include allowing the poor excuse for a human being to live.

14

THE room was hot, too hot, so hot he could barely draw in a breath without scalding his lungs. It was small and had no windows, no ventilation other than a small hole up near the ceiling. Most of the time they kept a bright light on him, forcing him to stand for days, beating him when he toppled to the floor or just plain sat down out of defiance—well, more necessity than defiance, but they didn't see it that way.

He'd been there weeks now, with no end in sight. Alone. Always alone. Occasionally they brought in others and tortured them—he could hear the screams and the sounds of brutality, the cries, usually in another language—and he was certain he was the only American prisoner they had. It was probably the reason they didn't kill him.

He wasn't certain he could have kept his sanity without her—without that voice, so soft and melodic in his head, taking him to another place, telling him she was with him, sharing her mind so that he felt he wasn't alone in that small six-by-six room. When she wasn't with him, he composed music in his head, long concertos and entire symphonies. Or he took apart weapons and put them back together, all in his head, paying attention to every detail. Sometimes it was bombs, making them and taking them apart. Complex math problems and then back to weapons— in his mind he traveled back and forth, trying to keep from going insane.

They were coming. He could hear them. He always heard them. His heart began to pound and his stomach lurched. Air rushed out of his lungs in anticipation. It was going to be bad. It was always bad. They'd reduced him to an animal—no—less than an animal. He had rope brands from the tight bindings on his arms after they hung him for days, beating him with chains and whips and cables. He knew his arms were infected, he was running a fever, but it was all about breaking him.

He'd been in the camp too long and had seen prisoners come and go enough to know that each time they came at him, he was either going to survive and be tougher, or they would break him and destroy him for all time. The voice—*her* voice—became his reason to be tough, to survive. He'd been buried in the sand up to his neck for three days. That had been one of the worst ordeals, with the heat and the insects and the pressure on his body. He'd ended up with three broken ribs and several raging infections that lasted weeks.

A guard came in and his heart sank. He recognized the man as one of the most sadistic, a man who took pleasure in torture. He'd seen him put a drill through the back of a man's hand and laugh before beginning to chop off body parts, slowly killing the man. He often sexually assaulted the prisoners, and then beat them for hours, pausing only to take breaks when he was tired. He favored blowtorches, drills and electric shock.

At once, she was there, almost as if a part of her never quite left him and when he despaired the most, she moved in his mind, filling him with warmth and strength, although he didn't want her to witness whatever might happen.

You have to go. Now. He's the worst.

She couldn't be there if the guard assaulted him and then began to beat him because he planned to resist. If she went, he would be more alone than ever and maybe this time he could get the guard so angry that he'd lose control and kill him. Jackson couldn't see any other way out.

I'm not leaving you. I know what I'm asking, but please don't try it. Cooperate until that moment comes and believe me it will. There's always a moment when they won't be paying attention. I'll be with you and I'll pour strength into you so you'll be able to escape.

She'd kept him from trying to incite the guards to kill him before. He'd been there for weeks and no one had escaped. No one had come. He couldn't tell her where he was so she couldn't send a rescue team in. They moved him often. He didn't see that there was much hope at all. He couldn't promise her, not the way she wanted him to, but he did the mental equivalent of shrugging, as noncommittal as possible.

The guard stepped in close to his thin, torn body. The second guard, a smaller man with a long beard, and eyes that said he was just doing his job, but didn't have to like it, threw a bucket of ice cold water over his head. It was a shock with the room so hot and his body temperature high.

"Wake up, pig fodder."

Jackson could never be certain he understood the various insults correctly but the loose interpretations never mattered that much to him. He opened his eyes and looked at the miserable excuse for a human being standing, legs apart, a sick, malevolent gleam in his eyes as he studied Jackson.

"Tell me about the unit you're with. You owe them no loyalty. They abandoned you to us. Where are they going to be next?"

Jackson gave a little sigh and repeated his name and rank and serial number as he had a hundred times before. This was always the opening to the macabre dance they did together. He barely got to his rank when the guard delivered the first blow, rocking him back. The beating went on for what seemed like hours. First with whips, the lashing shredding clothes and tearing open skin up and down his body. No part of him was left untouched. Then came the kicking and punching.

The guard paused to take a rest, going out of the room. The second man stayed in the corner and when Jackson looked at him, he looked away, but he didn't interfere when the first guard returned, this time with a cane filled with nails sticking out of it.

Jackson knew he wasn't going to go through that and survive intact. He'd been beaten with it once before and the pain had been excruciating. Worse, the infections had been everywhere, the untreated wounds festering with the heat and insects. He was done. It was over.

She knew the exact moment he broke. Not in his resolve to hold out against his captors, but to force them to kill him. He heard her broken cry.

I'm sorry. I'm not strong enough to go through this again.

Live. Live for me. I know what I'm asking, but please, don't do this. Don't give up.

The guard approached him, an evil smirk on his mouth, his face twisted with his hatred. Closer . . . closer. Jackson watched him coming, holding himself still. Deep inside he heard her sob and then she suppressed the small cry. His heart stuttered. For a moment, he thought he could find the strength to endure, but the guard swung the heavy nail-studded cane and struck him across the chest. The breath left his lungs in a harsh rush and he heard a high-pitched animalistic sound escape his throat.

The guard laughed and stepped close to spit in his face. Jackson reacted, whipping his head up and slamming it into the guard's nose, breaking it. At the same time, he lashed out with his feet, letting his arms take his weight as he kicked the man in the groin. Jackson landed hard on the floor, his arms stretched and burning.

The guard thrashed around for a few minutes, fighting for air, while the second guard rushed over to wrap another rope around both of Jackson's ankles. There was a silence broken only by the harsh breathing of the sadistic guard. He got slowly to his feet, his face a mask of blood. He swore, grabbing Jackson by the feet and began to drag him across the stone floor to the door. He stopped and viciously planted a boot in Jackson's ribs before screaming at the other guard to help him.

Blood and spit ran down his face and he kicked again at Jackson's head before once more yanking on his feet. Jackson was dragged outside and through a courtyard to the back of an old beat-up car. His mouth went dry. He'd seen a body come back after they'd dragged him through the pitted, rock-filled, sandy road. There hadn't been any skin on the body, it had looked like raw meat on a hook.

The guard lashed Jackson's arms to the bumper and signaled to the other man to get into the driver's seat. They argued for a couple of minutes and then the sadistic guard drew his weapon. The other man got into the car and turned the engine over. Not bothering to wipe off the blood, his captor spat on Jackson's face and then threw himself into the car. Jackson heard the door slam.

Leave me now. She couldn't be in his head when he died, not like this, dragged behind a car like a dead carcass. *Thanks for everything. You have no idea what you've meant to me.*

I'm not leaving you. I won't.

If there had been a heart left in his body, her emotion would have broken it, but at last, everything in him was gone. He felt the rumbling of the car, the blast of the exhaust, a terrible jerk on his arms as if they were being pulled from their sockets and then he was being dragged through the rocks and sand.

He had thought he knew pain, but he was unprepared for the excruciating agony rushing through him. He nearly lost consciousness as the rocks and sand ground away his clothes and then his skin. His head was positioned higher, so the sand thrown up acted like a grinder on one side of his face, burning until he thought there was nothing left but bone.

A car came fishtailing up beside them, honking wildly, the driver waving his arms and finally pulling sideways in front of them, forcing the guard to comply. The car slid to a halt, the spinning wheels throwing sand all over the open wounds in his face and the entire left side of his body. The sand had shredded the few clothes he'd been wearing, leaving him raw and bloody, pitted from head to toe with sand.

Jackson lay there, the sand burning through muscle to bone, but he didn't have the strength to even lift his head to see what was happening. His arms felt as if they'd been jerked from their sockets and he was fairly certain something bad had happened to his left shoulder. The pain made him nauseous and the world around him spun, until his focus was off and everything tilted insanely.

The car door slammed and the driver came around to the back of his car, his legs in his line of vision. The sadistic guard rushed from the other side, roaring with anger. The driver of the other car got out much more slowly and came around to straddle Jackson's body. He kicked sand in his face, but Jackson didn't think the man even realized he'd done so. Jackson, as a human being, was of so little concern, they barely glanced at him.

An argument broke out, with the sadistic guard screaming that he would kill Jackson, that he'd do whatever he wanted. The driver of the other car, a stranger to Jackson, didn't raise his voice, but insisted that he was valuable and not to be killed. The man drew a knife, grabbed the rope binding Jackson to the bumper of the car and wrenched his arms up to pull the rope taut. It hurt like hell. For a moment little stars danced on a black background and Jackson was certain he would pass out.

No! Her voice was sharp. *They aren't paying any attention to you. There's only three of them. You noticed the gun in his belt. When he shoves the knife back into the scabbard, that's your chance, Jackson. There's a car, water, and weapons and no one around. You have to do this. I'll give you everything I can, but you have to do this.*

She was right. It was now or never. It didn't matter how weak he was, how exhausted or hurt, if he didn't take this one chance, another might never come along. Her resolve became his. He strengthened it with his hatred of his captors. He had learned to pray, and he had learned to hate. He never prayed for anything but the strength to endure, to hold out, to keep his soul intact, but now, he prayed for the strength to kill and kill swiftly.

His arms screamed, his shoulder throbbed and pulsed with pain, but all of that was pushed aside. He hung by the ropes, eyes narrowed to slits, his body coiling into the machine he'd been trained to be. The knife sliced cleanly through the ropes and he fell to the sand and watched as the driver shoved the blade back into the scabbard inside his boot. All the while, the driver and the guards continued arguing, paying him no attention at all.

As the sadistic guard stepped closer, fury goading him to double his fists, Jackson felt strength and power pour into him. It was so much so fast, he could barely contain it. He'd forgotten what it was like to feel the rush of adrenaline coupled with full power. His brain was clear, precise, every step planned out in advance. He struck, ripping the knife free with his left hand, the smooth arc of his hand continuing to slice deep into the thigh, cutting through arteries as he reached for the gun with his right hand, ripping it from the belt and shooting the sadistic guard right between the eyes.

He rolled, his legs sweeping down the driver he'd cut. As Jackson rolled, he shot the second guard three times in the chest and once in the throat, driving him backward. Sitting, he shot the driver in the head and slashed through the rope binding his ankles together. Something moved behind him, brushed against his back and he twisted around, the knife in his hand, his heart pounding, his other hand swinging at the unseen enemy.

"Jackson!"

She moved in his mind. Fear. Compassion. *Elle*. Jackson found himself sitting upright in the bed, a knife in his fist, sweat gleaming on his body. His hair was damp with it, the sheets soaked. Elle sat nearly beneath him, her hands in her lap, her expression soft and loving. He looked down and saw the blade of the knife pointed toward her, inches from her body. His stomach lurched. He opened his fingers and let the knife fall to the mattress between them.

"I'm sorry, baby. Tell me I didn't hurt you." He wiped the sweat from his eyes, rubbing his palms over his face and then through his damp hair. "Hell. I could have killed you. What the fuck was I thinking, bringing you here?"

She reached out a hand to him, but he jerked away from her, backing to the other side of the bed, feet on the floor, hands still rubbing over his face in agitation.

"Jackson—"

"Don't. Just fucking don't. Call Sarah and tell her to come and get you. I'll come over in the morning. Take Bomber with you."

"I don't think so."

Temper hissed in her voice, making him turn his head and meet her glittering gaze. "What did you say to me?" he asked, his own voice lowering, taking on an edge.

"You heard me very well, Jackson. I'm not leaving. You had a nightmare. A flashback. Whatever. It happened. We'll deal with it."

He glared at her. "Are you out of your mind, Elle? I could have shoved that knife in your throat. Right then, in that moment, you were the enemy. You sat there looking at me, totally without defending yourself. You didn't even put up your damn hands. Who does that, Elle? Lies there offering herself up like some sacrifice?"

"I didn't want to add to your nightmare. I just talked to you to bring you out of it."

Now her voice irritated him. She'd gone all soft again, understanding. He leapt up, paced across the room to his jeans and dragged them over his hips. "Well, you didn't talk me out of it, did you, Elle? You became part of it. And I could have woken up with a knife sticking out of your belly and my hand on the hilt."

"Nothing happened, Jackson," she said, obviously struggling to keep her voice soothing.

"Don't use that voice on me. I'm not a fucking child."

"You're certainly acting like one. You think by saying 'fuck' to me that makes you Jackson the badass? I'm not afraid of you, Jackson."

He swung around, crossing back to her side of the bed with purposeful, long strokes, deliberately looming over her. "Well maybe you should be."

She refused to drop her gaze. "I'll *never* be afraid of you. Not if you come at me with a knife and not if you yell the 'F' word at the top of your lungs. I love you. I'm in your mind. You'd never hurt me, not for any reason. So get over your big bad mood."

He glared at her again. "Has anyone ever told you that you're not the most soothing woman in the world?"

"The idea isn't to be soothing," Elle said, "it's to knock some sense into your incredibly thick skull."

They stared at each other, Jackson breathing heavily. He shook his head, looking away first. "Damn you, Elle. You don't seem to have one ounce of self-preservation left in you. Do you think this won't happen again? It happens on a regular basis. I've stabbed the mattress more than once. I don't sleep for days on end. It isn't going to stop."

"No, you're right, it isn't going to stop. You have scars

on your body, Jackson, and the worst ones are where no one else can see them. They aren't going to disappear. You said that to me, because you've lived it and you know. What happened is a part of you. Sometimes everything will be fine, and other times it won't."

She threw his words back in his face. If they were good enough for him to tell her, then they were good enough for him to live by. "That's just going to be a part of our lives. I can live with it. And you'll have to live with my scars, because believe me, Jackson, I have plenty of them. You told me what happened to me wouldn't come between us. I'm not a coward, and I love you. I refuse to walk away and you're damned well not walking away from me."

She stood up, stepped right up to him, refusing to be intimidated by him. "Not after you made me live. Not after your promises to me. You don't have that option." He stood there, looking back at her, his black eyes glittering with heat. He looked savage, mean even, but she didn't blink, staring up at him defiantly, even accusingly.

"Do you know what they made me into, Elle? You think I was an animal crawling on that floor, blind and sick and broken. I was a monster learning hatred, finding ice in my veins, a place I can go where I feel *nothing*— nothing at all. A place I can go to kill. That's what you're living with. That's who I am. That's what Kate saw that night."

She didn't flinch or turn away as he expected—as she should have. Her eyes softened and he saw—*love*. "Kate saw what I see. A man who tries to save the world. A man who doesn't run from a fight. One who stands and can always be counted on. When I was alone and terrified and half out of my mind with pain and revulsion and even shame, I knew absolutely without a shadow of a doubt that you would come for me. I knew you would never stop looking, no matter how many weeks, months, even years. I knew it in my head, in my heart and in my very soul. That's the man you are. That's the man I see standing in front of me. And if you don't see him, get your ass in the bathroom and look in the mirror."

Jackson felt a burning behind his eyes. His throat was raw. She was a stick of dynamite when she got going, she always had been. He loved her so much it terrified him. He'd never needed anyone. He'd never wanted anyone. Elle was different. She'd taken hold of his heart and there was no getting it back. He was a danger to her, maybe to others, but she just stood there in front of him, small and delicate and made of steel.

He damn well wasn't going to let her see him cry. He turned on his heel and left the bedroom, striding down the hall in the dark, toward the one room in his home where he could lose himself. He didn't bother with lights; whenever he was like this, restless and edgy and screaming with rage inside, he needed the darkness and shadows.

Outside the windows the mist had enclosed the house like a blanket, cocooning them in a mystic embrace. The wind blew through the trees so that they swayed and danced outside and when he stood at the window, he could see vines growing up along the fence, thick and strong, entwined around everything, with heavy sprays of blossoms. Those flowers grew thick and strong all along the Drake home's fences—and they bloomed through the winter season.

He shook his head and turned away from the strange phenomenon and looked at his masterpiece—the one thing that made sense to him when the world was all wrong. The baby grand piano was beautiful. The lines, the shiny black, the ivory keys—he'd spent a fortune on it and it had been worth every penny. Perfectly in tune, without a single blemish, it was as beautiful to him as the music it created.

He sat on the bench and placed his fingers over the keys and everything in him that had been chaotic and wrong settled. He closed his eyes and let his fingers drift over the keys, listening to the pure notes that poured from the instrument, a perfect pitch, a melody from another place, somewhere without sadistic maniacs, without rape and torture, somewhere his mind could go and see the beauty of the world around him.

The music allowed him to see the ocean, the waves crashing, ebbing and flowing like the earth's lifeblood. He could feel the pulse of the earth, the hills and mountains rising majestically in the minor and major chords as the music flowed from him into the keys and out again into the room, filling it with the sound of peace, giving him a sense of peace.

And Elle, beautiful, fiery Elle. He was more broken over Elle than what had happened to him. He could escape his own past, he could let hatred and rage for his captors fade and die in him, but not Gratsos. He couldn't live with the threat of Gratsos hanging over Elle's head. The way the man terrorized her, the way the man had treated her. He could live with a lot of things, but not that. He knew he would hunt Gratsos and he would kill him and he would have to come back home and face her. He couldn't live without removing the man from the earth permanently and he wasn't certain she could live with him once he'd done it. His heart stumbled and so did his fingers.

He let the music carry him away from his thoughts and

back to what was his world. Back to sanity and peace. Elle. His fingers flew over the keys, pouring passion and fire into his concerto, seeing her in his mind with her long red hair spilling around him like a silken, fiery waterfall. Her skin, so soft, pale in the darkness, rose petals in the candlelight, his hands moving over her body, taking her into his, shaping and memorizing every sweet curve.

He closed his eyes and made love to her with his music, joined them in his mind without even knowing he did so. Each separate note was a stroke, a caress, a gift to her. The song was his message of love, one he could never adequately say, but this instrument could and did, the melody rising with his own passion.

Elle watched Jackson play, his head bent over the keyboard, eyes closed, body swaying as the music moved through him, out his hands and into the instrument. She stood in the doorway looking at his face. He was completely absorbed in the music, his fingers moving over the keys, his thoughts far away. He was in the shadows, with just the small glow of candles allowing her to see his expression. She knew he had the heart of a warrior, fierce and loyal and deadly in a fight, yet looking at him now, she knew he had the soul of a poet.

She looked around the room. It was obviously built for the acoustics and the sound was incredible. There was a gas fireplace built into the wall and the hardwood floors gleamed. Near the fireplace was a thick carpet with two deep armchairs and a small table between them. Little else, other than candles, decorated the room. The candles gave off a soft light, but otherwise the room was veiled in shadows, just as Jackson often was.

Jackson stole her breath with his song, with the images in his mind. The notes played over her body, teasing her senses into a leaping fire until she couldn't take a breath without breathing him in. She ached inside with need for him, with the need to please him, to take him from that dark place inside him, to sheer bliss, to the ecstasy of his music.

She entered the room, padding across the floor to the fireplace to light it. Flames glowed a mixture of gold and red, low, just skimming over the logs almost in time to the music flowing around her. She felt different with the music, the pulse beating through her, stealing her fears away. The lower notes resonated deep in her most feminine core, throbbing there so that the sensation traveled through her body like a molten stream of notes, teasing over her skin and tweaking her nipples into hard peaks.

She took her time, going back for pillows and a light blanket, arranging them on the thick rug in front of the fire. This room was safe. No one, nothing, could get in and disturb their world here. She added a few long-burning candles to the rock mantelpiece above the fireplace and lit them before signaling to Bomber to lay outside the door for added protection, an amazing warning system. Then she closed the door firmly, shutting the two of them into the room and the rest of the world out.

She closed her eyes and listened to the music as it swelled in volume. She could feel her heart pounding in rhythm to the melody. She let it take her away to another place, somewhere sensual, the heat spreading through her body as she stepped out of her drawstring pants, folded them neatly and set them aside along with her underwear. She unbuttoned the long shirt and folded it next, placing it on top of the pants. Only when she was completely naked did she turn and pad quietly across the hardwood floor to stand behind Jackson.

She leaned over his back, her arms circling his neck, pressing her body against his bare skin while her mouth drifted over his neck in time to the sensual music flooding her body with wicked heat. Her teeth nipped, found his earlobe and tugged. His playing changed, the notes building from sheer passion to a swelling climax.

Her heart beat faster and her body ached for him, empty and needing him to fill her. She kissed her way down his spine, taking her time, the pads of her fingers sliding over his muscles, tracing scars while her mouth followed, soft and persuasive, kissing and licking, occasionally nipping. She went to her knees, her face pressed against his lower back while her arms slid around him, hands at the waistband of his low-slung jeans.

She felt his swift intake of breath, his body going still. She felt his mind move against hers, the waves of pleasure as she slowly opened the front of his jeans. He wore no underwear. She'd seen him pull his jeans over his hips, and his erection was thick and heavy, straining to be free. She moved her head around to his side so she could lick and nip at his ribs and lower along his hip as her fingers stroked and caressed and played along his thick shaft, following the movement of his fingers on the piano keys. The music swelled as did his shaft, and she cupped him lower, first at the base and then lower still, caressing the sensitive ball sac.

He lost his breath in a rush of heat. There was no hesitation in his mind, no questions as he turned to her, no fear that she might reject him. Like Elle, he seemed to have the same sense that this room was sacred and no one could touch them here.

He turned all the way around on the piano bench, his hands framing her face, urging her to look up at him. Elle never once stopped the caresses along his shaft, sliding her hand up and over him, moving between his thighs as she lifted her face for his kiss. He took her mouth with a tenderness that brought tears to her eyes. She tasted love. She tasted belonging.

"Make love to me, Jackson," she whispered. "Make me yours."

"You are mine, Elle. You always have been."

He stood up, holding her gaze with his as he pushed the jeans down and kicked them away. He drew her up and found her mouth again, fusing them together and this time, his kiss was a demand, a promise, a taking.

He lifted her in strong arms and laid her over the piano, exerting pressure with one hand until she complied with his unspoken demand and lay back, giving him full access to her body. He kissed his way up her calves, then her inner thighs, before draping her legs over his broad shoulders. She looked so beautiful lying there, completely open and vulnerable to him, no fear, only trust on her face, only need in her eyes. He smiled at her, a wicked smile filled with the promise of pleasure and lowered his head to trail a series of bites inside her upper thighs.

Elle's breath exploded from her lungs. His tongue rasped a long velvet caress over the stinging little nips. Deep inside, her temperature shot straight to raging inferno. He stroked his fingers over her sex and she shuddered. He smiled at her, another wicked smirk that sent her heart climbing into her throat. She couldn't take her eyes from his face. The lust carved there, the love blazing in his eyes. He slowly sank his finger into her tight, wet channel, and she cried out, her heart giving another unexpected lurch as his eyes darkened and blazed.

His thumb flicked her clit and she moaned, her hips

surging upward to try to get relief as the heat swept through her and became a fire. His mouth moved over her inner thigh again, and he blew gently into her damp heat. Rather than putting out the fire, the feel of his breath against her only ignited her more.

His tongue slid over her sex in a long, languid, very lazy stroke, as if they had all the time in the world and he was enjoying himself thoroughly. Her entire body tightened, shuddered and she moaned low in the back of her throat. He found those little moans and whimpers vibrated through his entire body and hardened him even more. Each time he elicited a soft little cry he felt it was a claiming of her, a branding, his mark, his scent, his victory, giving her pleasure, wrapping her up in erotic bliss.

He kissed her, tasted her, and then stabbed deep, completely at odds with his earlier slow attention. She nearly convulsed in shock.

"Jackson."

His name hissed out between her teeth, another breathy little moan that vibrated through his entire body. Her face and body were flushed with arousal, her eyes nearly opaque, so glazed and dazed he wanted to keep her like that, head twisting desperately from side to side, her hips rising, searching for him.

He spread one hand on her belly, holding her in place while he lifted her hips to his mouth with the other and began to devour her. She went wild, bucking against his mouth while he played her body, enjoying the havoc he was wreaking, loving the way she panted and squirmed and tossed her head. Her moans were long and low and just as beautiful as the notes he created on the piano— more so. His tongue flicked back and forth over her clit and then he suckled, sending her screaming over the edge.

He felt the waves of heat, the miracle of pleasure flooding her body and mind and the flow went straight to his mind and rushed to his cock.

He gave one last lick, felt a satisfying shudder go through her and he dropped her legs around his waist and simply lifted her. Elle wrapped her arms around his neck and buried her face against his throat.

"I love you, Jackson. I know you're trying not to think in terms of me belonging to you, but honestly, I want to belong to you." Her voice was a whisper, a thread of sound. She was still trying to find her breath after her orgasm. "Make me yours. I want to feel you inside of me and know I belong to only you. I need that." She rained kisses over his face and found his mouth almost blindly, tasting herself as their mouths welded together.

He laid her gently in the middle of the thick rug. "You taste sweet, like strawberries. I'm already addicted. I'm going to spend a lifetime eating you up." He straddled her, leaning down to find her breasts with the heat of his mouth.

She gasped and arched into him. His hands came up, cupping the soft weight, thumbs flicking over her nipples, tugging and pulling and creating a continuous streak of lightning running from her breasts to her womb. She was frantic for him, for the feel and taste of him, reaching up to cradle his head to her breasts, her hips writhing beneath him. Her breath came in anxious little pants.

Jackson loved the way she moved against him, her body craving his. She held nothing back, a hot, sensuous woman needing him, wanting him buried deep inside her, stroking his cock with eager fingers, unashamed of her craving for him. It heightened his own pleasure to know she wanted him every bit as much as he wanted her.

Looking into her emerald eyes, he felt a jolt of something close to fear—no, not fear: terror. From the first day he'd heard her voice in that prison camp, so long ago, she'd been his world. He couldn't imagine what it would be like without her, he didn't even want to know, yet he'd tried to send her away tonight. What had he been thinking?

He rolled off her, lying beside her and caught her breasts in his hands, tugging at her nipples, until she gasped and came toward him.

"Straddle me, baby." He wasn't going to pin her down, not yet. Not until she could get used to his possession. There was no need to chance putting fear back in her eyes, not when they were so hot with passion. He guided her using pressure on her breasts, lifting his head to flick at the peaks with his tongue, forcing her to bend forward and down over the top of him.

He could feel the cool air on his jerking cock, enflaming him further. He wanted to feel the clasp of her sheath, tight and velvet soft, clamping around him. She moaned softly as he slid his hands over her bottom, his large palms rubbing and massaging as he lifted her over his aching shaft. He guided her with her body over his and pushed his hips up as he brought her down over him. The feeling of her body opening like a flower, unfurling petals to take him in robbed him of breath and sent flames roaring through his veins.

Elle shivered as she settled her body over his, her eyes half-closed, savoring the feeling of fullness as he stretched her almost to burning. He didn't move for a moment, allowing her to get used to his size before drawing her down farther, pushing through tight muscles and lodging so deep she thought he was nearly to her throat.

"Look at me, Elle," Jackson instructed. "This—us together—I feel like I'm home at last. This is where I belong. Inside you. Look at me. Keep looking at me."

The silken slide of her hair tumbled around her face as her gaze locked with his and she began to ride him at the urging of his strong hands on her hips. He moved with her, thrusting deep, fast and then slow, watching her face flush with desire, watching the heat in her eyes, the way her breathing changed to little frantic pants as her body coiled tighter and tighter around his.

Jackson cupped her breasts, thumbs teasing her nipples. Watching her eyes, he grasped her nipples and pinched, tugging her down and over him, seeing the heat flare in her gaze, her mouth open to give one of her sexy, mind-blowing moans as she bathed his cock in liquid fire.

He kept her body over his, taking complete control, reveling in her surrender as he took over the rhythm, impaling her hard and fast, driving her up the peak, seeking his own release in the pounding thrusts of his hips. His fingers dug deep into her soft flesh, holding her still, all the while keeping her gaze locked on his. He wanted to feel her surrender, to see the pleasure in her eyes. Then her breath caught in her throat. She whimpered as the first wave of fire tore up through her core and settled in her belly to spread like a fireball.

Her emerald gaze never left him. He watched the flush rise up her body to consume her. He watched her surrender to the hot rapture—to him. He watched her give herself over to him, body and soul completely. The beauty of her gift only added to his own release, and he let go of every thought, everything and simply gave himself to her.

The music of her soft moans surrounded him, taking

him to another place where there was only her body clamping around his like a hot velvet vise, the liquid notes of pleasure that vibrated between them, as his body erupted with glorious, bone-melting release. Never once did she look away from him, drinking in his expression as they both floated together.

It was a long while before he stirred to push her tumbling hair from her face and slide his hand over the nape of her neck. "You're where you belong, Elle."

She nodded. "I feel like I'm home, Jackson. At last. I'm here." Tears shimmered in her eyes.

He pulled her close to flick them away with his tongue. "I hope you're not too sleepy, baby, because I'm going to want to make love to you all night."

For an answer, she brought her mouth down on his and let her body melt around him.

15

JACKSON groaned and turned his head to look out the window at the dawn creeping across the sky. He was sprawled on his back on the thick carpet in front of the fireplace in his music room. Most of the candles had burned low and a few were out altogether. The scent of lavender and sex lay heavy in the air and he breathed it in. Elle and Jackson. It was a heady fragrance and his body stirred in spite of the fact that he'd made love to her all night.

Elle lay draped over his body, her breasts across his thighs, her lips against his cock, her hands cupping his balls. Every breath she drew, every time she exhaled, he felt it against his softened shaft. His cock jerked and pulsed in time to her breathing, but Jackson lay limp and drained, basking in the aftermath of the best sex he'd ever had. If he'd had anything at all left in him, he would have been all over her, but he couldn't move. He could only lie there feeling absolute satisfaction. Pure contentment.

He wanted to wake up every morning for the rest of his life, just like this, with Elle over the top of him, her soft

breasts on his thighs and her mouth against his cock. He felt
alive. He felt renewed. He felt he had a home for the first
time in his life.

He ran his fingers through the thick mass of red silk
pouring down Elle's back and spreading across his thighs.
Her hair looked like a sensuous waterfall of shimmering
red draped over his hips and legs making him wish he
could move. He was starving, but he wasn't altogether certain he had any strength left to even get up and cook let
alone make love to her again.

Elle stirred, her hair sliding over his bare skin as she
moved slightly. Her warm breath teased his cock. Her
tongue darted out and licked him. His body jerked.

"You're a little demon," he accused. "You're going to
kill me."

She nuzzled his groin, inhaling, drawing in his masculine scent, unique to Jackson, filling her mind with him,
and what she'd like to do to him. He matched her quick
inhale with one of his own, reading the erotic images in
her mind, knowing she was deliberately teasing him. Her
breasts pressed against his upper thighs as she shifted,
tantalizing him with the soft feel of them. Her nipples
brushed against him, hard, tempting peaks. All woman.
His woman.

"I love you, Elle," he said, meaning it with every bit of
his soul. He wrapped her long hair around his fist, shifting
as she nuzzled again, this time her mouth moving sensu-
ously against him. He closed his eyes. "A man could get
used to waking up to you."

Elle moved her head so she could easily reach her prize.
Her tongue teased again in a long, lazy curl. "I could lie
here all day like this." It felt decadent. For the first time in
months, maybe even years, she felt completely relaxed.

His hands massaged the nape of her neck. "You do whatever you want, baby. I'm just going to lie here and enjoy you enjoying yourself, because frankly, I can't move."

She blew out another warm breath, bathing him in heat. "So I have you utterly at my mercy?"

"That would be affirmative."

"I like you that way." Her voice purred with satisfaction. "You didn't tell me you play the piano." She stroked her tongue in a long, languid caress from the base of his shaft to under the crown. "That was very bad of you."

His body shuddered as her tongue did a dancing little spiral along the most sensitive spot beneath the head, deliberately forcing the air from his lungs.

He had to wait until he could talk before he managed an answer. "I didn't want to ruin my image."

"That's right." She hadn't moved her head at all, but somehow she managed to engulf his cock and just hold him in her mouth, swallowing, as if pulling him down her throat. His body swelled involuntarily, impossibly, aching with need just that fast, filling her mouth and throat. She released him and blew another long breath of warm air over him. "I'd forgotten about your badass image." She licked down his groin and gently drew his soft sac into her mouth.

Jackson shuddered with pleasure. There was nothing at all hurried or frenzied about Elle's movements. Her languid, lazy movements were both elegant and feline, arousing him even more. She nibbled and sucked, paying him little attention, as if she was a cat, lapping at cream. Her mouth drew him deep, held him for several long, extraordinary seconds and then she would release him and resume her catlike licking.

It was slow, exquisite torture. She brought him back to

life and then some. Every nerve ending he had became
centered in his groin. His breath hitched when she moved
down his legs and bit at his thighs, her hair dragging sen-
suously over his hard, thick shaft, causing every muscle in
his body to tighten.

"Mmm, baby," she said, her voice dreamy. "I love the
way you feel, hot and hard and so alive."

She drew him into her mouth again, sucking strongly,
tongue sliding around him in lazy curls that nearly stopped
his heart. He couldn't speak. He couldn't even think. The
world around him dissolved, went red and hazy. Her mouth
was wet and hot, an instrument of unbelievable pleasure.
His breath exploded out of his lungs in a heated rush. She
drew him deep, her throat closing around him like a tight
fist, squeezing, holding him there for a long count and
then, once again swallowing as if drawing him deeper, her
muscles working him over until bright lights exploded in
the back of his brain.

He tried not to move, knowing if she stopped, his heart
might cease beating. She was moving again, suckling as if
starving, and when he touched her mind, he found—
desire. Hunger. A craving for him, to please him, to take
him beyond every limit and give him not pleasure but ecstasy. Her driving need to please him was more of an
aphrodisiac than anything else could have been. Not only
was she enjoying giving him pleasure, she was deriving
pleasure as well.

She used her tongue, a velvet rasp that sent streaks of
flames over him, her teeth, gently scraping and nibbling
along his shaft, careful to watch his every reaction, the
hot suction of her mouth drawing him closer and closer to
the edge. He tilted his head, needing her now, needing her

to take him deeper, shocked at how it felt each time he thrust and she took him in, her muscles squeezing around him.

His moans were loud, filling the room, a sweet music that she hummed along to, the vibration adding to the intensity of his pleasure. She sent shock waves through his body as she began to take him deeper and pull strongly, milking him, her hand on his sac, her mouth a miracle of magic. He felt as if he was an inferno, a white-hot flame, as thunder pounded in his chest and a roaring began in his ears. His toes curled and every muscle strained. The tendons in his neck stood out and he felt every drop of blood center and pulse in his groin. Hot. On fire. "So fucking hot, baby," he tried to murmur, but he couldn't find enough air to breathe the words to her.

There was a light sheen of sweat coating his body. His hair was damp and every muscle in his body strained toward her—toward that mouth that was devouring him, milking him. His cock jerked. Pulsed. Swelled until he filled her mouth and stretched her throat. He felt it then, rising, rolling over him like a tidal wave, sweeping him into an explosive release that didn't seem to stop, the hot semen pumping out of him, jet after jet, the orgasm erupting through his body, until his thighs and belly were so tight he thought he might die from sheer bliss. He heard his hoarse cry—*Elle*—and the guttural, animalistic moans coming from his throat.

She held him in her mouth while he softened and then licked at him gently, lovingly, as he lay there with his heart pounding out of his chest and his lungs fighting desperately for air. She kissed her way along his shaft and then up his belly to lay her head once more on him. Jackson could only lie there, shocked, colors dancing behind his eyes, his body in a state of absolute ecstasy. If there was a nirvana, he had found it.

You have to have the most beautiful, talented mouth in the entire world, Elle. I don't think I'll ever be able to move again, but I'm going to die a happy man.

She pressed kisses along his belly, nuzzled him and lay back down, her arms around him and her head pillowed on him. His cock was nestled between her soft breasts and she straddled him, her mound against his thigh.

Jackson may have dozed off, he wasn't certain, but when he opened his eyes, it was significantly lighter in the room. He was content to lie there, his hands in her hair, her body draped over his. Elle made him whole. Elle gave him peace. She made sense of the world. She took away the ugliness and allowed him to see the beauty in the same way his music did. She brought him so much pleasure he could barely conceive of it.

He tried to puzzle out what was so different about being with her. There had been nothing mechanical about the way she had touched him. Every stroke, every touch, her mouth, her tongue, even her teeth, had all been used on him with love. He'd felt the overwhelming emotion in everything she did to him. *His.* His Elle. She amazed and humbled him with her determination to give him pleasure.

"Elle? Are you awake, baby?"

"Mmmm."

She sounded drowsy and contented. Like a little cat. He tugged on her hair until she was looking up at him.

"Thank you for making me feel like a human being again." He frowned, trying to find words that would express how she made him feel when there were none. "More than that, thank you for loving me the way I am. You've made me feel far more loved than anyone ever has in my life. You make me feel . . ." He choked out the last word, but no matter how stupid it made him feel trying to articulate emotions, she deserved it. "Worthy."

She was silent a long time. He felt the breath running through her body, he was so tuned to her. She felt soft and warm draped over him, a living blanket that was everything good in the world to him. His fingers slid through her scalp, trying to massage, to give her pleasure rather than declare possession.

"You're everything to me, Jackson," Elle said eventually, pressing her lips against his belly. "*Everything.* And you're more worthy than any man I know. I was loving you with everything in me."

"I know you were, baby. I felt it."

"It wasn't about proving something to Stavros or to myself." She pushed up onto her elbows to look at him. "I feel so much better, Jackson. I was so afraid he'd taken everything from me, but he couldn't take away the love I feel for you or the way I need to express it."

His gaze drifted over her face. God, he loved her. "You have to expect to have trouble, Elle, with this—with us. Trauma is a strange thing so once in a while you may knock me on my ass again, and if it happens, it will be okay."

"And you might have a nightmare. I'll put the weapons under my side of the mattress." She grinned at him.

A slow smiled answered hers and then he nodded. "It only matters to me that you love me enough that you not only want to bring me pleasure, but that you enjoy it."

A slow, mischievous smile curved her mouth. "I *really* enjoy the way you say my name."

"Do you, now? How about hearing it for the rest of your life?" His hands tightened in her hair, stroked little caresses over her scalp. "Let's get married, Elle. Now. Right away. Invite the whole damn village. No wedding plans, just tell everyone it's a village event and we want them to come and celebrate with us. Whoever shows up, it's all good."

She stared into his eyes for a long moment. "This isn't an impulse thing? An afterglow from great sex?"

"This is me wanting you to be my wife. Now. I don't want to wait. Let's just make it official. We can get a license and be married right away. And fuck Gratsos. Let's get married on the beach."

She laughed. "You're so crazy, Jackson. You don't even like people around, yet you're going to invite the entire village?"

He turned on his hip, propping up his head to better see her expression. "You and your sisters are a huge part of Sea Haven. I know your older sisters want a big white wedding, but we're beach people. This"—he waved his hand to encompass his house and hers as well as the beach and the sea—"this is who we are. The village worked to get you home, praying, lighting candles, doing everything they could think of to try to help find you. Let's not hide, baby. Let's throw it in his face and be happy."

"I don't know the first thing about planning something like that."

He grinned at her. "That's the best part. We don't need to plan it. We just need to call one person."

Her eyes widened. "You're going to call Inez?"

"The moment you say yes to me."

"If you call her, Jackson, you'll never be able to back out, you know that, don't you?"

He wrapped his arms around her, rolled over, pinning her down just long enough to give her a kiss, before releasing her and rolling to the other side of the carpet. "I'll give you the first phone call. Tell Sarah and then I call Inez."

"They'll all come over."

He shrugged. "They will anyway. And I want to see Abbey and make certain she's all right. So go call." He leaned over her and bit her luscious butt. He wanted her sisters over because he was going to make certain Kate tried to help heal Elle's talent. They were going to need her at full strength.

"Ow!" Elle rubbed her bottom and glared at him. "Fine, I'll call her. You can go make us something to eat."

"I just fed you, greedy little thing." He brushed a kiss on top of her. "Don't worry, I'll make certain I take care of you like that every morning."

She couldn't help the color that swept up her neck to her face. "I'm telling everyone you play the piano." As a snappy comeback it wasn't the best, but it was all she could think of when he was looking at her like she was candy and he was about to devour her. He could make her insides melt with one look, and she grew damp and needy when his hot gaze moved over her.

Jackson gave her one warning look, snagged his jeans and went to take Bomber out while she called Sarah. She rolled over onto her back, savoring the feeling of the soft carpet against her back as she stared up at the ceiling, smirking a little as she replayed the sounds Jackson made and the intensity of the pleasure in his mind when she'd brought him to a climax. He hadn't believed she could do it either.

Maybe he'd think twice before he underestimated her powers again. She laughed to herself and looked around the room. She loved the room. She was tempted to use her talent, just to see if she could, just do something simple like snuff out the flames on the candles . . .

Don't even think about it. And stop feeling so smug.

I deserve to feel smug. It did hurt to use telepathy, but she didn't bleed and she took that as a good sign.

"Knock it off, Elle," Jackson snapped, sticking his head in the door and glowering at her.

"You started it," she pointed out and stretched her arms over her head. She loved the feeling of freedom.

"Do you have to be so damned beautiful and sexy?"

He sounded so irritated with her, Elle laughed. "Go away. I'm calling Sarah and then taking a shower." She forced herself to get up when she could have spent the day languishing there on the carpet.

Sarah didn't seem in the least bit shocked at her news, but then Sarah often had precognition and sometimes knew events before anyone else. Elle took a leisurely shower and dressed carefully knowing her family was coming over after breakfast. Even with Jackson making her feel as if she was the most beautiful, desirable woman in the world, she still felt ashamed that she had been taken prisoner.

She had extensive training, and she had tremendous psychic power. She had relied so much on her psychic abilities and her training that she hadn't believed anyone would be able to fool her. Her own arrogance had made her vulnerable. Facing her sisters, knowing that they knew, at least on an intellectual level, the humiliating depravities Stavros had inflicted on her, was so difficult. She didn't understand why she could face Jackson, and yet be so ashamed when her sisters were close.

She bit her lip and stared at herself in the foggy mirror. Whoever she loved could certainly be in danger and no matter what Jackson said to her, she knew that if Stavros could fool her for as long as he had, if he could keep her prisoner, then he was an extremely dangerous and powerful opponent. She wasn't about to underestimate him again, or overestimate her own strengths.

"Come eat, Elle," Jackson called.

Elle took a breath and let it out. She was going to call into work and let Dane know she was alive. It was the right thing to do. She didn't have much information to help anyone break the human trafficking ring, but she had enough to at least confirm suspicion that Stavros was involved and that his brother was alive and probably responsible for kidnapping women. Law enforcement would have to find a way to take them down and it would take time, but at least she would have contributed.

Jackson looked up from the table when she entered the room. She knew by his lack of expression and his dark smoldering eyes that he'd been in her mind, reading her thoughts. She sank down into a chair and reached for her teacup.

"No."

He'd made the tea just the way she liked it, with milk. It tasted delicious. Elle looked at him over the rim. "I don't want to argue, Jackson. You know I'm going to have to call Dane and let him know I'm alive. I can't hide forever. And it isn't fair to him."

"Once he knows, Gratsos will know. Gratsos bought the police. Hell, he probably bought his share of police around the world. The minute your report is filed, he's going to know you're alive for certain and he'll move heaven and earth to find you. We're not ready for him," Jackson pointed out.

"He's attacking us already."

"He's attacking anywhere psychic energy shows up," Jackson said. "You know he is. And I'll prove it. I'll go on the website today and look up strange events around the world. I'm willing to bet several areas had undertows where there are no undertows and jellyfish that shouldn't have been there, everything that happened yesterday. So just wait until you're at full strength."

"We can't know I'll heal all the way, Jackson. The longer I wait to file a report, the less time the authorities have to shut down this ring. I need to know that what happened to me will at least help someone else."

He set down his fork and leaned toward her, locking his gaze with hers. "Then you let Kate try today."

Elle pressed her fingers to her eyes and toyed with the eggs on her plate. "I'll try, Jackson." When he didn't respond she looked up at him. "I really will. I'll need you to help me, but I'll try to let her."

He reached across the table and covered her hand with his. "We won't let anything happen to her."

"He scares me, Jackson. I know you think he's not all-powerful, but look what he's done so far." She didn't want Jackson underestimating their enemy. She'd done that once and paid the consequences.

"When your family gets here, and I presume they're on the way . . ." At her nod he continued. "We can discuss Gratsos. Right now I think you should hear what Inez had to say."

Her mouth fell open. She stared at him. "You really called Inez and told her we were getting married?"

He shrugged, but she caught the gleam of amusement in his eyes. "Not precisely. What I said was, we wanted to get married immediately with the village invited to a beach wedding but we had no idea how to go about it."

She covered her face with her hands and peeked out at him through her fingers. "You didn't."

For one moment his teeth flashed at her and then he recovered and kept sober. "And then I called the Dardens on Inez's instructions. Apparently they operate some kind of village event calendar that can activate immediately and brings in all sorts of volunteers, which Inez said she will need."

"I'm trying not to hate you right now."

He picked up the tea mug and drank, unsuccessfully hiding his grin. "You liked the idea this morning."

"In the after-sex glow! Inez? Do you have any idea what you've let yourself in for? She'll put on the event of the year. She'll have you in a tux and top hat."

He openly smirked. "It's a beach wedding. She'll have you in a bikini." He leered and wriggled his eyebrows. "I'll be in board shorts. We'll both be barefoot."

"Dream on, my man. Inez is going to knock your socks off all right, but it won't be anything like you think."

The smile faded to be replaced by a small frown. "I'll have a little chat with her."

"You've had enough little chats with her. I'll be talking to Inez." She gave an indignant sniff.

"We're getting married, Elle, and I don't much give a damn if we do it here with the dog as our witness or in front of the entire world, but it's getting done. So get your birth certificate and have it ready. We're getting the license."

She rolled her eyes. "I see big bad Jackson needs another lesson. You need to be taken down a peg or two."

"Just how do you think a little girl like you can manage that?" he challenged.

A wicked, sexy smile curved her mouth. She let her gaze drift speculatively over his face, down his chest to disappear lower. "I could crawl under the table while you're eating your breakfast and see who's boss."

She licked her lips, a slow swipe of her tongue that had his cock jerking to instant attention. He eased his body in the tight jeans, trying to get comfortable with a raging hard-on. The sultry look on her face wasn't helping. For an instant, he caught the erotic vision in her head—Elle sliding from her chair and crawling on her hands and knees beneath the table, slowly opening his zipper and taking his engorged shaft into her talented, eager mouth.

Elle was looking right into his eyes. She ran her tongue along her teeth, leaning toward him across the table, letting him see her smirk. "My sisters are here. Would you mind getting the door while I clear the table and put the dishes in the sink?" Her voice dripped with innocence.

He caught her hand as she rose gracefully and pulled her to his side. "You think you're going to get away with that?" His mouth nuzzled her breast, his hand cupping her mound through her jeans. "They have to leave sometime and then you aren't going to be so safe."

She laughed softly, a clear taunt, knowing full well she'd gotten the best of him. He watched her hips sway as she picked up their plates and walked to the sink. She made anywhere she was home. And she made him feel alive. He carried the tea mugs and came up behind her, trapping her body between his and the sink, setting the mugs behind her so he could cage her in.

Elle looked up at him and he felt his breath hitch in his throat. And then he kissed her. Her taste was addictive. Her mouth sweet and hot and as hungry as his own. She stretched up to circle his neck with her arms, opening her mouth to his, tongue dancing with his, stroking and caressing and making love, long kisses that went on forever until the pounding on the door brought them both back to reality.

"It's a good thing you're letting your beard grow. My face would be hacked up. I have sensitive skin. I won't be able to kiss you if you shave again."

He kept his hands on her waist, holding her still. "I'll have to quit my job. I can't have a job as a sheriff unless I can go undercover. That's why I was grew this." He rubbed the light beard.

"You look like a gruff old mountain man."

"Mean." He sounded pleased. "Jackson the badass."

She rubbed her hand over the front of his jeans. "Jackson in trouble."

He put her firmly away from him and forced his body under control so he could walk to the front door without every step being painful. There was a congregation on his front porch. Bomber tilted his head to give him a look.

"Yeah, you let her signal you not to bark. Whose side are you on?" He glared at his dog, the traitor, and opened the door wide to let Elle's family in.

All of them. The entire Drake family. Sarah with Damon. He really liked Damon, the quietest among them and probably the most brilliant, although Tyson, Libby's fiancé, was in the running for that title as well. Damon was older and much more settled. He had a calming influence on everyone, never saying much, but when he did, they all listened.

Jackson had a fondness for Sarah. The oldest of the Drake sisters, she really looked out for her sisters—and everyone else. Sarah had a good head on her shoulders. He felt her touch Elle's mind, the lightest of brushes and something inside her stilled. She squeezed Damon's hand and smiled before flicking Jackson a quick look. He knew she was very aware he and Elle had made love. Sarah leaned in to kiss him on the cheek.

"Thank you, Jackson. She feels happy," Sarah whispered.

He glanced back at Elle and was surprised she wasn't in the room yet. Sarah meant they could feel the difference in her and he realized he could as well. Her spirit was lighter. Stronger. Elle had come back to them. All of her sisters were looking at him with stars in their eyes. He squirmed under the affectionate gazes, unused to being the center of attention.

"How are you, Abbey?" He turned to his partner in crime, avoiding Aleksandr's glare. The man had an arm wrapped tightly around his woman's waist and didn't look as if he'd be letting go for a long while.

"In trouble. Aleksandr is worse than the shark." She winked at him. "Mostly bruises. Some stitches."

"Infection," Aleksandr snapped.

Abbey made a face. "I had intravenous antibiotics last night and Libby's helping so I'll be fine. The dolphins are alive and that's what counts. Thank you for helping me last night."

Libby stepped in with Tyson. Her large eyes searched his face and something in her seemed to settle. "Inez called Sarah this morning."

Jackson couldn't stop the grin from spreading over his face. He felt the impact the moment Elle walked into the room. She took his breath and stole his heart. He just stood there like an idiot with a big silly grin on his face and nothing at all to say. She walked to him looking like a queen. Head up. Regal. Her long red hair spilling down her back. Her eyes on his. His stomach tightened. She fit right under his shoulder, her arm slipping around his waist, standing with him at the door as her family came inside their home.

He felt like a goof, not mean and badass, so happy about such a dumb little thing, but still, no one knew but him. Elle looked up at him. He sighed. Okay. No one knew how big of an idiot she could make him but her, and he could live with that. He felt her smile. In his mind. In his heart. And it warmed him.

Kate came in with Matt. He tightened his hand on Elle's shoulder. Kate looked strong and well rested, serene as always. She could bring calm to the stormiest situation. She sent him one of her special smiles and he felt included in her small circle. Matt had served with him, trained with him, helped him rescue Elle, never once hesitating. Jackson couldn't help feeling a little guilty that he was going to ask Kate to do something so dangerous. As if reading his thoughts, or just reading his body language, Kate reached out a hand and laid it gently on his arm. At once he felt at peace. He smiled his thanks when she nodded and moved into his living room.

Hannah came in. He loved Hannah. It was that simple. There was something elegant and charming and sweet about Hannah. And she belonged to Jonas and she would pretty much walk through fire for Jonas. Hannah hugged him. She had always hugged him and he knew she didn't touch too many people so he'd always felt privileged and a little humbled by her acceptance of him.

He kissed her on the cheek. "How are you feeling, honey?"

"Aside from Jonas hovering over me and me throwing up constantly on account of this . . ." She rubbed her hand over her small baby bump. "I'm fine. Do you mind if I make a few cookies to go with our tea? If we're going to do another healing session with Elle, we might need a little extra sugar."

"The kitchen's all yours." Hannah made everything taste a little bit better.

She puts love into everything.

"Damn it, Elle. Will you knock that off?" Jackson snapped. "You're so fu . . ." He trailed off with all the sisters looking at him. "You're hardheaded."

She laughed, damn her, not in the least afraid of his wrath. Out of the corner of his eye he caught Jonas shaking his head and mouthing words at him that looked suspiciously like "whipped." Behind Elle's back he gave him the finger. Jonas just laughed at him.

Joley came in last with Ilya towering over her. She instantly brought energy and brightness to the room. She was like quicksilver and Jackson was a little astonished that Ilya had actually managed to get her to agree to marry him. He figured the ceremony had better take place soon. She, like Hannah, was pregnant.

"I like your house," Joley said.

"Wait until you see his piano," Elle answered smugly.

The shocked silence hurt his ears. He could tell they were red-tipped and burning. *You treacherous wench. You're paying for that later.*

Elle laughed out loud. "He's amazing on the piano.

Joley, you have to have him play the songs he's written. They're amazing pieces."

"You compose?" Joley asked, obviously interested.

She loved anything at all to do with music and Jackson could see it was going to take a lot to slow her down now. He cleared his throat several times. "She's exaggerating. I tinker with it a little bit, nothing special."

"You play the piano?" Jonas demanded as if it was a sin.

Jackson leaned down, lifted Elle's hair away from her neck and bit her. She yelped and he soothed the bite with his tongue. *Get me out of this.*

She glared at him and rubbed her neck.

"Where'd you learn?" Sarah asked.

Desperately he took Elle's hand and bit down on her finger, then sucked it into his mouth, his tongue moving over the small sting. She yanked her hand away. *You're very oral, aren't you?*

It was a sign of his desperation that he didn't even reprimand her. "My mother taught me when I was boy," he admitted, blurting it out.

Elle took pity on him. Jackson didn't like to talk about his family or childhood. She flashed a smile at Libby. "I thought maybe if you all were willing you could work another healing session on me—everyone but Kate—and then Kate could try to work on my talent." She looked at Sarah. "Or do you think it should be the other way around, Kate first, just in case anything goes wrong?"

"Wrong how?" Matt asked.

As distractions went, it was a good one, Jackson decided as he settled into an armchair with Elle flopping gracefully at his feet. The Drake sisters liked to sit together on the floor. He'd discovered that a few years earlier when he'd first met them.

"I don't know, Matt," Elle answered honestly, leaning her head back against Jackson's chair, "but I don't want to take any chances with Kate."

Kate lifted her chin. "I know I can do it, Elle."

Before Matt could object, Sarah leaned forward and laid her hand on Kate's knee. "Of course you can, Katie, no one doubts that. But at what cost? I think that's both Elle's and Matt's question and a legitimate one. We can't risk you, especially now."

"I could do a controlled healing," Kate offered. "I would do a single layer at a time. Depending how much damage there is, it would work, but it would be over time—days. I'd have to work on you every day, Elle."

"Is there a risk to you, Kate?" Matt asked directly.

"There's always a bit of a risk," Kate admitted. "You see us after we work. We're drained. Libby has taken a lot on herself and it can be harmful. She has to be careful and I'm guessing I'll have to do the same. But healing Elle is not only worth the risk, I think, given what is happening here, it's one we all have to take."

The scent of freshly baking cookies filled the air. Jackson turned his head toward the kitchen. Hannah smiled at him from the doorway. As much as Kate could keep everything peaceful, Hannah seemed to add a touch of home, of comfort to the atmosphere. He realized his home *felt* like the Drake home. He'd always gone into their house and come out different, with a sense of a family and love. He wasn't certain if it was their deep faith in God, their magic, or the family itself, but they lived the way others dreamed of living—the way he was determined to live.

Elle reached back and took his hand. "I'm going to call Dane." She had to before she lost her nerve. There, with her family surrounding her and the smell of cookies and the teakettle whistling, everything seemed normal. She could call, promise her report and be done with it. One more thing out of the way. She was taking baby steps, but she was emerging from that place of terror she'd been living in for so long.

Jackson's music room, his home filled with her family, all made her feel strong again. She'd made Stavros into an invincible monster. She wouldn't underestimate him, but she wasn't going to be so afraid that she was paralyzed, afraid to live anymore. She looked at Jackson, knowing he disapproved.

"Please understand. I have to do this, Jackson. I need to. For myself. For all those women out there who don't have a family that can rescue them. Afterward, Kate can try her thing and if everything goes right, my sisters can work on healing me again." She showed him her arms, pushing up her sleeves. "See how much better I am?"

He swallowed. A muscle ticked in his jaw and then he nodded his head—barely.

"Is this a blocked number, because I don't get cell phone service here."

He nodded again, his mouth tightening.

It took a few minutes for Elle to make the international call to Dane's private cell phone. She was the only one with that particular number. Elle drummed her fingers on the tabletop as she waited for Dane to answer the phone, carefully avoiding Jackson's frown.

"Hello, Sheena," Stavros's voice purred. "Are you looking for your late, lamented boss?"

16

ELLE'S blood ran cold. Every vestige of color drained from her face. For a moment she couldn't breathe, fighting for air. Her entire body cringed at the sound of that velvet, taunting purr. Instinctively she reached out to Jackson, throwing out her other hand while her fingers clutched the receiver to her ear.

"Poor Dane couldn't endure. He's rather dead right now. Perhaps you'd like to talk to me instead."

Jackson reached around her without a word and depressed the phone with his finger, cutting off the contact. Elle dropped the receiver and buried her face in his lap. He put both hands over her head protectively. He'd been in her mind. He knew what those chilling words had done to her—destroyed every bit of confidence she'd begun to build in herself again.

He stroked her hair, offering comfort in her mind, not aloud, knowing she didn't want everyone to see her in her weakest moment. Bomber pushed close to her, closing in on one side as if to shield her.

Hannah crossed the room, breaking the silence first. "Drink some tea, Elle. He's a long way away and he can't touch you here. He wants you to think that he can, but you're safe here."

Elle swallowed hard, not yet having the strength to control the tremors in her body. "How do you know, Hannah?"

"I just know. Sit up and drink your tea. He wants you afraid because he can better control you that way. But you're home, here with us, and we're going to heal you and make you strong again. He can't win. He believes in his own power because he's never had anything or anyone stand in his way." She crouched down beside her youngest sister, gently pushing her hair from her face. "Look at me, honey." She waited until Elle lifted her head and their eyes met. "You aren't alone. You have all of us. You have our men. You have Jackson. You have this town. But most of all, you have your own talent, your own strengths. He isn't going to win."

Elle drew in a deep breath, turned and leaned her head back against Jackson's legs as she took the teacup from her sister. She looked around the room at the people who loved her—the people who would fight for her—fight with her. "He killed Dane. My handler. Dane's the only one who knew my identity. I was loaned out and he was afraid someone in his agency worked for Stavros. He claimed that Stavros had police on his payroll throughout Europe and even possibly here. He didn't want to take any chances. We built the Sheena MacKenzie cover very carefully over a period of time in order to bring her into Stavros's world."

"I'm sorry, baby," Jackson whispered gently. His fingers found the nape of her neck and began a slow massage to ease the tension out of her.

"Dane was a good man. He didn't deserve to die on my account."

"It wasn't your account, Elle," Sarah corrected. "He was trying to stop a human trafficking ring. You and I both know how dangerous that is. It's becoming the number one moneymaker, edging out drugs and weapons trafficking all over the world. Every branch of law enforcement everywhere is concerned, and all of them know the risks, just as they do when they're trying to bust a drug ring."

Elle bit down hard on her lip, not wanting to think about Dane. He came from a long line of law enforcement and his family had spent generations working for their country trying to stop crime. Dane had requested help from the United States and he'd gotten her. She hadn't done very well for him. Stavros had gotten to him, which meant Dane had been right—someone in his office was on Stavros's payroll. It was only a matter of time now. Even if Dane had protected her identity, Stavros knew Sheena MacKenzie was an undercover agent. He'd never stop now until he found her.

Jackson said nothing, knowing how the Drake family worked. He'd been around them enough times. He knew he was an intelligent man, but several in the room were better thinkers than he was. He was the quiet, action type, finding little reason for a lot of talk and a lot of reason for action.

For him, it was all quite simple. Stavros would never go to prison. Even if he was caught red-handed, he had too much money and too much clout for the evidence to stay untouched. It would disappear or be destroyed. Even in the unlikely case that he was convicted, he would be running his empire from where he was and reaching out to destroy Elle's life. No, Stavros wasn't going to prison.

Jackson glanced up and met Ilya's knowing eyes. The Russian just nodded at him, a small, barely there assent. There were two of them that felt the same way and Ilya was a good man to have at his back.

"I think the real question we need to be asking ourselves is, why is he so strong," Damon ventured. "When any of you use your talents, it drains you. He's a sea away yet he sustains power. That makes no sense."

Jackson's attention jumped to Damon. The man's brain was a machine. He was on to something. Whatever it was had to be important and valuable or he wouldn't have brought it up. He'd been giving it some thought and if he asked the question, he had an idea of the answer.

Damon shot him a quick glance and Jackson had to struggle to maintain his expression. Damon also knew that Jackson was planning to go after Gratsos and he wanted in, it was there on his face. Damon was no fighter, but he could plan a battle—hell, he'd developed defense systems for the United States.

"Maybe it's because he's a male," Jonas said, using his logical voice.

Hannah cuffed him hard. Joley smacked him as well, not once but twice.

"You're such a freakin' chauvinist, Jonas," Joley accused him.

"He has a point," Ilya said, straight-faced. "Look at me."

Joley punched his arm. "Don't flatter yourself, Prakenskii. I'm looking and all I'm seeing is a lot of hot air."

He caught her by the back of her hair and pulled her head back, finding her mouth with his, unapologetically taking possession. When he lifted his head, his eyes laughed. "I've obviously not been doing my job lately."

Joley grinned at him. "You do well enough."

Sarah made a little sound in the back of her throat, bringing everyone back to attention. "Actually, Damon brought up a good point. How is he able to maintain his energy?"

"He's not really using his own energy," Damon said.

Tyson leaned forward, a puzzled frown on his face, hands clasped together in his lap, his gaze locked on Damon in that focused way of his. Nothing and no one else was in the room at that moment. "You think he sets the energy seeking in the fog? Free from him?"

Damon nodded. "It has to be that, Ty. How else? There's no way he could sustain an attack in so many places at once. I looked up the Hidden Currents website and the fog was in sixteen places around the world at *exactly* the same moment. Now, most of those weren't even in the same time zone, but still, the fog hit precisely at the same moment regardless of what time it was in that particular region."

Tyson snapped his fingers. "I see what you're getting at. Clever, clever man."

"I don't understand," Jonas said, his voice irritated. "Enlighten me."

Damon's brows drew together. "He creates the fog to find psychic energy."

"I get that," Jonas sounded disgusted. "How does he sustain it? If he doesn't feed the energy, his fog would collapse, just dissolve. Something has to sustain it." He looked to Hannah for confirmation.

Hannah's attention was on her sisters. They were all looking at one another. "Could he do that? Have any of you ever tried? Ilya?" She looked to her brother-in-law.

"What?" Jonas exploded. "Try not to make the rest of

us feel like idiots. All this hoo-do crap is annoying as hell."

"Don't you see, Jonas?" Tyson obviously didn't notice that Jonas was about to lose his temper. "He sends out the fog, sustaining it himself until it finds psychic energy." His eyes lit up, admiration gleaming for a moment. "Then the fog feeds off the psychic energy available to it, leaving him free to create another trap in the water. Because he uses anything natural to the environment, he just basically has to set things in motion for his traps to work. He used kelp, sharks, fishing nets, wind, and he's got to be traveling on the hidden currents on the water. If there isn't one available he creates his own."

"If he's adept enough, he might be able to do the same thing, prepare a trap and the user of the psychic energy might be feeding the power to him," Damon said. "It's just a theory, of course, but where else would he be getting the energy? All of you are feeding it to him, and it explains why you were all so drained even when you were doing a surface healing on Elle."

There was another long, stunned silence.

Jackson tightened his fingers on Elle's shoulder to get her attention. "If he can do it, you can do it. And maybe on a much larger scale."

Elle shook her head. "I don't know how."

"You zapped him, baby. We both know you did. In that moment, before you went down, when you stopped that wall of water, you lost your temper . . ."

"Big surprise there," Jonas muttered.

Joley kicked him halfheartedly and Hannah glared at him.

"Well it isn't," he defended. "Is anyone here surprised?"

Elle felt the knots in her stomach loosen. Surrounded

by her family, the familiar teasing in the face of dangerous threats, she was beginning to feel safe again. Jonas loved them and she felt secure in his love—at home—in the same way she did with her sisters. She found herself looking around the room.

I'm very lucky, Jackson.

"Damn it, Elle." He reached down and caught her around the waist, dragging her up and onto his lap. Her tea fountained into the air, but simply stayed there, hanging while he wrapped his arms tightly around her and hissed into her ear. "You do that again before Kate works on you and you won't be able to sit down for a month."

Elle burst out laughing. The overturned teacup on the floor righted itself and the liquid streamed back into it. Elle threw her arms around Jackson's neck and hugged him, burying her face against his throat. "Did I tell you this morning that I'm madly in love with you?"

His large hands framed her face. "As a matter of fact you did." He trailed kisses over her, from the corner of her eye to the corner of her mouth before brushing her lips with his. "But that isn't going to get you out of trouble. Every time you use telepathy, I can feel the lesions in your brain increasing. You have to stop."

"I'm honestly trying," she admitted, shocking her entire family.

Elle rarely enlightened anyone to what she was thinking or feeling. The fact that she was explaining herself to Jackson was very telling to them all, especially that she was doing so in front of them. If any of them had doubted her feelings for the deputy, they were convinced now.

"I don't realize I'm using telepathy. We're so bonded it just seems natural."

"I know." His voice was so tender, Elle leaned in to kiss

him again. "Just try harder." He looked at Kate. "Really, Katie, I don't know what to do."

Kate looked at her younger sister, struggling to keep emotion from her face. Jackson had never called her Katie, not once in all the time they'd known one another. And the expression on his face when he looked at Elle brought tears to her eyes. He looked as if the sun rose and set with her, and more than anything, all of them wanted Elle happy.

"We brought some candles and a few other items, Elle," Kate said, her voice a little wobbly. "We've talked a little on how best to try and still give you privacy. Are you willing?"

Jonas stood up. "Maybe we'll leave you to it. We can go out to the deck and drink some manly coffee for a change."

There was a note in his voice Jackson understood. Jonas wanted to talk. Jackson flinched inside. Jonas was law enforcement all the way, but he knew Jackson, and he knew Jackson's way of thinking. He would want to arrest Gratsos, believe there was some way to take him down within the law and Jackson didn't feel much like arguing.

Jonas sighed and jerked his thumb toward the door.

Jackson set Elle's feet carefully on the floor. "I'll be back in a few minutes, baby. But don't worry, I'm not letting you go." He stirred in her mind, reminding her he was helping to create a strong barrier between her and her sisters so they wouldn't feel what she'd gone through.

The intimacy between Elle and Jackson had grown fast, ever since she'd connected with him when he'd been in the prison camp. The more they shared their minds, the more tightly woven the connection had become. He had been alone most of his life, not just alone, but a loner by choice, and now he couldn't imagine his life—his mind—without Elle in it. Her touch, not just physical, was addictive. The warmth she shared with him, her unreserved, uncompromising love that she poured into him was so much a part of him now. When he looked around at his home, he knew it was home because she was there.

Jonas made a sound in the back of his throat. He caught the grin Hannah and Joley threw at each other. The Drake women loved Jonas. He was more than Hannah's husband, he was truly their brother in their hearts. The only one they had. Their fierce protector and their biggest pain. They knew he wanted to talk to Jackson in spite of Jonas's attempt to keep it a secret.

Elle flashed him a small smile and he winked at her. Her smile widened.

"You're going to do this, then, Elle." Jackson made it more of a statement than a question. "Once you do, we move back to the Drake home. It's the center of power and we'll have even more ammunition against the son of a bitch. In the meantime, that house can protect you better than I can."

She shook her head. "No, it can't. He'd be all over me if you weren't stopping him, Jackson." There was quiet conviction in her voice. "He can't get past you."

Damon stood, leaning heavily on his cane. "Are you certain?"

"Absolutely certain. I can't keep him out. I don't know if it's because of the lesions and I can't maintain a natural barrier against him, or if he knows exactly every weak point. But as soon as Jackson pulls away from me, I can hear Stavros whispering to me, telling me he's coming for me. That if I don't come back to him he'll kill everyone

I love and that sooner or later he'll get to that one person who matters above everything to me." She looked at Jackson and there was pain in her eyes. "He means you."

Jackson curved his palm around the nape of her neck and drew her to him, tilting her head back with his thumb, pressing his forehead against hers. "Then he's in for a big disappointment, baby. We both know I don't kill so easy."

"I couldn't bear it if anyone else was hurt or killed because of me," she whispered, pressing closer. "I don't know how to live without you anymore."

"Look around you, Elle," Jackson said. "Take a good look at your family. Nothing is going to happen to any of us. In this one thing, you trust me. He isn't going to win."

Jackson turned abruptly and left the living room, Bomber at his side. He shoved open the door and went out onto the deck, rage welling up inside him. For a brief moment it consumed him, ate at him, until he felt the boards under his feet shift.

Damon and Ilya followed him, Damon dropping into one of the deck chairs. "You're going after him."

"I won't have to go after him. The son of a bitch is going to come right to me," Jackson said. "He's so full of himself he thinks he can come onto my home turf and take my woman." The edge of a glacier was in his voice.

"You have a plan."

Ilya and Jackson exchanged a long, knowing look. Jackson shrugged. He just needed his gun and the man in his sights and Ilya was with him 100 percent on the strategy.

Damon smiled at him. "I think we might need to rethink your plan a little bit." He patted the chair next to him.

"The bastard isn't coming out of this alive." The grim finality gave no room for argument. Jackson looked at

Jonas, who had followed them out, Tyson, Aleksandr and Matt close behind.

"Jackson," Jonas cautioned. "You can't kill someone in cold blood. You're a deputy sheriff, sworn to uphold the law."

"You can have my badge, Jonas," Jackson said quietly. "I'll write up my resignation and have it in your hands in five minutes." He started back into the house.

Jonas stepped in front of him. "Don't be an asshole. What are you going to do? Shoot him and go to jail?"

"That's pretty much the plan."

It was Damon who answered. "I might have a better one. Why don't you sit down and hear me out. I've been giving this a lot of thought and while I don't have all the details worked out, I think we can get rid of him without anyone going to jail. While I have to agree with Jackson on wanting the man dead, I'm not too keen on losing a brother-in-law. Jonas, if you think it best you don't listen, maybe you should go inside and see if Hannah needs anything." He looked around at the others. "If any of you don't want to hear what I have to say, now's the time to walk away."

Jonas shrugged. "I can't exactly be a hypocrite. I just don't want Jackson in trouble. I went out to sea to kill the man threatening Hannah. And if I got to Gratsos, I'd kill him. I may be hardheaded, Damon, but I know arresting Gratsos isn't going to stop him."

"Well, I've got a plan." Damon sounded smug. "Or at least the beginnings of one."

"Let's hear it," Jackson said, and sat on the rail, slamming up a barrier so Elle couldn't read his mind. He needed to stay in hers, but he couldn't have her knowing what they were discussing.

Elle felt it the moment Jackson put up a shield between them. He hadn't been subtle about it either. She glanced toward the deck where the men huddled together around Damon. Frowning, she looked at Sarah for an explanation. "They're up to something."

"Damon has a very level head," Sarah reminded her. "He'd never be involved in anything crazy. He's always the voice of logic and reason. He's probably calming everyone down. We have a few hotheads in the family."

Hannah grinned at her. "You wouldn't, by any chance, be referring to my husband, would you?"

They all laughed and began to arrange the candles around the room as they talked. "Jonas is never going to change," Joley said, "but we love him the way he is, Hannah."

"He's gotten so bossy since we've been married."

The sisters burst out laughing and Hannah put her hand on her hip. "What?"

"He's always been bossy, you dolt. You've just stopped blowing his hat down the street," Abbey pointed out. "Jonas comes with a label, 'Dominant Male Right Here.'"

"Well, I rather like it and he's not as bad as Ilya."

Joley blushed a deep crimson. "I get around him."

"I'll just bet you do," Elle said and nudged her sister with her foot.

"So what about Jackson?" Libby asked. "Sarah says you're getting married in a couple of days. Are you really, Elle? Are you sure that's what you want? Jackson has always put your back up. Are you prepared for what it's really going to be like living with him?"

Abigail glanced out to the deck to look at Jackson. With his scruffy beard he looked like a fierce mountain man. She knew he often went undercover for other counties. He was at home in the role he played, but sometimes he was intimidating. "You've suffered a terrible trauma. It might be better to make huge, life-changing decisions when you've had time to recover."

Elle found herself the center of attention, in the middle of her sisters with all of them watching her closely. She pulled her sweater closer around her, suddenly wishing she'd worn more clothes. They couldn't see the lash marks crisscrossing her body, but she was acutely aware of them, of the trail around her breasts and even over her sex. The inside of her thighs burned and for a moment she couldn't breathe.

Baby, do you need me to come in there and rescue you? Jackson's voice was a velvet rasp in her head. She felt instant warmth pouring through her and hadn't realized how cold she'd become. She was shivering and she made herself take a deep breath.

She looked through the window and he was looking at her. He put his hand up in the air, palm out, fingers spread wide. She put her hand up, palm facing him and felt the brush, first skin to skin, then his lips as if he'd pressed them into the center of her palm. She closed her fingers around the spot, holding the sensation to her. At once she felt steadier.

I'm fine. Thanks. And don't reprimand me, you started it. She ignored the stabbing pain in her head, needing the brief communication.

Wait until we're alone. His voice promised everything but punishment.

Elle turned her attention back to her sisters. "Jackson makes me whole. He gives me back everything Stavros took away. I'm not well, not inside yet, and I know that, but Jackson makes me better every day."

Sarah smiled at her. "I want you to get to the point, we all do, where we can put our arms around you and hold you. It's difficult for us."

"I know. I'm sorry. I hope you understand why. Knowing what happened to me and experiencing it are two different things. Until I'm strong enough to keep that from happening I don't want to take any chances with any of you, and Joley and Hannah are pregnant. We don't know how much their babies feel." She kept her chin up, trying to stay outside herself and not let those images and memories flood into her mind.

Jackson's mind moved against hers and she felt stronger, as if he stood beside her, linking hands, linking souls. There was no way to explain to her sisters, but she could see they were trying to understand.

"No one will cross that line without your permission," Sarah agreed.

"Kate has to stay safe. Promise me, you won't take too much on yourself, Katie. You can't burn yourself out in order to help me," Elle said.

"I've been thinking it might be best to try this in three sessions," Sarah said. "Libby and I talked it over and she said when she's healing something difficult, she's found if she attacks it in thirds, it conserves her strength and keeps her safe from being overwhelmed. Her body can absorb the disease or wound better."

Hannah blew on the candles to light them. At once the room was filled with the soothing fragrance of lavender. Sarah, Hannah, Libby, Abigail and Joley formed a circle around Kate and Elle, joining hands. They swayed back and forth in time to the swelling chant Sarah began. Kate moved closer to Elle until she was standing inches from her, eyes closed, her lips moving in prayer as she asked for strength to help her sister.

Joley's voice began to swell in volume. Abigail joined her, the blend of their voices strong and pure, a counterpoint to Sarah, Hannah and Libby as they chanted, a call and answer, building energy in the room. Kate smiled her serene smile and reached out to Elle again, her hand hovering just a breath from her sister.

"Are you ready?"

Elle couldn't help it. She reached out to Jackson for reassurance.

I'm here, baby. I've got the shield up and it's strong. She's not going to feel anything but love from you.

His voice was quiet. Strong. Protective. Her heart turned over. A part of her wanted to weep tears of joy for the way he loved her. She nodded her head at Kate.

Kate placed her hand on Elle's head, the lightest of touches, almost a caress, a stroke of love from one sister to another. At once she could feel warmth flowing from Kate's hand to her head. The throbbing pain that seemed ever present lessened. She could almost imagine the deepest layers in the lesions healing. Tiny sparks of electricity tingled, leapt and flickered, as if Kate was repairing an electrical current in her head.

The warmth grew to heat. The tingles became charges. Outside on the deck, Bomber suddenly lunged at the screen and began to bark. His entire body faced the women, ears forward, his teeth showing, his barking extremely aggressive. Hannah and Joley both jumped back, breaking the linked circle.

Kate's face paled and she pulled her hand away quickly as though burned. She swayed and Elle caught her around the waist, helping her to sit on the floor. Immediately Libby reached for her.

Kate scrambled backward, avoiding Libby's touch. "Wait, Libby. Just wait one moment."

"What the hell's going on in here?" Jackson demanded, yanking open the screen. Bomber bounded in, rushing over to Elle. "Dismiss," he snapped to Bomber and the dog ceased barking.

Elle paled. "Did something slip through, Kate? Didn't I protect you?"

Kate wrapped her fingers around Elle's slender wrist. "You protected me just fine. I didn't feel anything of what you went through. The barricade you and Jackson have together is astonishing." She dropped her head between her knees, drawing in great breaths to keep from fainting.

"Kate?" Sarah asked.

Hannah floated a plate of sugar cookies into the room, caught the plate and stood by anxiously as Joley maneuvered a teacup.

Kate looked up, her face very white. "I heard him."

"Jackson?" Sarah asked.

Kate shook her head. "*Him.* Gratsos. He was reaching for her, but he can't get past Jackson's barrier. He was so angry. Enraged. And he battered at it. I felt him." She paused. "And then he felt me."

Elle gasped. "Is he in your head? Tell the truth, Kate. Abbey. Make her tell the truth." She was totally panic stricken. Her heart beat so hard she actually pressed her hand against her chest.

"I pulled out the moment he felt me. I don't think he can find me again, but he has to know we're related. If he doesn't have your real name and address, he has another clue. I wasn't trying to hide or protect myself because it didn't occur to me that he might 'see' me or feel me as I worked at healing you." She took a sugar cookie and bit down into it. Joley thrust the teacup into her hands as she shivered. "He's a scary man."

Elle sank down onto the floor. First Hannah. Then Abigail. And now Stavros had frightened Kate. Sweet, serene Kate. It seemed almost blasphemy. Was there no one safe from the man? And Dane. She didn't even know if Dane's family knew he was dead, or if he'd just disappeared as she had.

She pressed her fingers to her eyes, fighting the burning tears. A part of her wanted to get on a plane and confront Stavros. Walk into a room and fight him—psychic power to psychic power—but she wasn't nearly well enough. He was going to find her—he *had* found her and he was systematically attacking every one she loved. Who would be next? Whose death would she be responsible for next? Hannah could so easily have died, taking her unborn child with her, and Abigail still had the bruises and stitches. Why? Because all of her sisters were conserving energy to heal her. They had nothing left for themselves.

She was destroying her family by staying. She closed her eyes, wrapped her arms around herself and tried to face what it would be like to put herself in Stavros's hands once again. A shudder went through her body. Every touch, every act he'd forced on her was so vile to her, such a violation of everything she was and what she stood for, and now, after being with Jackson and knowing love—the touch of love—she couldn't face it. She'd never be able to go through with it. A single sound escaped, one of complete despair.

"Baby, come here." Jackson crouched down beside her, his movements slow and gentle.

Almost immediately everyone went quiet and Elle's sisters moved back to give him room. It was evident in that moment that Elle, their strong, fierce sister, the one they'd all come to know as a protector and fighter, was fragile and in need of someone to lean on.

Elle rocked back and forth, barely aware of the others in the room. Jackson didn't touch her, simply stayed inches from her, his body heat warming her. *Elle. Look at me. You're retreating and wherever you go, you know I'm just going to be following you. Look at me, honey. We're here, in our home, and you're surrounded by everyone who loves you.*

Her eyes flickered. He could feel her, small and light and rolled into the fetal position, tucked into a corner of her mind.

That's it, baby. I'm right here. Right beside you. Look at me. See me.

The sound of his voice—soft, compelling, strong—penetrated the wall she'd erected to try to protect herself from a threat she couldn't face. Elle forced herself outside her mind and back into her body where she could open her eyes and look at his face. A strong face. Beloved in every way. Every line. Every scar. She knew his face as if it were her own. She could trace the bone structure, the firm jaw, his sensual lips and straight nose with the little crook in it.

Jackson's eyes were so dark, so compelling, and once she looked into them she couldn't look away. She felt safe there, held there, not captured, but sheltered. Tears blurred her vision and she blinked rapidly so she wouldn't lose sight of him.

Jackson, all too aware of their audience, gathered her into his arms, pulling her against his chest, his arms wrapping her up so no one could see her face. He knew Elle's family loved her, but she would be so embarrassed to be seen in a moment of weakness. Pride was a big thing to Elle and, where he'd already been through the first stages of trauma and knew what to expect, she had no idea that these moments would come at the most unexpected times.

Elle burrowed close to him, her face tight against the hollow of his shoulder. He stood, taking her with him, sitting in a chair with her on his lap, his arms effectively sheltering her from everyone.

"Katie," he asked softly, "are you all right?"

She nodded. "He didn't get inside my head. I pulled away as soon as I felt him. I think we both recognized we weren't alone at the same time."

"Thank you for working on Elle. I can feel a difference already inside her brain, with just the one healing. When you worked with her, could you get an idea of the damage?" Jackson really wanted an answer, but even more, he wanted to divert attention away from Elle until she could recover enough to face everyone.

As soon as he asked the questions Libby leaned in, anxious to hear the answer. Kate took a thoughtful sip of tea, taking her time, assessing the situation before she spoke. As always she brought a sense of calm, of peace to the room. She looked up serenely and smiled at Matt as he settled beside her, slipping her hand into his. She looked pale, but very much Kate, elegant even in her white blouse and faded, soft jeans. She wore no makeup and no one would ever guess that she wrote bestselling murder mysteries sold worldwide.

"I'm not going to try to minimize the damage to her, especially as I know we need Elle at full strength. The lesions are deep. She needs rest and she needs to relax and not use any part of her talent. I healed the first layer, but there are several. I'll work on her again tomorrow." Before Matt could voice a protest she tightened her fingers and looked at him, eyes pleading for understanding. "I'll be more careful next time."

"I thought we could send a little message next time," Jackson said. "Although I don't know if it's possible. He's obviously trying to harass Elle. Abbey, you can work with animals, can't you?"

She frowned, puzzled, but she nodded her head. "Fairly easily as a rule."

He indicated the dog. "What about Bomber?"

Abigail held out her hand to the German Shepherd and let him come to her, sniffing her open palm. The dog looked up at her with adoring eyes and wagged his tail. She stared into his eyes for a few moments and Bomber instantly lay down at her feet, still looking up at her eagerly.

"He's very responsive. He actually has a psychic energy all his own."

"He alerts to Gratsos's psychic presence," Jackson explained. "His ears go forward, his hair goes up, he stands and points, and gives his intruder bark. He knows before any of us when Gratsos sends his energy toward us."

"You think we can use his energy to attack Gratsos when he intrudes on Elle," Abigail mused, her expression thoughtful. She glanced at Sarah.

Jackson noted all the women were looking to Sarah. Even Elle stirred and sat up a little, turning her head, looking toward Sarah as if for the final verdict.

Tyson leaned forward, his gaze on Damon. "It's all about energy waves, right? It would work. Be kind of funny, have the son of a bitch touch Elle's mind and get a protection dog in his face, all teeth and roar." The grin faded. "But is it worth it? Is he going to just shrug it off and ask if that's all we've got?"

Sarah shook her head. "Gratsos was able to give Elle the sensation of choking her. She feels his fingers closing around her throat."

"Ilya can do things like that," Joley admitted, turning to smile up at her fiancé. "Only much nicer things, of course."

"So can the dog attack him?" Jackson asked.

"I think it could be done," Sarah said. "Abbey could connect Bomber with Gratsos through Elle and give the attack command. I don't know how much damage he'd do, or how long we could sustain the attack, or even if it's worth the effort, but I'm betting it could be done."

"And if he asks himself if that's all we have, more to the good," Damon said. "Let him think we don't have much."

Sarah glanced at him sharply, but Tyson stood up and looked at his watch. "I'm pulling a shift tonight at the fire station. One of the men is sick and they want a couple of us there. We've been losing divers lately. The sea's been so unpredictable and they keep coming up from Southern Cal, thinking they know more than the locals." He bent to brush a kiss over Libby's mouth. "Don't do anything without me."

"We're heading out tomorrow morning to get our marriage license," Jackson said. "We'll try another healing session in the evening. If we're going to let Bomber loose on Gratsos, that's the most likely time we'll try. You'll be back by then."

Libby blew him kisses and then stretched out her hands to Elle. "Before we leave, we're going to do another quick healing session for your body. All of us are participating and we aren't using much energy, so don't panic. And I've got plenty to help Kate." She glanced toward her sister who hadn't attempted to move from Matt's arms.

When Elle still hesitated, Sarah leaned forward. "Listen to me, Elle," she said, using her big sister, this-is-a-lecture voice. "When we're together, we're very strong, strong enough to stop him. You have to have faith in us. You're so busy trying to protect us that you've forgotten what it's like to be part of our circle. He's attacking and he's getting closer. We're all in danger now, whether you like it or not. We need you at full strength. So it's time to heal you. Do you understand me, Elle? It's time."

Elle looked at her sister for a long time and then nodded. She would welcome whatever they did for her as long as they maintained their distance. She could tell Libby was healing her from the inside out. The whip lashes were still fresh, but no longer hurt or felt raw. With this session the wounds would fade. She was looking forward to looking at herself in a mirror without wincing at the sight.

Elle's sisters lined up behind Elle, this time without Kate, and lifted their hands into the air, the soft melodic chant rising as the warm energy surrounded her.

17

ELLE kept her hand firmly in Jackson's, her fingers tangled with his tightly as they walked into Inez's grocery store with the marriage license in Jackson's pocket. They'd had to go inland to the courthouse, an hour and a half drive, in order to do the paperwork. But it was done and they wanted to drop by and consult with Inez. Bomber walked close to Jackson on his leash, prancing a bit, showing off.

It had taken most of the morning to complete the round-trip and the sun was peeking through a small cloud layer as they walked along the wooden sidewalk toward the grocery store. Several people stepped from their shops to greet Elle and wish her well, all with wide grins, saluting Jackson as if he had stolen the prize.

"We're creating quite a stir," she observed, a little nervous with all the attention. Having Bomber helped, because often people started out talking to her, asking her questions about her disappearance, but Bomber distracted them quickly.

She waved as Irene Madison and her son, Drew, came

out of the bookstore, Drew with a pile of books in his arms. Irene looked glowing, although when she first saw Elle, she stumbled a little. The last time she'd seen Irene, the woman had been bashing Libby over the head with her purse, demanding she cure Drew of leukemia. She had blamed Libby for the boy taking a risky prescription drug that had nearly driven him to suicide. Elle hadn't been very forgiving as she rushed to her sister's aid, and if it hadn't been for Jackson, she could have done the woman real harm. Still, Elle had a difficult time feeling remorse when Irene had hurt Libby.

Irene flashed a tentative smile. She looked a little leery of the German Shepherd, and Elle was secretly glad. Bomber might have picked up on her dislike of the woman, because he didn't act friendly; rather he positioned his body at a slight angle, as if protecting Elle, or intimidating Irene. Elle clung tighter to Jackson's hand, and forced a smile. "Irene, how nice to see you. Drew looks well."

"I am, Elle," Drew announced before his mother could speak. "I'm playing basketball this year." He grinned at her. "Of course I ride the bench a lot, but I made the team." His grin widened. "It helps that the school is so small we hardly have enough players to field a team, but still, I'm there."

"It's been fun going to all the games," Irene admitted. "Drew's been in remission for months now."

"That's wonderful," Jackson said.

"It's thanks to Libby and Tyson," Irene conceded. "They've helped me work with Drew and he's in a new study with a drug Ty developed."

Elle swallowed hard and nodded her head. It was the best she could do. She would never forget that moment when she felt the wrench, Libby going down, sick, disoriented, broken. They'd nearly lost her, and, although it wasn't entirely this woman's fault, she'd actually struck Libby when her sister had been defenseless. The wind came in from the sea—a soft breeze ruffling her hair and carrying the soothing touch of her sister Hannah.

Elle turned toward the Drake home and blew a kiss back toward the captain's walk, her hands going up to shift the wind back toward her sister. She noticed the dog looked back toward her family home as well and she dropped her hand on his head to stroke a grateful caress over his fur. He was definitely making her first real public appearance easier.

Jackson cleared his throat. "They're always doing that sort of thing back and forth," he explained.

Drew laughed. "Everyone knows that. We all like it the most when Hannah blows Jonas's hat off his head."

"Is she still doing that?" Irene asked.

"Oh yeah. He was chasing a couple of us when he saw us skim boarding at Big River and she slowed him down with the wind in order to give us a chance to get away," Drew happily told them, missing Elle's quick shake of the head, and forgetting his mother was standing right there. "Man, it was so funny. He started yelling at the wind and every time he went to pick his hat up, the wind caught it and blew it just out of reach. It kept going closer and closer to the water and he kept yelling, 'Hannah, don't you dare,' but eventually we got out of there so I don't know if she actually put it in the waves."

"She does like to do that," Elle said, hoping to divert the attention back to her. "It's good practice and keeps Hannah's skills sharp. She's very precise at it, you know."

Irene's hands were on her hips, a frown on her face. "Just when were you skim boarding at Big River, Drew?"

He turned bright red and began to stammer.

"Did you cut school?" Irene demanded.

Jackson took Elle by the arm. *I'm guessing now's a good time to get out of here before she realizes Hannah helped the boys get out of trouble. Jonas would most likely have taken them to their parents.*

"We'll see you later, Irene, Drew," Jackson said. "I hope you're both coming to the celebration."

Irene beamed at them, diverted for a moment. "Your wedding. Of course. We wouldn't miss it for the world. And, Jackson . . ."

He cringed, the tips of his ears going red. The hand on her back was urging Elle to move forward, but she turned back deliberately, forcing Jackson to wait politely.

"Thank you so much for helping us get Drew to that camp in Tahoe for AE week. We never could have managed it and he really enjoyed it."

"It was so cool, Jackson," Drew agreed. "I got to skateboard and swing on a trapeze and go sailing." His entire face lit up. "I even drove a race car, you know one of those little all-terrain ones. I've never done any of those things before."

Jackson cleared his throat, avoiding Elle's gaze. "I got your thank-you card, Drew. That was enough. I'm glad you had a good time." His voice was gruff and now his entire ears were red. Jackson pushed Elle ahead of him, hoping to make it to the safety of the grocery store before anyone else stopped them.

The day was a little overcast, with floating clouds, but it was bright out, the sun shining off the water, making it necessary to wear sunglasses. He shoved them on his face.

"This is worse than walking with a fu— a . . . er . . . a celebrity," Jackson hissed between clenched teeth. "No wonder Joley is marrying Ilya. She needs a full-time bodyguard to get her one block down the street."

"You wanted to walk." There was a hint of laughter in her voice. Now that Jackson was uncomfortable, the walk might turn out fun after all. Bomber must have agreed with her, because he looked up at her with a wide, toothy grin, his eyes laughing as well. "You didn't tell me you helped Drew go to a camp for Alternate Education week."

He shrugged. "The kid's never been able to do anything, he's always been so sick. And the other kids come back talking up a storm about all the places they've gone and the experiences they've had and I just thought it might be good for him."

"I'm sure it was."

"He's stuck with his mom all the time and she fusses over him until the kid wants to explode. He loves her, but he's a teenager, he needs a little freedom."

Jackson sounded a little defensive. Elle looked up at him. "What else have you done?"

"Nothing. There's just this program I've been working on getting him into for the summer. It's kind of like a foreign exchange thing. He'll tour four countries and see a bit of the world. He needs that, Elle."

She stopped right there on the sidewalk, circled his waist with her arms and went up on her toes, pressing kisses over his chin up to his mouth.

His hands settled on her hips, half holding her away from him. "What are you doing? Everyone's looking."

"I'm kissing you."

"Well, cut it out."

"I like kissing you."

"Not in public. I mean it, Elle, get that wicked little smirk off your face."

"Big badass Jackson. What a baby," she taunted. Laughing, she caught his hand and began walking toward the grocery store, Bomber keeping pace.

Jackson heaved a sigh and ran his finger around the crew neck of his T-shirt. "It's hot today." Speeding up a little he guided her at a faster pace, hoping to reach the door before anything else happened.

"Is it?" The teasing note lent her voice a little lilt.

He glared at her, hoping for intimidation. She was in a "Drake" mood. When the seven sisters got together nothing stopped them from teasing the crap out of anything and anyone in their line of fire. He seemed to be lined up in the crosshairs with Elle today. With a sense of relief, he reached over Elle's head and shoved open the heavy door, stepping back politely to allow her through first. He followed her—straight into hell.

Jackson stopped dead, half in and half out of the doorway. Half the village was crowded into the store. He instinctively tightened his hold on Bomber's leash and the dog came to instant attention.

"Jackson!" Inez called out sharply. "You're letting flies in."

There were no flies. But she certainly knew how to draw attention to him. Everyone in the store turned around to stare at him with wide grins on their faces.

"You look like a deer caught in the headlights," Elle whispered, sounding smug.

He reached for the back of her shirt, half intending to drag her back out of the store but she had already slipped just out of reach as if she'd anticipated his reaction. A spattering of applause went around the store and he could feel the color rising under his shirt and up his neck.

"Congratulations," Reginald Mars said to him and clapped him hard on the back. "Good to know someone in this town had the sense to snap that girl up." He leaned close and lowered his voice, just enough to sound conspiratorial, but loud enough for Elle to overhear. "That one's got a little fire in her. You're going to have your hands full."

Elle laughed. "Keep it up and I'll be spilling every bad story I know about you to my aunt Carol."

Reginald Mars had his own hydroponic farm and his vegetables were sought after and considered the best. But the man could be very difficult and before the Drake sisters' aunt had returned to town, he'd just as likely throw his produce at a person than sell it to them.

He winked at her. "Don't buy any of this mass-produced, poison-covered garbage, Elle. I already left a box of vegetables on Jackson's deck. I owed for—"

"That was kind of you, Reginald," Jackson interrupted. "I'm trying to feed Elle as healthy as possible. I particularly like those tomatoes you gave me a couple of weeks ago."

As a distraction, it should have worked. Mars could talk tomatoes almost as well as Clyde Darden talked flowers, but nothing was deterring the man. He simply acted as though Jackson hadn't spoken.

". . . helping me with the paperwork for the permits. I couldn't have gotten through them without you. I was pretty sure you talked them into letting me extend my building and Darryl, over at the courthouse, told me you had."

"I don't sell poisoned tomatoes," Inez denied in the background, hands on her hips, glaring at all of them. "My vegetables are every bit as healthy."

Jackson wanted to sink through the floor. Elle was beaming at him. He gritted his teeth and forced a semblance of a smile. *Don't say a word. Not one word.*

Elle gave him a wide-eyed look of innocence that he didn't buy for one minute.

"Elle!"

Trudy Garret rushed Elle, nearly knocking her over so that Jackson reached out a hand to steady her, keeping it on her back to let her know he was there supporting her. He stepped close, crowding her body when he felt her instant withdrawal. She steeled herself and hugged Trudy back. Jackson helped her stem the flow of information, holding a shield for her to prevent invading Trudy's privacy. Beside Trudy was her little boy, Davy. Trudy was engaged to Matt's youngest brother, Danny Granite, and she worked at the Salt Bar and Grill.

"How are you doing?" Trudy asked, taking a firm grip on her son's hand. He tugged at her, trying to get to Bomber.

Jackson shifted the dog a little closer to give the boy access. Instantly he was petting and talking to the German Shepherd.

"Good. How are things?" Elle responded. She leaned back into Jackson.

"Awesome. Danny and I are thinking we might buy the Grill. It's for sale. His parents said they'd help us." She grinned. "Of course, I think they want us married first, which would be logical."

"Is anything holding you up?"

"I see. Now that you're taking the big plunge, you're going to get the rest of us to do it," Trudy teased, but her smile faded. "I just want to know that Danny really loves Davy. I don't want Davy to be pushed aside in any way."

"All Danny does is talk about Davy," Jackson supplied. "He's a good man."

"Nervy," Reginald supplied, "real nervy."

Elle patted his arm. "You're not helping the cause here, Reginald. We *want* Trudy to marry Danny."

"In that case then, stop living in sin in front of the boy," Reginald advised.

Inez glared at old man Mars. "Shame on you!"

"Well, she shouldn't be," Reginald said. "In my day that boy would be taken out behind the barn and taught a lesson. You don't play with a lady's affections."

"Danny asked her," Inez said.

Reginald's bushy brows came together and he turned his piercing gaze on Trudy. "You don't dally with young men unless you're serious. Not at your age. And not when you have a boy to look after."

Trudy blushed wildly. Jackson coughed behind his hand.

Inez leaned over the counter, taking matters into her own hands to get the attention off Trudy. "I've done a lot of planning, Jackson, and everyone is helping. It's going to be a wonderful celebration." She blushed a little and turned toward the quiet man sitting with her behind the counter.

Elle's eyes widened at the sight of Frank Warner, who must have just gotten out of jail. "Frank, how nice to see you."

He looked pale and much older, his silver-gray hair closely cropped, but still thick and wavy. He gave her a half smile, a little surprised, as if he expected her to ignore him. Inez moved in close—protectively. "It's good to see you as well, Elle. I hear you're about to get married."

Jackson put his arm around Elle's shoulder and held

out his other hand to Frank. "Inez has been working on it for us. Hopefully you'll be able to come. We'd love to have you. It's not formal . . ."

"Formal enough," Inez said. "I've had Sarah send for one of those couture gowns for beach weddings."

Jackson's eyebrow shot up. "I thought a beach wedding meant bathing suits, Inez."

She sniffed disdainfully. "You know better than that, Jackson Deveau. You will dress up decently for Elle."

He leaned down to whisper in Elle's ear. "I was looking forward to the bikini."

"I heard that, young man. I may be old but my ears are sharp." She cleared her throat and took Frank's hand. "Frank and I have been talking about getting married ourselves. We've known each other for too many years to count and thought we might grow old together, sitting in our rocking chairs on our front porch."

There was something on her face when she looked at Jackson, a need for approval, a hope that he would agree with her. Whatever she was feeling, she wanted something from Jackson. Elle understood then, the dynamics of the relationship were more than Jackson helping Inez out with her store, or Inez helping to plan his wedding. They were more like mother and son, or at the very least, a great beloved aunt.

Jackson's smile was slow in coming and his eyes drifted speculatively over Frank Warner's lined face. Fresh out of prison, he seemed an unlikely candidate for Inez to fall in love with, but everyone in the village knew she'd stood by the man and visited him regularly in spite of the long distance she'd had to drive to get to the prison.

"Well, Frank, you're getting the second most wonderful woman in Sea Haven. I hope you appreciate her and always take good care of her." His chin nuzzled the top of Elle's head, but she could feel a faint tremor running through his body.

She moved her mind through his. He was worried. He knew how much Inez loved Frank, but he didn't know Frank Warner, not at all, and it bothered him that Inez was making the decision so quickly.

Inez doesn't do quick. She will have thought about this for some time.

Women in love aren't rational, baby. Believe me, my mother loved my father and he was the worst kind of man. There was a small hesitation before he made the confession. *I loved him, too, but that doesn't mean we should have. We both would have been far better off without him. I don't want that—what my mother had—for Inez.*

Without hesitation Elle leaned across the counter and held out her hand to Frank. "Congratulations, I think it's wonderful."

Frank put his hand in hers and Elle closed her fingers around his. For a moment there was only the warmth of human contact and then Frank's emotions spilled into Elle's mind—into Jackson's.

Jackson felt the impact immediately, the distaste of knowing someone's private thoughts. Frank was uncomfortable, sitting in the midst of the villagers' scrutiny for Inez. He'd always loved her, but felt unworthy of her. He didn't want others to turn away from her because of him, yet he couldn't quite bring himself to walk away from her. He felt old and tired and worn, and just wanted peace again—with Inez.

Jackson became aware of the stabbing pain in Elle's head, and knew she was using her talent too much. She was going to destroy all the work Kate had done. He tugged at her arm to get her to release Frank's hand.

"Let me know what the two of you need, Inez," Jackson said.

Her chin tilted and quivered for a moment before she steadied herself. "We need a couple of people to stand up for us."

Jackson bent to brush a kiss on her cheek. "It would be a privilege, Inez. Name the time and place and we'll be there."

Relief flickered in her eyes and then Inez ran her hand back and forth over Jackson's beard and clicked her tongue in disapproval. "When are you getting rid of that scruff so I can see your face again?"

He grinned at her and circled Elle's waist with his arms, drawing her back against him. "She won't kiss me if I don't have a beard. I'm not going without kisses."

Inez frowned at Elle. Elle, under cover of the counter, kicked Jackson's shin. "It's my face," she admitted. "I have very sensitive skin and his whiskers rub and I get burned."

"Oh, that's not good," Inez said. She sighed. "I guess you'll have to keep the beard then, Jackson, but keep it trimmed. You go through periods where you look positively awful, like those bikers who come through the village."

He grinned at her. "How would that be, Inez?" Half the village wore long hair and beards.

"Don't give me sass," she scolded, knowing full well he was teasing her. "*Mean* is how they look. You don't want to scare off Elle before you marry her."

A bell tinkled, signaling someone else had come or gone and Elle angled herself better to keep an eye on everyone in the store. Irene and Drew had slipped in and were at the frozen food section. The Dardens were over by the bread rack talking to Jeff Dockins, another local. The store was filled with her neighbors and she let the talk flow around her, the familiar camaraderie soaking into her like nectar.

She'd always loved Sea Haven and this store in particular where all the locals came and hung out visiting. Some called it gossip, but she knew they were just exchanging news, all interested in each other's lives. They helped one another out often and genuinely cared. She leaned her head back a little, relaxing into Jackson.

Against her leg, Bomber pressed close, his body alert, quivering, fur and ears standing straight up. He was looking around the store, not at her. A chill went down her spine. The hair on the back of her neck stood up and she felt goosebumps rise. Her breath caught in her throat and she shifted, letting her eyes slide around the store. The Reverend RJ was lurking at the meat counter and she knew Jackson had already spotted him, realizing how protective his body posture was.

A young teenage girl stood at the Reverend's side, her lip, nose and eyebrow pierced. She wore dark lipstick and darker eyeliner. Her long hair hung straight to her shoulders, a shiny raven's wing of blue-black. She was very pretty, although she wore all black and there was no animation on her face at all. She didn't look at anyone, but stared at the floor.

Dropping one hand on Bomber's head, Elle let her gaze slide past them. The premonition of danger was strong. Urgent. Dark. Cold seeped into her body, first her skin, then her blood and bones. Jackson began to rub her arms as if to warm her. She let her gaze drift around the store. Several people were donning sweaters or rubbing their hands together as if cold.

Jackson. She whispered his name and tried to shield his body with hers.

"What is it, baby? I see RJ. I'm not going to let him get confrontational." His mouth was close to her ear, his breath warm, his lips brushing her earlobe in a secret kiss.

But it wasn't RJ. The air left her lungs in a little rush as she spotted a dark shadow sliding through the store, crouching near first one person, and then another, sniffing, fingers extending, beckoning. Frank looked toward the shadow and then Mrs. Darden. Elle pushed away from Jackson and inserted her body between Frank's line of vision and the slowly creeping aberration.

As she watched, the shadow crept around the store, lengthening along the wall until it formed a shape she was familiar with. Death. A faceless ghoul, long and thin with outstretched arms and a wide mouth gaping greedily, needing to feed the endless addiction.

She sketched a quick sign in the air as it crouched over Mrs. Darden and the ghoul spun around, eyes glowing for a moment, recognizing the enemy.

RJ, directly behind the shadow, must have thought Elle was staring at him. His face hardened and he clamped his fingers around the young teenage girl's wrist, yanking her forward toward the counter. Both RJ and the girl flowed right through the apparition as though Death was not there.

RJ set the shopping basket on the counter. "We're in a hurry."

Elle watched the shadow stiffen. His tongue slid out of his mouth as if tasting something. He sniffed the air. Abruptly he pulled his arms in tight against him, as if holding something locked to him, closed his mouth, and then he vanished and took the chill of death with him.

Jackson waited for the Reverend to speak to Elle, but he didn't. The man was notorious for taunting the Drake sisters, trying to get media coverage, offering to exorcise their demons. It was odd to see him without his body-guards. The girl's mother was nowhere in sight. Jackson had a bad feeling about that girl. And Bomber rumbled a warning, showing teeth.

Deliberately Jackson crowded next to RJ at the counter. "Surprised to see you still in town."

The Reverend cast him a smoldering look of hatred. "You shouldn't be. There's been a cop cruising by my house every half hour. In a town where there's no police, that seems a little excessive."

The girl kept her head down, eyes downcast.

"We suspect a pedophile in the area, Reverend. You want us to make certain all the children are safe, don't you?"

"That's an ugly word," RJ spat out.

"It's an ugly crime."

"And that dog is dangerous. You shouldn't have him around people."

"He's only dangerous to criminals. He particularly hates men who abuse women, rapists and pedophiles. Just a thing he has." Jackson gave a hand signal and Bomber snarled, showing a mouthful of teeth, then subsided at another signal from Jackson, but he never once took his gaze from RJ.

The Reverend glared at Inez. "Can't you hurry? If you weren't talking so much, you'd get a lot more done."

Jackson looked at the girl. "How old are you?"

RJ yanked the girl close to him, his face a twisted mask of fury. "She doesn't have to answer your questions. Her mother put her in my charge."

"Are you all right?" Jackson asked her.

The girl refused to look at him. She just shook her head.

"Don't make trouble, Venita," RJ warned. His voice seemed soft and soothing, even cautionary, but Jackson felt the psychic push of energy signaling something altogether different. "Your mother will be so disappointed."

The girl stiffened and averted her face further.

"You don't have to be afraid," Jackson said. "I'm a deputy sheriff. If this man has hurt you or threatened you in any way, I can help you."

"I'm a man of God," the Reverend proclaimed loudly and, gripping the teenager's arm, he tugged her away from Jackson, leaving his items on the counter.

Jackson watched them leave the store with a speculative gaze behind his dark glasses.

"Can't you arrest him?" Inez said. "He's a monster."

She looked at Frank. Clearly she believed Frank shouldn't have gone to prison when RJ so clearly should. She believed Frank had been duped, that he wasn't a malicious criminal. Jackson thought maybe a little bit of greed had come into play, or Frank wouldn't have been so easily duped, but he wasn't going to voice his opinion.

"He hasn't been caught committing a crime, Inez." Jackson glanced at his watch. He wanted to call a friend at the office and find out what they could about the teen and her mother and they had to get back to the house soon. Elle's sisters would be coming over to do another healing session with her.

"He's sleazy," Inez declared. "Every time he comes near me, my skin crawls. And Bomber didn't like him." She smiled at the dog. "Good boy. You're a very good dog."

Elle patted Bomber's sides. "He is a good boy. We'll see you later, Inez. And you, too, Frank. We're heading home."

"Elle could use a little more rest, Jackson," Inez advised. "She's still pale and has dark circles under her eyes."

Elle couldn't stop her fingers from creeping up to touch her face. Inez had seen her bruised and swollen face, but her sisters had made her look normal again, hadn't they? For a moment she doubted. She could still feel every punch, every slap, the vicious quick jabs and then the gentle strokes. Stavros's voice whispering to her, pleading and cajoling that she just needed to behave, that this was hurting him to have to punish her this way. She shuddered and turned to bury her face against Jackson's chest, uncaring of the people around her.

You're safe, baby. I'm right here. I'm always with you.

Inez looked stricken. Elle had always been self-sufficient and sure of herself, absolutely confident, even as a young child. Yet, she'd curled into Jackson and suddenly appeared quite fragile. "What did I say, Jackson?" she whispered, walking with them to the door.

"Nothing at all, Inez," he said. "You're fine."

Elle managed a small smile over her shoulder as Jackson took her out of the store. "I'm sorry. I don't know what happened."

"Nothing happened, Elle. You're going to be all right." He wrapped his arm around her shoulders, keeping her close. "You'll find you're going to have triggers and you just have to deal with them when they crop up. *We'll* deal with them."

She quickened her steps on the wooden planks, hurrying toward Jackson's truck. The wind blew in off the sea, just a breeze, ruffling her hair and touching her face. They could both hear the feminine voices singing a soft melody, a soothing balm to her raw nerves. Out in the ocean, several whales surfaced, blowing as they did so, as if saying hello, and then swimming silently past the headlines before slipping back under the water again. At once she could hear their answering song, the breeze skipping over the water to bring the healing tones, the melodic keening and groaning, accompanied by churring and whistling.

The whales sang to Elle, performing a masterpiece, a sonata, most likely directed by Abigail. The unusual music sustained her on the way home. Highway 1 wound along the cliffs above the ocean and the whales kept pace with them, gliding lazily through the water, singing to her, occasionally breaching so she could maintain a visual.

As they drove up the drive to his home, Jackson noticed the abundance of bird life and plants and flowers. The blossoms seemed thicker and more colorful. He could see herbs had sprung up in one section just along the back fence as he parked the truck. The Drake women sat on his deck, listening to the whales, singing back to them in low tones. Abigail and Joley singing a harmony while the other women's voices rose and fell in counterpoint like waves.

Jackson went up the stairs and stood, Elle leaning against him, listening to the song the whales and the girls performed back and forth. When the last note faded, he shook his head. "Unbelievable," he said. "Never in my wildest dreams did I ever think I'd hear something like that. I'm not going to ask how you did that."

Abigail smiled at him, even as she dropped down on her knees to greet Bomber. She scratched his ears and chest. "I've decided to try tonight, Jackson. You know, to attack Gratsos through Bomber. Kate's going to do another session with Elle and I'm going to join just before she withdraws. We think Elle is at her most vulnerable right then and he feels the barrier slip for a moment. You're maintaining it, but as Kate withdrew she sensed you holding yourself back to give her more privacy. And that made Elle's defenses just weak enough that he almost slipped through." She looked at Kate. "We're going to give him another opportunity and this time we'll be ready."

"I don't understand what you're going to do to him. How can Bomber possibly touch him?" Elle rubbed her throat as if she felt Stavros choking her.

Abigail glanced at Hannah and they exchanged a wicked little grin. Jackson frowned and stirred, suddenly uncomfortable. "What are you two up to?" he demanded.

"A little experiment is all." Sarah began to build a circle right there on his deck with candles.

"Where's Ilya? And Jonas? And Ty. Damon was going to be here. We have things to discuss. What's going on? Where's Aleksandr and Matt?"

The sisters burst out laughing. "You sound a little scared," Elle said. "Are you afraid of my sisters?"

"A little," Jackson admitted. "Things get out of hand fast when you're all together."

"Ty's pulling another shift," Libby explained. "They're very shorthanded with that flu going around. And Damon is with him. He drove to the Willit's station house to talk about something to do with energy and the Bermuda Triangle. I didn't really listen. When they get all technical I just tune them out."

"Matt's got this thing with his brother tonight," Abbey added. "And Aleksandr, Ilya and Jonas are doing some research for Damon. He wanted them to talk to the fishermen and divers in the area and get some data for some big project he's working on."

"Great," Jackson muttered and folded his arms across his chest. "They get the fun, and I get left unprotected with all of you."

Sarah pointed to the kitchen. "Make yourself useful. We'll need tea and cookies after the session."

"Cookies?" His eyebrow shot up. When she glared at him he sighed. "Fine. I think Inez or Mrs. Darden sent some over." He kissed the top of Elle's head and stalked into the house, feeling slightly guilty that he was leaving Bomber in the midst of women he knew were up to no good.

Elle sank down onto the mat in the center of the circle, Kate to her right, Abigail on her left. Bomber lay down with his head in Abbey's lap, ears forward alertly while she stroked his head. Libby sat facing Elle, and Hannah, Joley and Sarah made a semicircle behind her. The scent of lavender permeated the air.

Elle held up her hand before her sisters could begin a healing chant. *Jackson.*

Right here, baby. Can't you feel me?

She wrapped herself in him, in his warmth and strength. Letting out her breath, she nodded and Joley began the soft melody to draw energy from around them to heal Elle's tattered talents. She felt the familiar touch of

Kate as she entered, so light, so soothing, bringing her calm and serenity along with the rebuilding energy. This time she felt the difference immediately as her sister worked, building on her previous session, restoring and repairing faster and faster.

Just as she thought she might have to stop Kate from doing too much and burning herself out, she felt Abigail's touch. Truth. Purity. Then Hannah. Mischievous and determined. Sarah. A force to be reckoned with, a sword beyond measure. Joley, a thirst for vengeance and a need to protect her younger sister. Libby entered last, her sweet, healing touch spreading through Elle's body and then uniting them all until they were a solid unit.

Okay. Pull back a little, Jackson, Sarah instructed.

Jackson weakened the barrier in Elle's mind, so that her shield shimmered nearly transparent, giving her sisters glimpses of her memories if they'd chosen to look. They stayed focused on one thing—waiting in silence—staying to the back of Elle's mind, hoping their enemy would take the bait.

Abigail drew the dog's mind into their center. He was on alert, already sensing Stavros's entry. Before the man could set himself, they dragged one memory from Elle's mind. Stavros, stark naked, body exposed. Abigail hissed a command. The dog leapt. Roared. All teeth. Ferocious. Stavros screamed. High-pitched. Agony. And then he was gone.

18

"ALL right, baby, you're going to tell me why you insisted I go over to the Dardens' this evening and repair the stairs and look at the roof and every other thing in their house from the electricity to the generator." Jackson made it a demand. "What's up? You were tired and whether you want to admit it or not, you're a little intimidated by the Dardens. And why did you give them those large candles with the crucifix in them and ask them to keep them lit through the night? And then make me stop at Inez's to give candles to her and Frank Warner? Something's up, and don't give me your innocent look. It was a big deal to you."

Elle sighed and looked up at the sky. The sunset had been spectacular. She understood why Jackson had built his house in the exact spot he'd chosen. His deck had the most extraordinary view of the setting sun. Colors had streaked across the sky, all orange and red and pink, while the sun, a bright molten ball, had poured liquid gold into the sea. They hadn't gone inside, content to sit side by side on a blanket up on the dunes while the sky turned from orange to purple.

Jackson remained silent, outlasting her. She sighed again, knowing she was going to tell him and he'd probably think she was crazy. "I saw Death today." Her confession came out in a little rush. "Today in the grocery store, I saw Death."

He turned to her, studying her upturned, anxious expression and a chill went down his spine. She was very serious. "What does that mean?"

"I sometimes can see with a second sight. I don't know how else to tell you, most of my sisters can do it. Today, in the grocery store, he was there, looking for someone to take. Both Frank Warner and Mrs. Darden attracted his attention, but anyone in the store, including you, is at risk."

"That's crazy, Elle. Death isn't a person. It just happens."

"He looks for people close to death, a sickness, an accident, a suicide. He finds them. I saw him. You don't have to believe me." She looked out over the ocean. "We all have a deep faith, and I know you do, too. I've seen you in church, Jackson, but even though there is good and evil in the world, it doesn't mean that there aren't anomalies as well. Some people think we're an anomaly, but obviously we want to believe our gifts were given to us for good. There are things you just can't explain. Death is one of them. We've always called the apparition that. He comes sometimes and looks for someone close to dying and speeds it up."

"Can you stop it?"

She shrugged. "We think it's like accidents and random occurrences, but that once he's in the vicinity, he isn't satisfied and won't leave until he's stolen a life. It isn't the same as a natural death, because he craves that life and succeeds in stealing it."

Jackson shook his head. "I don't even know what to say."

"He looked at everyone in the store and he has their scent, the essence of their life. I saw him take it in and he'll not stop until he's satisfied."

"Did you tell your sisters?"

"I took Sarah aside and told her. She's seen Death before, when he came here on Damon's shoulders. Damon had slipped away and Death wanted him back, but he took someone else. Whether we helped fight him or not, none of us really know."

"But there's nothing you can really do about it?"

"Not unless we're there when he tries to steal life—and even then we might not be strong enough to stop him."

"You can't save the world, Elle," he said gently. "Sometimes, when I'm working, I have to repeat that to myself a dozen times a shift."

"I know." She produced a tentative smile. "But sometimes we can get in a little strike for justice." The smile faded. "He was closer, Jackson."

His head spun around and he locked gazes with her. "What do you mean? He? Death?" But he had a sinking feeling she wasn't talking about death—not from the look on her face.

Her stomach churned and she pressed a hand there. "Stavros. I felt him and he was closer. He knows where I am and he's coming."

He let his breath out and nodded. "It's okay, baby. I figured he'd come. As soon as he answered Dane's phone, I knew."

"And you're not afraid?"

Terrified. She wanted to say terrified. He knew that and understood. Jackson shook his head. "No, I think it's a major tactical error for him to come onto our turf. He's arrogant and used to getting his way. He thinks he'll buy off the cops or the locals and get help to reacquire you, but he's going to run into a little problem with that plan."

The confidence in his voice steadied her. "I'm not going to think about him tonight. At least he's not feeling very well."

"I still can't believe your sisters did that," Jackson said, leaning back, linking his fingers behind his neck. "You're all a little out of control."

Elle pillowed her head on his chest, giving him a tentative smile. "Actually, I thought they were very controlled. No one even peeked at my memories and you shielded them beautifully from my emotions."

His hand stroked her hair. "Let me just say, you're all a little crazy and I never want to get on any Drake woman's bad side."

"It was your idea." She felt compelled to point this out.

He tipped his head up to look at her. "Oh, no. I was thinking to go for the throat."

Elle laughed softly. "I think that's just as bad." She tightened her arm around his waist, snuggling closer. "Whatever happened, I think we scared him enough that he won't be visiting me for a day or two." This time there was satisfaction in her voice.

Jackson rolled over until his body was half blanketing hers. He framed her face with his palms and looked down at her, looked into her eyes. "Have I told you that I love you?"

His wide shoulders blocked out the sky and then his

face was descending slowly toward hers. She could see his long lashes and straight nose, the compelling hunger in his eyes. He always managed to make her heart beat a little faster and her body just melted, right there in the sand, soft and pliant and accepting.

She took a breath and he kissed her, long and leisurely, his hunger growing as he fused their mouths together. She pressed her body closer, wishing they were skin to skin, wanting the feel of his chest rubbing against her aching breasts. Her fingers settled in his thick, wavy hair and she gave herself up to the pleasure of his marauding mouth.

It took moments—or hours—before she realized he had somehow opened her blouse and exposed her breasts, and was now making his way down her throat and over her sensitive skin. A jolt of electricity went from her breasts to her womb, so that she felt the clutch and the emptiness and needed him to fill her.

"Undo my jeans," he whispered and bent to feed at her breasts.

With his teeth and tongue wreaking havoc, her fingers fumbled at his zipper. It took forever for her clumsy hands to free him from the opening. At once she felt the hot brand of his heavy erection lying along her thigh. Now she needed her clothes gone. All of them. She desperately wanted to feel him against her skin.

Jackson lifted his head from the soft pillow of her breasts, and let his gaze drift over her flushed, aroused body. He slid his hands inside her shirt, feeling the heat of her soft skin, inhaling her scent. Elle. He just wasn't whole without her. His fingers slid around to her ribs so he could lift her slightly, forcing her breasts to thrust upward toward his mouth. She looked beautiful, exotic, so sexy his blood heated, sizzled, and rushed through his veins like a drug.

She moaned when his mouth closed over her breast and his teeth tugged at her nipple. Her body writhed under his. She was so sensitive. So responsive to him. Her fingers slid up and down his shaft, stroking and caressing, nearly driving him out of his mind. He could feel her heartbeat against his mouth, along his palm, knew she could feel his heartbeat through his pulsing, eager cock.

He bit her ear and then her neck, tiny little nips that took her breath and then he licked and kissed each spot. "Let's go into the house, baby."

She could only give him a little whimper as he rose, dragging her with him, leaving the blanket behind. Her breasts spilled out of her shirt and he pulled her around after three steps and kissed her, his hands cupping the soft mounds, thumbs sliding back and forth in small caresses.

They never made it into the house. They were too hot for each other. Even the breeze coming off the ocean did nothing to cool the heat raging between them. They got as far as the deck and he shoved the shirt from her shoulders so that it floated to the deck a little distance away. He caught her around the waist and brought her up on her toes, kissing her again and again, welding their mouths together, his tongue stroking and caressing, while his hands tugged down her jeans. Without taking his mouth from hers, he ordered, "Take them off, kick them away."

She couldn't think with his mouth raging against her, devouring her, so hungry he was ravenous. Her body throbbed with need, wet and hot and desperate for his. He never stopped kissing her, as she struggled to kick away her jeans until her body was bare and she was pressed against his. His shirt was long gone, but his jeans still covered his legs. It didn't seem to matter and there was something a little primitive and sexy about being totally naked when he was partially clothed.

Elle could hear the blood pounding in her ears, a roaring, a need that wouldn't stop. She couldn't get close enough, her hands cupping him, stroking and caressing the thick hardness, so velvet soft and hot. She groaned and felt the shudder run through him as if she'd ignited a fuse. He simply lifted her, taking a step so that her back hit the wall and steadied her.

"Wrap your legs around my waist."

His voice was hoarse—sexy, so needy she felt another rush of welcoming liquid. She hooked her ankles together around him and clasped her hands at his nape, head back, hair cascading in a long fall. His body was so hard. So perfect. The air on her nipples added to her arousal, the wind teasing over her body like fingers.

Jackson was slightly shocked to hear a growl rumbling in his chest and throat. He felt like a mad animal, consumed by lust and love, a need to be inside her so strong he brought his hands to her hips and using his strength, pushed her hips down hard, impaling her on his thick cock. He felt her body sheath his, drawing him in, so hot and tight and wet, gripping and squeezing and taking his breath.

As he drove upward, he felt the resistance of her body, her breath slamming out of her lungs, the thrill of pleasure in her mind that went from breasts to belly to her hot core so that her muscles clamped around him hard. The pleasure burst through him, shook him, consumed him until nothing mattered but driving deep into her, over and over, feeling the hot clasp of her body, the tight, burning sheath gripping at nerve endings determined to drag his release right out of him.

Her body tightened. She shuddered, her eyes going wide. A whimper slipped from her throat. As his hands forced her down, she moved her hips in a tight circle, riding him, rising and falling, matching the intensity of his frantic rhythm while her body coiled tighter and tighter around his. Her body was scorching hot now, a fire that roared through his veins and pulled every part of him to the center of his body. Mind and blood and strength. Building . . . building.

He heard her moan, and his body jerked in response. He knew she was close. That soft sound was a musical symphony to him, a song he played in his mind, and he wished he could transfer to the keys on the piano and hold forever to him.

Another rising moan. She chanted his name. Soft. A whimper. She threw her head back again, her soft hair sliding over his arms, her face flushed with arousal. He loved her like that. That perfect moment before her body clamped down like a vise on his, drawing out his hot release. Her unknowing song, her heat. The look on her face. It all combined to give him a fierce, primitive satisfaction and added to the wicked pleasure swamping his own body.

The first wave hit her hard, consuming her. He drove deep, his cock stretching her tight channel. A ripple went through her, from her womb to her belly and up to her breasts. He actually felt it. Another loud moan and her entire body locked around him, a vise that clamped down so hard for a moment he couldn't separate pain from pleasure. She shuddered again as another wave built. He felt the contraction move through her, through him, swelling like the tide, a shock wave jolting outward from her feminine sheath, surrounding him, vibrating through him. He felt her heart beat against his.

He thrust again, heard her soft cry, her music crashing in his ears, and then there was that moment, that perfect, glorious moment when he felt the power coil in his body, gathering, and his blood roared—the sound of thunder—racing up through his body, his balls tightening, his cock rocketing pulse after pulse of hot seed deep so that his body shuddered with hers as the burning pleasure washed over him and her tight muscles gripped him hard, milking his shaft until he was empty. For a moment, everything blurred around him and he felt spent, deliriously happy, and totally, completely at peace.

Elle pressed her face into his shoulder while her body trembled with aftershocks, each quake rushing through his body like an electrical current, spiraling pleasure through him. He waited for the air to come back into his lungs and his legs to get their strength back. He kept his body tight in hers.

"I dreamed about you for years, Elle, of this, taking you over and over. I love hearing your moans and that little whimper you give when you can't talk anymore. Your eyes go unfocused and you have this sexy as hell dazed look on your face. I see you like that every time I close my eyes and my cock gets hard as a rock and I'm desperate to be inside of you—I see you soaring into another place."

He stroked his hands over the curve of her bottom, reveling in the feel of her soft skin. "I swear, Elle, you really were made for me. We fit. You're so damn perfect I lose my mind when I touch you."

Elle licked at the hollow of his damp shoulder and then pressed kisses up his shoulder to his neck. She nibbled and bit at him, her body moving in languid circles, still coming down from her powerful orgasm. "You make me feel as if I'm flying," she admitted, her voice drowsy.

"I'd better get you inside before you catch cold out here."

"Libby says the cold air doesn't give you a cold. Germs do," she murmured, snuggling closer to him, making no attempt to put her feet on the ground. "Besides, can't you feel? I'm still hot."

"Scorching," he agreed. "And you'll always be that way to me."

She moved her hips in another long, slow circle that sent waves of pleasure rippling over him. He was grateful she was so petite. It was obvious he was going to be carrying her inside. He managed to find the door handle and get it open and he staggered in through to the bedroom, collapsing on top of the mattress. Elle kissed his neck again and rolled away from him, her naked body sprawled across the bed.

"You think you're going to sleep?"

"Mmm."

Jackson laughed and went back to retrieve their clothes and the blanket. He stood over her for a long time, wondering at the miracle that had been handed to him. Not once, in the long nights on the bayou, in the humid heat and the utter loneliness of his childhood, had he ever dreamed of someone like Elle. He drew a sheet over her body and tossed his jeans aside before crawling in beside her.

Those days seemed so far away, yet he could remember them vividly, the utter desolation, trying to fish in the midst of swarms of mosquitoes, afraid to go home without some small thing for his mother to eat. By the time he was ten she'd retreated to some place inside her head, but she'd give him a distant smile and a brief kiss on the cheek when he'd take off to hunt or fish for them. Their mattresses were made of the moss he gathered and dried from the trees and stuffed in the cloth sewn together. He dodged alligators and scrounged for roots and anything pretty and colorful he could bring back to his mother.

And then his father would return and for a short time, his mother would come alive. Music would fill the house and his father would accompany him into the swamp, showing him how to set traps and run the nets and the better fishing spots. The brief good times would be interspersed with bouts of drinking and violence, screams and thudding fists, nights spent sitting outside bars and shivering in the cold or feeling sick from the heat.

And later, when he was older, there had been moments racing down the highway on the back of a powerful bike, feeling strong and invincible for short periods of time. His mother grew sicker and his father more violent and distant, but it was the only life Jackson had known and it seemed normal to him.

Elle's family was the fairy tale. Unreal. Impossible to believe. No one that he had known lived like that. They'd fought for their existence, mostly loners like him, with fathers that came and went. The camps were places of drugs and alcohol and men who were broken from wars looking for camaraderie and finding it in violence. The women were just as hard drinking and sold themselves for a place to belong.

Maybe his life had better prepared him for his capture and torture. Elle had only known a loving environment. Maybe, in the end, the fact that he'd started alone, spent weeks on end without anyone talking to him, had made him strong enough to survive and in doing so, had shaped his determination and will so that he could find and be there for Elle.

Elle stirred, turned over and opened her green eyes. Her gaze moved over his face. She held out her hand to him. Elle with her soft welcoming body and a mouth made in heaven. Elle with her loving heart.

"Turn toward me," he instructed softly.

She obeyed him without question, without hesitation, uncaring that she was tired, only wanting to give him whatever he needed. She made him humble with her generosity.

He pushed his pillow away and laid his head level with her breasts. Soft. Warm. Amazing. One arm circled her waist and he pulled her body to his, sliding one leg between hers. His hand slipped over the curve of her bottom, memorizing the texture and shape of her before sliding up her thigh to cup her warm mound.

He waited, but Elle didn't protest. "God, baby, I love you." He whispered the admission against her throat, kissing his way to her breast. He felt her heartbeat. Her breast was warm and soft as he gently covered it with his mouth, tongue sliding over her nipple. He felt the answering ripple against his hand. "I love how you want me, Elle."

"Always," she murmured, pressing a kiss against the top of his head. She drifted on a tide of pleasure as he suckled at her breast, his fingers exploring hidden shadows.

The phone jangled, a loud, unexpected disruption that set her heart racing. "Jackson?"

"It's all right, baby." He rolled over and snagged the receiver, listened for a moment and then sat up, a frown on his face. "I'm on my way. Meet you there."

"What is it?" Elle asked.

"Nothing, honey. Jonas needs some help. I'll take you to your house and leave Bomber with you."

"No way." Elle sat up clutching the sheet, looking panicked. She shook her head. "I'm coming with you."

"It's business, Elle." He hastily dressed, pulling on clothes, shoving a knife into his boot, strapping a holdout gun to his leg before pulling on his belt and weapons.

Elle mirrored him, dressing just as fast in warm clothes, determined not to be left behind. It was odd to her how at times she felt confident, like she was regaining herself. Then in the blink of an eye, she'd realize that she was still curled up in the fetal position in her mind, terrified to move one direction or the other without Jackson.

As if he knew, and he probably did, that she couldn't bear to be away from him, Jackson didn't argue with her and she ran out to the truck with him and watched as he ordered Bomber to load up.

"Are you going to tell me what's going on?" she asked as he reversed and sped down the highway, setting a red strobe on the dash to warn vehicles he was going to an emergency.

"Jonas got a call that a woman was screaming for help and running around the headlands. She was hysterical, claiming she'd been held prisoner and that her daughter was being exorcised of demons and something terrible had happened."

Elle sucked in her breath sharply. "RJ. He had that young girl with him."

Jackson nodded. "I thought something was off with her. I asked for information, but haven't had time to check on it."

"If she's in his hands, you know what he's done to her," Elle said in a tight voice.

"You don't have to do this, Elle. You can stay with your sisters."

Elle shook her head. "No, I can't. I need to be with you and if you find her, I may be able to help." She moistened her dry mouth. "RJ and that girl were in the store this afternoon."

He glanced at her pale face.

"When Death was there." She swallowed hard.

He reached out a hand and laid it over hers, but he didn't bother to try to reassure her. Nothing he said would make a difference. He could only get there as quickly as possible and hope nothing had happened to the teenager.

Vehicles were strewn in a haphazard fashion just off the road as emergency volunteers had raced to the site. Jackson parked and leashed Bomber before coming around to help Elle out of the truck. He took her hand and they jogged along the path out toward the edge of the cliffs.

Jonas looked up when they approached and waved them over. He'd obviously been watching for his deputy. Jackson saw a woman wrapped in a blanket sobbing, sitting on a rock, facing the pounding ocean below. Fire trucks were parked along the fence line and his heart sank. The water was treacherous here. Even on the beach below, one had to watch carefully when the tide was coming in, but if someone had gone over into the rocks, there was little time to get to them.

"What happened?"

Jonas glanced at Elle, who tightened her fingers around Jackson's and stuck her chin in the air a bit defiantly, daring Jonas to send her away.

"That's Lori Robertson. She's a single mother with a teenage daughter. The girl's name is Venita and she's fourteen, a bit rebellious, this is her mother's description, a cutter—the kids refer to them as *emo* around here. She dresses in black, has multiple body piercings, writes depressing poetry, you know the drill. She wears enough eyeliner for a roomful of people, according to her mother. Her hair is straight black and in her face all the time."

"I ran into her at the grocery store," Jackson said. "She looked like half the kids we know."

"Yeah, well this one has a mother who thinks her daughter is possessed by the devil. Her Reverend told her so. First they spent a week on their knees praying together, but Venita continued her demonic behavior."

"What's demonic about *emo* behavior? They like to color their hair and write poetry about life being depressing—which it can be at fourteen," Elle defended. "They're referred to as 'emo' because they're sensitive and emotional."

"I'm not saying anything against her, Elle, just filling you in on what the mother believed. Apparently the Reverend told her that the number of earrings she had in her ear was a sign of devil worship."

"And she believed him?" Elle said, disgusted.

Jackson put his arm around her, drawing her under his shoulder. "What happened?"

"When the prayers didn't work, RJ graciously offered to bring Venita to a house and work with her. They arrived together and the mother planned to leave, but at the last second the daughter fell apart and begged her mother not to go. RJ became angry when the mom decided to take her daughter back to San Francisco with her and he demanded she leave. He told her he'd gone to the trouble of arranging this time with her daughter and the expense of renting a house."

Jackson shook his head. "The man's such a bastard. He had a taste for the girl and didn't want to give her up."

"The mother still refused and RJ's bodyguards dragged her into one of the bedrooms and tied her up there. She was beaten and raped."

"Did we pick them up?"

Jonas nodded. "We've got the bodyguards. She should be at the hospital so we can have a forensic rape kit done on her, but she won't go. Evidently Reverend RJ had himself a good time with the daughter. Venita overheard RJ calling someone and arranging to sell her along with setting up an accident for her mother. The daughter snuck into her mother's room and cut her loose. They ran and the men caught them here."

Jackson walked closer to where the firemen were working, trying to get down to the rocks below. "Damn it. The daughter fell over?"

"Not exactly. RJ had Venita by her hair and was dragging her back. Her mother said she was sobbing and pleading, trying to get away. The mother kicked herself free and tried to shove RJ away from Venita, but the edge crumbled and he went over, taking Venita with him. Jeff Dockins and a couple of others saw the entire thing and held RJ's bodyguards until the deputies arrived."

Jonas saw the captain motioning toward him. They went over to him. He shook his head. "My men can't get down there, Jonas. We've called in the rescue helicopter and it should be here within ten minutes. She's moving down there and so is he, but they're both injured. The water is slamming that rock. I think the man has a broken back and the girl seems to have a compound fracture of the leg. Maybe one arm broken and there's blood on her face." He shook his head again. "I'm sorry, but I just can't risk my men. That cliff is unstable and we nearly lost one of our guys."

Elle blinked back tears. All those months she'd put in undercover overseas to stop this very thing and it was happening in her own hometown. She hated that she couldn't prevent any child from experiencing such a terrible fate. Jackson, his mind woven tightly with hers, brought up his hand and curved his palm around the nape of her neck, his fingers massaging gently.

Bomber gave a short bark, the hair on his body standing up, ears coming forward. A chill slid down Elle's spine and she instinctively took a small step to put her body in front of both Jonas and Jackson. She scanned the crowd of firemen and volunteers under the bright lights they'd set up, seeing familiar faces. Her heart jumped when she saw burly Jeff Dockins. He'd been in the grocery store. Who else? Clyde Darden was there, standing on the edge of the crowd, peering below with binoculars. She silently cursed him under her breath for being so nosy.

Trudy Garrett busily handed out coffee to the volunteers. Reginald Mars helped her, along with Drew Madison. They moved in and out of the crowd, Trudy closer to the cliffs as she gave coffee to the firefighters and paramedics. Elle glanced down again at Bomber and then followed his focused gaze. Her heart jumped. In the boulders ringing the small picket fence warning people away from the edge, she glimpsed a dark shadow moving slowly, skulking from one rock to the next, his head covered with a hood and a cape flowing around his body.

Death slunk along the ground, a shadow among the other shadows, weaving in and out of the crowd so that she caught a glimpse of him and then he'd be hidden again. His head was thrown back, although his hood covered him, and he sniffed the air like a bloodhound, searching for something unseen.

Elle stepped away from Jackson and Jonas, intent on protecting the townspeople. Jackson caught her arm and stopped her.

"What do you think you're doing?" he demanded.

"Death is here," she said. "He's searching for a life. He's chosen someone."

"It's not going to be you, Elle. You damn well aren't sacrificing your life because you couldn't stop RJ or anyone like him from hurting a child."

"What use am I if I can't help anyone?" She jerked her arm away from him.

Jonas hemmed her in from the other side. "Tell us what to do to help, Elle."

She shook her head. "Not you, Jonas. I'm not risking you, and Jackson was in that store. Death could have his scent."

Jackson actually pulled her body against his, bringing her up on her toes, his gaze fierce. "You were in that store as well. You're. *Not.* Doing. This." He bit out each word, enunciating them between his teeth.

Elle stared into his dark, implacable eyes and felt his iron will pressed against hers in her mind. There was no arguing with him. She wasn't going to win. She had to think of something else. "Fine," she capitulated. "Jonas, get Trudy away from the cliff. I don't care what excuse you give her, you have to get her away from there. Drew, Reginald and Mr. Darden should be moved into a safer zone."

"We don't see what you're seeing, but obviously Bomber does," Jackson said, following the dog's gaze. "We'll try to shield the others as best we can, but you stay right with us."

The sound of the helicopter could be heard moving toward them in the distance. The Huey was flying over the mountain, emerging just above the trees and heading toward the cliffs.

"Jonas! Ty is on that helicopter. He pulled a double shift." Elle was stricken. "Has he done a rescue since he fell?"

"Mandatory recertification is required every ninety days, Elle, you know that," Jonas assured her. "He's very experienced."

"Ty wasn't in the store," Jackson said gently, knowing what she was worried about.

"He cheated death before," Elle said. "Or rather Libby did. What if he's come back for Ty?" She pressed the heel of her hand to her forehead.

The helicopter flew overhead and headed out to sea to assess the situation. The captain had given them the information and now it was up to the helicopter rescue crew to decide whether or not they were willing to try a rescue. Over water, short-haul rescue was one of the most dangerous maneuvers and each crew member would have to agree the rescue was justified in order to save a life and they could perform it safely or they would return back to base and the victims were lost.

The helicopter settled in a nearby field to conserve fuel while the crew talked it over and planned a strategy. Jonas, with Jackson holding firmly to Elle's hand, used the distraction of the helicopter to move the crowd of volunteers farther away from the cliff. Jonas made certain that Clyde, Trudy, Drew and Reginald were among those in the center of the crowd, away from any potential harm.

Elle let her breath out slowly and climbed up on top of a boulder in order to get a better view of the rocks below.

She could see the two victims lying sprawled out, Venita's right arm dangling off the rock so that each time a wave crashed against the large mussel-covered rock, the water tugged at her, threatening to pull her into the sea. The rocks were slick and polished from the constantly pounding sea and the life growing on them. It had to be difficult to cling to the surface. RJ moved one leg, but otherwise, stayed still. He was lower than Venita and every few waves the water splashed high and sprayed over him.

The helicopter rose into the air and her heart began to pound as it circled above the victims and began to maneuver into position. She could see the crew through the open door, the strain showing on their faces as they approached the cliffs from the right. The winds were steady and Elle knew from talking with Ty that it was essential they stay that way, as gusts over twenty miles an hour made it impossible to perform a rescue along their coastline.

With her heart in her throat, she watched the helicopter slow and then the crew chief move to the skid and secure himself. "It's Ty," she whispered aloud as a second man moved to the skid. He would be the rescuer, the crew member going down the rope, putting himself in harm's way. "I knew it." Fate had a way of interfering, of repeating when it didn't get its way.

"Ty has nerves of steel," Jonas muttered, shaking his head. The last time Ty had performed a short-haul overwater rescue on the coast, he'd fallen and suffered major head trauma.

Elle couldn't imagine what was going through his mind, but she looked frantically for the shadowy, robed figure skulking somewhere in the rocks. *I can't see him.* Even to herself she sounded desperate. She clutched at

Jackson's sleeve as she twisted around, trying to get a visual on the others who had been in the grocery store. "Drew! He's over by the fence. Look at the ground along there." A faint crack had developed, whether from the firefighters and their equipment as they'd tried to get down to the victims, or whether Death could maneuver the ground to suit its needs, she didn't know.

"I'll get him," Jackson said.

"No!" Elle held him tighter. "You can't. Death is crouched right behind him. Don't call attention to yourself or Drew. Not yet."

She could see the apparition now; it wasn't facing Drew, but rather toward the helicopter. She glanced down toward the sea below. Ty was on the rock, crouched beside Venita. He moved over her, gently removing her arm from the water, obviously communicating with her. She could see the girl writhing in pain. Her heart pounding now so hard it hurt, Elle watched as Ty carefully, in a crouch, made his way to assess RJ.

She could taste fear and danger in her mouth. "The cliff is going to go." She gripped Jackson harder, afraid to look away from Ty, afraid to take her eyes off Death. Jonas sprinted across the grass toward Drew. Jackson tore free from Elle's hand and went after him. Death leapt into the air and came down hard. A tremor rocked the earth. Someone screamed. The ground began to crumple all along the cliff. Mud, rock, the fence and debris crashed down toward the sea and the rocks below.

Drew slipped, arms waving in the air to try to balance. For one moment, Death looked back over his shoulder, hesitating as he saw the boy waver in the air. Jonas dove, locked hands with Drew as the boy went over, taking his weight, just holding him there as Jonas lay prone in the tall grass. Jackson anchored Jonas's legs as the firemen rushed to help. Death turned back toward the sea, looking to the victims below, his face a mask of unholy glee, and then he leapt.

Elle looked below to see Ty's body blanketing Venita's. He must have covered the girl when the slide started and the rocks had bounced all around them. She could see RJ hidden under a pile of boulders and mud. Ty stood up cautiously and leaned over to look at the man crushed on the rocks. There was a slight movement. Elle saw the shadow reach RJ.

"Please," she whispered. "Please let that be enough."

The stokes—a basket the victim was put in for the ride up—was lowered from the helicopter as Ty made his way through the rubble to try to help RJ. The shadow crouched on RJ's chest, pressing his weight on him, leaning close to RJ's face. Ty leaned over RJ and began CPR, trying to save the man, but Elle could have told him it was too late. She saw the shadow look toward Venita.

The next wave crashed over the rock and the helicopter lurched a little. Elle lifted her arms to stay the gusts of wind. She held back the flurries, giving the pilot time to steady his craft and give orders to bring Venita up before the weather deteriorated. They would abandon the body to the sea and hope to recover later.

Elle's heart didn't stop straining until Ty and the teenage girl were safe in the helicopter and the pilot had set the craft in motion, bringing it back over land to set down in the field where the paramedics waited.

Death had faded away and she let her breath out, looking at Bomber, just to be certain, before she could believe everyone she loved was safe. She made her way to Jackson, who had escorted Drew to the paramedics just to make certain he was okay. Jackson immediately put his arm around her and they exchanged a slow, wordless smile.

19

"YOU look beautiful, Elle," Sarah said. "Absolutely beautiful."

Elle turned around, looking at herself in the mirrors. She hadn't considered that she really would be married in a white wedding gown on the beach, but the gown Sarah had chosen was exquisite, although daring. The bust was ruched silk georgette, a bikini top essentially with double spaghetti straps, hugging Elle's breasts. Asymmetrical transparent lace sprinkled with small leaf and poppy appliqué flowed over her midriff. The couture gown, by a popular and talented New Zealand designer, was perfect for a beach wedding. White satin hugged her hips low, beads sparkling to the ankles.

"It's breathtaking," Hannah proclaimed.

Elle couldn't take her eyes off her skin. Libby and her sisters had made certain that not a single line, not a scar, nothing at all remained of her encounter with Stavros. Her skin was flawless, not even a blemish showing. She blinked back tears as she looked at her oldest sister.

"I can't believe the lash marks are gone. I was afraid he'd permanently scarred me. I hated Jackson having to see those wounds. He never flinched at them though." She blushed a little remembering him trailing kisses over every lesion.

Libby smiled at her. "He's going to be thrilled when he sees you in that dress."

"Jackson wanted me to wear a bikini, but I knew I couldn't, even to a beach wedding. I didn't think I'd ever wear one again," Elle admitted.

"Thanks for looking after Ty last night," Libby said. "When I heard he was going to be the dope on a rope, I was terrified. It seemed such a coincidence, the same cliff, the same field, and he's the one up for rotation to do the rescue, or rather the man whose shift he covered."

"Jonas saved Drew," Elle said, looking at Hannah. "Drew would have gone over that cliff if he hadn't caught his arms. He really does have a psychic gift whether he wants to believe it or not. He was running before that cliff gave way."

Hannah blinked back tears. "He told me Jackson saved both of them. That if he hadn't been right behind covering Jonas's back, like he's done for years, he would have gone over the cliff with Drew."

"They do look out for each other," Elle said. She glanced anxiously at Sarah. "Is Mom here yet? She said they'd make it. They were in Europe again at their house there."

"Joley sent a small plane to pick them up. The pilot landed at the Little River Airport just a couple minutes ago. They'll make it in plenty of time," Sarah assured her.

"What about Aunt Carol?"

"She drove in late last night and is staying with Reginald," Abbey reported. "When I called she sounded a little flustered and I wasn't about to ask any questions. With my luck I would have blurted the word 'truth' and she would have told me far more than I ever wanted to know. I just got off the phone fast."

"I've got news," Joley announced, adjusting her dress and frowning at the tiny baby bump she couldn't hide. "Sheesh, I'm totally showing. I'm kicking Ilya when I see him."

"We already know you're pregnant," Sarah pointed out. "There's not much news after that. And you aren't showing at all."

Joley waited for the laughter to subside. "Very funny. All of you," she sniffed indignantly. "Just for that I'm not telling you a thing." She studied her figure again and drew in her breath. "Couldn't you have chosen something a little less clingy? It's beautiful, but honestly it looks almost like a wedding dress."

The dress was ivory in color, a halter top made of transparent lace beaded with platinum and pearls gathered together at the midriff with a sheer lace panel encrusted with more platinum and pearls. The dress showcased her generous breasts and left her back daringly bare. Sarah had chosen the gowns from the same New Zealand designer because they were perfect for the beach wedding and flattered them all. Silk satin crepe flowed to the ankle, creating elegance with every movement.

"It is a wedding dress. I loved it and wanted to be married in it, but because we were having a church wedding, I didn't think it was appropriate so I chose them for Elle's wedding. The designer is a friend of mine and she'd already made most of them for bridesmaid dresses."

"Great, I have a big baby bump in the front of a wedding gown. How attractive is that?"

"Very," Hannah said soothingly. "You look so beautiful, Joley. Don't be upset."

"Oh, for heaven's sake," Sarah said, "everyone knows you're pregnant. Why are you making such a fuss? Hannah's showing and you're not at all."

Joley looked uncomfortable. "Hannah's married. I wanted to wait until Elle was home."

"Joley!" Elle wailed. "I'm sorry. I shouldn't have done this so quickly. Maybe I should wait until all of you are married."

"No, you shouldn't," Joley said firmly. "I just feel funny facing Mom and Dad pregnant. You know I'm always the screw-up." She shrugged. "I suppose it's silly to want to be married when I'm always the one in the tabloids. And boy, is the press ever having a field day right now."

"Mom and Dad don't think you're a screw-up, silly," Sarah said, wrapping her arm around her younger sister. "They're proud of you. They love Ilya and they know why you waited. Of course you'd wait for Elle. I guess you'll just have to be impulsive like Jackson and be the next ones. We can put something together fast. Abbey and Aleksandr are getting married in their backyard with only family there."

Joley smoothed her hands over the dress again. "I'm crazy about Ilya," she admitted in a little rush, "but sometimes, I worry that I'm so crazy about him that I'll blow it all."

Abigail frowned. "Joley, Ilya is just as crazy about you. Where did you get all these insecurities?"

"I've always had them when it comes to Mom and Dad. And Ilya is my life. I'm so wrapped up in him, I sometimes feel like I'm obsessed." Joley ran her palm down her thigh. "I hate being away from him."

Sarah looked at her watch. "Well, honey, we've only got a few minutes to finish up or the bride will be late and Jackson will send a cop to pick her up."

"So tell us the news," Hannah urged.

"Sylvia Fredrickson is going to have a baby." Joley dropped the bombshell on her astonished sisters. "Inez invited Mason and Sylvia to the wedding and Sylvia wanted to make certain it wouldn't make us uncomfortable to be there. She was really very sweet on the phone and sounded happy. She said Mason didn't divorce her and they've worked things out. She asked to apologize again to Abigail and wanted you to know, Abbey, that her life is a thousand times better because of you."

"Of course you told her to come to the wedding," Elle said.

"I did," Joley confirmed.

"That makes me happy that she's turned her life around," Abbey said.

Hannah made a sound in her throat and waited until they were all looking at her. "I believe those of you who thought to lecture my decision to help Sylvia learn her lesson should apologize. I'm certain it was my help that put her on the right path."

"With a big red handprint on her face every time she lied?" Joley said. "That's right, Hannah, it was very helpful."

All of them laughed. Sarah shook her head. "How you manage to say that with a straight face and in that righteous tone, Hannah, I'll never know."

Elle looked at her watch again. "I really wanted to talk to Mom before I got married. Just for a couple of minutes."

Sarah rubbed her arm. "Give it a little more time."

Bomber gave a short bark and Elle ran to the window to peer out. "She's here!" She started crying.

Hannah wrapped her arm around Elle's waist. "Don't ruin your makeup."

"I never thought I'd see her again," Elle sobbed.

Hannah burst into tears with her. Their parents walked in to find them all crying. Mrs. Drake took Elle into her arms and held her. Mr. Drake wrapped his arms tightly around both of them and they just stood there trembling, holding one another, grateful Elle was alive and back home.

"I'VE never seen you so cleaned up," Jonas said, brushing an imaginary speck of lint from the suit jacket he was holding out to Jackson. "Somebody might just call you a pretty boy."

Jackson resisted giving Jonas the finger and adjusted his tie. "Somebody might get knocked on his ass. I thought a beach wedding would get me out of wearing a suit and tie."

"No such luck," Damon said. "Sarah wanted Elle to wear a beautiful gown and you have to look halfway decent standing next to her."

Jackson swung around away from the mirror as Ilya came in. "Is the yacht anchored out at sea like we suspected?"

"Yes." Ilya flicked a quick glance at Jonas. "I had to enlist Hannah's aid to help position the yacht where we could reach it. Sorry, Jonas, but no one can make the wind obey like Hannah."

"Did you tell her the plan?" Jonas asked.

All the men turned for the answer, regarding Ilya with

worried frowns. Ilya shook his head. "I just said we had one and were working out the kinks. Once I said Damon was helping she seemed to be relieved. Apparently Jackson and Jonas are regarded somewhat as hotheads."

Ty nodded in agreement. "Libby said Elle's worried Jackson might do something crazy and end up in jail. Hannah said if he did, her knuckle-headed husband would be in the same cell right along with him."

Jonas gave a derisive snort and scowled at Damon. "How have you managed to keep Sarah thinking you're as innocent as a lamb?"

Damon shrugged. "She admires my brain and knows I'm a logical man." He spread a map on the kitchen table. "And I have an innocent face."

"Mostly you give a good line of bull," Aleksandr contributed as he peered down at the map. "Make some sense of this for me."

"What we're going to do, gentlemen, with the help of the townspeople and our women, is create a new Bermuda Triangle. A ship is going to sink and with it, Stavros Gratsos, the billionaire shipping magnate, who will be, sadly, lost at sea. He won't be arrested. No one can be blamed for his death, and it will create a great mystery that people can speculate over for years to come. Not to mention, it will provide spectacular skies for the wedding and all the guests will swear all of us were together for a celebration and no one could have harmed Gratsos in any way."

Aleksandr shook his head. "You really think we can make a ship disappear?"

Damon nodded. "He uses the sea as his weapon. He's at home in it. He's going to stay out on his yacht and do as much damage from there as possible. But we're smarter than he is. We're going to create what is known as a 'credible physics anomaly.'"

Matt cleared his throat. "Actually, Damon, maybe you and Ty are, but the rest of us like to rely on weapons. Because this"—he spread his arms out over the map—"I don't understand a word of."

"We have everything we need. We're sitting right on a continental shelf. The San Andreas Fault runs right along this coast, right? In fact, we're the triple junction where three tectonic plates come together." Ty said. "Isn't the standing joke that the next earthquake is going to take us all out?"

Ilya scowled at him. "Bite your tongue. We don't want to give Gratsos any ideas."

"You can't trigger an earthquake, Damon," Jonas objected. "What do you want to do? Create a tsunami and drown the bastard? You'll take Sea Haven with you."

"No, I don't want a wave, even a rogue one. I agree that's far too dangerous. We have something much better. Methane clathrate, of which we have significant deposits on the ocean floor. These hydrates only form in the continental shelves and so typically are in shallower depths. In other words, in our reach." Damon looked pleased with himself. He beamed at the men and waved his arm as if he'd just performed a magic trick.

There was a small silence. Matt cleared his throat. "Methane gas? We're going to bomb him? Stink him out? What? Where are you going with this?"

Damon looked at Ty and raised his eyebrow. "I told you, we're going to sink his yacht. Didn't I explain that to you? We're going to give everyone a legitimate scientific puzzle."

Jackson swung a chair around and straddled it. "Lay it out for us, Damon."

"What we're going to do is quite simple. We'll be celebrating on the beach, and up in the sky, everyone will start seeing strange anomalies like those associated with the Bermuda Triangle. We'll give them everything we can find that's been reported down through the years. Flames in the sky, the water turning color, and lights, whatever we come up with. I've got Inez working on that for me."

"Inez?" Jackson snapped. "You can't involve her in this."

"She's sharp, Jackson. She came to me and said she was certain you had a plan and whatever it was, not to let you do it and to come up with a better one."

Jonas laughed and punched Jackson in his shoulder. "Smart old lady knows your brain capacity, bro."

Jackson rubbed his hand over his face. "This would be a whole hell of a lot cleaner if I just took the bastard out with a rifle."

"He's a billionaire, Jackson. You don't think a few people might notice?" Damon said. His look said he agreed with Elle and Hannah—that Jackson was a hot-head.

Jonas straddled a chair beside Jackson and pulled the map around. "Tell us how this is done, Damon." Jackson was liable to go the sniper route if he didn't think this was going to end the threat to Elle, and Jonas wasn't about to arrest his best friend for murder. "How do we sink a ship?"

Damon exchanged a gleeful look with Ty and even rubbed his hands together. "You give them the explanation, Ty."

Tyson nodded. "There are a couple of ways to sink a ship."

"Blow it up," Matt muttered under his breath.

"*Without* touching it," Damon reiterated. "All of you are obsessed with explosives and weapons."

"There's nothing more satisfying than a good explosion," Matt agreed. "But I'm listening. This is starting to intrigue me."

"Now that I have your attention." Ty scowled at him. "Try to stay with me. The easiest way to think about this is to picture a submarine. In simplest terms, it's filled with air and it stays on top of the water because it's lighter than the water, right? When it wants to sink, they remove some of the air and let in some water and down she goes, because now she's heavier than the water."

"So we're going to blow a hole in her and let in water," Jackson said.

Jonas frowned. "I suppose we could use one of the dolphins to plant the charge but Abbey might get upset and balk at that."

"Oh for God's sake," Damon burst out. "We're not blowing up the damn boat. Get over it. We're not setting charges, we're going to do this in a scientific manner and make it appear a physics anomaly, a natural phenomenon that occasionally occurs."

"In other words, shut up and listen," Ilya translated from where he was leaning against the wall, arms folded across his chest.

Tyson nodded. "We're not using that method of sinking the ship anyway. We're using door number two—the second method. We're going to make the water less dense than the yacht." A wide grin spread over Tyson's face, his gaze nearly reverent as he looked at Damon. "This plan is a thing of beauty. You're definitely the master, Yoda."

Jonas huffed out a breath, obviously grinding his teeth together. "Okay, Master, how do we make the water lighter than the ship?"

"We're going to break the hydrate seal over the deposit on the continental shelf. That will eject methane gas into the water. The gas will rush to the surface in a column, breaking into smaller and smaller bubbles on its way up. The key, and this is where our hidden current comes into play, is to have a very swift and contained escape of gas, providing a patch of highly agitated, tremendously fizzy water."

Ty took up the explanation, seeing the incredulous looks surrounding them. "Because the water is filled with tiny methane bubbles, it will be mainly methane gas, not air. And methane is half as dense as air. The air in the yacht is actually below sea level, allowing it to float, but now the craft is sitting on the one spot in the sea that's less dense and that baby is going to sink."

There was a stunned silence. "Are you certain?" Jonas asked. "Will they be able to get off the ship before it goes down?"

"It's going to sink like a stone, although the one drawback I can foresee is that the deposit I want to tap in to is located about halfway to the bottom. Which means when the ship goes down it will be trapped halfway, it won't sink all the way to the bottom," Damon said.

"I wouldn't worry too much," Tyson said. "Instincts will make them want to swim up to the surface using the shortest route, but they won't be able to. It's the Dead Sea in reverse."

Jackson rubbed his fingers over his eyes. "What's the Dead Sea in reverse? What are you talking about?"

Damon shrugged. "In the Dead Sea, there's such a heavy concentration of salt that the molecules are so close to one another and so dense that the water is extremely buoyant. One thing you really never want to do is dive perpendicular into that sea. If you were to dive straight down, you could get stuck, literally stuck, head down, feet up, with no way to get out. The buoyancy of the water would just trap you in that position and you'd drown."

"You're making this up," Matt said.

"Nope. It's true. And if Stavros were to realize he's in methane gas, which he won't because he'll be panicked and disoriented, he could, in theory, swim down and then away, getting clear of the localized patch of gas and back up to the surface. Of course the water is cold and if there's a storm at sea, he's not going to make it, but there's that slim possibility."

"What about other ships?" Jonas asked.

"Two things. Inez has invited every fisherman from here to hell and back to the wedding and we've created a forecast of an impending storm with warnings about the surf," Damon said.

"And I made certain it was backed with a bad feeling about going out on the water today," Ilya added.

"How long will we have to keep other ships away?" Jonas asked.

"The gas will dissipate rapidly. By that time the ship will have filled with water and it will sink to the bottom. If a trace of the gas is found, it will only add to the mystery. No other ship will be in jeopardy because it's the concentrated burst that we need to take him down and that will be over," Damon added.

"We're also going to make certain there's enough psychic energy occurring to entice him. Abbey's going to put on a display in the sea. Hannah will create a show in the sky. Everything done will, later in the retelling, look as though the events led up to a true physics phenomenon. Naturally, Abbey and Hannah and every other participant in the anomaly will be on that beach watching Jackson and Elle exchange vows," Damon added. "Perfect alibis for everyone."

Ilya pushed his fingers through his hair. "There's one other small problem."

"What would that be?"

"My brother. I've tried luring him off the ship with the idea of having him arrested for trying to bribe a public official," Ilya said. "I sent word that you'd only talk to him."

Jackson stood up so fast his chair went over backward. He kicked it out of the way and advanced on Ilya. "You never said you had a brother working for Gratsos."

"No, I didn't," Ilya said. "I didn't know until we went in to get Elle out. I talked to her and asked her to keep it confidential until I could figure out what was going on."

"When?" Jackson demanded. "She's been with me every minute."

"Not this morning. I was at the Drake house when you dropped her off to get ready."

Jackson swore under his breath, furious with Ilya, even angrier with Elle. *What the fuck, Elle. You don't keep something like this from me, you understand? It's my job to protect you and I'll be damned if you hold back information.*

Don't say the "F" word to me on our wedding day.

Is that all you have to say to me? I'm standing here with my dick hanging out because you didn't let me know Ilya's brother was working for Gratsos. Jackson stalked out of the house, away from Ilya, tempted to punch him. He paced back and forth on his deck.

Well, put that lovely treasure back in your pants and calm down. He asked me to keep it confidential.

I don't give a damn what he asked. We don't do that. You tell me everything.

There was a short pause. *I'm sorry, Jackson. I wasn't trying to keep anything from you. Ilya told me they had each other in their sights and put their guns down. He wanted to know what part his brother had played in the events on the island. His brother was a bodyguard, but he was the only one nice to me. He definitely wanted me off the yacht before Stavros took me to the island. He argued with Stavros.*

But he didn't help you escape and he sure as hell knew what Stavros was doing to you.

He never came into the room until the day Stavros brought that guard in and killed him. The bodyguard was furious.

Jackson erupted into language far worse than the "F" word. He didn't give a damn if the man was Ilya's brother, he hadn't stopped the torture happening to Elle. Maybe he hadn't known everything, but he was guilty and the man could go down with the ship.

He turned at the sound of the door closing quietly. Ilya faced him. "He's undercover. He was raised the way I was, Jackson, and he's undercover. You know you don't blow months or years of work to save one person. You have to look at the bigger picture."

"I don't want to hear bullshit excuses."

Something hard flickered in the depths of Ilya's eyes but he remained calm. "You've worked undercover. I'm certain you've had to make hard decisions. If you're trying to take down the ring, do you save hundreds, maybe thousands, or one?"

"You don't know that's what he's doing."

"I know. I can't tell you how I know, I just do." Ilya regarded Jackson steadily. "He has to live with himself and what he's done in order to get close to Gratsos, just as I had to live with very unpleasant things."

"He pulled his boss out of harm's way on the island. You can't tell me he didn't. So he'll do it again if you give him an inkling of the plan."

"Which is why I don't intend to. I've tried to lure him to shore, but if he doesn't take the bait, he'll die with Gratsos. I'm not willing to risk Joley and Hannah or any of the Drake sisters any more than you are. They're my family now, my first loyalty is to them."

"Tell me you didn't have Gratsos in your sights and let him go."

"Would you believe me?"

Jackson nodded and kept his gaze steady on Ilya. Ilya shook his head. "I didn't have a shot. I would have shot through his bodyguard to take him out."

Jackson let out his breath slowly. "Okay. Okay then. Let's just get this done. I'm sorry about your brother being involved in this."

Ilya shrugged. "It's the world we live in. The world we grew up in. We all know we take our chances. I don't have to like it, but I'll live with my decision to let him go."

Jackson? Elle's voice trembled. *Do you still want to get married?*

Jackson swallowed the love welling up inside of him. *More than ever. We're going to fight, Elle. You know we are. It's going to be loud and I'm going to slip up and use bad language and be pissed as hell at you. But that is*

*never going to take away how I feel about you. I prefer
a fiery woman. I don't want a yes woman. I want someone
who will stand up to me and argue her point when she
thinks she's right. Of course in the end, you'll realize I'm
right and we'll have great makeup sex.*

He felt the laughter in her and it warmed him. There
was a part of him that worried she was going to come to
her senses and walk out on him. His mother had retreated,
distancing herself further and further until she eventually
was lost to him. His father couldn't resist the lure of the
biker world. Although he'd wanted to stay, their lives together weren't enough for him, the bayou and home weren't
what he needed. Jackson wasn't enough for him to stay.
Sometimes he still felt like that boy desperately trying to
hold his family together and feeling he was never quite good
enough for anyone to want him.

I want you. Elle's voice was fierce. *I want you with every breath I take. Can't you feel me, Jackson? Can't you
feel my love for you?*

Such emotion poured into him, he nearly went to his
knees. *I feel you, Elle, all around me. I can't wait to marry
you.*

He moved back into his house and turned to the waiting men. Damon had gathered up his map and burned it in
the fireplace before donning his jacket. The others were
straightening ties, brushing lint from their suits and making certain they were going to make Inez very happy.

"You okay?" Jonas asked, putting a hand on Jackson's
shoulder.

Jackson nodded. "This is the happiest day of my life."

Jonas grinned at him. "I know what you mean."

Jackson turned to Damon. "You really think we can do
this? Sink his ship?"

Damon nodded. "I do. There will be enough energy at the celebration to draw on in order to combat anything Gratsos tries. It will work. You just concentrate on getting married. Tomorrow, Elle will read about the untimely demise of Stavros Gratsos in the newspaper, unless the sharks get his body first."

"If it doesn't work, I'll have this night with her," Jackson said.

"Technically," Damon said, "this won't even be murder. We may have planned it out ahead of time, but he's going to make his try and we'll be acting in self-defense. So Jonas can still sleep at night."

"Let's do this," Aleksandr said. "Inez is coming up the dunes and she's frowning."

"DEARLY beloved, we are gathered here to join this man and this woman in holy matrimony."

The preacher began and Jackson could barely make himself listen. Mostly he heard nothing but his heart thundering in his ears from the moment Elle had stepped into view and walked toward him. Barefoot. Her gown a bikini top and sarong covered in sparkling beads. Elle took his breath away with her beauty. Her red hair was swept up in an intricate knot and she stood there looking ethereal in her white gown with the long lace veil that seemed to float around her like a cape. Her flawless skin looked so soft beneath that transparent panel of lace that it was all he could do not to slide his hand over her bare midriff.

Behind him, huge white tents were anchored in the sand with long tables of food and drink and an intricate wedding cake from one of the bakeries. The townspeople pressed all around them, standing shoulder to shoulder. Soft strains of music drifted on the light breeze and the fragrance of lavender permeated the air.

He took Elle's hand, slipped the ring on her finger and felt an answering jolt in his chest. She put the ring on his finger and he caught her hand and kissed it.

Ilya stepped forward, pulling Joley with him. "Before you pronounce them man and wife, marry us." He patted his pocket. "I have the license and our rings."

Tyson grinned and caught Libby's hand. "You can't get out of it now," he said and stood very straight, almost caging her in. He held up two rings. "Marry us, too."

"Can you do this in front of all these people, Abigail?" Aleksandr asked.

She nodded and stepped up beside him, fitting perfectly beneath his shoulder.

Kate and Matt looked at one another, laughed and stepped up beside Elle and Jackson. "We're ready as well."

"And us," Damon said. "Everyone's already here, Sarah. Let's get married." He held out his hand and she took it.

Hannah and Jonas grinned at each other. "I guess we're everyone's attendants."

Jackson slipped his arm around Elle and held her while the preacher had each couple repeat their vows. He glanced at the sky as the wind began to pick up a little. Strange, dancing lights formed overhead, almost like the aurora borealis, over the night skies in Alaska. Colors of purples and blue, pink and white were nearly luminous. Several villagers gasped and pointed.

As rings were exchanged the sky changed again adding in more colors, green, oranges and reds dancing through the luminous colors, giving off the impression of flames in the skies. Jackson glanced out toward the horizon. He didn't have a visual on the yacht, but he knew it was out there. He felt the man now, felt him close. He glanced at Bomber. The dog was uneasy and had turned his body to face the sea.

Waves slapped the shore and poured over the rocks. Far out, the water appeared a dark green surrounded by the deeper blue. And then it foamed white. A cheer went up as the preacher pronounced them man and wife and each couple kissed and was presented to the crowd. It sounded a little strange to hear "Jackson and Elle Deveau-Drake."

Dolphins burst out of the water, somersaulted and dove, disappearing back under the foaming sea. Whales breached and birds flew overhead as if in salute. Several seals bobbed heads in the waves, looking toward the beach.

Applause broke out as the couples moved through the crowd, down the beach toward the white tents. Jackson kept Elle's hand firmly in his.

"I've never seen the sky like that," Elle said, uneasiness in her voice.

"Damon had some weird-ass explanation for it. Something to do with humidity and the barometric pressure. I don't know. I don't understand half of what he says." He shook hands with several people and kissed Inez, who kept wiping tears from her face.

"Look beyond the dancing lights, out on the horizon, Jackson." She squeezed his hand. "The fog is building and it's thick and dark. *His* fog. He's here."

He bent to brush a kiss on top of her head. "Not here, baby. He's out there somewhere on the ocean."

"And he's going to do something. He's going to be

angry that I married you." Her voice trembled. "And I did turn two of his attacks around on him. His pride won't take that."

"Don't think about him right now." The band started up and Jackson pulled Elle into his arms, sweeping her over the sand, her bare feet sliding between his as he kept her close to him, his body warming hers. "Have I told you how beautiful you look? Honestly, Elle, I don't deserve you."

She pressed her face into his shoulder for a moment, but was too worried to stay there long, looking back out toward the sea. Her breath caught in her throat as he whirled her around, forcing her to look at the tents and people who had gathered to help her celebrate. "Look at all the people who love you, baby. Everyone is here."

"Everyone I love, Jackson." Her voice choked now. "He's going to attack us."

"I know." He said it quietly. "He'll try—and you'll stop him."

Elle looked up at his face, saw the resolve there and spun around looking for her sisters. Their husbands danced with them, yet they formed a line between the ocean and the townspeople, as if they were guardians.

"Feel the energy, Elle," Jackson whispered. "It's all around us. These people care about us, and they're dancing and singing and celebrating out of love for us. The beat of the music, the laughter, the energy here is tremendous and it's all positive."

She drew in a breath and looked out to sea again. Lightning flashed in the sky, far out, tearing through the dark fog. Thunder rumbled, and beneath them, the ground vibrated. No one noticed as they danced and sang. Elle stepped away from Jackson and joined her sisters as they turned and faced the roiling water.

"Send the animals away, tell them to swim along the coast up toward Point Arena," Damon suggested to Abbey, "just to be safe."

Abigail did so, and the dolphins and seals dove deep and were gone, leaving the water churning and restless.

"He's here," Elle whispered. "Look at the kelp."

To either side of a fifty foot strip, the kelp stood up in the water, bobbing and floating as it should, but along that fifty foot stretch in the middle, the kelp stretched flat, as the water on the surface ran in a current, a river racing through the sea. A wave burst over the sand, riding up toward Elle, stopping inches from her bare feet when Hannah stepped forward and waved her hand. In the water was a mass of reaching kelp, moving as if alive, seeking prey.

Jackson contemptuously kicked driftwood onto the greedy vines and the current receded fast, heading back toward the ship anchored somewhere beyond the dancing lights. The fog deepened to a darker hue, spinning now. Lightning blazed along the edges of the darker clouds and thunder cracked. Again the ground beneath their feet shivered.

Elle's body tensed. "He's coming at us," she warned.

Her sisters stood with her, shoulder to shoulder, Elle in the middle. She could barely breathe with fear. Far out now she could see the wall of water forming, building into a massive tower. Her throat closed. The rogue wave was coming in fast, a monster, driven by rage and hatred and a savage need to control. Stavros was bent on destroying everyone she loved.

The air thickened around them, pressure building, the force sucking at them as if trying to draw them into a maelstrom of violence. Libby took a step forward, along with the water receding. Sarah and Abigail both caught at Libby, holding her still while the sand was drawn from under their feet. Yards of water rushed back to join with the oncoming wave. Elle glanced over her shoulder, realizing there was an eerie silence. No one ran. No one tried to save himself. The townspeople stood there, watching the wave gather in strength and speed. They had to know, had to realize that the wave would kill everyone, smash houses and cars and destroy everything in its path.

Elle couldn't believe that no one moved and then she realized they were looking at her with faith, with complete confidence. They believed in her. They believed in her sisters.

Stavros! I won't let you. She flung the words at him and raised her arms, stepping deliberately into the surge. She opened her mind to connect with her sisters, melding with them, throwing her fears away because it was now or never. She *had* to stop Stavros. She had no choice. Everyone was counting on her and he would *not* destroy her family. He wouldn't take the love of her life from her. And he wouldn't take her friends or her beloved town.

She felt the power swamp her as she tapped in to the vast supply of energy all around her. The force hit her hard, slamming into her with such vigor she nearly went off her feet, but she stood her ground and faced that wall of water as it gathered more speed and towered a hundred feet in the air. As the wave approached them, it split in two, coming at the beach from either side of that fast-moving current. There was so much vile hatred and rage mixed into the tower of water that she was afraid to meet it with any violence of her own. She didn't know what might happen. She needed something else . . .

She took a moment to glance at Ilya for help, but he

was turned away from her, facing some other threat she didn't see, expecting—believing—that with her sister's help she would keep all of them safe. She saw her mother step up beside Sarah and her aunt Carol beside Abigail and she felt them waiting for her direction. She turned her head one last time to look at the people behind her. She caught sight of a child, blowing bubbles from a miniature container and she quickly turned her head to look at Jackson. His eyes were on her. His mind in hers. He caught her idea and a slow smile softened the edges of his mouth.

Jackson had inadvertently given her the very tools she needed with his lecture on positive energy. A burst of confidence rushed through her and she felt the instant reaction in the joined minds of her sisters. Elle faced the oncoming wave and a small laugh escaped. Meeting Stavro's attack with violence would only feed him power. She had to give him something else, something he couldn't understand and it was all around her. Not power. Not control. Not even anger or revenge. Friendship. Love. Faith.

The wave separated, speeding around the current running on the surface of the water back toward Stavros's yacht. Her sisters spread out in a V-shape, with Elle forming the point and they all lifted their hands. Elle began to direct, feeding them all the energy around her, the positive, happy, celebratory energy.

Just as in chemistry classes from all those years with her teachers frowning at her, Elle began to mix the ingredients needed. Thicken the water, provide warmth, heat bursting up through the bottom as the wave rolled over it, reduce the surface tension of the water, a bit tricky and she lent her mother and aunt a little help. The wave rolled closer but now it was superheated and much thicker, the composition already changed. She could see the blossoming colors, like an iridescent rainbow rolling through the water. And then Hannah and Elle provided the fierce wind, stepping together, hands up, grinning at one another like two children, agitating the mixture, blowing hard, and the two waves began to break apart.

Large spheres rose into the sky, filling the open spaces so that for a few moments the blue was blotted out and there was only a canopy of large, shiny bubbles, a myriad of colors shining through the translucent spheres. Behind her she could hear the laughter and applause, as if everyone thought this was an amazing part of the celebration, thousands of bubbles floating over the sea, back toward the horizon, the rush of warm air carrying the joyful mood of their celebration across the ocean.

Elle staggered and Jackson was there, his arm around her to steady her, kissing the side of her face, love pouring over and into her. Weak, she clung to him, looking over his shoulder at her brother-in-law. Laughter and conversation poured all around her as the music started up and children ran up and down the beach as if mountainous waves and thousands of bubbles were an everyday occurrence. None of them seemed to notice the rip current going from shore out to sea increasing in strength, the kelp lying flat now as pressure from Stavros sucked the water back toward him for another try.

Ilya closed his eyes briefly and beneath the water a small seal burst on the continental shelf, ejecting methane into the fast-moving current. The rapid stream carried the methane bubbles back with it. He concentrated on pushing the riptide under the yacht so that the power and energy Gratsos was generating took his boat farther out to sea in spite of the anchor. The Greek was forced to abandon building another wave for just a few moments in order to stop his yacht from being carried away.

Stavros stood at the front of his opulent yacht, hands on the railing facing the shore where the celebration continued as if he were nothing at all. *Nothing.* Discounted as a nuisance, not a formidable opponent, a man to be reckoned with. She was mocking him with her bubbles, laughing at him, making him look weak. It was a slap in the face, an insult not to be forgiven. She had dismissed him, hadn't taken him seriously, but she would learn, she would know, just before he destroyed everything that mattered to her, how powerful he really was. His face was burned from the backlash of Elle's first psychic retaliation, unexpected and shocking, the pain still excruciating. And he could barely walk, every step agony. He couldn't be with a woman for a long time, and she was going to pay for her betrayal—letting another man touch her body that belonged to him—everyone she loved was going to die.

The tiny methane bubbles frothed and agitated the water surrounding the boat the moment Gratsos stopped feeding the hidden current. The yacht staggered, shuddered and abruptly plummeted as if into a hole, sinking in one long drop. There was no time to do anything, his crew diving into the ocean around him and sinking as well in spite of kicking strongly. He tried frantically to swim to the surface, but he couldn't get his body moving in an upward motion.

From the corner of his eye he saw his bodyguard drop deeper, obviously disoriented, swimming in the wrong direction yards from him, going under and away and then Sid disappeared in the darkness. Around him, his crew seemed suspended in the water, most already motionless, a couple struggling feebly in the cold and dark.

Stavros fought, kicking and pulling with his hands, try-ing to go up. The cold seeped into his very bones, as if the water soaked into him, became part of him. He held his breath, lungs burning. He was Stavros Gratsos. He owned the world. No one, nothing could oppose him, certainly not some worthless woman. He commanded the ocean, yet he couldn't drag water through his hands. He had to take a breath. He shook his head, feeling as if he might explode with the need for air. Frantic now, he opened his mouth to scream and took in nothing but water.

The residents of Sea Haven looked out to sea and saw what appeared to be phosphorescent lights dancing be-neath the water. Often when seals stirred up the ocean floor, the phosphorescent colors of red and green and yel-low would glow through the water. In the distance, the fog dissipated as if it had never been and the lights in the sky danced with the rhythm of the music. They turned back to their celebration, crowding around the couples, insisting on dancing.

Elle frowned and looked at her sisters. "I don't feel him, do you? I don't feel a threat at all." She turned to Jackson and followed his gaze, first to Ilya, whom she caught nodding, and then to Damon, who just grinned and winked at her.

"What have you done?" she asked suspiciously.

"Kiss me, wife," Jackson said, drawing her back into his arms. "This dress, bikini and sarong, whatever you call it, is driving me crazy. We'll have to go home soon."

20

THE gate stood open, welcoming them home. Jackson lifted Elle into his arms and followed the path of rose petals strewn along the way leading up to their house—the Drake family home. Elle's parents had officially turned over the estate and Drake legacy to them, looking very happy as they kissed their youngest daughter good-bye.

Each stepping stone vibrated beneath Jackson's tread, the symbols blazing with light as he cradled his wife in his arms and put his foot on the stones. He kissed her every other step he took, savoring her soft, willing mouth and the taste of passion and love combined. Her soft laughter floated around them, teasing his senses.

"Look, baby," Jackson said, "toward the sea."

Elle turned her head and looked out over the deep blue water. Dolphins performed a water ballet to the song of the whales, leaping and twisting and somersaulting at spectacular speeds. She gasped and held him tighter.

"They're welcoming us to our home."

"I believe they are," he agreed.

The wedding celebration had lasted long into the night. Elle felt like a princess, dancing the night away with her prince. Stars scattered across the sky like sparkling diamonds, and she held out her hand to study the radiance on her finger. "Look at that. It's so beautiful, Jackson. How did you think of it in the middle of everything else?"

"We couldn't get married without a ring," he said and kissed the corner of her mouth. "I had it made months ago."

"I love it."

He stepped onto the porch and frowned, turning around, still holding Elle high against his chest. Her long gown shimmered in the moonlight as he twisted around. "The deck looks a little different. When did they change it? There wasn't an overhang before, and it wraps all the way around the house, but I can't tell what's new and what's old. It all blends seamlessly."

She nuzzled his shoulder. "It looks like the deck you built at your house."

He stood for a moment longer, studying the deck, trying to figure out how the new wood appeared aged, as if it had been there for years. He felt Elle shiver in the cool night breeze and he turned back to the house. The front door opened, as if by an unseen hand, spilling light onto the porch. The front room should have been dark and cold, but warmth seeped out, enveloping them, the scent of cinnamon and apple spice drifting with the heat.

He carried Elle to the threshold and looked inside. The front room was transformed. Hardwood floors and high, cathedral ceilings gave the house the look of the one he'd designed. The large rock fireplace was still there with an ornate glass screen around it, the symbols glowing various colors from the flames dancing behind it.

"When did your family do this? I was just here." He looked down at the large mosaic in the entryway. The tiles danced with light, throwing a multitude of stars on the ceiling. Tiny little sparks leapt and crackled in the air, a mini-fireworks display overhead. He hesitated, leaning close to her ear. "Baby, I've got to tell you, this house is freaky. I think it's alive."

She turned her face up to kiss him. "It's just welcoming the new generation. It will settle down as soon as we step inside."

"You're certain?"

She laughed. "Take the step. You already married me and changed your name around for me. You may as well go all the way and accept the house, too. I noticed it's already been rearranged to your preferences."

He took possession of her mouth, maybe gathering courage, he didn't know, or it could have been the joy rising like champagne bubbles in his blood. She was beautiful. And she was home. She was his. "You're my preference," he stated and stepped across the threshold.

The tiles glittered, throwing off a purple-pink hue, but she was right, the moment his foot touched the floor, the house was just that—a house. No, it was home. It smelled like home and comfort, a haven for them.

He kissed her again. "We need a bed."

"This minute?" She nuzzled his neck, smiling at the urgency in his voice.

"Right this minute," he insisted.

Laughing, Elle started to point up the stairs to her old, childhood bedroom, to the floor where seven bedrooms waited to be occupied, and then realized the master bedroom was now theirs. She inhaled sharply and pressed closer to him, the enormity of their legacy swamping her.

"We'll be fine," he whispered, following the direction in her mind.

He started down the wide hall, frowning a little, thinking even that seemed wider with higher ceilings. Doors stood open and as he passed one, he caught sight of a brand-new baby grand piano. Abruptly he stopped in the doorway. Jackson slowly allowed Elle's bare feet to drop gently to the floor. He circled her waist with one arm, looking around the room in amazement.

"Look at this. A music room." He stepped inside, his gaze sweeping upward toward the ceiling and all around. The room was built with acoustic tiles, obviously soundproofed. Again, a spacious room with only two wide, comfortable chairs and a thick carpet. Candles adorned shelves and the gas fireplace was built into the wall, almost an exact duplicate of his sanctuary. But the piano . . . He went over to it almost afraid to touch it. "This is extraordinary."

"Each of my sisters left us a gift. This is from Joley."

He shook his head. "This is too much."

She took his hand. "You'll need this room for solace, we both will. There will be times we'll need to shut out the rest of the world and just find peace. Joley gave that to us."

"I'll never be able to repay her."

"We're giving the Drake family the next generation, Jackson. Each of my sisters is contributing to our children."

The concept was almost more than he could understand, the way the sisters felt about one another, tied so closely together, giving so freely to one another without any thought of return.

Smiling, Elle tugged at his hand. "Come on. Let's see what our wedding gifts are."

Jackson was almost afraid to look after seeing the

piano. They peeked into another room, this one quite massive, and discovered a library, floor-to-ceiling books with a rolling ladder that ran along all four walls. High-backed plush armchairs with small tables between each set provided cozy places to read, the lighting as perfect as Kate could get it for them and their children. There were reference books, classics, a foreign language section, every kind of fiction with Kate's books prominent on a shelf.

"She signed them," Jackson said, slipping one back onto the shelf. "And there's an entire section of children's books as well as parenting books." He flashed a grin. "I'll bet she had me in mind when she selected those."

"Some of these are very rare," Elle said. "This is so Kate."

The next room had to be from Sarah. High-tech gadgets of every kind were positioned throughout the room. Advanced computer systems, weather stations, interactive stations, and gaming were set up throughout the room. Jackson leaned over one item. "This is for you. A pretty little anklet bracelet so I know where you are at all times."

Her eyebrow shot up. "Really? Because I'm certain my sister wanted me to keep track of you."

"I don't know what half these things are," Jackson admitted.

"Oh, don't worry, Sarah and Damon are certain to teach us," Elle pointed out. "Both are big on security and I'm betting . . ." She crossed the room to open the door to a much smaller room. It refused to open until she pressed her palm over the screen. Inside were weapons. Lots of weapons. Elle stood back so Jackson could peer in, whistling softly, a wide smile on his face.

"*Now* I feel I'm home."

She pushed open another door. This one was far different, made of steel, fitting snugly into the frame. She looked around. Beds. Chairs. Shelves. Well-stocked first-aid kits. Bottled water. Candles. She looked at him. "What is this?"

"A panic room. I can shove you and the girls inside and know you're safe."

Elle, still wrapped tightly in his mind, felt that last bit of tension leave him. She put her hand on his arm. "You've been worried."

He shrugged. "You're my life, Elle. When we have our children, they'll be included in that circle and I'm not a man to lose everything. I want you as safe as possible."

"So you don't think three protection dogs, a room filled with weapons, a panic room and house that eats people isn't just a little overkill?"

He gathered her up, pulling her to him. "I think we'll need three dogs, a room filled with weapons, a panic room and a house that eats people the moment we have our first daughter."

She laughed. "You're so crazy."

"So which sister gave you the panic room?"

"Libby. No doubt about it. She'd want us all safe at all times. And did you notice all the first-aid equipment in there? Definitely Libby. We've got a lifetime supply of Band-Aids."

He laughed and moved her down the hall, his body making urgent demands. "How do we take that top off without ruining it?" He had been looking at the temptation of that bare expanse of soft skin all evening. His hands were already sliding over the lace, unhooking and opening the delicate material so that when she stood in the doorway of the room closest to the master bedroom, he could cup the soft weight of her breasts in his hands.

Jackson put his chin on Elle's shoulder, peering into the nursery. He knew immediately this had to be Hannah's gift to them. Stars spun on the ceiling. The room looked celestial, a mural painted on all four walls. Symbols of protection were woven into the theme of the universe, the room in soothing colors, designed to bring peace.

"I want to make a baby with you right now." He bit the lobe of her ear, his whisper wicked. "We can try and try until we get it right. We need practice, Elle."

"Hmm," she mused, turning her head, one arm going back over her shoulder to cradle his head so she could kiss him. "I don't think you have too much of a problem in that department."

His hands went to her hips, pushing at the satin material. "If I was that good, I'd have you out of this dress already."

She shimmied until the long drape of material slid down her thighs to pool on the floor, leaving her in a white lace thong that left her buttocks bare. Both his hands immediately went to cup the tempting invitation, and he pulled her to him, lifting her onto her toes. His mouth fused with hers and he walked her backward right out of the dress and toward the master bedroom. Elle's hands went to the buttons of his shirt as they moved down the hall, opening the thin white tuxedo shirt so she could run her hands up and down his bare torso. The moment he lifted his head, she trailed hot kisses down to his flat belly.

Jackson inhaled sharply, looking in wonder around their room as Elle's fingers busily worked on his trousers. She knelt, pulling the slacks down, pushing the material onto the floor so he could step out of them. Two walls of the room were glass, filled with salt water, where coral and fish lived and swam in the giant tank. Soft lights threw off a glow as the brightly colored fish with strange shapes moved peacefully behind the glass. He knew this was Abigail's gift to them. The ocean in his bedroom.

He looked down at the woman kneeling at his feet and his heart swelled. This was a fantasy he'd never imagined, not in his wildest dream. He reached down and pulled the pins from her glorious hair so that it spilled down her back, the silky strands caressing her breasts so that her nipples peeked out at him enticingly.

"Elle." He said her name. Waited until she looked up at him. Very slowly he drew her to her feet. "Tell me that I'm *your* choice. Not the house. Not fate. *Yours,* Elle. It has to be your choice."

She brought both hands up to frame his face. "Forever and always, Jackson. You'll always be my choice."

She went up on her toes, tilting her head to reach him. He simply swept her up and took her to the bed strewn with rose petals, laying her down, coming down with her, and Elle knew, in her heart, in her mind, that she was home.

The wind rushed up from the sea to the house just below the Drake estate where Sarah and Damon lived, swirling around, listening to the soft sounds of love coming from the bedroom. The wind moved over the old mill where the new bookstore and coffee shop stood proudly looking out to sea. Kate and Matt hadn't quite made it inside their home just beyond the mill. They lay on the deck together, hands frantically moving over each other's body. Moving along the coast the wind found Abigail and Aleksandr's beach home overlooking the sea, where Abigail sat on Aleksandr's lap in the hot tub, a glass of sparkling champagne in her hand, holding it to his mouth while her hips moved in a slow, sensuous rhythm. Just a bit farther up the coast in the huge estate, Ty pressed Libby against the glass, his mouth fused with hers. Across the highway, the wind traveled to find Hannah wrapped in Jonas's arms, their bodies intertwined on the huge four-poster bed, and then it whipped through the acreage of trees to the large house next door where Ilya had Joley pinned against the wall, her ankles locked around his hips. Kicking up leaves and twigs, the wind circled back, heading home, heading out to sea, stopping only to surround the Drake home for a moment, caressing the windows as, inside, Elle and Jackson made love.

Drawing back out over the sea, the wind rushed in playful little gusts, in celebration, before it rose off the ocean, carrying a soft whisper into the small village of Sea Haven. *The Drake sisters are back. They've all come home to stay.*

Turn the page for a special preview of

DARK SLAYER
by Christine Feehan

Available in September 2009
from Berkley Books!

SWIRLING mist veiled the mountains and crept into the deep forest, stringing layers of white through the snow-laden trees. Pockets of deep snow hid life beneath the cap of ice crystals and along the banks of the stream. Shrubs and fields of grass rose like statues, frozen in time. The snow gave the world a bluish cast. The forest where icicles hung and the stream with its water frozen in bizarre shapes seemed an eerie, alien world.

Clear, crisp and cold, the night sky shone bright with stars and a full, glowing moon that spilled a silvery light over the frozen ground. Silent shadows slipped through the trees and ice-coated bushes, moving with absolute stealth. Large paws made tracks in the snow, a good six inches in diameter, single file, the trail winding in and out through the trees and thick shrubbery.

Although they looked in good health, strong with steel muscles rippling beneath thick fur, the wolves were hungry and needed food to keep the pack alive through the long, brutal winter. The alpha suddenly stopped, going very still,

sniffing the trail around him, lifting his nose to scent the
wind. The others halted, wraiths only, silent shadows that
immediately fanned out. The alpha moved forward, staying
downwind while the others sank low, waiting.

A yard away, a large piece of raw meat lay on the trail
as if dropped there, fresh, the scent wafting temptingly
and drifting back toward the wolf. Wary, he circled, using
his nose to detect potential danger. Scenting nothing but
the meat, with his saliva running and his belly empty, he
approached again, coming in downwind, angling toward
the large piece of lifesaving food. He came in three times
and backed away, but no hint of danger presented itself.
He nosed in a fourth time and something slipped over his
neck.

The alpha leapt back and the wire tightened. The more
he struggled, the more the wire cut into him, strangling
the air from his lungs and sawing through flesh. The pack
circled, pacing, his female rushing to aid him. She began
to struggle as another wire snared her neck, nearly knocking her off her feet.

For a moment there was a hush, broken only by the
gasping breath of the two trapped wolves. A twig snapped.
The pack whirled and dissolved in a rush of fleeing shadows, back into the thicker cover of the trees. The bushes
parted and a woman stepped into the open. She was
dressed in black winter boots and black pants that rode
low on her hips. She wore a vest of black that left her midriff bare and had two sets of steel buckles running down
the middle. The six buckles were shiny, almost ornamen-
tal, with tiny crosses running up and around, embedded in
the squared silver pieces.

A wealth of blue-black hair spilled beyond her waist,

pulled back in a single thick braid. The long, hooded coat she wore, made of what appeared to be a single silver-tipped wolf pelt, fell all the way to her ankles. She carried a crossbow in one hand, a sword at one hip and a knife at the other. Arrows were in a quiver slung over her shoulder, and all down the inside of the long wolf skin were small loops containing various sharp-bladed weapons. A low-slung holster adorned with rows of very small, flat, razor-sharp arrowheads housed a pistol on her hip.

She paused for a moment, surveying the scene. "Be still," she hissed, both annoyance and authority in her soft voice.

Both wolves instantly ceased struggling at her command, waiting, bodies trembling, sides heaving and heads held low to try to ease the terrible pressure closing around their throats. The woman moved with fluid grace, flowing over the surface rather than sinking into the ice-crusted snow. She studied the snares, a multitude of them, disgust in her dark eyes.

"They've done this before," she scolded. "I showed them to you, but you were too greedy, looking for an easy meal. I should let you die here in agony." Even as she rebuked the wolves, she withdrew a pair of wire cutters from inside the wolf pelt and snipped the wires, freeing them. She pushed her fingers into the fur, over the cuts deep in their throats, and clamped her palm over the slashes, chanting softly. White light burst under her hand, glowing around and through the wolves' fur.

"That should make you feel better," she said, affection creeping into her tone as she scratched the ears of both wolves.

The alpha growled a warning and his mate bared her teeth, both facing away from the woman. She smiled. "I smell him. It is impossible not to smell the foul stench of vampire."

She turned her head and looked over her shoulder at the tall, powerful male emerging from the twisted, gnarled trunk of a large evergreen fir. The trunk gaped open, split nearly in two, blackened and peeled back, the needles on the outstretched limbs withering as the tree expelled the venomous creature from its depths. Icicles rained down like small spears as the branches shivered and shook, trembling from contact with such a foul creature.

The woman rose gracefully, turning to face her enemy, signaling for the wolves to melt back into the forest. "I see you have resorted to setting traps to get sustenance these days, Cristofor. Are you so slow and foul that you can no longer lure a human to use as food?"

"Slayer!" The vampire's voice seemed rusty, as if his vocal cords were rarely used. "I knew if I brought your pack to me, you would come."

Her eyebrow shot up. "A pretty invitation then, Cristofor. I remember you from the old days when you were a young man, still handsome to look at. I left you alone for old time's sake, but I see you crave the sweet release of death. Well, old friend, so be it."

"They say you cannot be killed," Cristofor said. "The legend that haunts all vampires. Our leaders say to leave you alone."

"Your leaders? You have joined them then, banded together against the prince and his people? Why seek death when you have a plan to rule every country? The world?" She laughed softly. "It seems to me that this is a silly wish, and a lot of work. In the old days, we lived simply. Those were happy days. Do you not recall them?"

Cristofor studied her flawless face. "I was told you

were pieced together, one strip of flesh at a time, yet your face and body are as you were in the old days."

She shrugged her shoulders, refusing to allow the images of those dark years, the suffering and pain—agony, really—when her body refused to die and lay deep in the earth, stripped of flesh and open to the crawling insects abounding in the dirt. She kept her face serene, smiling, but inside she was still, coiled, ready to explode into action.

"Why not join us? You have more reason than any other to hate the prince."

"And join the very ones who betrayed and mutilated me? I do not think so. I wage war where it is due." She flexed her fingers inside the thin, skintight gloves. "You really should not have touched my wolves, Cristofor. You have left me little choice."

"I want your secret. Give it to me and I will let you live."

She smiled then, a beautiful smile, her teeth small and pearl white. Her lips were red and full, a teasing, sexy curve inviting him to share the humor. She tilted her head to one side, her gaze moving over his face, assessing him carefully. "I had no idea you had become such a fool, Cristo." She called him by the name she had used when they were children playing together. *Before.* When the world was right. "I am the slayer of vampires. You summoned me with your traps"—she waved a contemptuous hand—"and you think I should be intimidated by you?"

He grinned at her, an evil, malicious smile. "You have become arrogant, Slayer. And careless. You had no idea the trap was for you and not your precious wolves. You have no choice but to give me what I want, or you die this night."

Ivory shrugged her slender shoulders and the silvery full-length coat rippled, moved as if alive. One moment it loosely flowed around her ankles and the next it was gone, settling over her skin until six ferocious wolf tattoos adorned her body from the small of her back to her neck, wrapping around each arm like sleeves.

"So be it," she said softly, her eyes on his.

Spinning, she drew her sword with one hand, rushing toward him, going up and over a snowcapped boulder to launch her body into the air. She felt the bite of a hidden snare, and inwardly cursed as the noose closed around her neck. Already she was dissolving, but blood spattered across the snow in bright crimson drops.

Cristofor laughed and leaned down to scoop up a handful of snow and lick at the droplets, savoring the taste of pure Carpathian blood; not just pure—the slayer was Ivory Malinov, from one of the strongest Carpathian lineages in existence. He followed the arc of blood, saw her forming a few feet from him, closer to the treeline, and satisfaction made him cackle.

Ivory saluted him with two fingers, touched the thin line running across her neck and put her finger in her mouth, sucking off the blood. "Nice score. I did not see that coming and I shall have to apologize to my wolves for scolding them. But, Cristo, if you believe your partner back there in the woods is going to help you after slaying my wolf pack, you are doing some serious underestimating of your own."

She ran forward again, her hand low, drawing and throwing the small arrowheads, snapping them with tremendous strength so each buried itself deep into his body, in a straight line from belly to neck. The vampire roared and tried to shift. His legs disappeared, melting into vapor. His head swirled and disappeared. Fog drifted in from the trees in an attempt to help conceal him, congealing around his body, forming a thick veil. The torso remained, that straight, damaging line from belly to neck, exposing his heart.

Her sword sank deep, her body weight, strength and momentum from her run driving the blade through the body right beneath the heart. The vampire screamed horribly. Acidlike blood poured from the wound, sizzling over the sword and splattering across the snow. The metal should have been eaten through, but the coating the Slayer used protected it and also prevented that portion of his body from shifting. She turned her body in a dancer's spin, sword over her head, still stuck inside his chest so that she cut a circular hole around his heart.

Ivory withdrew the sword and plunged her hand deep. "I've shown you my secret," she whispered. "Take it to your grave." She withdrew the heart and flung it away from her, lifting her arms to call down a sword of lightning.

The jagged bolt incinerated the heart and then jumped to the body, burning it clean. "Find peace, Cristofor," she whispered and hung her head, leaning on her sword, tears shimmering briefly for her lost childhood friend.

So many were gone now. Nothing seemed to remain of the life she'd once known. She took a deep breath, drawing in the crisp night before cleaning her sword and all trace of the vampire's blood from the snow. She retrieved the eight small arrowheads and slid them into the loops on her holster before holding out her arms for the silver-tipped pelt. The tattoos moved, emerging, sliding once more over her body in the form of a coat. She allowed the silvery full-length coat to settle over her body slowly before picking up her weapons and drawing up the hood. At once she seemed to disappear, blending seamlessly with the layers of white fog.

Ivory moved in silence, feeling the hostile energy radiating from her pack. They were under attack and her wall of protection was weakening. She'd thrown the shield up around them hastily when she scented the second predator. Had he not been quite so eager for the kill, and stayed downwind, he might have managed to kill her wolf pack. She couldn't use the arrowheads on him; the vampire's acidic blood would have eaten through most of the coating. She had very little time to kill her enemy once she buried the small lethal wedges in the vampire's body, before that acidic blood ate through the coating and allowed her enemy to shift.

Weaving through the trees, the slayer stayed low to the ground, taking on the shape of a wolf. With her silver-tipped pelt it would be difficult to distinguish her from the other wolves in the area as she slipped through the trees toward the second vampire. She sank behind a fallen tree, studying the figure hurling fireballs at the wolves. He had cornered them just at the water's edge where the ice was thin and dangerous. She could see cracks spreading along the thin shield she'd thrown up where the vampire continually battered at it.

She took a breath, let it out and let herself find that place deep inside where there was stillness. Where there was resolve. She stood and ran at the vampire, firing the crossbow as she went. Again, her aim was for his torso. She caught him as he turned, one arrow slicing into his lower back, the second missing altogether. He flung the fireball at her and Ivory somersaulted on the ground, letting it fly over her head. Then she was up on her feet, still running, always advancing, shooting at him with the crossbow.

The vampire howled in rage, the sound cut off abruptly as an arrow slammed deep into his throat. Her wolves threw themselves at the wall, frantic to come to her aid, but she knew the vampire would simply destroy them all. On the other hand . . .

The slayer shrugged, this time sending her thick silver-tipped wolf pelt away from her. The heavy coat landed in the snow, spread wide, the fur rippling as if alive. The hood stretched and elongated; each sleeve did the same, moving with life as the body of the coat formed three separate shapes to match the merging ones of the hood and sleeves. Ivory didn't wait for her companions to shift to their normal forms. She rolled across the snow, coming up on one knee, firing two more coated arrows into the vampire's chest while he was distracted by the six emerging wolves.

The vampire hissed, his eyes glowing hot with hatred. He tried to shift, but only his legs, belly and head took the shape of a multiarmed beast, leaving his heart exposed. He realized he was trapped, but was fully aware of the small arrow weakening in his back as the metal was destroyed by his acidic blood. He whirled, sending up a spout of snow, gathering the wind to him and hurling it outward, creating an instant blizzard as the snow was drawn into his circle and flung out around him.

It was impossible to see the vampire in the center of that storm, but the wolves leapt through the swirl of icy snow, guided by scent to attack, tearing at his legs and arms, the alpha going for the throat in an effort to bring him down. The slayer followed them into the circle, knife in hand, hurling herself into the frenzied fray. One of the wolves yelped, and then screamed as the vampire ripped open its sides with curled, slashing talons and flung its body at Ivory.

She dropped her crossbow and caught the wolf as it slammed into her chest, driving her backward. The blizzard slashed across her face without mercy, tearing at her exposed skin as she went down, the wolf on top of her. She put the animal's silvery body aside as gently as possible and crawled forward quickly, covering the snow-capped ground like a snake, picking up the crossbow and loading it as she slithered forward. Firing rapidly, she struck him three more times, exploding to her feet right in front of him, driving the knife deep, her hand, wrapped around the hilt, following as the blade sliced through bone and sinew in an effort to get to the heart.

The vampire reared back, spittle and blood foaming around his mouth. He slammed his fist at her chest, trying to get at her heart, striking the double row of buckles. Howling, he withdrew his hand, the burn marks evident in the flesh of his knuckles. The tiny imprints of crosses woven into the silver and blessed with holy water burned through his flesh almost to the bone.

The vampire roared, clubbing at Ivory's throat in spite of the wolves hanging on his arms. His nails scraped across her neck and shoulder, gouging flesh away as he struggled wildly. The alpha male hit him full force in the torso, driving him back and away from Ivory before those poison-tipped talons could pierce her jugular.

Ivory leapt on him, punching down and through with her fist, reaching for the heart, ignoring the acid as it poured over her coated gloves and began burning through quickly. The vampire thrashed and ripped at her, but the wolves pinned him down as she extracted the pulsing black heart, flinging it from her and raising her hand toward the sky.

Lightning zig-zagged, streaked down and slammed into the heart, jolting the ground. The wolves leapt out of the way and the bolt of cleansing energy jumped to the body, incinerating the vampire and cleaning her arrows. Wearily, Ivory bathed her gloves in the light and then sank down into the snow, sitting for a moment, hanging her head, struggling to draw in air when her lungs were burning with need.

One of the wolves licked at her wounds in an effort to heal her. She managed a small smile and laid her fingers in the fur of the alpha female, rubbing her face in the soft pelt for comfort. These wolves, saved from death so many years earlier—more even than she remembered—were her only companions, her family. They were her true pack and she owed no loyalty to any other but them.

"Come here, Raja," she crooned to the big male. "Let me take a look at the damage."

Still trapped behind the shield she'd created to protect the natural wolf pack from the vampire, the alpha roared a challenge. Raja ignored him as he'd done so many others over the years. The natural pack lived and died, the cycle of nature intervening, and he'd learned such petty rivalries didn't touch him. He sent the natural alpha a look of pure disdain and crawled to Ivory, lying on his side so she could inspect his wounds. She'd healed him countless times over the years, just as his sisters and brothers healed the slayer's wounds, their saliva containing the healing agents.

She scraped snow from the frozen ground and dug deep until she had good soil. Mixing her saliva with the soil, she packed the wounds and then hugged him. "Thank you, my brother. As so many other times, you've saved my life."

He nuzzled her and waited patiently while she inspected each of the pack. The strongest female, Ayame, named after the demon princess wolf, cuddled close to him, inspecting his wounds and passing her tongue over the other scratches he'd received. Their littermates formed the rest of the pack: Blaez, his second in command; Farkas, the last male; and Rikki and Gynger, the two smaller females. They crowded around Ivory, pressing close to her battered and bruised body in an effort to aid her.

The littermates were very distinctive with their thick, silver-tipped coats and a shimmering fall of luxurious fur. All were larger than normal, even the two smaller females. Each had the blue eyes from their puppy days when Ivory had tracked blood and death back to the den, finding the mangled bodies of her natural wolf pack all those years ago. Even then, she'd become a scourge to the vampires, a whisper, the beginnings of a legend, and they'd sought to destroy her. Instead, they'd killed and mutilated the bodies of the wolf pack she'd befriended.

She'd found the puppies dying, their torn bodies wriggling across the blood-soaked ground, trying to find their mother. She couldn't bear to lose them, her only family, her only contact with warmth and affection, and she'd fed them her blood out of sheer desperation to keep them alive. Carpathian blood. Hot and healing. She'd stayed in the den with them, back away from the light of day, nearly starving herself and, again out desperation, having to take small amounts of blood from them to stay alive. She hadn't realized she was giving blood exchanges until the largest and most dominant of the pups underwent the change.

The pups had retained their blue eyes as they'd grown, the Carpathian blood giving them the ability to shift. Their ability to communicate with Ivory had saved them, giving them the necessary psychic brain function to live through the conversion. They had been wounded a thousand times in battle, but over the last century they'd learned how to successfully bring down a vampire, the seven of them working as a team.

She lay back in the snow, catching her breath, letting her body absorb the pain of her wounds. The one in her neck throbbed and burned and she knew she had to clean it immediately. She was impervious to the cold, as all Carpathians were. Her race was as old as time, nearly immortal, as she had discovered, to her horror, when the prince's son had betrayed her to the vampires for his own gain. She'd never known such agony, an endless battle deep in the earth as years went by and her body refused to die.

She must have made a sound, although she didn't hear herself. She thought her cry was silent, but the wolves pressed closer, trying to comfort her. Behind the shield, the natural pack took up the cry. Looking up at the night sky, she let her wolves soothe her, the love and devotion a balm to her whenever she thought too much about her former life. Time was creeping forward. This time of day was as much an enemy as the vampire. She had to hurry to get to her lair; there was still much to be done before dawn.

Ivory pressed her fingers to her burning eyes and forced her body to move. First, she removed the poison from the lesions in her flesh, where the vampire's poison-tipped claws had torn her open. The vampires who banned together used tiny, wormlike parasites to identify one another, and those parasites infected any open wound. She had to push them through her pores fast, before they could take hold and require a much more in-depth healing. Again she brought down the lightning to kill them before mixing soil and saliva to pack her own wounds.

"Ready?" she asked her family, picking up her weapons and shoving the used arrows back into her pack. She never left a weapon or arrow behind, careful that her formula didn't fall into the hands of the vampires, or worse, Xavier, her mortal enemy.

Ivory stretched out her arms and the pack leapt together, forming the full length coat in the air as they shifted, covering her body, the hood over her head and flowing pelt surrounding her with warmth and affection. She was never alone when she traveled with her pack. No matter where she went, no matter how many days or weeks she traveled, they traveled with her, keeping her from going insane. She'd learned to be alone and had the wolf's natural wariness of strangers. She had no friends, only enemies, and she was comfortable that way.

Striding through the snow, she waved her hand and allowed the shield to disintegrate. The wolf pack milled around her, weaving in and out between her legs and sniffing at her coat and boots, greeting her as a member of the pack. The alpha marked every bush and tree in the vicinity to cover Raja's scent marks. Ivory rolled her eyes at the display of dominance.

"Males are the same world over, no matter what the species," she said aloud and checked the wolves one by one, assuring herself the vampire hadn't harmed any of them.

"All right. Let's get you fed before dawn. I have a ways to travel and the night's fading," she told the pack. Catching the alpha's muzzle, she looked into his eyes. *Find and drive prey to me and I'll bring it down for you. Hurry, though. I don't have much time.*

Although she talked to her own pack all the time and they understood her, it was easier with a wild pack to convey the order in images rather than in words. She added a sense of urgency at the same time. She needed to begin the trek back to her lair. Ordinarily she would fly, and each of her weapons was made of something natural that could shift with her, to transport her arsenal over long distances. But first she had to help the pack find food. She didn't want to lose them over the winter, and another storm was coming in soon.

The wolf pack melted away, once again fading into the forest to look for prey. She shouldered her crossbow and began walking through the wilderness in the direction of her home. She'd only make a few miles before the pack would flush something her way, but she would be that much closer to home—and to safety.

She understood little about the modern way of life. She'd been buried beneath the ground for so long, the world was unrecognizable when she'd risen. She'd learned over time that the prince's son, Mikhail, had replaced him as the ruler of the Carpathians, and his second in command, as always, was a Daratrazanoff. She knew little else of them, but even the Carpathian world had changed drastically.

There were so few of her species, the race nearing extinction. And who knew? Maybe it was for the best. Maybe their time was long past. So few women and children had been born over the last few centuries that the race was nearly wiped out. She wasn't a part of that world any longer, no more than she was a part of the modern-day human world. She knew little of technology, other than from the books she read, and she had no concept of what it would be like to live in a house or village, town or—God forbid—a city.

She quickened her steps and again glanced at the sky. She would give the wolf pack another twenty minutes to flush game before she took flight. As it was she was pushing her luck. She didn't want to be caught out in the light of dawn. She'd spent so much of her life underground, she hadn't developed the resistance to the sun as many of her kind had done, able to stay out in the early morning hours. The moment the sun began to rise she could feel the burn.

Of course, it might have something to do with her skin taking so long to renew itself, scraped from her body as it had been until she was nothing but bones and a mass of raw tissue. Sometimes, when she first woke, she still felt the blades going through bone and organs as they chopped her into little pieces and scattered her across the meadow, left to be eaten by the wolves. She remembered the sound of their rasping laughter as they carried out the orders given to them by her worst enemy—Xavier.

The wind began to increase in strength and dark clouds drifted overhead, heralding the coming storm. She sought the haven of the trees and took refuge, closing her eyes to seek the wolf pack. They had discovered a doe, thin and drawn from the winter, hobbling a bit from an injury to her old body. Giving chase, the pack had taken turns, running her toward Ivory.

She whispered softly, asking for the doe's forgiveness, explaining the need to feed the pack as she lifted her weapon and waited. Minutes passed. Ice cracked with a loud snap, disturbing the silence. Hard breaths burst from lungs in a rapid puff of steam as the deer broke through the trees and ran full out over the icy ground.

Behind the doe, a wolf ran, silent, deadly, hungry, moving across the expanse of ice on large paws. Surrounding them, the pack came in from various angles, keeping the doe running straight toward Ivory. They'd hunted this way more than once, bringing the prey to her in desperate times.

Not wanting the doe to suffer, Ivory waited until she had a kill shot before releasing her arrow and taking the animal down. Before the alpha could approach the carcass, snarling at the others to wait until he had his fill, she hurried to it and retrieved her arrow, striding away fast, not wanting to use energy to control a starving pack when there was a banquet in front of them.

Increasing her speed until she was running, Ivory sprang into the sky, shifting, the wolves sliding over her skin to become the ferocious tattoos as they streaked through the clouds with her. She always felt the joy of traveling this way, as if a burden was lifted from her shoulders each time she took to the air. Spinning dark clouds helped to ease the light on her skin as she moved quickly toward her home. Maybe that was what made her feel less weighted down—that she was heading home where she felt safe and secure.

She'd never learned to be relaxed and at ease aboveground where her enemies could come at her from any direction. She kept her lair secret, leaving no traces near her entrance, so no one had the opportunity to track her. The entrance wasn't protected with a spell, so if a Carpathian or vampire found it, they wouldn't know it was occupied. Many years earlier she'd learned the areas underground where her enemies were most comfortable, and now she avoided them.

Ten miles from her lair, she went to earth, landing, still running, skimming across the surface, arms outstretched so her wolves could hunt. They all needed blood, and with all seven of them spreading out, they'd run across a hunter or a cabin. If not, she would go into the closest village and bring back enough to sustain the pack. She was very careful not to hunt near home, not unless she absolutely had to.

As she slipped through the trees, the mountain rising high in the distance, she came across tracks. An early morning wanderer out to get wood perhaps, or hunting himself. She crouched low and touched the tracks in the snow. A big man. That was always good. And he was alone. That was even better. Hunger gnawed at her now that she'd allowed herself to become aware of it. Ivory ran in the footsteps, following the male as he made his way through the trees.

The forest gave way to a clearing where a small cabin and outhouse sat, a stream dissecting the meadow surrounding it. Ordinarily the cabin was empty, but the tracks led through the snow and inside. A thin trail of smoke began to float from the chimney, telling her he'd just come home and lit a fire.

Ivory threw her head back and howled, calling to her pack. She waited on the edge of the clearing and the man stepped outside, rifle in his hands, looking around at the surrounding forest. That lonely call had spooked him and he waited, quartering the area around his house.

Ivory took to the sky again, moving with the wind, part of the drifting mist surrounding the house. She stood above her prey on the roof while he studied the forest and then, with a small curse, went inside. She saw the shadows flitting among the trees and gestured to them. The pack sank down, waiting.

The crack beneath the cabin door was wide enough for the mist to flow through and Ivory entered the room, warm now from the crackling fire. Only one room, with a small fireplace and cooking stove, the cabin had the barest of amenities. In modern times, even the poorest of the villagers had such meager trappings. She watched him from the hidden corner of the room as he poured water into a pot and set it on the fire to boil.

Crossing the space, she materialized almost in front of him, slipping between him and the fire, her will already reaching for his to calm him and make him more accepting. His eyes widened, and then glazed over. Ivory led him to the chair where she could seat him. She was tall— much taller than many women in the villages, a gift from her Carpathian heritage—but this mountain of a man was still taller. She found the pulse beating on the side of his neck and sank her teeth deep.

The taste was exquisite, hot blood flowing, cells filling and bursting with life. Sometimes she forgot just how good it was to feast on the real thing. Animal blood could sustain life, but true strength and energy came from humans. She savored every drop, appreciating the life-giving blood, grateful to the man, although he wouldn't remember he had donated. She planted a dream, slightly erotic, wholly pleasing, not wanting the experience to be unpleasant for him.

She flicked her tongue across the puncture wounds to close the two holes and erase all evidence that she'd been there. Before leaving, she got him a drink of water and pressed it to his mouth, commanding him to drink, and then she set another glass beside him and tucked a blanket close to keep his body heat up.

The pack met her in the deeper woods, surrounding her the moment she called to them. The alpha male came first, leaning against her knee as she knelt and offered her wrist, the blood welling up. He licked the wound from her left wrist while the female fed from her right. She fed all six wolves and then sat in the snow for a moment, recovering. She'd taken quite a lot from the woodsman, although she'd been careful to ensure that he could still function, not wanting to risk him freezing to death before he recovered, and she was a little drained after the fight with the vampires and then feeding the pack.

She rose slowly and held out her arms, waiting for the wolves to shift back into tattoos covering her skin. As they merged with her, she felt a little more revived, the wolves giving her their energy. Again she ran and leapt into the sky, shifting as she did so, giving her body wings as she flew over the forest and headed home.

The clouds were heavy and full, and small gusts of wind blew in the mist, blotting out the rising sun. The mountains rose in front of her—snowcapped and high— hiding warmth and home beneath the layers of rock. She found herself smiling. *We're home,* she sent to the pack. *Almost.* She had to scout before she dropped down, check for strangers in her area.

She felt the wolves reach out with each of their senses, just as she did, never taking safety for granted. It was how she'd managed to stay alive for so many years. Trusting no one. Speaking to no one unless far from her dwelling. Leaving no tracks. No trace. The Slayer appeared and then vanished.

She worked her way in an ever-tightening circle, closer

and closer to her lair, all the while scanning for blank spaces that might indicate a vampire, or for the disruption of energy that meant a mage, might be in the area. Smoke and noise might be humans. Carpathians were more difficult, but she had a sixth sense about them and could hide herself if she felt one near.

As she began her spiral downward, unease rippled through her body and then through the wolves. Below her, through the layers of mist, she caught glimpses of something dark lying motionless in the snow. The snow began to fall, adding to her loss of vision, and she knew by the prickly sensation crawling over her skin that the sun had begun to rise. Every instinct told her to increase her speed and make it to her lair before the sun broke over the mountain, but something far older, far deeper, deterred her.

She couldn't turn away from the sprawled body lying in the snow, already being covered with the new powder falling. *O köd belső—darkness take it*. Cursing ancient Carpathian oaths that would have shocked her five brothers in the old days when she'd remained their protected, adored baby sister, she set her feet down in the snow and threw her arms out to allow her pack to leap down.

The wolves approached the carcass wearily, circling in silence. The man didn't move. His clothes were torn, exposing part of his emaciated torso and belly to the gleaming, hungry eyes. Raja moved in, two steps only, while the pack continued to circle the body. The alpha female, Ayame, stepped in behind the male and Raja turned and snarled at her. Ayame leapt back and whirled around, baring her teeth at her mate.

Ivory took a wary step closer as Raja resumed sniffing the motionless man. He'd once been a powerful male, no doubt about it. He was taller than the average human by several inches. His hair was long and thick, a black-gray pelt that was loose and unkempt. Blood and dirt were caught in the thick strands, matting his hair in places. She leaned over Raja to get a closer look and something inside her shifted.

Gasping, she pulled back abruptly, her body actually turning, ready to flee. He had the strong bones of a Carpathian male, a straight aristocratic nose and deep lines of suffering cut into his once-handsome face. But what really caught her attention and terrified her was the birthmark showing through his torn, thin shirt. She could see the dragon on his hip. It was no tattoo; he'd been born with that mark.

Dragonseeker. Her breath rushed from her lungs in a long gasp. Around her the snow continued to fall and the world became white, all sound muted. She could hear her heartbeat, too fast, adrenaline pumping through her body, her blood roaring in her ears.

Raja nudged her leg, indicating they leave the body where it lay. She took a breath, although her lungs could barely drag in air. Her body actually shivered. She turned away, signaling to the wolves to leave him, but her feet refused to work. She couldn't take a single step. The man with that ravaged face and too-thin body held her to him.

She raised her gaze to the heavens, letting the snow cover her face like a white mask. "Why now?" she asked softly. A plea. A prayer. "Why are you asking this of me now? Don't you think you've taken enough from me?" She stood waiting for an answer. Waiting for lightning to strike, maybe. Something. Anything. Her whispered entreaty was met with implacable silence.

Raja gave a series of whines. *Come away, little sister.*

Leave him. He obviously disturbs you. Come away before the sun is high.

For the first time in hundreds of years, she'd forgotten the sun. She'd forgotten safety. Everything she knew, everything she'd learned, it was all gone because of this man. She wanted to go away. She *needed* to go away, but everything in her was drawn to this one man. *Päläfertiilam— lifemate—her* lifemate—the curse of all Carpathian women.

CHRISTINE FEEHAN

Dark Slayer

The Dragonseeker Razvan is considered an enemy of both Carpathian hunters and vampires. But when Ivory, a rare female Carpathian, frees Razvan from his prison cage, she senses that Razvan is more than what he appears to be, and is willing to go against the entire Carpathian race to help him. But will her belief cost them their lives?